The Astral Shore

Elizabeth Genovese

Published by Silver Sword Publishers, 2017

THE ASTRAL SHORE

First edition. October 21, 2014

Written by Elizabeth Genovese

For my mother, Anne J. Genovese, a great lady and greatly missed.

1. THE AKA THREAD

THE PSYCHIC WORE a kabuki lion mask with eyes dramatically framed in black and red and a platinum mane that hung to the waist. From a secluded corner of the party room, Laurel wrapped her arms around the taxidermied cat and narrowed her eyes. There he stood, in the shadow of glowing skulls and lighted pumpkins, her channel to the man of her dreams. Was he the real thing? *You have to be. I need you to be.*

He called his next subject forward, a guy wearing a diaper and crocheted baby hat. "A few steps closer," the psychic said. "Okay. That's good." He lowered his head and thought a minute. "Lake. Cottage. There's an old camera in the cottage that's important to you. Nikon or Konika. Get it out of there. But call your broker first and check for third-party liability."

The baby man widened his eyes. "Impressive."

She heard herself whimper. Yes, impressive.

"I do have an old Nikon. But about this third-party thing?"

"Could be a sewer or septic issue," the psychic said. "*Beyond* your property line. Promise me you'll call your broker first thing Monday."

The guy crossed his heart. "Promise."

"Now promise your wife."

The baby man turned to his wife, a diminutive brunette dressed as Mary Poppins, "I promise to call Tom Mac-Something-or-other on Monday. Thanks, Michael."

The guests clapped and whistled. She dug her nails into the taxidermied cat.

This Michael Johnstone could be the answer. Nancy said he made big bucks as some sort of psychic parapsychologist or parapsychologist psychic. Whatever. Nancy said the guy wrote two books and travelled the world on business. And he cared about his subjects. Well, good on him. She could use that.

"Come on, Laurel," Nancy said. "I'll introduce you to Michael."

"Need a glass of liquid sin first."

She aimed the cat at the bar and edged through the crowd in her polka-dotted pinafore, black patent Mary Jane shoes and white straw hat with matching bow. This was her third Halloween wearing the costume. Oh to be a little girl again.

"Well hello, little girl," a gladiator said, licking his lips. "What's your fancy?"

She propped the fanged cat on the bar. "I brought my own fancy, thanks."

"Is that a real cat?"

"Not anymore."

Laurel grabbed the cabernet she'd left breathing behind the bar and squinted at the mirrored glass. It had been a year since she visited Nancy in her home. Truth was she hated mirrors and Nancy had mirrors everywhere, mainly around the bar. Mirrored ceiling above the bar, mirrored walls around the bar. Wherever she went in this house, there she was. Tired old joke. She uncorked the wine with her back to the mirrors.

"It wasn't *your* cat, was it?"

"My mother's." She took a swig. *My crazy, twisted mother.*

The cat even resembled her—black hair, teeth bared, back arched. All good little girls owed their mothers at least one commemorative day a year. Mother's Day. Birthday. Christmas. Her lucky mother got Halloween.

On the far side of the room, the guests surrounded Michael Johnstone like mystery around the Sphinx. She wiped the sweat from her lip, topped up her wine, and plotted ways to abscond with the guest of honour. Priority One—a private powwow with the psychic. Priority Two—get his take on today's incident with the two men at The Royal York Hotel. If not for the incident, she'd be home sipping a fruity Beaujolais and dreaming of Mark Grant.

A week ago, she couldn't care less about hiring Nancy's psychic friend. She planned to bring Mark Grant into her life with no help from anyone and was doing okay. Until today. Fate revised the plan today when it lobbed those two men at her. She pressed in on her stomach. Things happened for a reason, of course they did. There were no coincidences. She absolutely believed that, and Nancy said this psychic was the best in his field.

While *Thriller* blasted from six house speakers, a different song thrummed in her head, an instrumental piano tune she heard waking, drifting off to sleep, and during thoughts of *him*. The song, something between a dreamy piano nocturne and prelude, was too familiar for comfort. Who was playing? It wasn't Mark because she'd memorized every song he ever sang and every note he ever played. Maybe this Michael guy would hear the song, even identify it.

A guest shot her a flirty look as he swaggered by, dripping in spicy aftershave. The same aftershave Mark wore in the dreams, the same scent that wafted into her nostrils every morning. She ignored him and looked away. Familiar song, familiar scent. Not so familiar God. If only He approved of her. If only He'd jet propel Mark Grant into her life via this psychic top gun. And if He would just do that little thing, she'd try—okay, she'd try for sure to *consider* forgiving her mother. Dizzy from a surge of adrenaline, she anchored her hand on a barstool.

"You okay?" the gladiator asked.

She ignored him some more. It was time to approach Michael Johnstone. *Shiny shiny, mister cat. Won't you tell me where I'm at?*

Laurel stashed the cat behind the bar and snaked through the crowd, wedging herself up front beside Baby Man and Mary Poppins. Talk about yer dysfunctional-looking family.

She knew about dysfunctional families. She was a walking almanac on 'Everything You Ever Wanted to Know about Dysfunctional Families'. Sipping and plotting, she watched Johnstone read eager palm after eager palm.

For the first time today, her heart settled down to a dull thud. Of course the cabernet helped, and judging from all the tittering, he'd impressed the guests but seemed reluctant to delve into futures. The guy didn't like crossing lines. Well, she'd knock that out of him quick.

A pesky husband and wife team insisted he go ahead and get personal. When the wife got teary after he said their daughter's marriage was kaputski, he spent the next few minutes consoling her. The guy really and truly cared and she sure wasn't one to rush the judgement on nice guys. Although reading futures clearly disagreed with him, she'd contract him to investigate hers. *Her* little psychic prediction for the night.

Suckering this gentle, caring, sympathetic man would be child's play.

Okay, her turn now. When a chimpanzee staggered off after hearing of an impending liver ailment, she stepped forward waving her schoolgirl braid at him. The lion's eyes studied her a moment, something he hadn't done with the others.

He held up his palms. "You're fine where you are," he said, sniffling.

After more sniffling, he breathed deeply. Several guests joined their circle. The chimpanzee returned with a fresh drink and whispered to a ghoul. She did the right thing coming here tonight, because the man *felt* something happening to her, felt it big time. *Yessss!*

When he closed his eyes to concentrate, someone lowered Mike Oldfield's *Tubular Bells,* better known as the intro to *The Exorcist.*

"You're walking along the shore, and it's snowing," he said, then cleared his throat. "I hear the ocean and gulls. The surf pounding the shoreline. I hear music in the surf. Do you play the piano?"

Her stomach fluttered. "No."

"Did you ever own a red toy piano?"

"No." She held her breath.

"Well there's something about hands on a piano, young hands. Wait ... a boy's hands. There's a bandage on his finger. And ... ocean again."

While she skipped through fields of clover in her mind, he stepped back and pinched his nose. "Sorry folks, I'm a little drippy."

The room thickened in a fog of whispers.

"You okay, Michael?" Nancy asked.

"Nasally challenged but fine." He nodded at her. "Is this *your* little girl, Nancy?"

She smiled flirtatiously while Nancy introduced them.

"Michael Johnstone, Laurel Ariss. Laurel, Michael."

After Nancy excused herself to mingle, they strolled over to the bar. Michael poured himself an Amaretto on ice and noticed her turn away from her reflection. Geez, observant guy. She distracted him by yanking out the taxidermied cat from behind the fridge. A couple stopped to uncap a Budweiser and the girlfriend frowned at the cat.

"Oh my, that's real isn't it?"

"Used to be," she said, dangling the cat at her. "A relative of my mother's."

Michael had been studying her again. Good.

"Now explain the cat to me," he said, "because I don't see the connection between it and your costume."

"I was in the Halloween 'Come As You Aren't' fashion show at the Royal York today and used it as a prop." She also used it to mess with her mother. "So why not bring it tonight? It is Halloween." That sounded stupid and defensive.

"Oh so you're the model. Nancy's spoken of you."

"Uh-oh."

"Uh-oh?"

Laurel tightened the bow at the end of her long, black braid and whipped it over her shoulder. "Nancy's seeing my brother and sometimes I tease her about it." She had to steer him back to Mark Grant. "Coming here tonight was calculated on my part. Nancy tell you that?"

"What, that you're calculating? You always refer to yourself so favourably?"

Since God didn't approve of her, why should she? "Don't like to brag, what can I say."

"Okay. You should know I mostly do this for fun. I'm not a fortune-teller, Laurel."

"I'm not looking for one. I already have a fortune."

"Then what are you looking for?"

Conscious of the sick, fluttery feeling in her gut, she pasted on a smile. "I'm having a supernatural or paranormal experience. So I uh, need your help before I end up in the cracker barrel." Close call. She almost said *before I end up back in the cracker barrel.* "If you could just give me time to tell you what's happening, at least what happened to me just this afternoon—"

"Could just?"

What, he was teasing her now? He was sure picking one helluva time. "I'd like to talk. Set up an appointment. Your convenience. Name the place and the rate. Doesn't matter."

"You always speak in short, choppy sentences?"

"You keep asking me questions."

"That's my job," he said.

"Does that mean you're hired?"

Michael laughed and so did she, for real this time. "Sorry, Laurel. It's been a long day for me, too. Sure I want to hear your story, and we'll discuss rates only if I can help you. Tell me about this afternoon."

"I can't talk here. There's an order to the story and I don't want to be overheard."

"Fair enough. So you don't play the piano and never owned a red toy piano," he said, topping up her wine. "Do you have an interest *in* piano?"

Damn, he didn't bite and suggest they leave. "Very much so. Richter, Helfgott, Gould. Gould died, you know, of a stroke three weeks ago. And Mark Grant." Saying Mark's name flooded her with warmth.

"And you're interested in the supernatural. I got that from your intense focus. You certainly know how to monopolize the spiritual energy in a room."

She softened her eyes. "Maybe the subject of my intense focus is you."

Using the thespian flair he'd demonstrated during his readings, he lifted his chin and stroked it. "Nice, but I'm not buying. We both know it's not my leonine physique that interests you."

The lion seemed suspicious, not easy to win over. No matter. She'd offer him a good buck, because with the exception of the red toy piano, the man had already proven himself. Michael Johnstone would make a great destiny guru, so said her fluttering, trustworthy gut.

"Alright, yes, I am interested in the supernatural." Maybe she could fire him up by playing the woman in distress. "Something's going on with me. I think you got that part. But what's going on, I have no idea, except that I think I'm losing control of, well ... me. Doesn't that make me a slave to this thing, whatever it is? That's where you come in. If I get you interested enough." She motioned him away from the bar, over to a vacant corner in the hall, but for some reason he didn't budge. "I seem to be obsessed with someone, someone I know of but haven't met. At least not on this plane. We're connected and I want to find out how, what it means."

"A man?" he asked.

She started munching on a cuticle. "A man. And when you find out who he is, you'll probably want to tell me I need a shrink, not a psychic investigator."

≈≈≈

Given the aura loaded with violet and deep blue, an almost blinding, swirling mass of it, Michael acknowledged the paranormal snatching at her. And the emergent black form in her aura was interfering with his extrasensory acuity. The form seemed charged with something resembling static. Whatever was going on with this woman had him intrigued to the knees. Who was the man that had her melting into pools of drool? Too, what about the piano and pounding surf? Standing beside her was like living in a giant conch shell.

Plainly disturbed by the mirrors around the bar, she kept scratching at the backside of her neck. It was mean of him to keep her in the bar area when she kept trying to steer him away. But he wanted to determine whether it was the mirrors bothering her or something else in their space. So far he couldn't tell, though earlier from across the room he saw her take the cat off the bar and stash it, which was strange. Given the occasion, why not leave it on display? The cat meant something to her, that's why.

"We could go," he said, noticing her brighten at the suggestion. Fine, he'd let this mistress of manipulation take the lead. He wouldn't mind having a look at her place, be among her things. He waited for the lady to play her trump card and she did. But she seemed unstrung suddenly.

"This will be the first time I've told anyone this," she said, clutching the cat against her chest. "I'm a private kind of gal. Would you mind if we left right now?"

"Not at all. You seem tense. I can give you a lift home if you'd like."

"My car's across the street. I hate hanging around crowded places, unless it's a concert. Mild case of claustrophobia, I guess."

Laurel told him to meet her out front then sliced through the crowd, down a dark hall lined with lighted pumpkins and a creaking and moaning soundtrack.

"Can I help?" he asked, out on the porch. Nancy was right behind him.

"Thanks, but no. Told you, a mild case of claustrophobia, eh Nancy? Nancy's used to this."

"Oh well, terrific," Nancy said, "considering we'll be at the Grant concert tomorrow night with sixteen thousand other people. I think we should pass, Laurel. Taking you into that crowd's been worrying me."

Laurel's eyes blazed in anger. *"Taking* me? Well you can just march in there and get me my ticket. Katherine and I will go. The last thing I need is you mothering me all night."

"Alright, alright," Nancy said with a show of palms. "I'll call you tomorrow." She thanked him for everything and returned to the party.

Laurel sneered after her. "A six-foot tall skinny woman in a Wonder Woman costume. She should've gone as a skyscraper."

"You have a friend who cares," he said. The lady sure didn't want to miss that concert tomorrow night.

"True. But she cares too much sometimes. Come on." Full of vinegar now, she slipped her arm into his. "I'm in the blue Porsche. Follow me back to my place and we'll de-mask."

She lived in the Circle Court townhouses, a heavily-moneyed area three streets over from Yorkville Village. Lucky lady. He followed the Porsche to visitor's parking and Laurel rolled down her window. After flagging his spot, she screeched around a couple of tight corners and disappeared in the underground maze. He stepped out of his Cressida wagon and put the headpiece back on. Okay, where'd she go? He started counting exits and was up to six when he heard an 'over here' about ten yards off. Feeling her eyes on him from somewhere in the gloom unnerved him. She hadn't moved, hadn't made a sound.

"Right here," she said from a doorway crevice.

He jumped and Laurel seemed to find this amusing.

The exit led to a courtyard with old-fashioned lampposts behind ten townhouses shaded by tall pines. Hers was the third down on the left and most private of all, framed by a five-foot hedge and divided by a high, wrought-iron gate. The woman had 'private' stamped on her soul. He detected an ambiguous significance in the large A enclosed in a lopsided square on the gate.

"Unusual," he said, observing her stiff walk, the stiffness most prominent in the shoulders. Though the pathway had room for two to walk side by side, she preferred to walk ahead of him. The lady liked to lead. As they passed through the gate, the crooked square that framed the 'A' pulled him in like some disembodied hand.

The townhouse had a perfectly symmetrical face right down to the yellow mums in fat Roman amphoras on both sides of the door. She'd trimmed the mums in the pot on the right to match the shape and number of mums on the left. After passing him the taxidermied cat, she opened the door and flicked on the lights. All he could see was blue. She had everything matchy-matchy in a light shade of blue—the rugs, draperies, carpets, kitchen tile. What kind of woman had he met tonight?

"Your, uh, this is beautiful," he said, tugging off the mask. "You're a very symmetrical lady." Wasn't symmetry synonymous with balance? How balanced was Laurel?

She nodded. "The colour blue understands me. Let's sit."

Progress, good. Things would seem less *Halloweeny* once she relaxed and removed her mask. Maybe she wouldn't seem so peculiar. He puzzled over the surfboard-shaped mirror above the fireplace, a blue-tinted mirror. Blue obsessed this woman. Why? In fact, she had several obsessions. Blue. The ocean. The weird gate. And Mark Grant's music.

He observed the fish netting, diametrically suspended from two corners on the living room ceiling. Besides dust, the net supported shells, sea horses, pieces of coral and small, funny shaped bits of driftwood. Adorned on the living room wall were six elegantly-framed seascapes. With no people in any of them, or any photos of loved ones, for that matter. There were no pictures of her, either, which impressed him. Nancy said she made the cover of Vogue three times.

The feeling was blue, the main floor was blue, the lady was blue. Take off the mask, lady, take off the mask. But she hadn't taken it off. Instead, she sat staring at him from the loveseat across from him, while he sat tangled in the Kabuki lion mane, sopping in the armpits.

"Your turn," he said, untangling himself. He put the headpiece under the coffee table. Maybe she'd be more comfortable sitting and talking beside him, just like regular folks.

Well sweet dreams and jelly beans, she finally removed the mask and smiled. With her lips. He found no smile anywhere in those beautiful green eyes. "Lovely," he said, sincere. She had that classy Bryn Mawr look, like a brunette Grace Kelly. "Don't think I've seen eyes that shade of green before."

"You look like Richard Dreyfuss. Can I get you anything?"

A psychological profile would be good. "Naw, I'm okay, thanks."

She stiffened in her seat. "Can you help me, maybe?"

"On second thought, I'll take a Coke or Pepsi if you have it. Let me process, Laurel."

"Okay," she said in a childlike voice. "I'll get you a Coke."

If he took her case, he'd have to cancel Ireland and the entity-infested castle. Oh what the hell. Who needed Ireland in November? Besides, Laurel needed him. She needed someone to help her and from what Nancy said, she didn't have a lot of 'someone's' in her life.

He sensed an extraordinary, possibly dangerous event heading her way. In a vision clip, which was how he referred to these things when they came to him, he saw several grim-looking, winter-clad people on a beach, all crouched over something he couldn't make out. It had been two years since he'd had a clairvoyant flash this vivid, and there were no ghosts here, no satanic evidence, so he could nix demonic interference. It was not reincarnative. Great, he was positive about what it wasn't. So then what the hell was it?

"I'm a captive audience, Laurel," he said, when she returned with the Coke. "Really. I meet a girl at a party and an hour later, I'm whisked away like some egg in an omelette. So wherever you want to begin, I'm all patience."

She hardened her shoulders and gazed up at the netting. "Now that I have you here, I don't know where to start," she said, eyes solemnly fixed on a starfish.

"How about you identify the man for me? You said once I found out who he is, I may suggest a shrink rather than a psychic. Why?"

"Because he happens to be famous." She said this defensively. "At least a million women want him. The thing is I don't know how he got into my life. I don't remember the first time I ever saw him, or heard his music, or dreamt of him. It was like he came from nowhere and landed in my head, in my life. There have been ... flashing incidents ... *revealing* incidents that show we're connected. Some *Thing* is bringing us together. So like I said, I have no control. How can you have control when you're obsessed? Yes I realize it's an obsession. It's also more than that, Michael."

Still visiting with the crowd of people in his head, he'd already guessed the man's identity but wanted to hear her say his name. "Who is he, Laurel?"

She sighed and resumed focus on her friend, the starfish. "Mark Grant."

Laurel slipped into a mini reverie after saying his name, so he let her have this quiet moment to collect her thoughts. He certainly needed a moment to collect his. So, it was more than the man's music. It was the man. How much should he tell this strange lady, obsessed with the colour blue, the ocean and a famous man who fit in nowhere?

For a lady obsessed, there was a conspicuous absence of Grant's albums, concert programmes and souvenirs. Yet in the entrance hallway, she'd hung framed posters of classical pianists David Helfgott, Sviatoslav Richter and his favourite, Glenn Gould. Ah, those shimmering notes. He knew Gould had just died, but let Laurel have her moment at the party. She wasn't the only fan.

Laurel taped Gould's obit to the bottom of the poster, stuck it right on the glass—

Glenn Gould, one of the most celebrated pianists of the 20th century, passed away on October 4, 1982 after suffering a stroke. He had just celebrated his fiftieth birthday.

Fourth in line on the wall of fame was Roger Williams and as a popular music pianist, he didn't fit the classical genre, nor did Mark Grant. So why Roger and not Grant? Why had she completely omitted him from her gallery? Though Grant sang, danced and played sax, he too was renowned as a popular pianist and often opened his concerts on piano.

There were no posters anywhere else of Grant, at least not on this floor. No sign of her obsession for him. That's why he fit in nowhere. He had to get a look at the rest of the house.

The intensifying black in Laurel's aura made him cringe. If not for the ocean, the piano chords hammering his eardrums and the frozen-like crowd vision, it might be time to think about leaving. He could simply tell himself the girl needed to see her doctor and to check back with him once the Clozapine kicked in.

He cupped his hand over his mouth and exhaled. Maybe he should take her connection with Mark Grant to the next level, which he could do by linking her to all the blue around here. Still staring at that ridiculous starfish, she appeared dazed.

"Laurel, why is this thing with Mark Grant more than an obsession?"

It became clear that Laurel wasn't in a daze. While he'd been sitting here totally preoccupied with his thoughts, she had gone into a trance.

He observed her for several minutes. She didn't move, didn't blink. The black had evaporated from her aura. In fact, her *aura* had evaporated. The aura was absent from the body in only two ways—either the person was dead or the spirit had left the body to wander elsewhere.

Where are you, Laurel?

He needed a mirror and the surfboard mirror over the fireplace was too big and too blue for his purpose. He slipped off his shoes and tiptoed about in search of a small one, remembering she hung her purse on the hall coat-rack. Models carried purse mirrors. Models had hundreds of mirrors all over the place. Not this lady. Except for the surfboard, no mirrors. And no Vogue covers. Hmm.

Impatient to raid her purse and get back to her before she snapped out of it, he felt the sweat trickle down his back. Sweat, his personal gauge for intensity of interest and exhilaration. He yanked a pocket mirror out of her purse and made it back in two minutes, leaving a trail of soggy sock prints in the carpet.

Michael eased the mirror upright to the left of her face, about three inches from her head. From this position he could see half her eye, hairline, and beyond. Staring into the partial view of her eye, he used his peripheral vision to look left. This was how the novice trained to see aura, but he wasn't looking for the aura, rather something the Hawaiians called the *aka thread*. This thread linked spirit to body, so he needed to source one end to track her spirit.

It took five minutes to locate the thread, which extended to her left, past him, and up the stairs. He continued holding the mirror in front as he walked toward the stairway. The reflection showed a vast amount of tension in the thread, taut, like a rubber band about to snap. At the top of the stairs, with his heart hammering like a steady beat on a monster drum, he called to her as tremendous amounts of energy jerked the hidden end of the thread.

"Laurel?"

After losing the thread in the shadows on the second floor and no light filtering from downstairs, he let intuition guide him. He took a step left and felt nothing. After three steps to the right, a flash electric current jolted him toward the door in front of him. Laurel's spirit was obviously behind this door and quite busy. Hand tight on the doorknob, a strange shuffling noise intensified when the current tugged him into the room. *Thud! Pitiful whining!* He gulped down several breaths. The whining sounded agonising, inhuman. Suddenly every light in the place flicked on and he froze, gaping at Laurel tearing up the stairs.

"Oh God, not again," she said, breezing by him. "Not again!"

"What, not again? What's going on, Laurel!" She acknowledged neither him nor his question and smacked the door open with such force that it busted a hinge.

An animal lay on the floor, whimpering, its paw scratching at the wall.

The dog, a sort of terrier, seemed oblivious to its bloodied snout. It continued to lie there, pressed against the wall in an unnatural position. Laurel got down on her knees and stroked it, spoke softly to it, but the dog, mesmerized, continued to scratch at the wall.

Nerves raw and mouth dry, he listened to Laurel comfort it. What the hell just happened here? Why had her spirit separated from her body? He recalled the strange sound before Laurel snapped out of it downstairs. There had been a thud, a whack against something. The crazy dog had taken a flyer at the wall. Why would a dog do that?

Under these bizarre circumstances, he found it difficult to think straight. There was Laurel, Laurel's dog, and the odour of sea air and marsh invading his nostrils. He inhaled deeply. He'd never encountered a paranormal glitch of this magnitude.

"Laurel? It's like Davy Jones' locker in here!"

"What do you mean?" she asked, casting him a sideways glance.

"The sea!" The dog yelped, probably because he was shouting like a fool. "This room reeks of the sea. Ocean! Can't you smell it?"

"Yes. Parts of the house often smell this way. Now you see why I need you?"

He nodded, robot-like. "How's your dog?"

He'd be fine, she said. A trip to the vet could wait until tomorrow. It was an easy bet that she and the dog had previously experienced these *episodes.*

"How many times has this happened?" he asked twenty minutes later. They were sipping tea across from each other at her kitchen island while the dog, whose name was 'Mouth' bobbed his way through a bowl of chow. Laurel had an abundance of circled real estate ads strewn about the kitchen, all for waterfront property.

"Three times in the last month," she said, following his eyes along the ads. "I'm afraid he'll seriously injure himself next time. Maybe I should let my brother take Mouth until I sort this out. I don't know. I'm too tired now. Too tired to think straight."

"At the party you said something happened just this afternoon. Did you want to save the story for another day?"

"Oh not at all," she said, suddenly animated, excited fingers dancing on her chin. "If you have time now, I'd love to tell you, to get your take on it. I promise not to keep you much longer."

He felt her adrenaline spike. Tonight he'd get the highlights and save the rest because her emotions were all over the place—the sea, the dog, Mark Grant, something about a bandaged finger. The rest could wait until she was calmer, hopefully sometime before the millennium.

"What happened this afternoon?"

"I had this dream last night about the Piano Bar in the Royal York Hotel. So after the show, I ... well I had to go and have a drink. I was seated two minutes when I noticed the two guys at the table beside mine. Staring at me ..."

"Understandable—"

"No, no. It was a look of recognition!"

"They were at your show in the hotel?"

She rubbed the back of her neck. "No. I had this dream last night and I think one of them was actually *in* the dream. I remembered the tie he wore, navy, with a blue diamond in the middle."

"Wow. Go on."

"I don't recall much of the dream except snippets. The guy's tie. Mark's ... Mark Grant's face. And his hand, or someone's bandaged hand. Not the whole hand, though. A finger."

"Oh?" he said, fidgeting with a cufflink.

"Yeah. And then the guy with the tie said, 'Excuse me, Miss, but weren't you in here last night with Mark Grant?' I said I wasn't and he said, 'Not to be a pain but I was in here last night and I wouldn't mistake you for anybody.' Then his friend said, 'You probably remember her from the show here in the hotel. It's been on all week.' The guy said no. He was positive I was in there with Mark Grant last night.

"Then the waiter comes over with my wine, and get this— the waiter says to the guy, 'I've been following Grant's tour and last night he was in Philadelphia. No way was he in here, sir.' Still, the guy insisted. It was a stalemate. We all stopped talking at once. Then the pianist sat down to play so I went and took a seat at the piano."

The dog jumped in her lap and she kissed his head. "That's certainly something to explore, Laurel."

"But listen to this. I'm finishing my wine and notice the pianist has a bandage on his finger. So I ask him does he have difficulty playing with a bandaged finger. And he says, 'No bandage, miss'. So I look again and there's *no* bandage!"

"God."

"So now I have to get out of there. Everybody around the piano's lookin' at me like I have three heads and on the way out when I'm paying my tab, I hear my waiter talking to the new waiter coming on shift." She shook her head absent-mindedly and patted the dog.

"What?" he asked.

"The new waiter said he saw me there last night. He said 'Philly or no Philly, that guy is right. *She* was in here last night with Mark Grant. I know because I served them.'"

He was dying to talk about the dream and the dog running into the wall, wanted to touch and console her, but she'd become raggedy around the edges. And she had this untouchable quality, a kind of hands-off vibe.

"I'll help you figure it out, Laurel. I'm fascinated. Guess you knew I would be. You get some rest now and we'll pick this up after the Grant concert."

He tried reading her while she packed the Kabuki mask in a Christmas bag, handling it as if it was a Fabergé egg, the black in her aura shifting like the tide. He groaned to himself. He'd had enough of *tides* for one night. Of one thing he was certain—the lady had a hidden agenda. He'd have to recommend that her personal life, present and past, be accessible to him. But not tonight, and so he suggested they hook up again in two days.

Laurel spoke dreamily of tomorrow's Grant concert as she walked him to the door.

"I can't wait," she said.

Too bad he couldn't be there with her to observe because somehow, Mark Grant was at the core of this ... this paranormal glitch, or whatever it was. Come Tuesday he wouldn't know which question of at least twenty to ask first.

As sure as ghosts in the graveyard, he'd have twenty more by Wednesday.

≈≈≈

Laurel dimmed the lights in the living room and curled up on the couch with the dog. She kissed Mouth's bandaged nose. "My sweet Mouth-man. We know what's really going on here, don't we? And we don't want Michael to know, do we?"

The dog lapped at the space between them.

"My baby." She could count on her little friend, who never disappointed, was never cruel or backstabbing. She could always trust him. Unlike certain maternal family members. "Want to hear a bedtime story? Yes, you say? Okay, hon.

"Once upon a time, a daddy came home from a business trip and gave his seven-year-old daughter a present—a magical diamond-shaped aquamarine stone. At five inches in diameter, she'd balance it on overlaid palms, always holding it with reverence. She called it her *Blue Diamond*."

Laurel crisscrossed her palms and Mouth slobbered them with kisses.

"Anyway, the daughter immediately realized the stone was magical 'cause she saw the ocean in it, a magnificent aquamarine sea with that wonderful briny smell coming off cool breezes. She'd taste the salt and feel the sand squish between her toes. She'd hear the waves lapping the shore and see herself building sandcastles on the beach. It was a peaceful, private place with chalk cliffs gleaming like gemstones, and always *always* the yucca-yucca of gulls. Thing of it was, she grew lonely in the beautiful blue diamond place and longed for a playmate to share it with."

Mouth whimpered adoringly when she kissed his head and set him at her side. "We're going to put on Mark's *It's Always After Eight* LP. Start setting the mood for his concert tomorrow night."

The dog yipped and raised his ears. She smiled. Mouth recognized Mark's music. For all she knew he recognized Mark.

She put the dog on her lap and patted him. "Come on now, settle down. Back to the story. So anyway—wishing never made it happen, so the little girl continued to play alone in her blue diamond place.

"Then one November before a family Christmas trip to England, her beautiful place changed into a place with a black thunderous sky and a ravenous mouth of an ocean. Something on the shore must've harmed her because she awakened in her room two whole days later with the diamond glistening at her from her night table. Her crazy wicked mother called her a liar when she insisted she remembered nothing of her nightmares.

"'Then how do you know you're having nightmares if you don't remember?' her wicked mother hollered, and she mocked her for years about it. Dreading her mother's ridicule, she never again spoke of her belief—that the diamond world was real and had passed pieces of its magic on to her, the scariest most powerful pieces.

"The time came for her family's Dickens Christmas vacation to England. So one snowy Christmas Eve they all went, including her crazy wicked mother, to a cozy seaside restaurant. The little girl's life changed forever that night. Because there she heard the most beautiful music and saw the most enchanting ... most enchanting—

The dog shot off the couch and ran barking like hellbeast into the living room. "Mouth, don't you want to hear the rest? No, Mouth!"

Charging after him, she caught and reeled him in by the tail a second before he smacked his head again. Poor, sweet crazy mutt. She carted him upstairs and spent a good hour settling him in his doggy bed, which was empty when her alarm went off at 6 a.m. Holding her breath in spurts, she padded down the stairs calling to him.

"Mouth, honey?"

She found her adorable guard dog posed on his haunches, nose to the dining room wall.

Did Mouth get to meet you first, Mark?

I'll be at the concert for you tonight, Mark.

2. ENCHANTING BOY

AFTER A PRE-CONCERT MEAL in Fran's Restaurant, they cut their way slowly through the crowd toward stadium entrance D. Every few seconds, Laurel glanced up at the huge marquee blinking his name. She clutched the collar of her sheepskin coat up around her ears and snuck a forefinger beneath her turtleneck, stroking the tiny half-moon scar on her throat. Mark would heal all the old scars.

"Hey, Laurel!" Nancy shouted from a vendor booth. "Come check this out!"

Nancy stopped to consider the hottest thing in rock emblem jewellery while Katherine warned her off because it came from China and she had to cut that out. People crammed themselves into stands buying T-shirts, buttons and junk food. Bodies' crowded bodies' and money flipped from hand to hand. Ticket scalpers and dope dealers huddled in corners. All this was happening because of Mark.

"If you wait till after the concert, you'll get it half price," she said, rapping impatient knuckles on the booth. Stung by a bolt of pain in her hand, she shook it out. The girls' voices softened as a light-headed rush blazed through her, the kind one gets when they say someone walked over your grave. Tonight had to be the start for them, the real start in the world Mark loved, in the world she tolerated. She held her breath, gazed at the marquee again. Oh God, did he feel her presence, too? "Let's get to our seats, girls."

"We have forty-five minutes, Laurel," Nancy grumped, then handed the vendor back the item.

"True, but let's get to our seats, anyway." Katharine said.

She smiled. She and Katharine met while competing for a modelling job and after a decade, were about as close as cats and commotion. And Nancy? She supposed Nancy was her best friend. Nancy was also her brother's girlfriend and slightly over-zealous with her affections. For sure, Nancy'd blab to Courtland and for that reason she couldn't be trusted. From now on she'd only trust Michael, who needed to know of all supernatural episodes for obvious reasons. Well, maybe not all. She'd keep private what she needed to keep private, like her emotional climate. If issues developed between her and Michael, she'd deal. Later.

"So," Nancy tugged at her jacket sleeve as they moved with the crowd through the turnstiles, "you never really did tell me last night why you wanted to meet Michael Johnstone."

"It's time I fixed some of this stuff with my mother." She sighed for effect. "I'm tired of dodging her calls. Vomiting at the sound of her voice."

"Really? Wow, good for you, Laur. Courtland would love to see you two make peace."

"But what can a psychic do for you and your mother?" Katharine asked, narrowing her eyes.

She stared ahead into the crowd. "Oh, you know, these people have a way of reading your aura. Calming you. Maybe Michael can keep me from stabbing her with one of her stilettos."

Nancy laughed and Katharine pulled a face.

Everything had worked so perfectly last night with Michael. Even that blank-out in his presence turned out to be rather timely. Bet he wanted to be here tonight so he could observe, study. She was a case to him. So what. She'd been a case before, starting at age eight when she got the blue diamond, and her mother would have no argument with that.

"She spends too much time in a dream world," her mother said to anyone who would listen. "Even her teachers say she daydreams too much."

Where in blazes did Santina the daydream specialist think she got it from? Unable to convince anyone that Santina owned acres of prime property in La-La-land, she eventually gave up trying.

Shortly after her thirteenth birthday, Santina nearly died from strychnine poisoning. Now why would anyone want to poison Mother? It must have cost her father a fortune to keep the cops out of that one. Unable to recall most of that time suited her fine, thank you very much, considering she spent most of it in some kind of head void. Once she recovered, her father whisked Santina off on the first of several vacations spanning the globe. Gulliver had nothing on the jet-setting Ariss's.

"He doesn't want her near me," she told the psychiatrist. "In a way I'm glad. Anyway, Dad's great with long distance phone calls and presents. Don't know how Mother does it. She's enchanted him away from everything."

Mark would believe her about Santina, and he would end the blanks, heal the scars. As the catalyst, Michael had the psychic credentials to teach her how to use the power and the magic. He'd discover the paranormal connection between her and Mark Grant. Once he'd accomplished this, she'd write out the check and say bye-bye. People served purposes for a time and with their purpose served, there wasn't much need for them.

By the time they found their seats, that rush feeling, that destiny-rush, had spread throughout her body, hanging images in her memory like tinsel on a tree. Piano keys, a forehead, small hands, a stormy ocean. She rotated her finger around the scar again—she deserved the hurt and could therefore justify the self-punishment. So much blood and doctors and nurses and worried looks. So many days in the hospital and nights when the tingling came back, along with frag memories of the blue diamond—and the strange silent boy who sat by her bed in the night. The boy no one else could see. The boy who brought the ocean sounds. Blue, blue ocean. Blue, blue. Diamond blue.

Damn these hazy memories! Laurel shifted in her seat. Time to focus. Section Reds were pretty good seats. She really wouldn't need the binoculars, but she had to see his eyes up close. And his hands. Filling the two rows directly behind them was a rather annoying group from Grand Rapids, Michigan. Already stoned and excited, they passed their pipe down to Nancy while the kid with the goody-bag inside his jacket broadcasted to everyone within hearing range that he was Detroit's Frisbee champion.

"I shoulda brought it, man," he complained to Nancy, "because right now I'd be on the floor shakin' my buns. Guess you girls don't got one?" He directed this question at her.

"I couldn't fit one in my purse."

"Can you believe this poor kid's broken up that he forgot his Frisbee?" Nancy whispered.

"Yeah," the Frisbee kid nattered, "we boarded that bus at seven this morning. But this concert's gonna be kick-ass, man. Real kick-ayass!"

"Do you get the feeling we're the oldest ones in here?" Katherine said to her.

She waved away the Frisbee kid's pipe. "That doesn't bother me. What'll bother me is if these people keep bugging us for our binoculars. Why does Nancy have to get so friendly right off the bat?"

"Knead your shoulders a bit," Katherine said. "It'll help relax you."

"My shoulders don't need kneading. What I *need* is to be undisturbed when Grant comes on. I've been waiting a long time for this concert."

"Nice to see our fantasies in the flesh," said Katharine, Miss Junior Psychologist. "Hope he doesn't disappoint."

Katherine knew nothing of her fantasies, which were not fantasies. Mark was always as real as this power of hers, and with their fated connection they'd soon be together. From the *Diamond world* to here. Then once she learned how to work the power—back to the blue diamond world. They'd be happiest there. Because everything that mattered came from there.

When the lights finally dimmed, the sold-out stadium glowed with flicking lighters and sparklers. The crowd whistled and clapped until their palms stung. Laurel struggled to calm her erratic heartbeat. No fantasy here. Just the reality of two worlds uniting. The rush still with her, the tingling moved along her arms to her right temple. The erratic heartbeat dulled to a gentle pulse. She inhaled deeply, smelling not the Frisbee kid's marijuana, but the scent of marsh and seaweed. The ocean! She leaned forward, rested the binoculars on the bridge of her nose, and waited.

≈≈≈

Five minutes to show time, the audience had no knowledge of the commotion backstage. Mark Grant's request for a last-minute change in the opening number had two of his musicians practically unhinged.

"Freddy, I don't comprehend this at all, man. Did Mark say why he wanted to open with *Carolina Blues*?"

"No. He wants to open on keyboards, so listen, it's cool. We just switch the tunes and run with it. No hassle."

"Mark's kickin' back on some other planet and it's no hassle? Keyboards, man. Don't comprehend any of it."

≈≈≈

With the soft-white strobe on him, she savoured Mark Grant's sleek, majestic stride across the stage to the piano. He wore an ice cream suit over a black high-collared shirt with no tie or jewellery. He'd styled his trim, sandy blond hair off his face, revealing a long passion line from temple to mid-brow. The line seemed mysteriously evocative. She'd never seen the line on his forehead, yet she had stroked it. *How? When?*

Through the lens, she found herself most attracted to his hands. Such fair, smooth hands. Young hands. Her body began to drift and float. *God, oh God, don't blank me out now.* Please. She needed this so bad, needed to stay in the present and *see* him.

The piano grew larger. No, no! His hands grew smaller ...

"Oh what happened to his finger? How can he play, Daddy, when his finger's all bandaged up like that?"

"It doesn't seem to be hurting him, dear."

"I'm gonna give him something that'll make him feel better. You'll see. It's a surprise."

She would wait for him to leave the piano, then put the surprise on top and he wouldn't even see her do it. The surprise throbbed in her hand and when she set it tenderly on the piano, it sparkled at her. So pretty–I'll miss you.

He left the piano for some time, busying himself with other things. She loved the way he moved, the way he smiled at the customers. She wanted to watch him like this forever. If only he would see her, smile at her, but then maybe he'd think her silly, too little for him.

After a while he returned to his piano, spotting her surprise halfway through the song. It sparkled so that he had trouble concentrating on his playing. He must have wanted to hurry and finish the song so he could hold it. He looked around a little bit, even struck a funny note. This made her giggle because he loved her surprise and didn't know where it came from. He kept looking

at it, struck more funny notes. For a second or two he stopped
playing altogether. Something kept jabbing at her shoulder.

"Stop Daddy. Let me hear him finish his song."

Jab, jab.

"Please, Daddy."

Jab, jab, jab.

The full weight of her body returned. The marshy shoreline
now smelled like sulphur and marijuana. Mark's finger had no
bandage. But she had a memory. Yes, yes. A memory. This
blank she remembered! She had felt this somewhere else
happiness, this somewhere else electricity. But mostly she felt
power surge through her consciousness like a high-voltage spike
in the brain, though it wasn't bright or freeing. The power
loomed from a dark and lonely place. But who in their right
mind would care about that now?

The grating jab was more of a shoulder poke now and she
spun around, nearly butting heads with the Frisbee kid, overly
excited for some reason.

"Please, please! Let me borrow your binoculars? I just wanna
see what's goin' on down there. One second. I'll just keep 'em
for a second!"

Fine, anything to sedate the kid. She handed them to Nancy
to pass back to him, but Nancy, all squinty-faced, was acting as
strange as the crowd. Where was Mark?

She grabbed Nancy's wrist. "What's happening, what's
going on? Where's Mar, I mean where's Grant?"

"Where you been, Laur? Didn't you see what happened at
the piano!"

"No, nothing. What happened?"

"He seemed rather preoccupied during that last song,"
Katherine said so calmly it irritated her.

"How *rather* preoccupied?"

"He started playing at the piano. Then he started looking at the piano, not the keyboard, but the top of it. Then he looked around a bit and hit the most gawd-awful chord—"

"Then a couple more bum notes," Nancy said, "and then the band took over and he just walked off the stage. I don't think he's feeling well. Something's wrong with him."

Destiny. The connection. It had happened again and glory hallelujah, for once she remembered. It was real. True. Here—in this place. What was the significance of the ocean, her father, the bandaged finger? All she could recall of the long ago memory were the music sheets. She kept seeing music sheets on a piano top.

When Grant returned to the stage after a brief absence, he took the microphone and apologized to the audience, saying he'd recently experienced some nasty cramps in his right hand.

"Not to worry, please," he told the crowd. "Now let's have some fun."

Grant performed brilliantly for the rest of the concert. His agile hands took command of the keyboard, his beautiful voice carried to the rafters. He cajoled with the band, delighted them with his sax and danced over every inch of the stage. He gave three encores and by the end, the audience forgot all about the hand cramps. It was a five-star concert memory.

≈≈≈

Laurel said an abrupt goodbye to the girls after the show. "I'm tired," she said, "Hope you guys don't mind if we skip the wine and brie. The crowd zapped my energy, I guess." With her two Mark Grant programmes in hand, she left them on the street by Fran's parking.

"So much for wine and cheese at Chez Ariss," Katherine said.

"She's got things on the brain," Nancy said, perusing Fran's menu. "I noticed it last night when she left with Michael. Can't get her to talk."

"It's still inconsiderate, Nancy. Laurel will never change."

"She has from the old days."

Katherine raised her eyebrows. "True. She's gotten worse." She started to say something else, hesitated, and took another sip of her Grand Marnier.

"What? Tell me."

"Okay, but don't say anything to Laurel about this. I know she's your best friend. Just that I have reasons for not wanting her to know. Not yet."

Nancy didn't like it, but promised to keep her mouth shut.

"I got a letter from Guy. Things are going really terrific for him out in L.A."

Nancy edged closer to the table. Though Katherine and Guy busted up when he moved to California four years ago, she still had a thing for Guy Sweet. Somehow they managed to salvage the friendship.

"His work is taking him places out there, important places. Get this—he's been doing a lot of rock photography and I don't mean the mineral kind."

"You're kidding. Like who?"

"The latest is Dale Mith." Katherine laughed when Nancy's jaw dropped four inches. "Katherine, I'm having heart palpitations. Okay, so why aren't we telling Laurel?"

"Think about it. Dale Mith is the biggest rock star on the planet. And he and Mark Grant are best friends. Laurel finds this out and she'll start pushing Guy at me. I won't give her the chance to use me again. Remember Bridebook?"

Nancy shook her head.

"I told you. Mind you, it was years ago. I was still modelling at the time, had visions of moving to New York, the whole schmear. I'm sure I told you this. Anyway, Claudine's appendix burst so she couldn't do the Bridebook layout and Claudine owed me a favour. So she got the client to see me. I mean we had the same colouring, height, measurements. Funny how

Laurel picked the day of my big interview to treat me to a pre-birthday luncheon at Truffles.

"'I'll go with you to the Bridebook office,' she said. 'It's just down the street from Truffles.' Right. I was so stupid. The client took one look at Laurel and I was out, colouring or no colouring. Didn't matter that Claudine and I were fair and Laurel was dark. And Laurel's career soared after that, remember, spreads from New York to Paris? Claudine hit the roof. She could never stand her.

"She used me to get in that office, Nancy. Okay, so the client preferred Laurel, but what hurt is that all I got was a shrug from Laurel. There was no remorse, no nothing, except, *well, that's the way things go in this business, eh Katherine?*' Then stupid me goes off to lunch with her. I know it was a gazillion years ago, but still ... if I tell her about Guy's shoot with Dale Mith, she'll start pushing for an introduction to Mark Grant and I'm not sure where Guy and I are at right now, or at least where we're going. And Laurel doesn't back off when she wants something and I *know* she'd want to meet Mark Grant."

Nancy wiggled playfully in her seat. "Hey, so do I, and Dale Mith. You kidding!"

"I'll tell her, once I know more from Guy. Besides, beautiful women barely faze these guys, at least beyond a one-night stand. Mark Grant wouldn't take a second look."

"Oh I don't know. Laurel loves animals and kids. And Mark Grant has a kid. I think he'd know she was sincere."

Katherine slid back in the booth. "Okay I'll give ya that one."

"Give Laurel that one. She has changed, you know." Nancy sighed and clutched her sweater.

"What?"

"Lately she's been like a bat in a cave. Flitting around in the dark. Hiding. Secretive. More secretive than usual, that is. I may have a talk with Court about her soon as he gets back."

"Ooh, I wouldn't wade into that pond."

"Well, aside from the fact they still fight like mad about Mrs. Ariss, they're tight. Maybe she won't be as secretive with her brother."

"They still fight about her mother?"

"Yep, that fire's still raging. You think Laurel is antagonistic towards her mother? Noooo. Laurel *hates* her mother. And that's why she and Courtland argue. He's close to both parents."

"Mrs. Ariss still battling depression?"

Nancy shuffled her feet under the table. "If that's all it is." She nearly let it slip that Mrs. Ariss was seeing a psychiatrist now, but caught herself. Court wouldn't like that repeated. And Laurel ... well, Laurel could care less. "Anyway Mr. A's building that hotel in Cordoba and Mrs. A's right by his side."

"I'm surprised her father hasn't tried to reconcile them."

Katherine was fishing but Nancy wasn't biting. Her father had tried to reconcile them, several times after Laurel's recovery from that ugly breakdown, but his attempts failed. "Maybe he has. But you know Laurel. She's not exactly chatty Patty when it comes to the family dynamics."

"You really think you should tell Courtland how weird she's been lately?"

Nancy closed the menu and put it aside. "Don't think I'm hungry. I haven't made up my mind."

"When's he getting back from Europe?"

"Two weeks. Miss the man like hell. Did you see how she zoned out tonight? How touchy she is? I don't want to spoil Court's homecoming, nor do I want to rag on Laurel. I don't know what to do."

"Stay out of it, that's what you do. Courtland's perceptive enough. She is his sister."

"Tall order, Kath. What if she's picked up a gene from her mother? Now there's this Michael Johnstone business from last night."

"Did you buy the bit about his helping with her mother?"

"Sure, I got all excited at the prospect of that. What? You didn't?"

Katherine fluttered her lips. "Yeah, right. When Claudine grows a second appendix."

≈≈≈

Mouth went into his jumping bean routine soon as she opened the door.

"He's mine, sweet thing!" She swept the little dog into her arms. "Now we'll have everything Santina has. Even more!"

Mouth licked off her cocoa butter lip gloss. Her precious boy knew stuff. She'd have that special love, a quiet world for the three of them. And Mark had that adorable little son. She'd be such a wonderful mother because she knew what not to do. Her crazy mother was the prototype of what not to do. And when Fraser was grown with a family of his own, they'd all spend Christmases together. She and Mark would grow old, have wheelchair races at the country home, and at night he'd sing and play piano for her and she'd scold him about his sodium intake and remind him to take his calcium pill. Mark and Laurel. Laurel and Mark.

"I've done it, Mouth," she said, tugging playfully on one of his ears, whispering into it. "I've really done it. I've tapped into something so powerful. I'm powerful." Then she headed up to celebrate in her secret room, her Sea Room where she would spend the night drinking Scotch and try to remember more.

≈≈≈

Laurel walked into the upstairs closet carrying a bag with everything she needed for the night—scotch tape, scissors,

Mark's two concert programmes and a tray of ice cubes. Hearing the dog scratching at the door after closing it behind her, she called out, "Not tonight, Mouth-man. Go to sleep and I'll see you in the morning."

Having turned on the Phase Four sea music from downstairs, the surf melodies greeting her marked the perfect end to a perfect evening. She adored this room. To anyone else it was just a large closet used to store winter clothing. It had a top shelf lined with five boxes. Hat-boxes, she told everyone, hat-boxes and junk boxes. Hanging in it were two fur coats, a number of gowns, one guest bathrobe, and a heavy bedspread draped across the bar beneath the box shelf. Several pairs of boots lined the floor along with two lumpy garbage bags filled with casual summer clothes. At least that's what she told the stay-overs. Actually, the hatboxes were hatless and the lumpy garbage bags were filled with ancient newspaper and Christmas wrapping.

Seeing *Whatever Happened to Rosemary's Baby* gave her the idea. When Rosemary heard the baby crying behind the linen closet, she had the good sense to realize something more than linens lurked there. So Rosemary took down the shelves and voila! A door leading to another room! Brilliant idea. Only it would be a drag always having to take down the shelves and put them up again when she wanted to get in. The closet effect worked better. She could disappear behind the clothes, open and close the second door behind her and no one would know. If anyone went looking through the house for her, good luck to them.

It was really a small spare bedroom with the ceiling papered in clouds and sky, three walls in ocean murals and the fourth plastered with photos of Mark, a cluster of them inside a huge lopsided square from ceiling to floor. In the middle of the cluster was a childhood picture of herself, the photograph taken on somebody's cottage dock—father in the background,

Courtland in the middle and Laurel sitting cross-legged on the dock in the foreground. She cut her mother out of the picture. It was a rare and treasured photo and to her knowledge, the only photo of the *blue diamond,* which she held in her cupped hands.

Tucked in the corner was a rollaway bed, squeaky rocking chair beside it and a bottle of Glenlivet atop an occasional table made of driftwood. Beige carpeting. One wall speaker. An intercom. She never knew why she put the intercom in here. To hear Mouth, maybe? Or the phone or the door? For some reason, the intercom seemed important at the time.

Looking eerily animate on the floor next to the rocking chair was where she kept the black, hissy-looking taxidermied cat, back arched, green eyes wide. The day she brought the cat to the taxidermist, he tried unsuccessfully to talk her into three alternate poses. 'That's the way I remember it', she lied, offering no further explanation. Of course the taxidermist had the good business sense not to ask the customer for the cat's story.

The object most prominent in the room was a four-foot display stand covered in a floor-length, royal blue velvet spread, six-inch square rise on top—and nothing displayed on it.

Laurel cranked up the Phase Four and poured herself some Glenlivet. Carefully removing the staple from one of the programmes, she unfolded the eleven by fourteen poster of Mark. Damn foldout had a paper line all the way down the page. Well, she'd simply cut out his full-length frame and tape it to the wall. And since she'd run out of space in the photo cluster, she decided on a section of ocean in the mural. Within minutes Mark looked like the mighty Poseidon holding the sea in place.

Halfway through her third Scotch by this time, she felt light-headed and tingly. The carpet was sand, the blue lighting night sky and the mural rolling waves. Having switched to

Mark's music two drinks ago, she pictured him on a Montreal-bound flight, the last stop of the tour. Poor darling had to be wondering what happened to him at the piano. If only he didn't have to catch that flight right after the show. If only they could have met backstage. She would have taken him to Rudy's in Yorkville. Afterwards, she'd have brought him back here and made sweet love to him all night long. *Soon, darling. Soon we'll be together in some quiet place. No madding crowds for us.*

She stripped down to her teddy and stretched out on the rollaway. Softly calling out for Mark, she collapsed her arms at her side, allowing the tingling rush to overpower her. Summoning the courage to enter the void to be with him, she let her body drift into weightlessness. This time she would have to return with more of him. She choked back tears as she spoke.

"I demand to remember more. Make me remember more."

Laurel crossed the threshold into the blackness...

≈≈≈

...Rudy's intimate setting glowed with candlelit tables and torchy music. The patrons stared at them in a non-intrusive way. He held tight to her hand, running her fingers softly around his lips. She memorized his eyes, smiled at the sound of his voice, delighted in his touch.

He leaned forward and kissed her. "You're different tonight," he said. "A little unsettled. Tell me what's bothering you."

She scanned the people in the room, felt her chest tighten. Before, nothing had been negative in this place. "Everything's different tonight, haven't you noticed? Even these people."

"What about the people, love?" he asked.

"Before they hardly noticed us, even after they recognized you. Tonight they're all looking and whispering."

He glanced around, smiled. "So? Different people tonight. Different people unaccustomed to celebrity. Oh baby, baby, we're due for more of the real world, don't you think? Maybe it's time we found a way into it."

She shook her head emphatically. "No. It's always been so perfect here, the way we love each other, everything. And tonight I'm remembering glimpses of you, even hearing the waves rolling in at your father's house. I've never remembered anything of you from there before, everything else about my life, but not you. So why now? Something's happening, Mark, and I'm worried."

"Worried? No, baby. Don't you know every enchanting thing that's happened to us has been predestined? I want you happy. I want us to find a way to get there. I want us to make it there. I want to love you there."

A chill passed through her. "Are you sure that's what you want? Because I'm not happy there. I don't like anything about it. I don't even like me. I ..." Finally convinced she could trust another human being with this information, she said, "I HATE me there."

Eyes bold and confident, Mark cupped his hands over hers. "Stop now. If that's true I will help you find out why and we'll fix it. Don't be afraid of remembering me there. Lord, I wish I were remembering you. With luck, soon I will, too. Then we can find a way to make us happen all over again." Mark removed her star sapphire ring from her right hand and slipped it on her left hand. "Only there," he said, "can I replace this with a wedding band."

Partially blinded by a flashbulb they caught sight of a man scurrying away from the proximity of their table, another man chasing after him.

"Hey, Ben!" the man shouted, "I don't have enough cash to pay the tab, man. Wait up."

"Let's get the hell out of here, Laurel," Mark said. "As out as we can get."

≈≈≈

The phone woke her. The damned intercom was good for something after all. A blush came over her as she ran naked from the Sea Room, suffering a slight loss of dignity stumbling through the closet. Mouth started licking her foot when she picked up the receiver in her bedroom. She didn't like being naked in front of the dog. *Why* was she naked?

"Uh, hello?"

"Laurel, it's Michael. Michael Johnstone. You sound out of breath. Did I get you at a bad time?"

"No, no, I um ... I just got in."

"Really? Must've been a great night. Listen, he's not there or anything is he?"

"He who? What do you mean?"

"Laurel, I know you met Mark Grant last night and I want to talk to you about it. Actually, I assumed you'd be wanting to speak to me today. But since you just got in—"

"Michael, what are you talking about? I didn't meet Mark Grant last night. Think you can go a little slower? I'm in kind of a fog here."

After a brief silence on Michael's end, he said it was important they talk and asked if he could come over.

"Of course. But what's this about my meeting Mark Grant last night?"

He told her he'd explain when he got there and hung up.

When she put the phone down she noticed her ring was missing. She kept thinking of Mark, about what Michael had said, about the concert and what happened there. Something else happened last night in the Sea Room–another blank. Something wonderful. And when she felt the weight of her star sapphire on her *left* hand, she collapsed on the bed, ecstatic. She held up her left hand and laughed at the ring.

She remembered.

≈≈≈

Michael arrived about forty minutes after their phone conversation, a copy of the *Toronto Sun* folded neatly under his arm. Before he got there, she remembered nothing of showering, dressing, applying make-up or even stepping on the dog's tail when he got underfoot at one point. When she returned to the Sea Room to collect her clothes from last night, she detected seminal odour in the room. A powerful memory trigger, smell had become her most dominant sense. Dominance. That's what she had now in the form of power. Anything she wanted she could take.

≈≈≈

"You've got me baffled," Michael said, joining her at the kitchen counter. "Do you still want me to help you with this thing or not?"

She looked at him questioningly. "Of course I do. I need you to tell me exactly what this thing is, how to use it."

"Then why lie to me, Laurel? I know you and Grant got together last night."

"I keep forgetting what a psychic can do. Yes, we were together. And it was beautiful."

"Did you go backstage after the show?"

"No," she said, feeling something out of sync with their conversation. "How would I get backstage?"

"Well then how did you two meet, Laurel? Did you run into him somewhere after or what?"

"Michael, I had a dream about us, a very real dream and we were together. And it's the first dream where I've remembered everything. At least most of it. We were talking about here and there, whatever that means. Then he took my ring and slipped it on—"

"He took what? Uh ... w-what do you mean–ring? What ring? You mean that ring?" Michael stood up and pointed a shaky finger at it.

"Yes, of course this ring," she said, watching his complexion pale.

Michael took a breath. "Laurel, have you seen today's *Sun*?"

"No. Truth is I haven't been out."

"Here," he said, thrusting the newspaper at her, "page 103. One picture's worth a thousand words."

Given her racing pulse and heightened senses, it was next to impossible to control her excitement. But she managed, barely reacting to the photograph of Mark dining with a woman whose back faced the camera. He was smiling while slipping a ring on the woman's finger. Though she didn't recognize the woman's dress, she did recognize the long black hair, the star sapphire ring, and the surroundings. The place was Rudy's in Yorkville, one street over. And the woman was herself.

≈≈≈

He told Laurel he'd drop by again later in the evening. It was still a working day and he had some business to take care of. What he didn't tell her was that this business concerned her little tête-à-tête with Grant last night at Rudy's. She said it was a dream and he knew photographs didn't lie. Maybe she believed it to be a dream. Maybe she was lying. And if she was leading some kind of dual life, then yeah, she needed a shrink, not a psychic. Michael left his car in underground parking and took a walk over to Rudy's for a quick beer, thinking he might learn something, even feel something.

The lunch crowd dined early at Rudy's. With one available table by the door, Michael grabbed it and shut his eyes for a few seconds to fine-tune his senses into the atmosphere. The central focus seemed to be on two men having an argument on the other side of the room. He couldn't quite make them out but one of the voices had a familiar ring. As he sat there sipping on his Lowenbrau, thinking about this thing with Laurel, it suddenly dawned on him who the voice was. His old pal Lonnie Fletcher. Both he and Lonnie attended Queen's University together about five years ago and played on the university hockey team for two semesters. A lot of carousing went on back then and he and Lonnie shared some good times.

After Queen's, Lonnie had one good season playing pro hockey with the Leafs until he busted his knee. So six months after the busted knee and busted dream, he received an offer to work for Canadian Press International. Rumour had it he tossed words better than he ever tossed a puck, so Lonnie married the job. Although he wasn't a journalist for C.P.I., he was more of a getting-the-facts-straight man. Michael had no idea what title went along with that but when he heard Mark Grant's name shouted more than once, he knew Lonnie was here for the same reason as himself.

He didn't want to walk over and interrupt them. Instead, he ordered another Lowenbrau and waited. Since he was sitting by the only exit, Lonnie would have to walk right by him on his way out. About ten minutes later, Michael nailed him by tugging on his scarf. Same silly looking multi-coloured scarf. Same Lonnie.

"Hey, Fletch," he said. "How you doin', buddy? Been a long time."

"Stoner!" Years ago Lonnie had shortened Michael's surname from Johnstone to Stoner. He never called him anything else. "How the hell are ya? Still in the spirit business?" Lonnie asked, joining him.

"You bet. Still going strong."

"Glad to hear it. Feel like lifting *my* spirits any?"

"Yeah, I couldn't help overhearing part of that. What's going on?"

"C.P.I. sent me down here to straighten out a mess," Lonnie said, gesturing for the waitress. "Seems Mark Grant was in here last night, that is according to the owner and numerous waitresses. A freelance shutterbug even got a shot of him with some mysterious woman and the picture winds up in today's *Sun*."

"I know. I saw. So what's the problem?"

"Problem is we get a call this morning from Grant's press agent. Now get this–Grant was nowhere near this place last night. Directly after the concert, he was in one of our limos on his way to the airport. I checked it out and it rings true. His private plane took off at 12:45 for Montreal. He even signed an autograph for the limo driver.

"Now I come over here," Lonnie spoke quickly, dabbing the spittle at the corner of his mouth, "and I find out Grant was here last night at the same time he was supposed to be on that plane. And the *Sun* has to do a retraction and say it was some look-alike, but they insist here that it really was Grant. He even used a gold American Express to pay his tab, waitress says it was his name on the thing–everything. Go figure it, Stoner, you're the psychic."

"Was Grant told about the credit card?"

"That presents another problem. Shortly after the alleged Grant and his lady left, the receipt, now get this–the receipt, which includes both the bank copy and the house copy– vanishes. Yeah, vanishes. They've turned this place upside down and they can't find it anywhere."

Michael didn't want Lonnie to know this, but the vanishing receipt was the most intriguing thing he'd heard so far. He felt all gooseflesh under his windbreaker. "Did you speak with the photographer?"

"Yeah," Lonnie said. "Poor guy. He's so bummed about this because he swears it really was Grant. He's being pressured to include an apology in with the *Sun's* retraction. I mean, Grant would know where he was last night and he's got the limo driver, along with the autograph, along with numerous people at Toronto Airport to back him up. This is really weird but we have to go along with Grant's wishes or somebody's gonna get shot with a wooden bullet. Pay checks will start vanishing faster than you can spell 'missing receipt'. After all, when a celebrity as big as he is is seen slipping a ring on a lady's finger and it turns out it's not him at all ... let us say that CPI frowns on words like *legal action, claim, litigation.*"

"Any word on the lady, Fletch?"

"None. Great looker, that's all I know from what Ben said."

"Ben?"

"Ben Sidenko, the shutterbug."

≈≈≈

Michael got Ben Sidenko's address from a contact at the *Sun*, then phoned Sidenko and set up a meeting. By late afternoon he was sitting in the photographer's apartment watching him knock back what must have been his fifth or sixth gin and orange juice. Like everyone else directly connected with this boner, poor Ben Sidenko was having a bad day.

"My credibility's really blown now," Ben was saying. "Some jerk-off at the paper this morning told me I have such appropriate initials, that before long my name'll be shit all over this town. Not exactly in clover here and now I find myself sitting with a psychic investigator of all things who wants to keep our conversation hush-hush. Like I told ya on the phone, man, it's cool. So what can I do for ya?"

"Well, your print in the *Sun* was in black and white," Michael said, putting Ben's misaimed orange pit in the ashtray, "and you said your film was in colour. So I was wondering if you'd let me have a look at your own colour prints and the negatives."

"Negatives'll be no good to ya, man," Ben said.

"Why's that?"

"They show more distortion than the prints if you can believe that. I didn't even expect the prints to turn out. I only developed the film because I had other stuff on it, which turned out fine. Only the Grant negatives were screwed. Excuse, I mean the *alleged* Grant."

Michael asked if he could see them anyway and a moment later, Ben returned with both the prints and the negatives.

The colour prints were as fuzzy as the black and white shots but clear enough to emphasize a substance resembling coloured flecks of snow framing Mark's body. Laurel didn't have the snow. What she did have was grey, chunk-like matter around the head, the matter appearing solid, though split or broken. The negatives were something else again.

"Um ... uh ... would it be alright if I took a set of these negatives?" Michael asked. "I'll be happy to pay for them."

The photographer shrugged out a yes, then staggered off into the kitchen for more ice.

He'd never seen anything like this. Their bodies were transparent, with everything around them reflected *through* them, like ice or glass. Lines and lines of colour surrounded Mark. On a negative! And that peculiar grey matter around Laurel's head on the colour prints turned out to be solid black squares, or lopsided boxes. It looked like someone had suspended a small, black box mobile over her head. Michael didn't like the look of these black things. They gave him the creeps.

"I'll be on my way now," he said, taking out his wallet. "How much do I owe you?"

"Forget it," Ben said, leaning on the refrigerator for support. "If you can clear this up for me, even raise a question or two, I'll be back in business."

On the way out he dropped a fifty-dollar bill on the plant stand. Listening to poor Ben Sidenko cussing the ice-cube tray, he was amazed the guy wasn't the least bit intrigued by the strange photographs or a parapsychologist coming to pay him a visit.

≈≈≈

Michael decided to go home first and unwind before returning to Laurel's. For now he wouldn't tell her what he suspected but later he'd run his idea by her, once he connected a few more of the dots. He turned on the cassette, his third recording since meeting Laurel the other night. Just the other night. Amazing.

"Thursday, November 2nd, 1983. For the first time in my career I've come across what I believe to be a clear case of astral projection. Of the two forms, Laurel Ariss falls into the second category. The first is called 'asomatic' projection where the subject rises above his body, has a new point of view and does not appear to have a body at all. One can be anywhere around his physical body and be watching himself, but he will be watching himself from nothing. This is the form of astral projection with which most people are familiar.

"However, the second form termed 'parasomatic' is a buzz-theory generally dismissed among scientists. That aside, in the parasomatic astral state the subject is located in a duplicate body–*his* duplicate body. He can literally be in two places at once.

"Today's circumstances led me to conclude such is the case with Laurel Ariss and Mark Grant. Somehow they have met and connected on the astral plane, have had frequent meetings and have even been, I suspect, lovers. However, on this plane they have little or no recollection as to what's been happening to them, though Miss Ariss is beginning to recall what she describes as 'very real dreams'.

"But more is involved here than the parasomatic astral state. Miss Ariss is a striking woman who has I fear, a delusional concept of her own importance. Also, her predominant colour-aura is black. Disturbing. I also believe or should I say perceive, that she is capable of aggressive paranormal skill. Some form of volatile energy or power has taken root inside her and is rapidly developing. I don't know exactly what it is or its point of origin, though it's clear that Mark Grant is the receiver. I need to learn to what extent he is affected.

"Not much to go on, but I do know this–Ariss and Grant are destined to meet on this plane and when they do, God knows what will happen. I do have an idea, however. I will be seeing Miss Ariss again tonight and will suggest to her that there may be a way to expedite their actual meeting. I will suggest that during their next astral encounter she leave Mr. Grant with a simple written message. Nothing too elaborate, but a suggestion giving no names, addresses or phone numbers. Rather, something like 'Come to Toronto'. He will then be instructed by her to keep this note in his hand at all times. If he places the note in his astral clothing, it will dissolve when he comes to.

"This is all so fantastic. I don't even know if the note experiment will work. But of this I'm certain—they must meet soon. Spending too much time in the astral could damage their hearts, emotions, and minds. And with Miss Ariss mysteriously holding all the power, Mark Grant could be especially vulnerable. I strongly recommend they meet as soon as possible. Again, it would help if I knew how Mark Grant is feeling."

Fortunately, as a fan of Grant's, Michael had his latest LP– *It's Always After Eight*. Maybe an analysis of the lyric sheet would give him a glimpse into the man's subconscious. Why not? Something could register. Why not exercise the gift?

After re-playing the tape, he settled down with a beer and Grant's lyric sheet. An hour later, with only the title cut left to examine, it appeared Grant's subconscious was unaffected by Laurel. Then one-third of the way through the title cut he developed gooseflesh for the third time in one day—

IT'S ALWAYS AFTER EIGHT

I follow your shadow through corridors to Oblivion,
where Oblivion has your eyes burning into mine.
You've made my mind a steel case.
So why can't I get close in this obscure place?

Need more time in this romantic blue space.

CHORUS
Accentuate, accentuate
Elaborate, oh elaborate
It's always after eight
Oh it's always after eight

The idol says, dear Lady of Shadows, I am fearful of a sham.
Will the shadow lady answer saying not a sham but
a house of dreams that flower?
Space stretches time, dear Lady of the Clock Tower.
Space stashes time, and the idol doubts the hour.

CHORUS

Waiting years in minutes as this form covets her shadow.
Wanting a key encounter to get back on the lovers' track.
No time to miss time necessitating facts.
No time to blow time anticipating facts.

CHORUS

Please accentuate, accentuate
Elaborate, please elaborate
The time is after eight

It's always after eight
Ahhh, formulate
It's always after eight

Though these lyrics seemed vague on the surface, she got to him, all right. Grant *had* been affected—but to what extent? If only he knew. If only he knew what was going on in Mark Grant's head right about now.

3. THE ASTRAL SHORE

 **Malibu, California**

TEN DAYS AFTER the Montreal concert, Mark sat nursing one of his best friend's lethal cocktails on the upper deck of Dale's Malibu beach house. His five-year-old son, Fraser, was on the beach playing fetch with Heathcliffe, Dale's Irish setter. Soon as he stepped out of the car, he asked Dale to not cuss around Fraser and to drop the bags, he'd unpack later. He just wanted to kick back and count the clouds.

He needed this down time with his two favourite people. Because of that weirdness at the Toronto concert and bizarre conversation with his father two days ago in London, he hadn't slept in two weeks. Mark stole a peripheral glance at Dale and smiled. Dale, who'd been studying him from the corner of his eyes while pretending to squirt butane into the table lighter, had more of the stuff on his jeans.

"You'll be going up in flames in a moment. Here, let me do that."

"Forget it." Dale took a whiff of his sweatshirt. "Talk to me, mate."

He exhaled quietly and smiled, which felt good considering he'd been smile-deprived for days. "Alright then. Have to say I missed you and my kid down there." He stopped to give a holler to Fraser. "Fraser! Away from the water. Wait for me!"

"'K, Dad!" the boy shouted back.

"I feel like I've been away for years and now that the tour's over, now that I'm finally here, it hardly seems real."

"Yeah, I know," Dale said. "Jet lag. Mind lag. But tell me, have you not been feeling well?"

"Well I'm naturally a bit trashed, but feeling well–considering."

"So what in blazes was that hand thing all about in Toronto then? Justin gave me the crack on things. I mean, you just walked off the stage, man. You've never done that before."

"My hands are fine, Dale," he said, relieved at the chance to unload. Justin didn't know swot, neither did the crowd in the Gardens that night. They knew what he wanted them to know.

"Then what's this story of Justin's? Unless my hearing's been scrambled by aliens, that's what he said."

Mark looked down for Fraser.

"Heathcliffe's watching him. Don't worry."

He tightened his posture in the chaise. "Justin hasn't a notion and I'm sure as hell not discussing it with him. Something strange happened at the keyboards that night, Dale. I had some sort of regressive thing happen to me. For a few incredibly alarming moments, I was a boy again, at my father's in Rottingdean, sitting at that ancient piano of his. And the house was still the restaurant with customers and clanking in the kitchen, tables arranged exactly like when I was a kid. When I walked off the stage, I saw myself as a boy. Bloody frightening. I had to anchor myself in a corner backstage, willing it to pass."

Dale rolled the lighter absentmindedly in his hands. "You know, you should've postponed this tour. I mean, Gil's death last May, your dad's stroke a few weeks afterward. Then you had to keep it together for Fraser and put the London digs up for sale. Settle your dad in that convalescent place. Seems you never got time to grieve. It's caught up with you now, Mark. I know you've got good survival power, but you've been through hell. Gillian's death was—"

"Considered all that." Thinking back on the horror of it, he grieved more for Fraser than himself. As for his father's stroke—no shock there. He'd had two small strokes in ten months. Dale had to understand that what happened the other night had nothing to do with belated grief, but something quite different. "You know Gil and I had stopped loving each other long before she ... we had gotten together again after a year's separation only because of Fraser. I cared deeply for her, we were friends and I still miss talking to her but I went back to her because of my kid. I couldn't bear losing custody if a divorce went down. He means everything to me, you know that. And Gil was a great mother.

"But I still wonder how all that water got into her lungs when she was nowhere near the pool. I mean, how can a person drown in the bloody living room? If it was a drowning. They never really did make sense of it. And her poor body. I never told you what the coroner said, did I?"

Dale set down the lighter. "No. I've been waiting."

"He said she looked as though she'd been pummelled by a thousand tons of water. Justin and I had quite the time keeping the press off it."

"So sorry, mate. So sorry."

He wanted to tell Dale what he never had, what he never told anyone. "But now listen, Dale. Listen. When the coroner unveiled Gil's body for the postmortem, she looked lovely as always. What he saw on the examining table was not what he saw in our living room. He couldn't explain it. Still can't."

"Am I processing right? She was unrecognizable at the house and normal for the post?"

"Yes. And Fraser caught a glimpse of the *before*. Just a glimpse because I hollered at him to leave the room. At first even I didn't know what I was looking at. He's never going to hear about his mother that way, Dale, unless some well-connected smutraker in the coroner's office digs it up and sensationalizes bloody hell out of it. I still worry about that happening. It's a miracle it hasn't happened yet."

"Maybe it was some kind of illusion when you pulled back the drapes—"

He waved Dale's idea away. "And what? Both of us, including the coroner's people having the same illusion? No. Can't be explained. It's a mystery horror we'll never solve."

Mark walked to the railing and waved down to Fraser. "And my father's stroke came as no surprise. They cautioned him about the high blood pressure for the longest time. 'Til I went completely off my wick I warned him about his health, but he's so damned stubborn he wouldn't listen. Odd though, we believed he had his act together before it happened, that he'd been taking better care of himself."

"How's he doing?"

"He's still partially paralysed on his right side, but slowly getting the use of his hand again. And he's talking a little now. Doctors feel confident he'll have an eighty percent recovery. But when I told him I was going to check the house in Rottingdean for him, he got all knotted at me. Over and over again he kept mumbling, 'Close the restaurant 'til I get back there. Don't go back there'. He still thinks we've got the restaurant. I've heard stroke victims often regress, though. But for some reason he didn't want me near the place."

"So did you go?"

"Sure I went. I had this urge to see the place again. Fraser and I stopped on the way and picked up some surf gear in Brighton. Got a new surfing mask. No more blue face for me. Even broke down and got a leash for the board."

Dale jerked his head back. "A leash? You?"

"I know. Absurd, isn't it? But with the kid, I can't take the chances I used to."

"You're still a shark in water and you've kept fit. Though it's beyond me why you winter surf. I know it's big at home, but ..." Dale scratched his jaw. "So? The house?"

"It looked like there'd been a break-in. No, nothing serious. More of a *Goldilocks* thing. My old bed had been slept in and there were two empty wine glasses on the piano, one with lipstick. I kept smelling perfume all over the place, perfume mixed with my own cologne. Strange. But I didn't notice anything missing. Probably just a couple crashing for a night.

"But I felt so weird in the house, strangely magnetized by the place. All the memories–the swimming meets, the surfing, shuffling around as busboy at thirteen, playing piano for the customers, doing everything to help Dad keep it together after Mum died. He missed running that restaurant without her. I remember the sadness when he gave it up, flipped it back into a house again. You know, if not for our get-together here, Fraser and I might've stayed on a bit. Though, Fraser didn't mind leaving. He kept telling me how dopey I looked, which brings me to something else I wanted to tell you."

"Alright then."

"Something similar to what happened at the concert, only this time I don't remember anything of it." He leaned on the rail and examined his hand. "I uh ... well, according to my son, I went and sat down on the couch next to the piano and my mind went off on some sort of strange tangent. Fraser said I spoke to him but I sounded like his robot toy. And I know something did happen, Dale, because when I snapped out of it I needed to get my bearings all over again. Maybe it's just being on the road so much and this thing in Toronto. Two things in Toronto, actually. Did Justin tell you about the newspaper photograph?"

"Yeah," Dale rounded his eyes. "Seems you've got a double. Fascinating. Did they find out who he is yet?"

"No, not yet. And I don't find it fascinating. It makes me shudder. It looks so much like me I tried to remember when it was taken. The photo's in my luggage. When I unpack I'll show you. This guy is my twin. Wait 'til you see it. Dale, believe me, it's not grief. Something weird's going down. And after I catch a few Z's, maybe I'll be able to explain myself better."

As he primed for that nap, Fraser came running into the house insisting he and his Uncle Dale have a romp with him on the beach. Anxious to show Dale the photo, he preferred to unpack first.

"This is too bloody much," Dale said, staring at the picture while he shoved things in drawers. "I'd swear this was you, absolutely swear."

"It is Dad, Uncle Dale," Fraser said, pinning on one of his father's boyhood swimming medals, "only Dad doesn't remember the camera shooting him."

Dale grinned and play-punched Fraser's jaw. Mark had often heard Dale express the wish that a kid had come out of his marriage to Carmen instead of a divorce and a three-million dollar settlement. He sat down on the edge of the bed and plunked Fraser on his lap. "Fraser, it's not Dad. Didn't I explain all that to you?" He tapped his son's nose.

Unconvinced, Fraser gave him a weak nod.

"Now would I lie to you, kid?" He said this in his best Bogie impression and the boy giggled.

"No, Dad," he said, staring adoringly at him. "But I'd know you anywhere."

He shook his head in exasperation. It was like trying to separate surf from swell. "Go get into your jeans and jacket and unpack our lucky rock. Then we'll all take that romp on the beach."

"You still carrying that thing around?" Dale asked, laughing at the way Fraser bunny-hopped out of the room.

"Oh man, now listen to you. I've never once seen you perform without that Peruvian coin thing of yours. Come to think of it, you're still number one even in your old age. Maybe I should put my rock on a chain and wear it around my neck. What do you think?"

"My ass, old age! Let me remind you I happen to be the youngest thirty-eight I know and you're only three years younger than me. And you'd look flippin' ridiculous with that blue thing pounding you in the chest. I mean my coin is class, mate, and your rock is—well ... it's a rock, isn't it."

Mark and Dale tossed a Frisbee around on the beach while Fraser and Heathcliffe occupied themselves building a sandcastle. Fraser decided he'd have to find a very special place for the rock. It didn't look right as a moat. He loved his father for trusting him to play with it. His dad knew he always took good care of his things and he'd had this rock since he was a teenager so it was extra special to him. But lately it had been making Fraser sniffle and cough a bit.

Heathcliffe, rapidly developing a fascination for the rock, kept licking it. When the dog put it in his mouth, Fraser gave him a couple of gentle conks on the head. Heathcliffe dropped it in the sand.

"I didn't mean to hurt you, Heathcliffe." The boy's voice broke at the sight of the droopy-eyed dog. "But Dad would throw a wobbler if you chewed up his rock." The dog looked affectionately on as Fraser wiped the drool and sand off the stone with his windbreaker. Then Fraser began to cough, just a few little coughs as he continued wiping. When Heathcliffe started to whine, he told him all was well, probably flu coming on.

After cleaning the rock, Fraser held it up and stared into it. Even though doing this plugged up his nose and made him cough, he couldn't seem to help himself. The rock looked like its own place, like its own planet or something. Once he saw his mom in there looking out at him, smiling. Taking no notice of Heathcliffe's whines, Fraser began to wheeze and gasp for air. He had never lost his breath like this before and it frightened him.

The rock fell from his hands.

"Dad. Daddy—"

He tried to call out for his father as loud as he could but his voice broke. Pounding his chest with two small fists, he fell onto his side, felt gurgling in his ears, felt faint and terrified. Then he felt nothing.

≈≈≈

Mark didn't realize how far down the beach their Frisbee play had taken them until he heard Heathcliffe barking and saw Fraser lying on his side, his small body rising and settling in a slow jerking motion. Running to his son, he called to God for the first time in years.

God, please! Please!

Fraser lay taking slow protracted gasps, eyes open and focused on Mark's rock, half-buried in the sand. "Daddy's here, sweetheart." He positioned the boy on his back, turned his head to the side, then back to the center and began mouth-to-mouth. Was he doing it right? Oh, God! And Dale had run for an ambulance. After a few drops of water trickled down his face, he pinched the boy's nose and blew four hard breaths into his mouth. Fraser coughed and gazed lovingly at him. By the time he was breathing normally again, Dale was making a beeline for them, followed by two stretcher-bearers.

The medics checked him over and told Mark he'd done the right thing. The boy would be fine. All he had to do was get him into bed and keep him there until tomorrow.

"He'll sleep for hours, Mr. Grant," one of the medics assured him. "You don't have to worry. Your son will be fine now."

Mark patted Heathcliffe and thanked Dale and the medics. Then he scooped his son into his arms and carried him into the beach house.

Dale stood watching the large blue stone glistening in the sun.

≈≈≈

Still pacing and restless at midnight, Dale suggested he go get some air. With Fraser sleeping soundly he didn't need to be cooped up inside. A stroll along the beach this time of night would relax him and God knows he needed one quiet hour to himself. Fraser had been fine for hours, had bounced back from his ordeal. He had comics all over the floor by his bed, an empty ice cream bowl on the night table beside his bed, and a seventy-pound Irish setter sleeping on his bed. Fraser was great.

As he walked away from the beach house he looked up at the three-quarter moon and followed its rays into the water. The glistening whitecaps on the waves brought warm childhood memories of rising and going to sleep to the sound and smell of the ocean. Fraser was safely with him. The tour had ended, which left a boy sitting at a piano to contend with and an all-consuming feeling of desire. Now what of this double?

For years there had been imitators, people who styled their hair the same, wore ice cream suits matched up with white coronets slightly cocked over the left eye. They moved like him, danced like him, so naturally they resembled him after a while. But the double? The double was identical, a mirror reflection, and a bloody weird experience.

Thinking about the girl in the photograph, he wondered if the view from the front was as pleasing as the view from the back. Were they lovers? Was she with the double because he resembled him or because she genuinely cared for him? The double loved her, though. He looked totally blissed while slipping on that ring.

Soon, he'd be replacing it with a wedding band.

He stopped on the shore and fixed on a moonlight beam riding in on a wave. He wasn't looking at *her* when he slipped on the ring. He was looking at her hand. In the photograph he was looking at her hand, her finger! And a wedding band? He tried to force his mind to freeze this thought or flash, whatever the hell it was, but couldn't. Too fleeting. Yet the memory of what just happened in his brain stayed solid, as real and solid as his blue stone.

Each wave rolled in slower than the last. The ocean breezes and sounds lengthened like four beats on a whole note, and his lungs didn't seem to require air. A musky vanilla fragrance attached to a spectral figure, swooped by him toward the beach house. And while his *body* heard Dale report on Fraser's condition and heard himself say good-night to Dale, then undress and slip into bed—his *essence* was somewhere else ...

... It always began this way. He would leave the world and just float away. He could walk through doors, fly over cities, watch his thoughts become real things. Everything appeared to move quite normally, yet he could be in Canada one minute and in England the next. He could reach up and touch a star. Then looking down at the beautiful life he had made for himself, worked so hard to get, somehow seemed insignificant and this worried him. His son was there, his friends, his livelihood, and from this plane they were too far away to touch. He couldn't even tell them stories of his adventures on this plane because he remembered nothing when he got home to them.

This was a duplicate world, with a Moulin Rouge identical to the one in Paris, ruins like those in Rome, a Times Square no different from New York. Only this really was Paris, Rome and New York, with a slight difference–the people he saw here were either in dreams like himself, or dead. And the dead refused to leave this world for higher planes due to their earthly obsession for material things when they were alive. All they had to do now was 'think up' whatever they wanted and it was theirs. They didn't have to work or set goals. They needed no visions, had no dreams. They had everything and they had nothing.

In the beginning, it was the most fascinating experience of his life to be everywhere, see everything, feel omnipotent, until he realized he'd seen it all before. The desire for invincibility had left him. Hard work realized one's dreams. With that standard absent in this world, there could be no sense of accomplishment. So why return to a place filled with dreamers and the apathetic dead?

It had all become complicated, confusing. For the first time the other night, this astral world seemed uncomfortably real, real in the sense of an emerging third world. Those people at Rudy's were neither asleep nor dead. Laurel was right. Something was different. Something was happening to both of them. Perhaps now he could convince her, talk her out of her love for this world. And he had to do it from here because when he awakened, little of her stayed with him.

As always, they met in the same place, at his father's house in Rottingdean, England. It was morning when he found her cross-legged on the beach, staring at the ocean. For a moment he watched her long black hair surf the wind. He studied her lovely profile, realizing once again that it was she who called him here. If not for Laurel, he'd never bother coming back. He'd had enough of this astral world, a world that didn't seem to want his son.

He slid in behind her and put his arms around her waist.

"When will we be together always?" she asked, running her hands over his.

He brushed his lips along her neck.

"And why do I still feel so lonely?"

He kissed her, knowing the kiss to be real here, but could they take it with them? This was a place of isolation. Separateness. This was not a world for lovers. Why were they here?

She seemed to float onto the sand as he laid her down. He removed his windbreaker and cushioned it beneath her head. He looked at the weight in those lovely eyes—passion with confusion. Love with fear. The time had come to take their love and run. But where to run? This beautiful place appeared to be slowly disintegrating. And he knew this insight was not coming from his mind, but from hers. Laurel had the power, yet fear ruled her. Why was she afraid?

"Beautiful girl, where do you go when you leave me?" he whispered as they made love. "Come with me. Come home with me."

"But we are home," she said, eyes pleading. "It's safe here. Our world evolved here. By this ocean. It's haunted me for years, you know. As a child. As a woman. I've always wanted to be near it. And I want to be near it with you."

Their lovemaking climaxed into silence. How could he convince her that life in this place was over? Even the magic it took to get here no longer impressed him. He wanted to leave. This stagnant astral shore was no place to begin their life. Didn't she have family to miss, friends to miss? He had asked many times in many ways and received nothing but vague answers.

He asked her again, "Why do you not want us to go home, Laurel?"

≈≈≈

From a quarter mile down the beach she saw the tall, formless shadow looming toward them. Watching it multiply and circle them frightened her. At least Mark could not see this sinister thing. A relief, since he had grown restless here. The thing disregarded her command to wash over her. Did it sense her waning confidence in her power? A foot away now and Mark still hadn't flinched. Why was it only she who saw it? What did it want with her? Would she have to pay a price for loving Mark in this world?

She rested her head on Mark's chest and closed her eyes. If the shadow passed, she would convince him to stay, at least a while longer. And if it hovered, she would acquiesce. She would help Mark move their love into the real world. But she would not do this without first expressing her fears.

The shadow hovered.

"Make love to me once more," she said, voice breaking. "It's going to be the last time here, isn't it?"

Mark acknowledged her question with a kiss.

"I'll go anywhere with you, Mark. I'll go home with you."

"I know you're reluctant, Laurel. I know you'd rather stay, but we can't."

The sinister shadow enveloped her. "I do have fears."

Mark swept a strand of hair away from her eyes. "I promise you we'll put all those fears to rest, one by one. A long talk tonight, baby." Then he reached for his jeans and stopped, rubbed the base of his neck. "Remember the first time we met here, Laurel? It was freezing that night and all you had on was a sundress. I was wearing shorts and a T-shirt. Now we seem to be appropriately dressed for the weather. The other night in Toronto—it was the same thing."

She pretended to ignore his comment and continued dressing.

"Why is it," he asked, "that I can remember There from Here, but I can never remember Here from There?"

"I don't know," she said, avoiding his eyes.

Mark cupped his hands on her face. "Laurel, what are you afraid of? I'm not into having snatches of time with you in a double life and it's beginning to present a problem in the familiar world. We've been photographed. Together. Now how could that happen? And at home I think it's somebody else, somebody who looks exactly like me. Here I know it is me. I want to put an end to this confusion. And I don't think it's a good idea that we spend so much of our time here. What's happening to us at home right now, don't you want to know?"

She pulled him closer. "All I know is that at home I'm beginning to remember a bit of our life here. That when I'm home, I want you with me. I know it's going to happen, that some strange thing is forcing it to happen and I'm thrilled about it. But thinking about it happening from there frightens me. Mark, when we meet there, what if you find me different? What if you don't love me? What if I really am different?"

"There. Here. How can you be different? Perhaps your fear will be put to rest when we find out what brought us together in the first place. Something happened to us at home. We did something that brought all this about. All the answers are there, Laurel, not here."

"Mark, I think all this happened because of me. That you had nothing to do with it. That you had no choice and that's what scares me." Her eyes grew dark. "When I get a picture of myself at home, I don't like what I see. I feel insecure and unlovable. I feel like a user. Or worse."

Mark gave her a bear hug. "Well you're not going to be feeling that way much longer, I promise. Not with me around. We'll get answers, beautiful girl, for everything. And we'll rid you of your fascination for this place, too. You'll want to spend the rest of your life in the real world only. With me."

They went into his father's house, bathed and made love again. Afterwards they stretched out on the bed he slept in as a boy and talked about the evidence suggesting they were no longer in the astral, but some embryonic midpoint. Even though they could still travel with the speed of light, they felt cold and heat and now had to dress for the weather. People in the real world had seen and photographed them. The same mysterious thing that had forced them into this world was now forcing them out. For reasons unknown, they had to begin all over again—from home.

She told Mark all about Michael and how he must be the one to help them find the answers. He had experience with the unknown. He also had an idea that might get them out of here for good. But they had to go back to Toronto tonight, to her home. From home she would write him a simple note and if Michael's plan worked, this note would find its way back to the real world, with Mark. It might also help trigger more of the life they shared here. Then Mark suggested they deliberately set themselves up to be photographed again. The devil's wrath couldn't keep him from going to Toronto after that.

"One thing, though," Mark said. "Wouldn't it be simpler to just leave me with a photo of yourself and put your name and number on the back?"

"No," she told him. "Michael said that could be dangerously overwhelming for both of us. He said our second meeting should happen naturally, or at least seem so to us. The other way would be too jarring, for you more so than me. You'd be confused and want all the answers at once and of course I wouldn't be able to give them to you. Everything has to happen a little at a time in the beginning."

"Alright, baby," he said. "Let's go. Why don't we casually stroll into the Imperial Room at the Royal York Hotel? I'm sure to be seen there."

As their thought-forms readied them to leave, she thought about her blue stone and wondered why she'd kept it from Mark. It just seemed important, maybe safer, to keep it to herself. Secretly, she named this place her Blue Diamond World, and trembled as she said goodbye to it. They didn't have much time left here. Seconds from now they would be in the Royal York Hotel and once Mark was photographed, they'd return to her place where she would leave him with the note. They decided the message would read, 'Record in Toronto.'

Less than an hour later, or so it seemed since she had no conception of time, they heard a key turning her front door lock.

Her voice shook as she whispered to Mark, "I believe that's me coming home from somewhere. That means we say goodbye now, doesn't it? Because as soon as I walk into this room, you'll be on your way."

Hearing footsteps coming closer, Mark held tight to the note and kissed her. "This has been so astonishing but I'm glad it's over." He spoke quickly. "Next time we meet we won't be forced away from each other. Don't be afraid, Laurel."

Then a shudder flash zipped through them. The footsteps stopped in the hall, beyond the corner of the room. As they dematerialized, she sensed someone or some thing watching and listening. And their surroundings transformed to a deep clear blue ...

... A slightly disoriented woman walked into her living room and for a moment covered her eyes with her hands. When she took them away, an unnatural smile crept into her face. She said to her dog, "I know he was here, I can smell his cologne. Next time I'll see him. Next time he'll have to stay."

≈≈≈

Many things popped into his mind when he awakened close to noon with Fraser cuddled up in bed beside him, one being that Toronto photograph, and the second and most important—the woman. He had been wondering about her last night on the beach and today he felt an obsessive desire to meet her, to know her. How could this woman, a stranger, arouse him so?

It had been a long time since he awakened with an erection. That blasted woman was somehow becoming increasingly familiar to him. He'd dreamt of a ring on her hand, her long black hair flying in the wind. And though he couldn't remember seeing her face, he did remember what she made him feel. Why did this kind of passion only exist in dreams? And why was he so emotionally hung-over today?

Following a hard knock, Dale and Heathcliffe let themselves in.

"So here he is," Dale said, grinning at Fraser who was tucked in beside him. "I went to check on him then figured he'd snuck in here. How you doing?"

He took a long, lazy stretch. "I am inconveniently aroused."

"Well take a cold blast then, that'll fix you. What's the matter, you have a dirty dream?"

"More than that. Don't think I'm feeling quite right."

Dale sat on the edge of the bed. "You weren't feeling quite right last night either, mate."

Should this surprise him? "Really. You sound like my son."

Dale's gaze flitted about the room. "When you came in from the beach last night you looked like a man who just downed five or six bevvies."

He sat up and ran his tongue along his teeth. "Ugh. Sand in my teeth—" He glared at Dale.

"Okay, Mark. What?"

Nothing like starting the day clammy and crazed. And feeling this way brought back the days when he took beans so he could stay up and work for seventy-two hours straight, followed by the heavy-duty ludes to get him down. Still sensitized to the things, he hadn't gone near them in two years, vowing never to touch that trash again.

Dale grabbed the rock from the night table and returned the glare. "Tell me now or I'll strike you with this."

He checked to see that Fraser was still asleep. "Dale ... something happened to me on the beach last night. A kind of out of body experience. For an instant and it was only an instant, I thought I saw the shadow of myself heading away from me toward here. After that I don't remember anything. I also don't remember that plane ride to Montreal last week or going into that daze Fraser spoke of at Dad's. Then of course we all know what happened on stage in Toronto.

"And here's the creamer—my subconscious is obsessed with that woman in the Toronto photograph, even to the point of dreaming about her. I couldn't even see her face. It seems to me that every time I turn around, something strange goes down. And I'm positive there's nothing wrong with my mind. That much I do know."

Dale shivered. "Creepers. Can you pinpoint when all this started?"

"Not sure, but it's been going on for some time, though I hadn't taken any real notice of it until Toronto. That's when I began feeling it might be time to start calling for the doctor. Mind you, I've got the shakes now but I'm so bloody curious."

"Mark, I hate it when you get curious. The last time you got curious you had us chanting in India with that quack."

"Well he taught you how to relax, didn't he? You're too suspicious. You never trust anybody, especially women."

"Yeah, with bloody proper reason. Now I suppose you're gonna go digging for your double and his lady friend."

"Dig up what exactly? There's no digs to be dug. Besides, I've got enough to do. I've got to get the flat ready in New York, get Fraser straightened away with his new governess and tutor."

"I don't want a tutor," Fraser said, choosing this moment to awaken. "I want to go to a real school."

"And how long have you been awake?" Mark asked, giving him a playful frown.

"Oh, I came in around India," he said, avoiding his father's eyes, "and I got your mail, Dad. I found it on the floor."

Fraser yanked a folded piece of blue paper from his pajama pocket, took a whiff and handed it to him. "Smells good."

Since when did the mail come so early in the day? His heart started to pound. No one had to tell him it smelled good. He knew. He knew because he had smelled the musky vanilla scent before. The pounding moved to his groin as more of the dream came back to him. He had made love to this woman, had told her not to be frightened. He tasted the sand in his mouth, felt his erection harden. He thought of his father's house. He thought of Toronto. And once he read the note, he knew it didn't come from Malibu.

"Don't arse about, Mark. What's it say?"

"It's a note," he said quietly, his dove-grey eyes twinkling, "written in a feminine hand. It says, 'Record in Toronto'."

≈≈≈

By four o'clock in the afternoon, the rain was hitting the pavement so hard it looked like it wasn't raining. Stay indoors, the weather guys advised. The thunder and lightning storm was expected to last through the night. Like his father, thunderstorms fascinated Fraser and Mark realized it was a waste of energy trying to keep him in bed for the rest of the day. Yet the storm anaesthetized the boy and he sat quietly on the ledge of the enormous bay window in the game room staring hypnotically at the sheets of rain pounding the shoreline. Courtesy of Rachel, Dale's housekeeper, Fraser sat, wrapped in a blanket, mug of steamy hot chocolate by his side.

Apart from the steady hum of Rachel's vacuum cleaner, the beach house was strangely quiet. Dale had reclined on the porch, beer in hand, watching him pace, sit, stand, and read the note for what had to be the hundredth time. Maybe he should get to packing and head for Toronto. Fraser was fine, so no need to stick around.

"Been thinking." Dale's voice was a thunder crack in the silence. "Me and the guys have booked studio time in New York in two weeks for the new album ..."

Mark stopped pacing and looked at his friend. As long as he'd known Dale, there was always a plan attached to 'been thinking'.

"... and I've been sitting here toying with the idea of un-booking it, maybe doing the new one in Toronto."

He smiled warmly at the best friend on the planet. "Dale, that message was meant for me. I think you're terrific, but I don't know if I want to involve you in this one." He meant that with all his heart. If anything happened to Dale—

"Look man, you need an excuse to go. And your tour's over, your new album's out, so what do you intend to do once you get there? How do you intend to fish out the people involved with that note? People have to know you're there. I mean, everybody has to know you're there. So I think your best bet is to use me."

Dale was right. What was he going to do, put an ad in the *Toronto Sun* personals? This thing was a happening in the making—he knew it in his soul. A shame patience was not one of his virtues.

"I wish I was more like you," he said. "You don't have a romantic bone in your body. That's the problem, you know— this metaphysical thing, the dreams, the girl, everything. It's all so incredibly romantic."

"So then it is more the girl than the mystery," Dale snapped. "Well then, I'd better be with you because if the only reason you're going is because of a broad, you're headed for trouble. And to tell you the truth, I don't buy into all this out of body stuff, you know that. I don't give a rat about any of it. What I think is that somebody's playing games. Somebody probably slipped you that note from right here in Malibu. Maybe somebody's been following you. You ever consider that idea?"

He waved the idea away. Could Dale really believe what he was saying? How could anybody from Malibu break through his security system long enough to get into the house and slip in a note? This place was about as vulnerable as punk rock. Dale obviously didn't care for the idea of his traipsing after a strange woman. Although Dale had loved many women, he never trusted them, especially since his marriage to Carmen went sour. All women were devious as far as Dale was concerned.

"Don't worry, old man. It's not romantic love I'm after. It's my fascination for the paranormal, which you know exists, so don't give me any more of that agnostic crap. Now let's get back to the idea of your recording in Toronto. If I use you, you'll have to use me, so how about I make a guest appearance on the album. We could also go one step farther and really blow Toronto on its ass."

"Yeah, how?" Dale asked, startled out of his lounge by a lightning bolt.

"They've got the El Mondrago Club there. What say the great Dale Mith performs live and on stage with Mark Grant? Performing together for the first time? Think of it. Fantastic promo for your LP and it'll be your show. What we'll do is spread the word that I'll be making a guest appearance. The town and the papers will go wild. What do you think?"

He got his answer from the big toothy grin on Dale's rugged face. But the smile faded as quickly as it came. "What's wrong, Dale?"

"It's something I've dreamed of us doing for a long time. I only wish we weren't doing it for the wrong reasons. Mark, this whole thing still gives me the willies. It could be dangerous, man. You've faced all kinds of danger before but this is different. Your mind is involved here. Something has actually been working its way into your head. I'd hate seeing anything happen to you is all."

"I know that." He gave Dale's shoulder a squeeze. "But what better way to conquer this thing and get it out of my head than to meet it head on?"

"Aw that's bad," Dale laughed weakly, "but I suppose it makes sense. Alrighty then, off to Toronto we go. Don't have too much time to get hold of all the guys, though, so we'd better roll with this change in studio arrangements and El Mo thing. Brilliant that Justin's coming in tonight."

≈≈≈

Justin Poppman had been friend and manager to Mark for ten years and Dale for fifteen. He'd discovered an impoverished twenty-three-year-old Dale performing in a Charing Cross dive, the kind of place that motivates success seekers, mostly because the landlord needs to get paid once a month. Within four years, under Justin's guidance, Dale and his three-man team had become the number one rock and roll band in the world.

Mark, on the other hand, practically stalked Justin until he got an audition. It took Justin one minute to make up his mind. Mark was a soloist first, and with that toned core due to years of swimming, he'd developed the lung capacity to carry out those long flowing notes. The voice lessons Justin insisted he take for the first three years of his career had paid off big time. Mark Grant was a gifted songwriter, pianist and dancer. And as a singer, there was no finer, more gifted voice in all of Rock Royalty. The industry moguls determined that Justin Poppman was the man behind Grant's success. Justin would agree with them.

Up with the dawn, Justin phoned Dale from New York and asked him to get the guestroom ready for tonight. He wanted to talk to Dale about the new album and discuss the possibility of a European tour this summer. Also, he knew Mark was visiting and wanted to speak with him. When Dale told him it would be like old times, Justin said he didn't think so and admitted that speaking with Mark was priority number one, the real reason for the visit.

Dale tried quizzing him but Justin was saving it. "We need a powwow," he said. "Just make sure Mark stays put. The press are after his whereabouts." Justin ended the call in typical abrupt fashion, leaving Dale scratching his head. Dale decided to abridge Justin's message. Mark had enough on his mind. Best he sit tight until Justin arrived and personally told Mark whatever the hell it was he had to tell him.

≈≈≈

Even though Dale had a limo waiting at Los Angeles International for Justin, the storm delayed him two and a half hours. The plane landed on time but the torrential rain was blinding to everyone foolish enough to be out. He arrived shortly before 9:00 p.m., a nervous soaking wreck, detoured by downed power lines, one mother of a mudslide and inching traffic along the Ocean Parkway. His greeting held a modicum of civility as he complained about the lousy California weather, how the rain had destroyed his new three-hundred-dollar Spanish leather attaché case, he was probably coming down with pneumonia and the limo driver had to be high on something. Mark decided that Justin was in a state over more than the weather.

After changing clothes, Justin joined him and Dale in the game room. Rachel, who was spending the night because of the storm, had a fire going and a heated double Courvoisier waiting for him. He took a healthy swig of the brandy and the impact of his attaché case on the coffee table sent the head flying off Dale's beer.

Dale scooped the barley cloud off his cigarette pack. "Alright, Justin. Lay it on us. What's got you all buggered?"

Frowning, Justin ignored Dale, clicked open the case, took out a brown manila envelope and handed it to Mark.

"What's this?"

"Well Mark, once you open it, look at it, then read the clippings attached to it, I'm hoping you'll tell me."

The envelope contained two enlarged photographs, the first of which he'd already seen, not only in the newspaper but repeatedly in his mind. There he was, his double, slipping the ring on her finger, plus the clipping—

Mark Grant relaxes over a drink in Rudy's of Yorkville with unidentified lady friend. Whoever she is, it looks serious. Has Grant got a secret?

One glance told him this man was not his double. Fraser would know, too. *This is you, Dad. I'd know you anywhere.* But how in God's name could it be? He wanted to shout it to Dale and Justin, wanted to hear himself confirm yes, this *is* me. He wanted to go off somewhere and bask in the wonder of it all.

The second photograph showed him laughing with Craig Russell, currently starring at the Imperial Room in Toronto's Royal York Hotel. Also in the picture was a cut-off profile of her, the girl with the long black hair, the stranger who wasn't a stranger. It was obvious she had purposely turned away from the camera. He felt the need to comfort her, to protect her. For what reason did she turn away? Who was she? Suddenly tormented by the question of her identity, he felt this manic urge to find her. From the *Toronto Star* he read the second clipping—

Mark Grant, back in Toronto after winding up a successful American-Canadian tour, enjoys a joke with Imperial star, Craig Russell, last night at the Royal York.

Justin asked if he was listening.

"I'm sorry, what?" he said, trying desperately to focus on the dream flashes.

"Mark," Justin sighed out his name, "for the past week I've been on the phone, ad infinitum, with *C.P.I.*, the *Toronto Star*, the *Toronto Sun*, and other important notables connected with this Rudy's and Imperial Room, not to mention Tony Vettese, who for the past week has been doing his job insufferably."

"Thought you fired Tony and got a new press agent," Dale said.

"Fired him. Got Tony back," Justin said, annoyed by the interruption. "And even though Tony and I don't agree on much, for once we agreed on this–that first photograph was not of you. We put retractions in the papers. A limousine driver came through with a legitimate autograph. So alas, we calmed the seas.

"Now it turns out that Mark Grant was on the town in Toronto the night of the day he landed at L.A. International with his son. Remember, they photographed you here, too. And what all this boils down to, Mark, is the fact that your ability to bi-locate has, of this morning, made news in three major cities. The papers are running impostor and secret life theories, with most of the attraction centred on the former. Everyone is looking for this double of yours and it seems that when they meet up with him they can't tell the difference.

"So I know three things, Mark. I know you could be mistaken for your double, which could prove extremely embarrassing for you. I know you're going to have to provide details down to the dreck for Tony until they locate this guy. And I know you knew about this since the beginning.

"Also, I spoke with Craig Russell today, who swears that was no impostor last night. So if it wasn't an impostor and it wasn't you, who the hell was it? And why didn't you inform me?"

He counted silently to five. "For the past few days I've been in Canada, the United States and the U.K. I've just begun to get my bearings and you surprise me, Justin. You should know that when I know I let you know. You know?" He didn't get so much as a smirk from him. "Okay, seriously, we need calm so we can come to heads on this."

After Justin had two more brandies and recovered from the shock of the second photograph, they set the wheels turning for the Toronto recording and subsequent El Mondrago concert. By six the next evening, they'd booked Sounds Interchange Studio from November twenty-third through December eighth. Dale contacted the band, who was pleased to hear Mark would be joining them on this project.

Justin had left for Toronto to meet with the owner of the El Mo and choose the concert date. Tony Vettese was already at work on the press releases and Dale had selected a young L.A. photographer and illustrative artist by the name of Guy Sweet to do group shots and design the jacket cover.

The wheels were in motion. In two weeks, Mark Grant would be on his way to Toronto, and—Laurel Ariss.

4. MOMMY'S LITTLE GIRL

COURTLAND BROUGHT THE *TORONTO SUN* with him, probably guessing she'd get all secretive about this latest photo at the Imperial Room. If she had to choose one person on the planet she 'sort of' trusted, it was her brother. But then, one could be sort of betrayed, or sort of abused, or sort of batted around like a mouse on the wrong side of a cat's paw. While Michael was still trying to figure things out, Courtland wasn't going to know the secret behind that picture. But she needed information from him today, so good luck getting it without telling him too much.

Waving the *Toronto Sun* at her, which he brought folded, page number highlighted in shocking lime green, Courtland wasn't about to let the mystery pic go.

"You and I have the same profile. So don't tell me this isn't you in this picture with Mark Grant and Craig Russell, because I'm not buying it."

"So don't buy it."

"Fine. If you insist. So if this isn't you, what are you doing with two copies?"

Damn, she forgot to take them off the kitchen island and hide them upstairs where she had three more. "I picked up one for Nancy."

Her brother smiled, came over and massaged the back of her neck while she scooped the ice cream. "You always look like you have a pole stuck up your back. So? Why would you give Nancy a newspaper clipping that isn't of you?"

Courtland, the Philadelphia lawyer. "Because it looks so much like me, even with the head turned away from the camera."

He stopped the massage, sat down beside her. "Why did you turn your head away?"

"Because I didn't want ..." Man, he was sharp. "It's not me, Courtland. Leave it."

"Uh-huh. If you say so."

"I do. So? We're at dessert and you haven't mentioned seeing the folks yet. What's up?"

Courtland made a sweeping gesture with his arms and she had to laugh. "*You* are asking about the folks? *You?* Okay, who's taken over my sister's body?"

Funny, she'd been kind of wondering the same thing herself. "Dad used the hotel as an excuse to call me last week. Said it's almost finished and he wants me there for Christmas. I told him I couldn't make it."

"I heard. I arrived in Cordoba the next day. What was your reason now? Let me see. Oh yes, your realtor has two houses to show you in The Beaches." Courtland rolled up one of several real estate sections she'd spread over the counter and peered at her through it. "I know you're still shopping, but really, over the holidays? Come on, Laurel."

She put the ice cream back and sighed into the freezer. "Okay. I just don't have the energy to go another round with Santina."

"You ever going to call her *Mother*? The anxiety's worsened, Laurel. Doctors have her on Klonopin and Xanax, but at least she's sticking with the shrink this time. Anyway, the drugs aren't working."

"The upshot of a bad conscience, maybe? Try a general anaesthetic. Anyway, I'm sorry about that but I can't make her head problems disappear. I'd like to make *her* disappear, though."

"Laurel! What does that mean?"

God, she hardly recognized herself these days. What was happening to her? For a second she actually entertained the idea of her mother dying. And hurting Nancy with digs and barbs had become a source of amusement. Her mother was mean before she went crazy. Was she going crazy like her mother? Maybe she should follow Santina's example for once in her life and have a talk with the shrink again.

Her brother fanned his hand in front of her. "Hello? You still with me? What did you mean by that, Laurel?"

"It means Santina exhausts me. It means she still won't own up to the past. And I'm tired of working myself up about the past, Courtland."

"You said. She said. We're all tired. And I think she will own up to the past now. She wants very much to talk to you, Laurel. Says there's something important to discuss with you. She wouldn't tell me what."

"Tell her to put it in a letter. Or, hey, tell her to *phone* me. Dad can show her how to use the phone."

Courtland sighed. "You're not the only one who's exhausted. Can't you let it go for Christmas?"

She passed his glass of Chardonnay over the island. "No. I can't." Her flat refusal seemed to knock the wind out of her brother, sadden him somewhat. Too bad. He'd get over it.

"Then explain Michael Johnstone to me. Nancy told me you hired this psychic guy to put some emotional salve on your issues with Mom."

"Michael's a parapsychologist. And no, I didn't hire him because of my issues with Santina. I lied to Nancy about that. And I'm not ready to discuss my reasons with you yet, either."

"Laurel, will you ever stop keeping secrets from the people closest to you?"

"Sure, okay. So I tell the truth and they lock me away in the whack shack for six months."

"Oh puh-leeze. Not that again," he groaned then patted the scar on her neck. "You carved up your neck. What the hell was Dad supposed to do—send you to Disney World?"

"I was falsely accused of poisoning my own mother and killing our cat. And how would you know everything that went down? You were off playing football or something."

"I'm sorry I wasn't there for you. But if we all get together, maybe we can wrestle the truth into a corner. I think Mom wants that. Come to Cordoba for Christmas, Laurel."

"I can't, Courtland. I have stuff going on here. Really."

"Michael Johnstone?"

"Yeah."

"Anything of a romantic nature?"

"No. All I will tell you now, and please keep this between us, is that he's helping me with some unsettling dreams I've been having. And I thought maybe you could help me, too." Courtland probed her with his eyes, taking way too long to consider. Uh-oh.

"Gee I hope I can. Think I'll make it conditional, though. A trade-off?"

"I am not going to Cordoba for Christmas. Not saying it again."

"This is something different." He reached inside his blazer and pulled out a small gold box. "An early Christmas gift."

"Aw thanks, Court—"

"Not from me, Laurel. From Mom."

It was like holding a dead fish. "So what's the trade-off?"

"That you keep it. That's all I ask. I don't want to have to return it to Mom."

Her neck and shoulders ached from circling this same wagon. Would he ever give it a rest? "I'm not calling her up, either, if that's what you're after."

"I didn't ask you to. Just open it, Laur."

She flipped open the lid and laughed at the brooch. Sick woman, her mother. Like mother, like daughter?

"Uh, excuse me," Courtland said. "That happens to be a 3D 18 karat gold cat and those blue eyes are pure Tourmaline. Vintage. Wanna explain the joke?"

Laurel laughed again, though it wasn't so funny now. "It's just that the cat's back is arched." But Courtland didn't get it.

She appreciated the fact that he didn't insist she put on the brooch. A nice guy, her brother. They moved into the living room and while Courtland petted Mouth into a snore-fest and was half a glass of wine away from joining him, she figured she'd go for it. Besides, he had to know when she had stuff on her mind. Since they were kids, he knew. Probably had something to do with the fist she kept tapping against her mouth. She needed to ask him about that time in England and hallelujah, he wasn't rushing her. He sat, sipping and petting, and patiently waiting. Yeah, a real nice brother.

"These dreams Michael's been helping me with," she said, wondering how much to tell him. "They're about our Christmas trip to England all those years ago. About the boy we saw playing the piano. I remember leaving him my blue stone, but everything else is hazy."

"Hmm," Courtland said, eyeing her suspiciously again. "So you want to know what I remember?"

"Yes. For starters, where in England was it?"

"Well I remember we had left London after experiencing the Dickens out of it and Dad taking us to Brighton by the Sea. Then on Christmas Eve we went to this cozy little restaurant for dinner."

She broke eye contact and rubbed her arms. "Brighton? So you're saying we weren't in London then?"

"What, the place you left the stone? No. It was either Brighton or some little town nearby, right on the English Channel. What's wrong?"

"Nothing. Do you remember me giving away the stone to the boy?"

"Sure. How could I forget? For a year that thing was like an extra limb, and then you lop it off and give it to a stranger. Blew us all away when you did that."

"But why would I do it, do you think?"

"When we walked in, the kid was playing some dreamy concerto-type tune on the piano. He was really gifted for his age we all thought. And you ... well, you were totally mesmerized. By the music, the kid, the sea. Everything. You were instantly smitten, what can I tell you."

"So I just walked up and gave it to him? That's it?"

Courtland moved the dog off his lap and leaned forward. "No, not quite. He took a break or something and that's when you got up and left it on the piano."

"Did he come over after? Did we speak at all?"

"Not when I was around, Laurel. I did use the head. Maybe he came around then, but I can't say for sure."

"Did you catch his name, maybe?" Oh no. She hadn't thought this inquisition through and judging by the wide-eyes and yellow flashing bulb over Courtland's head, he had caught on.

He snapped his fingers. "That newspaper photo in the kitchen! You think the kid in that restaurant was Mark Grant, don't you?"

The air around her felt thick with gloom. "Not anymore."

"What do you mean?"

"You know what a fan I am of his. His family didn't have a restaurant. He grew up in fancy digs in Bath. An only child. Went to a private boy's school. And his father was an orthodontist, his mother a dermatologist."

"No wonder the guy has great skin and teeth. So maybe he was visiting somebody around Brighton that Christmas. You don't know. It could still be him."

She got up and stoked the fire, inhaled the smoky fragrance. "No, it couldn't. I remember reading that he never played in public as a child. His parents couldn't even get him to play school recitals. He didn't play publicly until he formed a band, years later. In his late teens."

"Well if you knew that, then what made you think it could be him?"

She sat on the flagstone hearth, remembering. "In the dream I strongly feel he's in his home somehow. I can't ... I just know. If it was a London restaurant, maybe he would've played. Christmas Eve, among friends—he may have played. But there's no way his home was in some obscure part of England. And the boy in my dream was at *home*. I know it."

"Disappointed?"

"Yeah. I feel silly. I didn't mean to tell you this much."

"But your dreams about the boy and the stone? Who's the boy then?"

"I don't know. Maybe Mar ... maybe Grant's astral twin. Maybe a relative."

"Laurel, you're keeping secrets again."

She glanced at the bandage on top of Mouth's little sleeping head. "Sorry, Court."

"Well I hope this Michael guy can help you find some answers."

After Courtland left around four, she considered a five-mile jog, but then Michael might call. She couldn't concentrate on TV and had done enough cooking for one day. Mouth was booked for a grooming on Tuesday, but maybe she should try grooming him herself. How much longer would she have to sit still when all she could see in her head was Mark and those two Toronto photographs? His music and presence were everywhere around her, inside her. She had been in his arms, made love to him, left him with a message that seemed surreal now.

Three days ago she walked into this living room knowing he had been here. It was fairly crazy envying that other part of herself, that other Laurel for having him and leaving her with nothing but fragmented memories. If only she could pick up the phone and call him, say, 'I'm the one. Come and get me.' She was the reason for all Mark's headlines these days, the double, the *woman,* and all she could do was sit around and wait like some wallflower with crossed fingers. Waiting for Mark, waiting for news of Mark, filled every minute.

Waiting for the kettle to boil, she rested her chin on white-knuckled hands. It was true, that old saw. It did take forever when you watched it. Same with Mark, who had the message now. So when would he come to Toronto for her? And when he did come, how in the world would they meet? How had this power arranged for that to happen? Didn't having it give her the right to demand answers?

"When?" She tightened her hands into fists. "When!"

A flush crept up the back of her neck and she glanced toward the kitchen door. Red-nosed and runny-eyed, Nancy and Katherine stood gaping at her through the window. Oh fine. She shuffled to the door and let them in.

"Laurel, for heaven sake," Katherine said, huffing from the cold. "Didn't you hear us ringing the doorbell?"

She noticed Nancy standing there looking strangely at her. Again. "Obviously not." She hardened her face at the kettle. "I was too busy taking out my frustrations on the tea kettle."

Nancy took off her coat and looked around. "Yeah, we noticed. What's up?"

She grabbed their coats and practically threw them on hangers. "I have been stuck in here all day waiting for that stupid phone to ring. I'm up for a fashion layout in *Glamour.*" It was sort of true. "And the agency was supposed to give me the word today. It's a good thing Courtland popped in for lunch. At least he kept my mind off it a bit."

"That's great," Nancy looked relieved. "Aw you'll get it, don't worry. Too bad I missed Court, though. Oh well, we have a date tonight. At least I'm here to see your face when Kath tells you the big news."

If Katherine was getting back with her ex, she could care less, but why would Nancy want to see her reaction to that? Her pulse throbbed. Since when had Katherine been anxious to share news with her, about anything? "Well, let's get comfortable quick," she said, leading them into the living room. Nancy dashed into the kitchen, shut off the kettle and dashed back.

"Tell her, Kath," Nancy said, flushed.

"You remember Guy Sweet?" Katherine asked.

Hopefully, Katherine wouldn't take her usual forever to come to the point. "Of course I remember Guy."

"He phoned me yesterday. He'll be in Toronto next week with friends and he wants to arrange a get-together."

"That's really nice," she said dryly. There had to be more than this.

Katherine shook her head impatiently. "Wait a minute. You know why Guy's coming to Toronto?"

She couldn't imagine, but she needed to know, like *now*.

"He's coming to design an album cover and to photograph Dale Mith!"

She felt the blood rush to her head, felt her heart pounding in her chest and ears the way it had at the concert. This was the power way. The destiny. It was all about to happen, *really* happen. "So we're going to meet Dale Mith," she said, fighting to keep her composure. "I can't believe it."

"Well, listen to this," Katherine continued. "Dale Mith is recording half of his new album at a studio here and the other half at the El Mondrago. It'll probably be in the papers in the next day or two. Anyway, guess who's making a guest appearance at the El Mo with Mith?"

Katherine and Nancy broke into a fit of giggles when Katherine lisped out the 'with Mith' part.

She couldn't laugh with them. Feeling his name hanging on Katherine's lips, she wanted to cry the first happy tears she'd ever had. Finally she could forget about the past. Santina and all the horrors were back there and they could damn well stay there. Everything had worked–the magic, the power, the note. Mark actually had a part of her with him.

Laurel felt her eyes misting in front of the girls and for once she didn't care. "Who?"

Both Nancy and Katherine answered in the same breath, "Mark Grant!"

≈≈≈

Michael Johnstone had spent the past four years of his life with the title, Assistant Director of Research of the Division of Parapsychology and Psychophysics at the Scarborough Medical Centre Department of Psychiatry. Quite a mouthful. He simply told everyone he was a psychic researcher since most people believed a parapsychologist was nothing more than a ghost hunter who spent solitary nights investigating haunted houses in various parts of the world. Not quite.

In fact, he found the whole idea of ghost chasing rather tedious. The power of the mind fascinated him most—the unused portion of the brain, simple human energy and metaphysics, the science that investigates ultimate reality, the first principles of thought. Soon after discovering they're different, a child believes he is either blessed or cursed. Though he didn't understand the extrasensory mechanism in his mind that separated him from his friends, Michael knew there'd be plenty of time to find answers.

The acceptance of the psychic sciences in the 80s made answers easier to get, easier to clarify. Since psychics were clairvoyant, psychokinetic or telepathic, Michael wondered if he had inadvertently stumbled onto a new order in the case of

Laurel Ariss. Was she psychic at all? Maybe she was parapsychic, a name he made up. It meant beyond psychic. So how did she achieve parasomatic astral travel for herself and one other? Perhaps Julian could provide him with some answers. On his own, all he seemed to do was raise questions.

Dr. Julian Wieler, an eminent metaphysician and parapsychologist, was presently lecturing at the University of Toronto. In his late fifties, heavyset and double-chinned with thick grey, wavy hair, he possessed the greatest capacity for calm Michael had ever seen. Five years ago he had studied under Wieler at Queen's University. He remembered Wieler always looking like he'd just stepped out of a retreat house, never ruffled, totally relaxed and soft spoken, a twinkle of curiosity in the eyes. The students in the front rows sat thoroughly mesmerized. The students in the back rows kept asking him to speak up.

Michael found Julian Wieler in the University of Toronto library, probably absorbed in Monday's lecture notes. Since students weren't big on Saturday study, few occupied the massive oak-panelled library. He found himself practically tiptoeing toward him since campus libraries majored in echoes.

"Michael," Wieler said, shaking his entire arm. "Yes the hair is thinner but the face looks good, free of worry lines."

"The scalp got the worry lines," he laughed. "How's my favourite scholar?"

"Good, Michael. Happily, the brain and libido have formed a truce. Now sit. We will leave the chatter and speak of the woman who brought you here. On the phone you said she had experienced parasomatic disembodiment. Fascinating. First you let me read your notes and then you tell me everything in your own words, yes?"

Within the hour, Dr. Weiler had the update on Laurel, including Michael's first meeting with her, the impressions he received, the trance she went into, the smell of the sea in her bedroom, the incident with the two photographs, the dog, Grant's lyrics and the dreams. But it wasn't until Michael began attaching special significance to the black in both the photographs and her aura that Wieler seemed to want to take issue.

"Michael, tell me now," Wieler said, "What have you become? The last time I saw you, you were a scientist concerned only with the natural order of things. Now I find somewhat of an occultist, a rebel, and I feel a conflict against that order. Do you want to undermine science structure and glorify the occult? Are you a scientist or an occultist?"

"I'm a scientist who happens to be psychic," Michael explained, "sometimes the thorniest of thorns for me. Julian, of course I don't want to undermine science."

"Then you must keep a clear head and stick to the natural order. You know that the scientist is mocked for raising more questions than answers. But people tend to forget that answers raise more questions still. Remember two things, your scientific training and the fact that what may seem supernatural is often unconfirmed scientific fact. Don't get all caught up in the occultist's romantic notions—auras, dreams. The next thing you know you'll be side-tracked by theology and the like."

"Spoken like a true scientist."

"Thank you," Wieler said. "Now, it seems you are dealing with thought and energy here. These go together like protons and nuclei. With thought, it is necessary to have a psychological profile. I'm surprised at you, Michael, no background information on Miss Ariss' childhood. Was there trauma? Were there imaginary playmates? Were there obsessions with objects and or people? We must know all this."

"Miss Ariss prefers to keep her past in the past," Michael said. "I know how important past trauma is, but what's happened to her is all quite recent. It's all happened within the last month."

"This I find hard to believe. A woman of her age doesn't wake up one morning with parasomatic ability. No. There is always evidence prior to puberty. Youth triggers it through trauma, intense desire, even a feeling of alienation. Often it will lie dormant for many years because the young conscious mind requires time to ripen before it can accept and understand it. This is not mere psychic ability we are dealing with here. What we are dealing with is psychic energy. Now something triggered it once, obviously something has triggered it again."

"The intense desire she feels for Mark Grant? The connection she spoke of?"

"Quite possibly the connection and it is that connection that will take us back further than one month. Psychic energy can be dangerous, Michael. You're aware of this. However, it is deadly when it is the upshot of trauma, alienation. It then becomes negative, misplaced in youth."

"How could it be misplaced?"

"The child's will, mind over matter, P.K.–psychokinesis. All children have the ability to make small objects move, to float down a flight of stairs. They inject their energy *over* matter, therefore the energy boomerangs from the child to the object, from the object to the child. But the still budding energy always returns to them. In their innocence they pay it no mind and soon return to toys and parents' arms, and their energy goes to sleep inside them. But it stays with them, grows with them as they mature and develop.

"Now the alienated child, Michael, injects energy *into* matter. Could be a favourite doll, a teddy bear, a lucky marble. The child begins to give the object the love it feels it isn't getting from family. It talks to it, thinks into it, takes it everywhere. Its energy is going into the object and not returning. The child is being slowly drained."

"Are you saying that human energy can be injected into a solid form and stay there?" Michael asked, finding this theory difficult to believe.

"Yes. Thoughts really are things, Michael. Kirlian photography proves this now. Human energy can be photographed with special equipment. If we can have mind *over* matter, surely we can have mind *into* matter. The theologian will argue–if the devil exists, then God exists. The metaphysician will argue–if energy thought-forms can be transferred from mind to mind, certainly same energy thought-forms are transferable from body to body. So then can not human energy pass from the brain into a smaller, inferior object?"

"I don't–yes, I guess it makes sense. All right then, so what happens to the child? What happens to the object?"

"The child will have lost a vast amount of psychic energy. Therefore, physically the child will be weakened if it is separated from the object which is not likely to happen since it is so attached to it. But it will still be weakened to a certain degree as one cannot get feedback from a doll. Psychic energy helps a child to think, to reason, to develop conscience. A substantial loss of the energy will confuse the child's reasoning processes, hinder its intuitive growth. It could become overly suspicious, even psychotic, becoming destructive to itself and to others."

"Is there no cure for the child?"

"Of course, Michael. There's always a cure for psychic damage if diagnosed early enough. Simple–the child must get back what it has lost. He must have the family's love. He must know he is loved. He must learn that an inanimate object can be nothing more than a curiosity, a plaything. Then he must destroy the object of his own free will. A normal child will simply outgrow it. An abnormal child who's suffered severe psychic damage through energy loss will never outgrow it."

"Will the energy always stay inside the object if it's not destroyed by its owner?"

"Of course. Where's it going to go on its own when it has no mind, no heart, no soul? It is simple energy and only its owner knows what to do with it."

Michael thought it strange that a scientist should use the world 'soul'. "What if it falls into the hands of another?"

"If the object falls into the hands of another, a psychic link may develop between the former and present owners. They may see each other in dreams though they may never meet in real life."

"Now who's talking like an occultist," Michael laughed.

"An open mind, Michael. Science needs open minds and psychic links are nothing new."

"Does the link usually occur right away?"

"Unlikely. The child will be too overwhelmed by the loss of the toy. He will be feeling alienated, deserted all over again, too busy blaming himself for its loss. His young mind will be clouded, troubled. Don't forget, he has lost more than he realizes."

"Then you're saying psychic damage has been done? The child has been separated from the object and will never be normal again?"

"His childhood will not be normal and this could affect his adult life, yes. He will always remember the special thing he had and lost. To a child, the loss grows big in his mind. In the case of an adult, he now has enough psychic energy for three people. We all have. Finally, we are discovering what we can do with it. But all that energy can be positive or it can be negative depending on the state of mind of the individual. Unfortunately, it appears that negative energy is more powerful in that it can result in suicides, dementia, disease, hallucinations."

Michael thought of the black aura but said nothing. Even if this toy theory applied to Laurel, it was still just the wave before the tsunami. She and Grant may be experiencing a psychic link but their dreams were not really dreams. They were real, only they were real on another plane, yet they were photographed on this plane.

"But what about the photographs? How can they be photographed in the astral by an ordinary camera? How can they be seen by ordinary people?"

"The etheric double can be seen, Michael. But it cannot be photographed by an ordinary camera, this I cannot conceive. Those pictures had to be taken out of the astral state, immediately after, which can explain the colours and shapes around their bodies in the negatives. Have you considered an etheric switch, the astral body with the physical body?"

"W-wait a minute now. Are you suggesting that somehow the astral body winds up in bed or wherever and the actual physical body is the one out on the town?"

Julian Wieler widened his eyes.

"No. T-that's incredible! Open mind or not, I can't handle that one. The etheric double theory blows me away. But an etheric switch? No, they would've turned up in places in their pajamas. They would've remembered everything. They would've been exhausted or hung-over the next day." It had been years since he'd seen Julian Wieler. He could be getting senile. "No, we're bordering on the question of dematerialization here—at will. I'm aware of how powerful psychic energy is, but it would take much more than that to dematerialize."

"The U.S.S. Eldridge dematerialized with a crew of 181," Wieler reminded him.

"That story's officially denied, Doctor. So it's hearsay."

"Have you ever known me to connect hearsay with my belief in something, Michael?"

Shaking his head in amazement, Michael wondered how he got this much out of the loop.

"It's been done," Weiler said, laughing at his saucer-eyes. "Not by me, but it has been done. I have seen it. But today we are here to deal specifically with your Miss Ariss and her psychic problem. I can discuss the etheric switch and dematerialization no further with you until you have more for me. Our time is too important to waste on scientific speculation.

"You go out and get for yourself that psychological profile, past and present, yes? Then you watch her, study her. Help her to meet this Mark Grant. There won't be much else you can do until this happens. He seems to be the higher truth where she's concerned. Since something about him has linked them, it would appear Mark Grant is crucial to her existence. Your job will be to find out why. In the meantime I will leave you my Manhattan number. My secretary always knows where I am if you should need me."

Michael thanked him and carefully tucked the number away in his wallet.

"Remember, Michael, don't get bogged down by details. Stay with the root of the problem once you find it and I'm certain you will." Wieler hesitated thoughtfully. "You mentioned in your notes that Miss Ariss is a Christian, a Catholic. Is this correct?"

"Yes."

"Obviously she is not practicing. What she is practicing, albeit unknowingly, is Gnosticism, a movement believing in the release of man's spiritual element from bondage *into matter*. This makes her a heretic treading dangerous, unhallowed ground, Michael."

"Aha! A closet Christian!"

Wieler ignored Michael's playful outburst. "But you must remember this—should you ever find yourself up against a torrent of negative energy from this woman, do everything in your power to keep her from turning against you. If you feel she has, stay away from her. Immediately drop all hold she has over you on the psychic level or she'll make schnitzel out of your mind. I guarantee it."

"I will, Julian," Michael said. "Thanks for this. You know, speculative theory always makes me crazy. But once I get Laurel and Mark together, the answers will come. Ahh. You know what's exciting the hell out of me?"

Wieler regarded him curiously.

"Me sitting ringside when Laurel Ariss meets Mark Grant."

5. IN THE FLESH

Banford Arms Hotel, Toronto—November 28th

AFTER SPENDING A FEW DAYS getting Fraser settled in the New York flat with his governess, Annie, Mark hi-tailed it to Toronto and caught up with Dale and his band. Mark loved the ambiance of the posh Banford Arms Hotel on Nicholas Street, neo-Gothic old world charm at its decadent best. A quaint little street in the downtown Bay and Bloor area, Nicholas was three blocks from the Bohemian-style Yorkville Village, home to the infamous Rudy's.

"Been to Rudy's the last two nights looking for your double," Dale chided. "No sighting yet."

Dale had the suite across the hall, with the rest of the band dispersed in other hotels downtown. Guy Sweet was staying at the home of Katherine Harding, a woman with whom he was once serious and still maintained a deep friendship. Guy asked Katharine if she kept in touch with Laurel Ariss, a model whose perfect-boned face landed him his first magazine cover. When Katharine said yes, he asked her to invite Laurel to his party two days away on the thirtieth. Although he never took to Laurel, perhaps for the subtle dominance or ferocity in those steely green eyes, he was short on women to invite and she sure knew how to dress a room.

"Since Laurel's still in the biz, ask her to invite some of her friends," Guy said to Katherine.

"She doesn't have any friends except me and Nancy, if you want to count me," Katharine said. "Even if she had, I doubt she'd invite them."

≈ ≈ ≈

From his bedroom window, Mark looked out at Yorkville's twinkling lights along the rows of galleries, boutiques, restaurants, and beyond to the swank and private Circle Court Townhouses. With the downtown core in the throes of a serious-looking storm, he studied the clouds, something he liked to do with Fraser. When separated they'd each pick a shape during their day and trade cloud stories over the phone at bedtime.

Fraser would love these storm clouds, all moving swiftly across the grey and orange-streaked sky, shaping themselves into large-limbed animals with long claws and tangled manes. One cloud looked like an angel until it joined the one beside it, mutating into a monstrous black form, black and sinister. Even the fashionable-looking young woman entering the hotel seemed sinister hidden behind the dark sunglasses and black and gold turban. Watching her stop a few feet from the doorway, he wondered if she were here for a rendezvous. She looked up suddenly to catch him watching her. She smiled.

Feeling his spine prickle, he stepped back from the window.

After unpacking, he took a second glance at the blue stone. He'd set it on a smashing antique chest of drawers in the bedroom, thinking how its hue appeared deeper against the soft violet backdrop. Fraser said he used to see ribbon-coloured skies that reminded him of *Alice in Wonderland*. Now, since the incident at Uncle Dale's, all he saw was 'mad water' and 'thunder skies'. He chilled remembering Fraser's parting advice in New York, "Feed your lucky rock nice thoughts, Dad. So it won't rot inside."

Unlike his son, the stone never revealed anything of itself to him, except maybe behind his back. As a boy he'd play the Turn-around game, trying to catch it giving hints of its world when he wasn't looking. But he could never seem to turn around fast enough. He'd grown so attached to it, not because of its beauty, because it came mysteriously one Christmas. As mysterious as a message in a bottle, he'd often imagine deciphering the stone's message since it seemed to radiate pure essence and energy. Had that energy grown stagnant? At least once a month, he wondered about the stone's history.

Mark took the stone into the living room and curled up on the couch, thinking about Fraser, wondering for the zillionth time how all that water got into his lungs from the beach. Fraser could've died, could have died the same way as his mother. He rubbed his brow. Gillian's death was still such a mystery and he hated unsolved mysteries, especially when they involved people he loved.

This waiting around was driving him balmy. If not for *her*, he'd be house-hunting with his son in New York now. Dale would be back in Malibu bickering with Carmen over where to spend the holidays. Some other band would be booked into the El Mondrago, some other recording artist breaking headlines. So here he sat and stood and paced, impatiently waiting for the dream to bust open, getting wackier by the minute with Fraser in New York and him in Toronto. He always got wacky when Fraser was away from him. The dark thoughts magically disappeared with Dale's double-fisted knock. He'd brought Guy Sweet along and they both looked like they'd been into the bourbon. Not a bad idea.

"So when's your bash, Guy?" he asked. "I could use some amping up right about now. A little high-balling."

"You keep that posh nose of yours clean," Dale said, stretching out on the couch. "No more trashing with that shit."

Mark winked at Guy. Dale's mothering always made him feel good. "Oh, c'mon, Dale. A little chang-a-lang. A little benny-bash. Ahh, formulate." Mark parodied this to one of his songs and he and Guy laughed.

"The party's Tuesday night," Dale said, pouting.

"I had lunch with an ex-girlfriend today," Guy said, "and she's invited some of her friends. One's a model I used to shoot and gorgeous."

"Oh you're not going to fill the place with models, are you?" Dale's expression soured. "I'm so sick of the cliché. They all look so much alike I can never tell them apart. The model and the rock star. Gawd."

"That's why they can sell anything," Guy said. "The face is beautiful but forgettable. You know, any other man listening to you would think you certifiable. Besides, this one happens to be dark."

"Good." Mark rounded his grey-blue eyes at Guy, "I got dibs on her."

"I'm just gonna get bladdered," Dale said and Mark suggested they might start the party now. Anything to keep his mind off his restlessness.

Saying he had to sober up and get back to the studio, Guy answered the door on his way out. It turned out to be Lawrence, Mark's star-struck valet. Both he and Dale had valets for their stay, courtesy of the Banford Arms. Mark pried the letter from poor Lawrence's clammy hand and graciously thanked him.

"Is there anything else I can do for you, Mr. Grant?" Lawrence asked.

"No, that's fine for now. Thank you, Lawrence." Mark noticed the absence of postage on the envelope. "Do you know who left this?"

"The desk clerk said a lady dropped it off a few minutes ago. That's all I know, Mr. Grant."

"It's Mark. Catch a glimpse of her?"

"No, M-sir"

"Never mind the questions," Dale coaxed. "Slit the damn thing open!"

Waiting until Lawrence left, Mark opened it carefully and withdrew a single folded sheet of the familiar blue notepaper. Smiling victoriously, he waved it at Dale.

"Looks like she's found me. Well," he said, clearing his throat, "let's give 'er a read, shall we."

He loved that he could never get used to this, and after reading this second note in the same handwriting, the same notepaper, same perfume, from the same woman, he was used to it less and loving it more.

"Hope you two get together before she runs out of notepaper," Dale said, deliberately indifferent, though knowing Dale, Mark expected an ambush of questions. "It's all real, Dale. It's all real and this second note proves it. Perhaps she's still here in the hotel. She did drop the note off personally. Come on," he said, already halfway out the door. "We're going down to the bar for a wobbly."

"Well let's have it, man," Dale hollered in the lift. "Let me see the bleedin' note!"

Mark handed him the note and practically flew through the lift doors when they opened. By the time Dale caught up with him in the Halcyon Lounge, Mark had seated himself at a table nearest the exit, his eyes carefully scanning the room. Winded, Dale sat down in the tub chair beside him and gestured for a waiter.

"Two double Jack Daniel's straight up, please. It's too dark in here, mate. You won't be able to see nobody. If nobody's even recognized us so far, how are you supposed to spot a broad you don't even know?"

"I'd know her," he said, still scanning. "I'd know her anywhere and it's not that dark."

"Believe me, it's a bat cave in here. Listen, chill and wait 'til the party. The note said *See you at Guy's party.*"

"Sure, Dale. Brilliant. Easy." Mark squinted at the silhouettes seated at the bar. "And before that it said, *so happy you received my note, Mark.* After that it said, *until then, sweet sweet dreams.* So you see, she *was* here. Seems she's everywhere around me, inside my head, my dreams. I can't sit around waiting for Tuesday, not if there's a chance she's here now."

"Nevertheless, I don't think she's in here, mate. You may have to wait 'til Tuesday."

"Maybe not. I almost feel ... let's say I'm smelling her perfume."

"Mark, you're smelling the note. She stunk it up with her perfume."

"No, Dale. I smelled it when I entered the room."

"Damn, you could be right. There's maybe a dozen people here. Three middle-agers over there and that woman wearing the turban and shades talking to the geezer at the bar. Might as well leave."

"I've got a better idea. Let's order some bevvies and chill for a bit. It's dark enough in here that we can be comfortable. They've got that nice quiet piano bar over there."

"Lord, you would have to mention the piano. Tell me, how does she know I'm here at the Banford? And Guy's party? How's she doing this, Dale? And what *is* she doing to me!"

"Mark, from where I'm sitting, this thing just gets creepier. I realize you won't rest 'til you meet the lady, and when you do, spend the evening with her, find out what you can, then as nice as you can, brush her off. I don't like the tone of that note. The woman sounds extremely strange."

Had Dale been living in a cloud through all this? "After everything's that's happened, you're saying brush her off? You can't be serious."

≈≈≈

The drunk babbled on and on about hard times, how the little guy didn't stand a chance, the national debt, New York on the verge of bankruptcy and Canada's next. She just kept nodding every two or three sentences. Under the dark sunglasses, the drunk couldn't tell who she was looking at.

Laurel smoothed her hand along the bar's cool surface, watching his eyes dart around the room as he held her note. *Her* note. Dizzy with the nearness of him, she snuck a deep breath. Then another. And another. She wiggled her toes in her boots, shaking her foot until it cramped. How long before he kissed her, ran those sensual piano hands over her body? She felt certain that by Wednesday morning, she would awaken with more than the dream.

Gazing at him through the sunglasses, her skin tingled as she remembered dreams for the first time, dreams she must have been having for years. They had been together during his marriage, his tours, when she felt lonely and frightened. Destiny must speak in dreams. Somewhere in the dream she had the night before Halloween, destiny's voice said, 'Alright, it's time for you two to get on with it. Act one, scene one, coming up'.

It had all come together, except for the first time she saw his face. His not being the boy to whom she surrendered her blue stone was okay now because Mark was real and near and getting nearer still. Yet something about those dreams of the boy disturbed her. In the dreams, an angry sea and turbulent grey-blue water the colour of Mark's eyes engulfed them.

The remains of the coaster she'd been nervously shredding dropped to the floor when Dale Mith strolled up to the bar. Mark was watching. They mustn't speak before the party. She only wanted to prepare today, see Mark's handsome face, deliver the note and have the upper emotional hand at Guy's. Unable to lift her gaze from Mark, she saw Mith peripherally, smelled the liquor on him, sensed his playful mood. Time to get the hell out of here.

"Bartender," Mith said, casting an eye in her direction. "Will you send another round to our table, please? The waiter must be out takin' a piss or something."

She swept the coaster fragments into a neat little pile and signalled for the cheque. Forget the cheque. Better to toss a twenty on the bar and make tracks outta here.

"Here, let me get that," Mith said, sliding the twenty back to her, smiling sensually.

"Thank-you." She slipped an arm into her coat sleeve. Oh God.

Mith gently ran his index finger along the rim of her sunglasses. "You don't really need those in here, darlin'."

The drunk finally stopped talking and zeroed himself in. "Yeah matey, you said it. Take the glasses off, sweetheart. Bet she's got real perty eyes."

Time to move. Fumbling through her purse for the car keys, she prayed Mark wouldn't come over. If he got this close, he'd know. He was looking strangely at her now. She wanted their meeting proper. Not at a bar. Not like this!

"Don't go," Mith said. "Bartender, buy this lady another whatever."

She shook her head at the bartender. "No thank you," she said to Mith, avoiding his eyes. "Gotta run."

"What's so important?"

"Swimming lesson."

Mith chuckled. "Won't take no for an answer."

She stood up. "Sure you can. And sure you will."

Having to pass Mark's table on the way, she stole one last glance. Would her heart ever stop pounding? Mark didn't suspect and she felt sort of happy about this, sort of relieved. Mark beamed at her, no doubt amused because his best friend had just struck out. As she passed, he raised his glass to her.

Her thighs quivered. *It's me, darling. I love you. See you Tuesday.*

≈≈≈

Laurel styled her hair the way he had seen it in the dreams, parted on the side and loosely waved. The shoes were from *Hallan's* of Yorkville, the simple gold jewellery 18 karat, perfume, Nina Ricci's *L'Air du Temps.* Outfit—St. Laurent with a scooped neck silk top, puffed sleeves gathering on the elbow in a black and royal blue Picasso print. The black crepe satin pants had a sashed-over drawstring braided waist with a purple hip yoke. Cuffs, trimmed in yellow matched the half purple, half yellow sash. She looked like two million bucks and she knew it.

Laurel turned on the intercom and waited in the Sea Room. Michael and Nancy were picking her up and Katherine was hostessing for Guy at her High Park home. She entertained the idea of making a lone grand entrance around eleven but decided it best to appear on the arm of an escort. So she asked Michael, knowing he'd be escorting Nancy as well. With Courtland in Ottawa on a weekend business trip, it worked out perfectly. This way, Mark wouldn't think she was exclusively with Michael.

She dimmed the lights in the Sea Room. Finally. Tonight was the night and she was psyched. Mark hardly seemed real the other day, nor did anything else in the Halcyon Lounge seem real now. She glued herself in that barstool and hid behind the turban and dumb shades, confident he'd walk in any minute and when he finally did, he looked around the room and failed to *sense* her presence. Was she disturbed because Mark didn't know her straight away?

Funny, with all the things to be nervous about tonight, why now did it occur to her how much time she spent 'standing' in this room? When she wasn't on the sofa bed walking in the dream with Mark, she was always standing by the display stand covered in the royal blue velvet spread. And tonight, the square rise on top seemed to vibrate under the cloth. No. No hallucinations tonight. No achy shaky. She had to stay focussed, keep the mind clear. Mark was on his way into her life—the real one.

The best thing to do now was change her thinking and enjoy the hallucination. Stranger, more magical things had happened in this room. The display stand vibrated so, dizzied her. She leaned against the wall and squinted at it. What did it want? What had she meant to display when she bought it two years ago? Maybe Mark would give her a little something. How perfect if it came from him. Nothing would have more meaning than a gift from Mark to display on the stand ... to complete the Sea Room.

The vibration stopped with the buzz of the intercom. Michael and Nancy had arrived. So had Christmas. The room smiled at her as she left it. She smiled back. 'Go for it, Laurel,' the room said. 'Go for it. Go get him. Then bring him back here'.

She flicked off the lights and hurried to meet her destiny-love.

≈≈≈

Michael showed up alone. They would fetch Nancy on the way, he said. "I wanted to speak privately with you before the party." Although she had no use for him anymore, she was curious to hear what he had to say. He had accomplished what she wanted and she supposed he deserved credit for that. If not for his 'astral note' brainstorm, there would be no party tonight. She and Mark would still be loving each other back 'There' rather than 'Here'.

"I figured you'd be more nervous," Michael said, tinkling the ice in his Amaretto. "I know I'm nervous as hell."

"I only get nervous when I'm feeling insecure. And I don't have anything to be insecure about anymore. Mark and I are happening exactly the way I wanted. Tonight we'll be meeting here in the real world and we'll continue on. Think of it as a transition."

"It's much more than a transition. And you won't be continuing on, Laurel. You'll be beginning all over again. The atmosphere, emotional climate, the world—everything's bound to be different here. And take into consideration that Mark doesn't remember, doesn't know as much as you."

"Well, he will." Michael the naysayer. Gawd. "Before the night's out, he'll know a lot."

"How can he when we don't know everything yet ourselves? This is happening to you for a reason and that reason has nothing to do with fate. Something in you caused this to happen, and my guess is it started long before last summer."

Her mouth started twitching, dammit. She couldn't let Michael get to her, not now. "You use the word 'cause' in a tone that suggests cure must follow. Destiny arranges certain things for us, Michael. I don't need all the answers now and the last thing I want to do is delve into the past. It's not necessary. I've got what I want and I want to leave it at that."

"Mark may not want to leave it at that. He's seen his double. A beautiful woman comes to him literally out of a dream. He's a curious inquisitive man. The world's seen this, from his interviews, through his music. The man won't accept anything at face value, not even you, especially not you."

"Our circumstances are a little different, Michael. He'll accept. The situation. And me."

"You can't be serious! And the man has a son, have you forgotten? Listen Laurel, something's happening to you and it's getting stronger. It may not be good for you. It may not be good for Mark. That's why we have to continue working on this. And now that I have you and Mark together, it's a cinch we'll find—"

"No way, Michael. No. I want some peace inside myself, and the quiet to go along with it. No more probes, thank you. I want to be left alone now and I want Mark left alone. We're going to have the life we had in the dreams. And don't you dare look at me like that. I can make it happen, you know I can. You're right. The power's stronger, so I'm not going to question it. But I'm sure as hell going to use it. Something knows I'm due for happiness and it's seeing that I get it. Listen to the wind blowing outside, Michael. Can you hear it? Listen ... it's blowing the past away, far away from me. Smell the crispness in the air. How exciting. So clean and so new."

"That's what I s-said, isn't it, Laurel? Not just a transition. A beginning."

"Call it what you like, Michael. And thank you for everything you've done. Really. But after tonight, Mark and I will want to be left alone. Now let's kill this depressing talk and get Nancy. We have a party to get to. God, I'm happy tonight. It's like Christmas, and I've never had a bad Christmas. Doesn't the place look nice? I've been cleaning for two days. Mark will love it here."

Michael helped her on with her coat and stumbled on the way out.

≈≈≈

Guy had Katherine's vintage High Park home professionally catered and decorated like he was expecting royalty in black underwear. Necklaces of white disco lights hung over the bar and he'd cleared two corner sections for dancing. The music, a blend of soft rock and rhythm and blues, cooed from six speakers on loan from Sounds Interchange, and three uh-huh waitresses and two cinderfella bartenders helped distract the edgy guests from the eighty mph winds on the heavily-treed street.

Katherine chose the caterer and menu—three entrées consisting of salmon in a Béarnaise sauce, roast leg of lamb and oysters Rockefeller. She went crazy with vegetables like candied sweet potatoes, ratatouille, green beans almandine, rice pilaf. There were salads, fruit and coconut, guacamole, stuffed zucchini, appetizers of breaded butterfly shrimp, puff pastries filled with mincemeat, crab stuffed mushroom caps. For dessert—black forest cherry torte, trifle, and Florentine pastries.

Guy began with a head count of fifty at seven-thirty and guestimated somewhere between seventy to eighty by eight o'clock. So he figured what the hell and ordered two more cases of Dom Perignon and loaded up on the Jack Daniel's for Dale. He made a second call to Information for the emergency services number at Ontario Hydro—just in case. Though Katharine said she trusted the resilience of the ninety-foot, century old black maple shadowing her roof, Guy wasn't taking any chances.

The after-eight guests arrived looking amused and windblown or grumpy and windblown, the majority involved in the arts in some way, most of them musicians, studio execs, concert promoters, photographers and of course, actors and models. It looked like an indoor mini Cannes Festival with the guests ogling the door every time it opened. No secret they were all waiting for Dale Mith and Mark Grant. Already the women had organized themselves in front of mirrors, fluffing, glossing, and de-tangling. And one man asked to use a private area upstairs to straighten his toupee.

≈≈≈

Uptown, Michael Johnstone, Nan Clancy and Laurel Ariss were about a half hour away. Nancy kept frizzing out her curly blond hair with an afro pick, saying she missed Courtland tonight, said it three times. Michael was thinking about Dr. Wieler and that clairvoyant scene he saw in his head a few weeks ago—a crowd of stone-faced people gathered on a winter beach. Laurel was wondering how long it would take Mark to remember he loved her. She touched the scar on her neck and smiled.

≈≈≈

Downtown, only a few miles away at the Banford Arms, Mark Grant paced Dale Mith's suite trying to hurry him. Having consumed two double bourbons, Dale was now engaged in choosing the proper cologne for the occasion. When Dale finally made his choice and spritzed, Mark berated himself again for his faux pas at the Halcyon Bar.

"I should've gone after her. She walked right by me. Left a trail of cologne all the way out the door and I sat there like I was filling the bowl."

Dale sighed at Mark's reflection in the mirror. "I know. So you said."

"Turban and glasses. Man! How could I fall for that? I saw her enter the hotel."

"It didn't occur to you 'til she was out the door."

"How could it not occur to me? I wake with that scent in my nostrils."

"Mark, enough. I talked to her and it didn't occur to me," Dale said, considering another spritz. "You're gonna meet the woman in an hour."

"And since when has fragrance become a vital accessory for you? So come on, man. Let's go!"

Stubbing out his cigarette, Dale looked up at Mark's disgruntled reflection. "You're not the only one who's gonna be checking out this broad tonight. I'm in this with you, remember that. Someone's gotta look out for you since you're all caught up in this romantic crap."

"You're too suspicious. You wouldn't be in a state if it were a man, would you. Dale, this is so incredible. Why can't you enjoy it with me?"

Dale crossed his arms and leaned back against his dressing table. "You and Carmen are it for me, man. The two most important people in my life. I just don't want to see you buggered by some deranged broad."

"Let's go, Dale. I've always had tremendous survival power and that's not going to change. You're my best mate. Always will be. So are you ready? Can we please leave now?"

≈≈≈

Katharine was rushing by the door carrying a bag of candles when she arrived clutching her winter trench up to her ears. "Branches down all over the street, Katharine," she said, worried that Mark might not come in this weather. Michael was still in the driveway clearing away fallen branches.

"And the power's been flickering," Katharine said, annoyed.

"They here yet?" Nancy asked.

"No. You guys can use my private bathroom to tidy up. Make yourselves at home." Then off she dashed with her bag of candles.

"Of all the nights to have a windstorm," Laurel said, straightening her outfit in Katharine's room. "Guy would know if they weren't coming, right?"

"Right," Nancy said, afro-picking again. "Besides, this is mostly studio people talking business. He'll be here, Laurel."

Nancy had been a good friend, really. "You're missing Courtland a lot tonight, aren't you?"

"Yeah. I could use him here. Not used to socializing with these famous artsy types."

She wanted to tell Nancy so much more than she had, but Nancy had a way of expressing her 'concerns' with those closest to her. This was best kept amongst Michael, Courtland, and Mark, for obvious reasons. And nobody but *nobody* was going to know it all. Not Michael. Certainly not Courtland. And especially—not Mark.

She took a few more deep breaths. "A bit nervous."

The lights flickered off.

"Shit!" Nancy said.

"No, not tonight," she groaned. "Oh they just have to come back on."

The lights flickered on.

Nancy laughed and opened Katharine's bedroom door. "Ask and you shall receive, eh. We should go down before they go out again."

Hearing the applause coming from downstairs, she exchanged a buoyant look with Nancy.

"Wooo hooo!" somebody hooted.

"Hey! Men of the hour!" she heard Guy say.

While the hooting and hollering continued, her stomach filled with butterflies. "They're here, Nancy."

"I just tripped over a bloody log out there!" she recognized Dale Mith's voice.

"Mark's with him, right?" she said, needing encouragement from Nancy. "Guy said *men* of the hour."

"Hey Mark!" someone shouted, "You bring that list, man?"

His answer was barely audible, but yes, he was down there. She beamed at Nancy again.

"I'm gonna go down first, Laurel," Nancy said, pulling a stray hair off Laurel's shoulder. "I think you should make an entrance going down the stairs, you know, like Meggie Cleary did in *The Thornbirds*."

She felt the urge to hug Nancy, but as usual, held back. "An entrance. Right."

Nancy wished her good luck and left her alone. Laurel re-checked herself in front of the mirror, massaged the tightness in the back of her neck and shoulders. *He's really here on the premises. Only a floor below me.* Did she actually hear Nancy getting introduced down there?

She smiled at her reflection. "Time to get your man, girl. Remember, confidence."

Once she passed the stairwell wall, she got a clear shot of the party room. Everyone was gawking up at her. Was Mark among them? She did a peripheral search for him while managing the descent in heels. *Don't fall. Don't fall.* That only happened in the movies. Bedevilled by trembling limbs and a subtle nuance of doom, she managed a few more steps and followed Nancy's voice to the bar.

That's where she caught sight of him standing at the bar surrounded by at least six drooling women. Decked in a grey tailored suit, white Mandarin collar shirt and a smile that turned her knees to jelly, there he was. Her Mark Grant.

Their eyes met and held.

In that instant she saw the desire in them, saw the flash of concern. *Mark darling, don't worry about us. We're on this side of the curtain now. This is what you wanted.* The lights flickered off, and she held her breath on the stairway.

"No." She'd whispered it to herself and stopped on the stair. Katharine had enough candlelight that she could see to the left and into the party room. But she couldn't see the bottom of the stairs, couldn't make out faces.

"Hang on, Laurel!" Nancy shouted. "Careful on those heels."

The room filled with whispers and low voices all talking at once. A flicker of candlelight moved slowly toward her and up the stairs. Aimed at the light, she took another step and another, her ears paining from the pulsing heartbeat. Managing one more step toward the candlelight, a gloriously scented aftershave filled her space. So taken with the scent she bumped the strong arm anchoring her at the waist.

"I came to get you," he said, raising the candle until their eyes met.

Oh God. "Thank-you ... for coming to get me."

"You're welcome," he said, eyes searching hers. "Mark Grant."

"Laurel Ariss."

"Shall we continue on, Laurel?"

Most definitely. Forever. "Yes," her voice croaked. "I'm so glad you're here."

Mark tightened his arm around her waist as they made their way slowly down the stairs. Trembling, she couldn't keep an unmuddled thought in her head.

≈≈≈

Laurel had handed him his cheque tonight. 'Good job, well done, Michael. Thanks ever so much and let's keep in touch.' Of course he was paraphrasing, but he knew she was done with him. Now that she needed him most she was done with him, and no way but no way could he get her attention now. What he'd have to do then, he was deciding this on the spot as that pesky reporter walked toward him, was help her behind her back. He could talk to her brother. And Dale Mith seemed like an approachable guy.

"So, she's quite the looker, eh?" said the reporter, Kevin something or other.

Watching Laurel and Mark slow-dance like it was their wedding night, he agreed, "You here officially, Kevin?"

"Not really. Here with a date who works at *Sounds*."

"Convenient." He didn't like the vibe from this guy. He liked conversing with him even less in the candlelit house.

"You came with her tonight, I understand?"

"A few of us arrived together, yes."

"Gotta be that woman in the photograph, right?"

Michael was about to excuse himself on some pretext when Dale Mith strolled over.

"Hey mate," he said to the reporter, "this all off the record tonight, buddy?"

"It is," Kevin said.

"Who you work for?"

"Freelancer. *Toronto Star* mostly."

"Full name?"

"Kevin McLafferty."

"Right, well let's save the questions for the press conference at the Royal York. Alrighty then, Kevin?"

"Understood," and McLafferty made a hasty retreat.

"I've had my eye on him," Dale said, shaking Michael's hand. "Dale."

"Michael Johnstone. Hi, huge fan." Obviously he and McLafferty hadn't been the only ones watching Laurel and Mark.

"Thanks. Bloody power's still out. Don't need to know what I just ate, man."

"I'm sticking with chips."

"Your friend Nancy said you're a parapsychologist. Ghosts, is it?"

Michael laughed, "I study anomalous phenomena through scientific means."

"I don't quite get it, sorry, though Mark is fascinated by that stuff." Dale cast the new couple, now moving toward a seat on the couch, an austere look. I heard that journalist quizzing you about your friend being the lady in Mark's mystery photo."

"Not to worry, I dodged his questions." Michael wondered if he could dodge Dale's. Then perhaps he shouldn't as people often told more than they asked.

"Good man. Mind if I plug one in?"

Just as Dale asked, the lights popped on and the partiers cheered and charged the buffet table. "Not at all," he said.

Dale looked about to see who was within earshot. "Now that you've met Mark, could you tell in some way that that photo is not him?"

Of course he could. "No I can't. Sorry, Dale."

Mith took a swig of his drink and eyed him suspiciously. "Well, you don't ask you never know, right? Was that your friend, Laurel, in the picture then?"

"It certainly bears a strong resemblance. But something like that Laurel would definitely remember."

Dale chuckled. "You're good. Guess we're both looking out for our mates."

Dale observed Mark and Laurel leave the room while Michael observed the eerie shadow tailing her.

≈≈≈

Standing near him was like getting jolted by tiny electric currents. The soft elegant way in which he spoke, the passion in his eyes when he talked about his music, the love when he spoke about his son ... the smell of him ... his essence. She hadn't felt this loopy ethereal desire in the dreams, only in the intensity of the sex. But that memory had faded now that they were together on this side of their curtain. She was glad their lovemaking seemed vague because it would be new for them all over again. It was going to be perfect. Mark had no choice but to be hers. Finally, a dream comes true.

Mark closed Katharine's office door behind him.

"Now it's time to get into it, isn't it?" He swept back a silky lock of hair from his forehead and leaned against the desk in front of her. "Did you want to start, Laurel?"

"Do you think this is the best place to talk with all these people walking in and out?" she asked him, uncomfortably aware of the marching band in her chest.

Mark seriously regarded the question. "Are you asking me to go home with you?"

"Well, we ... it is a good place to talk. You're making me feel like a little girl suddenly." He hesitated. His hesitation unsteadied her and she practically toppled off the heels. What, he had to think about this? *Mark?*

He crossed his arms, tucking his hands under his armpits. She felt closed off from him and it hurt. "Where does my little girl live?"

What the hell did that matter! "Twenty minutes away. Near Yorkville."

Mark smiled sensually then winced for the second time in the last half hour. "I'll call my driver."

"Mark, your hand. Is it bothering you still?"

"You're so sweet to ask and I'm having it checked again. Now come and meet Dale before we leave because he *knows*. You're right, we should speak privately. Besides, it's my excuse to be alone with you as soon as possible."

As they headed back in to meet Dale, she noticed him and Michael sharing an exchange that most definitely seemed personal, and this disturbed her. She was about to meet the famous Dale Mith and all she could think of was what Michael was telling Dale, whose forehead was full of creases. Michael would bloody well be in for it if he caused problems for her and Mark. But she couldn't think clearly. She was half here and half in the clouds, somewhere in a dream. Mark, Mark. He kept catching her looking at him, which meant he couldn't take his eyes off her, either. She was going to be absolutely everything to him. She'd have to have nothing less than all of him and that was that. Except for his little son, of course.

So this is what happiness felt like. She could get used to this in a hurry. How wonderful to hold back happy tears instead of sad. She pictured him making love to her in a few short hours. She'd have to cry then. She'd have to cry to Mark who was everything, all that mattered. Brought magically to her.

During their introduction she zeroed in on Dale's icy politeness. "Nice to have a man around the house, right?" he said, sarcastically referring to her 'escort' down the stairs.

"Heels." She clicked a heel on the hardwood.

"Right. I've taken a shine to your friend, Michael, here." Dale tapped his fingers on the bar. "So I've invited him to the El Mo gig next week. We might even get together and throw back a few before then."

Dale suppressed a grin, appearing somewhat delighted that his and Michael's instant chumminess seemed to rattle her.

Obviously, Mr. Rockstar senior didn't like her. So what. "I'm really looking forward to seeing you and Mark at the El Mondrago. That is I will be as soon as Mark invites me." She smiled at Mark.

"Of course you're invited." Mark set his arm lightly on her shoulder. "If it weren't for you, there wouldn't be a show at all."

Silence followed.

"Give a little credit to me and the band, mate," Dale spoke first, polishing off his bourbon in one swallow.

"You got that far already?" Michael asked her.

She didn't answer. Pondering Michael's heavyish conversation with Dale, she asked him in a sugary tone, "And how far have you gotten?"

"Halloween," Michael said, a bit defensively. "I was telling Dale how we met."

"Hey, Mark," Dale said, his eyes fencing with hers, "you know Michael here is a psychic investigator. I find that really intriguing, mate. That sort of thing really fascinates me."

"Since when?" Mark asked.

Dale grinned, showing all his teeth. He must've had about two hundred of them. What was his problem, anyway? Did he have a thing for Mark or what? "Michael's work is fascinating," she said.

"So are you," Mark said, massaging a cramp from his hand. "Shall we go?"

"Where we going?" Dale asked.

Mark narrowed his eyes at him. "Laurel and I are leaving, Dale. We thought we'd go for a quiet drink somewhere. I'll talk to you tomorrow."

"Me too," Michael said. "Just waiting for Nancy and we'll be on our way. Laurel? Talk to you in a day or two?"

"Sure," she said, avoiding his eyes.

"Mark, great meeting you. I'll look forward to next week."

Mark shook Michael's hand. Glaring at her like she was one of the Gorgon sisters, Dale shook hers, squeezing a trifle hard. Dale was trouble, no doubt about that, but she could handle Dale. Still, she preferred that Michael not get too chummy with him. Michael was kaput now anyway. He had served his purpose.

6. LOVE BRAND

THEY DIDN'T SPEAK during the limo ride to her place. Mark cupped her hand, giving it the occasional comforting squeeze and she envied him his steady hand when he poured her a glass of water. But he could've been feeling on the inside what she was so obviously showing on the outside. Given the dry click in her throat, she managed to direct the driver to the Circle Court underground parking and panicked when Mark asked the driver to wait. Wouldn't he be staying the night? Had she been presumptuous?

Mark got out of the car, walked around to her side and helped her out.

"Thank-you."

"You're welcome. Would you mind if I dismissed my driver? I can call him back ... if necessary."

Yes! "Not at all," she said, hanging off the sunbeam in her head.

Mark took the turns along the path in the same beat with her. He placed his arm gently around her waist and timidly, she reached up and placed her arm around his. Walking silently with him to the gate was like a dance. They must have often strolled along the path in their astral life, which would explain Mouth's headbutts with the wall during Mark's comings and goings. He seemed so contemplative. Was he remembering something of their life before? Was he dying to touch her? Oh God, she hoped so. At the door, it took forever to fish out the key from her purse and when she did, Mark took it and opened the door.

As her clumsy hand fumbled for the hall light switch, he caught hold of her waist and pulled her into his arms and rocked her. Mark brushed his lips along her neck and ear. Shy at first with her hands, she ran them along his back and through his hair, until he released her. *I want you so much.* Had she thought that or actually said it? After she switched on the light, a disconcerting flash of confusion passed through Mark's eyes as he took in the decor.

"I love the sea," she said, leading him into the living room. He of all people would understand this decor. "It's always held a fascination for me, so naturally blue is my favourite colour."

Mark looked up at the netting, remaining silent until Mouth came over and spring-boarded into his arms. Panting like a train leaving the station, he licked Mark's face. "Your dog is so shy," he said, giving Mouth's head a friendly tousle. "One would think he knew me."

"Mouth." She reached for the dog and Mark said it was fine. "I guess maybe he does. Note the pillows along the wall." Feeling more like her good ol' bolder self, because he was on her turf now, she hankered to test the waters.

Mark set the dog down and checked out the row of pillows on the floor along the wall connecting the living and dining rooms. "I give up." He had a hungry look in his eyes which made her want to jump into his arms. For the first time she envied her dog. If he could do this to her with one look ...

"What can I get you?"

He smiled sensually. "Any kind of soda. Doesn't matter, Laurel. I want to keep my head clear."

She laughed at Mouth, still panting at Mark's feet. "You start a fire, please? I'll get us a couple of Cokes and put on some music. Then I'll tell you about the pillows. Lionel Richie?"

"Perfect," he said, checking to see that the damper was open.

She took her habitual deep breaths in the kitchen before returning with the Cokes. "I know it's early yet," she said, lighting the Christmas candle on the coffee table, "but Christmas is my time. Never had a bad one." She smiled at his amazing face and joined him on the couch.

Mark took her hand and kissed the top of it. "So here we are nice and private. You were going to tell me about the pillows along the wall?"

"Mouth's been running into the wall, in my room upstairs as well."

Mark widened his eyes. "Any trips to the vet?"

"Two. He's okay. A couple of bumps is all and that's when I put down the pillows."

He walked over to the wall and squatted with a dancer's precision to examine it. Mouth padded over and joined him. "Do you think it's me the dog's been following?"

"Yes." He didn't have to do this now. Later'd be good. He could come back and sit close to her, tell her he loved her, propose marriage.

Mark stood and stared pointedly at her. "This is all ... my God ... where do we begin? I know, how about with this ..." In one fluid motion he pulled her off the couch and into his arms. "This is happening to us so fast and it's been happening for a long time, I know. Laurel, I want us to explore backwards and forwards, over and about the middle if we have to. I want us to learn everything we've shared that I can't remember. You've reached my mind, even my dreams. And the dreams. My God, the dreams. They were real. The photographs prove it. I was in two places at once. One place in a dream, one place here. And in both places, you were with me. We've made love before, I know. I know because I'd wake up wanting you, smelling your perfume, tasting you."

Mark kissed her deeply, explored her back with his hands.

She whimpered and sculpted her body into his.

"You're ... this isn't the first time, Laurel. We're going to know, baby. We're going to know everything. I could rape you.

I want you that much. And I want to satisfy you. Rape you and satisfy you. Rape you and ..."

He almost did, stopping long enough to put a cushion on the floor in front of the fire. Tears rolled down her cheeks as she tore at his shirt, mindless and searching, searching for the place to leave her mark. Brand him. She ached to brand him forever and on his lower back, she did, spiking his flesh with a quarter-inch thumbnail until his body went rigid from the pain. As if Mark realized her intention, he let her cut him. She heard that glorious piano tune then, delighted in the vision of those gifted hands sailing over the keyboard. And blood spurted into her palm as she carved a lopsided square on her lover's back.

≈≈≈

Though fleeting, Mark had the sensation of things moving too quickly and his lack of control with Laurel disturbed him. He'd made love to many women but he'd known nothing comparable to this kind of passion. There was no passivity or shyness between them. No shame. Everything they did, they did with an exchange of gratitude. This was not sex, rather a glorious truth and gift to one another.

Vague memories surfaced as they made love, snippets of dreams or perhaps snippets of reality he believed were dreams. She was there before his fame, sensitive and beautiful and longing to love. He could easily love her, but falling in love with Laurel was not enough to make their strange past end here. He stroked the half-moon scar on her neck. Something had happened to her a long time ago, something that caused her to suffer. He felt she had no choice but to suffer, and he realized he'd seen her before the newspaper photographs, as a teenager, perhaps. And before that? No, she was in her teens. *You see, I had this dream ...*

"What, Mark?" she asked, cuddled up against him.

He stroked the scar again and kissed it. "I didn't say anything."

"Oh, I thought I heard you whisper something."

"This scar. How did you get it?"

She stared into the fire. "I don't remember."

"Yes you do, Laurel. The scar was self-inflicted, wasn't it? And you were a teenager when it happened."

Astonished, she asked him how he knew.

"A dream I had a long time ago. It was about this young girl. She had long black hair and big sad green eyes. She was in hospital and late one night I went to visit her. I remember going into the room and sitting on the edge of her bed, with only the moonlight streaming in. I wondered who this beautiful girl was and what the hell I was doing there, how I got there. I diverted my eyes for a second to the silly-looking picture above the bed. Two daisies with a big sunflower in the middle.

"Funny, I remember thinking 'what a dreary Van Gogh knockoff'. When I looked back at her, her eyes were filled with tears and she reached for me. Touched my arm. But I couldn't feel her touch and it scared me. Then she spoke. Asked me something really strange. She asked me how my hand was. I apologized saying I didn't know what she meant, then I asked what happened to her neck. You see ... it was bandaged."

Laurel gave his hand a gentle squeeze. "What did she say?"

"She said, 'I did something bad and punished myself for it'. Then a nurse walked in and turned white when she saw me. That's all I can remember. You haven't changed that much, baby. The girl in the dream, in hospital—was you."

"I remember that dream," she said, moving onto her back. "You weren't much older than me. You were a boy."

"Why did you hurt yourself?"

"I don't ... I really don't remember the grim details. There was a long part of my life where I felt dazed. It was a horrible time, Mark. Please, I don't want to remember it now. Not tonight. Not ever, really. I'd rather not be made to *ever* remember."

She started shivering, even with the fire still blazing. He wrapped his body around hers. A few moments ago sweat poured off her and now, after talking about that terrible stretch in her life, she got the chills. He wanted to soothe her, to stop pushing painful memories at her. Still he had to know. He had a child to consider and she did lie about the scar until he called her on it.

"It's alright, baby. It's simply that if I came to you, you must've come to me, many times. Do you remember anything of that?"

"Not at present," she said. "Probably later I'll remember more. If you need me to."

He had to give it a rest for the night. They had tomorrow and another tomorrow after that. But he wasn't sure he believed her. Ah hell, it didn't matter, at least not for the moment. She had suffered so and here he was reminding her. Why would she want to drudge up all that misery on this night of all nights? He pawed a hand through his hair. How could he be so bloody insensitive? All his questions had wiped away her beautiful smile.

"Tell me something, *turban girl*?" Laurel giggled and he tapped her playfully on the nose. "Why the disguise at the bar?"

"I thought it would fix the nerves if I met you first."

"And are they fixed now?" He grazed his lips along her shoulder.

"Oh yes."

"I should get you up to bed. You're exhausted."

"We can't yet."

"Why not?"

"Because I have to fix *you* now."

"Say again?"

She disappeared for a few minutes, returning with a bottle of peroxide, cotton swabs and a box of bandages. Blushing all the while, she tended to that little passion scratch she'd made on his back, blowing on the cut as she applied the peroxide.

"I'm sorry, Mark," she whispered. "I got carried away."

"It's okay," he whispered back. She had him breathless, flooded with warmth.

She finished and smiled shyly at him, the flush still covering her face. "There. Any other repairs you need?"

He devoured her with kisses.

≈≈≈

Laurel watched him sleep, ran her fingers gently along his temple. This force, this power had brought him into her dreams, and now her bed. But who controlled the power, that's what she needed to learn. Did she control it, or was she merely its host? Something evil had used her mother. Could be history repeating itself, which had been gnawing at her since she saw Mark at The Banford Arms. Perhaps something was using her all over again. If she were to leave and take another walk into the darkness, with Mark *here* at her side this time—where would this power take her and would it take Mark? She lay on her back and waited.

Okay I'm ready for you, so let's have it. Oh, Mark. Already I'm missing our special place.

When the speckled lights came, she could never tell if they were behind or in front of her eyes. Tonight they seemed to be on the ceiling and she yielded to these twinkly little friends who always took her on adventures. They'd been with her since childhood, during her blue stone time, during all those black-outs.

The specks multiplied and formed into groups, a hundred or so at first, then hundreds, then thousands, transforming into one large square of light obscuring the ceiling. The brilliant square resembled a movie screen. By now, she and Mark would be passionately greeting on the shore. Not tonight. Mark was still here, asleep at her side and she was conscious. What had changed?

Show me.

Shapes shifted across the screen, bright splotchy colours, undecipherable at this point. She thought of awakening Mark until her mind filled with the sound of waves, high tide crashing to shore. The coloured shapes whipped across the screen like an angry cloud on the horizon. The tones became earthier in colour and began forming an image. Now what was this? A mansion came into view, a four-storey brownstone manor surrounded by brooding trees and stone walls that screamed privacy. To the right was a tennis court. To the left a greenhouse and what looked like the beginnings of a swimming pool curving toward the back.

Birdsong replaced the crashing waves in her mind. A gentle wind in the trees. The hissing of a lawn sprinkler. And footsteps. Someone, maybe two people, were walking around in the greenhouse. Something or someone else lurked nearby, not quite human, not quite entity, yet she felt its power, its strength growing exponentially by the second.

Smells. She could smell the place! The summer air. Chlorine from the swimming pool. The fragrance of roses. The grass. It all seemed so familiar, especially one fragrance accosting her senses, one simple fragrance. Sandalwood.

Yes, she occasionally wore sandalwood, but hadn't worn it tonight. She'd worn *L'Air du Temps*. So why was this fragrance so overpowering? Her body twitched in bed when the greenhouse door squeaked open. She checked that Mark was still asleep then continued to watch as a small-framed woman backed out of the greenhouse carrying a basket of flowers.

Laurel's eyes narrowed. She wanted to reach out and toss the basket into the air. Wanted to take the woman's cutting shears and clip at her hair. Wanted to take the shears and jab them into the woman's fragile body. Oh God, why would she want to do such horrid things?

Heading toward the house carrying her little flower basket, the woman hummed. Laurel's stomach lurched as the sandalwood-entity stalked the woman. Such a familiar tune the woman hummed. Mark's tune. It had been one of her favourites, one of Mark's early tunes. *Blue Shades of You* helped propel him to fame and this woman knew every note. The cutting shears seemed even more inviting once she recognized the woman. This small, plain-looking, irritating woman was Gillian Grant, Mark's dead wife.

She made a fist under the covers when Gillian set down the flower basket and shears on the kitchen table. She had no wish to hate Gillian. Mark was hers. So who or what was this black presence stalking her everywhere—the dining room, the bedroom, back to the greenhouse for more cuttings? Why did she find it so fascinating, and horrifying? The entity, distorted and black, was a good head taller than Gillian Grant and seemed to want her dead.

A child called for his mother. She attempted to stop watching, even turned her head toward Mark, to no avail as the scene unfolded in front of her eyes no matter where she looked. The outcome of this strange event taking place on her ceiling would disturb her for the rest of her life. Of this she felt certain.

"Mommy!" The excited child bounded into the kitchen as his mother arranged the flowers in a vase. "Where were you? Dad phoned!"

"Calm down then and tell me what he said." Gillian looked away from the boy for an instant and shuddered as she surveyed the room.

"Dad said I can come down to the studio and watch him work this afternoon. Vincent can take me."

"Did Dad say for how long?

"'Til supper. We'll be back for supper. Can I go, Mum? Can I go get Vincent?"

"Yes, if you promise to get your father out of there by six o'clock. Sometimes he forgets about the time and I won't have you missing your supper. Deal?"

The child started jumping up and down and the black presence moved closer, then backed off.

"Vincent's in the garage. But before you get him, you go upstairs and change your clothes. You're not going into Dad's studio looking like that." Catching her breath, Gillian looked around again.

The child bunny-hopped out of the kitchen and the presence chased him halfway up the stairs, watching until he disappeared at the top of the spiral staircase. Then swiftly, it returned to Gillian Grant, keeping its distance until the boy climbed into the front seat of the silver Mercedes with the chauffeur, waiting until the car disappeared a half mile down the road and off the estate.

Gillian moved the flower arrangement to the massive Queen Anne table in the dining hall, over which hung a six-tiered chandelier. Her puny flower arrangement looked lost and ridiculous on the grand table, much like Gillian Grant did in this room. The picture window in the dining room had to be at least fifty feet wide, facing the limestone fireplace opposite. Laurel held her breath as she caught sight of a glittery blue object on the fireplace mantle. The black presence saw it too, charging for it as one would its life force, passionately reaching for it as parched earth would to rain.

Laurel watched, scarcely breathing while the presence swirled around this thing, swirling and dissolving into it, creating a vortex of blinding blue light. Her head ached and her eyes stung. Suddenly, she felt a consuming hatred for Santina, her mother, as the blue whirlpool of light replaced the ceiling scene. Energy. Ectoplasm. Protons. Neutrons. Darkness. Hate.

Her pain faded with the blinding light, now nothing more than a penetrating blue beam. As it dissolved, portions of Mark's living room reappeared on this bizarre ceiling screen. Hearing the sound of the ocean increasing in volume, she saw the chandelier, the picture window, that ridiculous flower arrangement on the table. Blood coursed through her veins seeing Gillian, horror-stricken, and backed into a corner by the fireplace.

She cupped her hands over her mouth. Something had yanked chunks of Gillian's hair from her scalp and excrement stained her shorts. The screen gave way, allowing more objects into view. Laurel saw the *other* woman in the room now, standing there smiling at Gillian, holding the beautiful blue stone she gave to Mark all those years ago. The other woman— the *sandalwood entity*—was *her*. Laurel lay in bed watching *herself* in this horrifying scene with Gillian Grant.

The stone had come home. Mark was the enchanting boy! She had to think clearly, had to reason. How though, when all she saw was the stone, her *Blue Diamond*, small young hands on a piano and an evil clone in this neverending vision? She commanded the clone to leave, 'Take the stone and go. Leave Gillian Grant alone. You have the stone and you have Mark'.

The clone turned to look at her, smiled. 'Laurel,' she said, and Laurel heard her own voice in her mind. 'Have you forgotten? Gillian Grant is dead.'

The clone raised the diamond to its face and focussed on Gillian's image. The ocean seemed omnipresent in the room, churning, pounding, crashing. A gauzy blue film covered the ceiling scene as she watched Gillian gasping, choking, arms flailing in a desperate attempt to live. Gillian appeared to be drowning indoors, in a place with no water, weighted down by an invisible undertow.

Stop!

She smelled the ocean, felt it pummel Gillian's body and features into something that faintly resembled a human being. *Stop!* The clone continued to beat the last breath from Gillian Grant. *No!* Finally it stopped, observed the unrecognisable bloated form on the rug, grinned as small amounts of water trickled from what had been a nose, a mouth and ears. Gillian didn't have a hair left on her body. A sudden coldness hit her core as she watched the clone poke the remains with its foot before returning the stone to the mantle, kissing it before setting it down.

At last, her 'twin' took its leave of the mansion, briefly stopping beside a child's bicycle propped against the greenhouse. She gasped as the thing transformed into a dusty black cloud, then extended a shadowy arm and dissolved.

The ceiling returned to being a ceiling. Exhausted, mentally and physically drained, she shut her eyes, prayed to reason, to make sense of the ceiling images. Gillian Grant had had a heart attack, so what she'd seen could not be real. No. No! Tomorrow she'd be able to reason it out. It was time to sleep now. She curled up behind Mark and kissed his wound. Mark would tell her the truth about Gillian, and if it was true it meant three things. Mark was her enchanting boy. Her *Blue Diamond* would soon be home—and a part of her killed his wife.

Trembling, she whispered to Mark, "Oh please, forgive me."

Then she slipped out of their bed and locked herself in the Sea Room until morning.

≈≈≈

Mark awakened at nine and couldn't find Laurel anywhere. There were three eggs and a sliver of cheese in the fridge so she probably popped out to get breakfast for them. Strange that she didn't leave a note or at least come in to say good-morning. Laurel was different, though, everything about her—different. She was the only woman he'd slept with who wasn't there clinging to him in the morning. And damned if she wasn't the first woman he wanted clinging to him in the morning.

The wind rattled the panes and an odd creaking sound resonated from the upper floor. For a townhouse, how much upper could there be? He heard her get up sometime during the night but drifted off before she came back to bed. Where'd she go? Didn't she know he wanted to look at her, make love to her the moment he opened his eyes, and talk with her about a million and one things?

Even with today's mile-long to-do list he couldn't motivate himself with Laurel trespassing in his head. Thinking about their lovemaking after the first aid made him want to hop in a cold shower. He'd probably need a fresh bandage as well. A shame she wasn't here to apply it in the smashing way she had last night.

While searching her upstairs bathroom for bandages, it dawned on him that apart from her not storing the first aid kit up here, she didn't seem to have much of anything else up here, either. The women he'd known kept jars, bottles, do-dads, and mysterious-looking feminine objects all over the place. Not Laurel. All she had was a toothbrush, toothpaste, soap, shampoo and shaver in the medicine cabinet. And a pen knife.

His heart flip-flopped. Poor baby, growing up in the absence of warmth while he'd enjoyed nothing else but. Actually the entire house seemed devoid of warmth. With the exception of the odd sea motif in the living room which he didn't fancy at all, the townhouse was beautifully decorated, everything in the right place. Nothing out of order. No magazines or albums scattered about. No family pictures. Only a few doggie toys, and of course those wonderful black & whites in the entrance hall of Helfgott, Richter, Michelangeli and Williams. He reached down and patted Mouth who had been following him everywhere.

"Your mistress left me out of the gallery. Don't mean to brag but I am considered *up there* with Roger Williams. And she knows of my classical training." Mouth's ears tuned in to the annoying creaking sound. "Do you have an old lady in a rocker for a neighbour?"

The creaking intensified. It couldn't be a neighbour because it was coming from above. Maybe it was a partially opened window in the attic with the wind blowing an old rocker about. Most women, young and old, loved rockers, but a rocker didn't exactly fit with the decor, so maybe Laurel stashed it in the attic. Why in blazes was he thinking so much about the damn sound? This place felt cold without Laurel, cold in all respects. The warmth of last night with the crackling fire, that home feeling and finally finding the woman of his dreams, was gone.

He picked up the dog and walked around looking at the stark blue walls and odd blue mirrors, the pieces of lacquered driftwood in the dusty netting. Suddenly everything appeared simulated. There was something wrong with this house, very wrong. Poor little girl. Immediately after the El Mo, he'd get her out of here, find her and Mouth a real home with him and Fraser. A home? Maybe he was rushing things a bit.

Alright. Enough of this bloody creaking. Seemed the only way to end it was to source the sound. The closest he got to it was a hall closet at the top of the stairs to the right. Mouth tugged at his trouser cuff.

"Come on now, puppy," he said, scratching the dog's ear. "Give me a break, I'm new here. Need to explore a bit."

Finding the closet jammed with a variety of bags and boxes filled to the brim, he smiled. So this is where she stashed the clutter. But forget the clutter because he was closing in on the noise, in or around this closet. Could that be? If he could get his hands on a light switch—maybe behind one of these green garbage bags. He dragged out three extraordinarily light bags and felt along the inside wall for a switch. Nothing.

"You know what, Mouth, there probably isn't even a switch in here."

With these words the creaking stopped. Mark stood for a moment, staring blindly into the closet, unknowingly focussing on the Sea Room panel. Something wasn't at all right about this place, like the day he and Fraser returned home from the studio and called Gil. There was something not right about the house that day, too. That horrible day. He'd ask Laurel about the noise when she got home. She'd know what it was. For now, he preferred to get his mind on something else.

Mark put the garbage bags back in place and stopped. The bags were so light, and crunchy. Ignoring the cold spot on the bottom of his spine, he twisted off the tie from one bag and found it filled with newspaper, nothing but crumpled up newspaper. He noticed two more like it on the left side of the closet. After a moment's hesitation, he reached in and pinched them, discovering they were the same. Following that, he heard a creak start and suddenly stop, almost mid-creak. He stared into the closet for several seconds then slammed the door shut.

"Come on, Mouth. Downstairs for a coffee while we wait for the mistress."

≈≈≈

She sat awkwardly in the chair, head frozen to the right, fixed on the exit. What would he think if he found her here? What would he think of her? She couldn't exactly tell him she sat up in this dumb chair all night, feeling sick, stupid and scared because she had to convince herself she could still act normal. Mark must never suspect she was troubled, or worse—disturbed. No-no. Not disturbed. Never disturbed. Santina was disturbed, but she wasn't Santina. She broke down and spent that time in the hatchery because *of* Santina, not because she was *like* Santina.

The intercom was on all night, so she could track him in case he got up at some ungodly hour and went looking for her.

But he'd slept, and now he was moving around downstairs, probably wondering where she got to. God, she had to get herself together, get the hell down there to him. But she couldn't move. Gee, could last night's ceiling horror have something to do with it, maybe? Why did she have to see that on their first real night together? Where did that vision on the ceiling come from? Maybe she hadn't seen it. Maybe it wasn't real.

For an instant during the wee hours, God flashed through her mind. So fleeting. Memories of being a little Catholic girl. Memories of something pushing God away. Everything that had ever given her comfort was always taken away. *Oh stop whining, Laurel!* Well nothing or no one was ever going to take Mark away. Just let them try. Just let them goddam try. Because without Mark, there'd be nothing left of her. So what purpose would this power have served?

If she was little again–if she was little and her father hadn't given her the Diamond–if she hadn't felt abandoned–if her childhood was happy–if her mother hadn't shown signs of lunacy on that trip to England, maybe she would've left the enchanting boy something different. She could have left her name and address. They might have become pen pals and eventually visited, fallen in love in a normal way. There wouldn't have been any Gillian. Would've. Could've. Should've. Youth had been a nightmare, a time forced to spend in dreams.

"I was never really little," she whispered to the taxidermied cat.

She had to get downstairs and hold him. There was nothing wrong with her. Mark was here now. Mark had been here since England all those years ago and he was here to stay. Never again would she have to hurt herself for feeling guilty. Mark had accepted and returned her love. The Diamond magic was real. Finally she could sweep away the past, so everything would be all right. But God still didn't approve of her. Really, how could He?

She found Mark rummaging through a cupboard, Mandarin shirt open and un-tucked, nibbling on a cracker. "Good morning, handsome man," she said, making a beeline for him. "I think I can do better than that."

Mark caught her in his arms. "Hey! Where were you? I woke up missing you."

"In the attic looking for an old photo album." She had to look okay. He had to not see anything strange or different in her eyes. "There's this old album of me and my family. I woke up thinking of the dream you told me about, about the girl, well, *me* in the hospital. I thought if you saw some pictures, you might remember more."

"Didn't you find it?"

"No. It wasn't up there. My brother must have it."

"Why would you keep it in the attic?"

See, she knew it! Already he was looking strangely at her. "I don't know. I keep all kinds of things up there. Why are you looking at me like that?"

"Laurel, I'm concerned, that's all. I wake up and you're gone. I heard you get out of bed last night. Then I hear all kinds of strange sounds around here."

"As I said, that was me fumbling around in the attic."

"Do you have a rocking chair up there?"

"Yes."

"Were you rocking or looking, baby?"

"Both, Mark. I had some thinking to do. You know, I'm still in a state about us. But I love you so much. I wanted to tell you that again first thing, here in the light of day." She put her arms around his waist and hugged him. "I've loved you for so long."

"You must never keep things from me," he said, stroking her hair. "When things bother you, you must tell me. I've sensed what you've been through because I feel I've been through much of it with you somehow. So let the love grow, okay, right here in the real world."

"Okay." He didn't say it back, didn't say *I love you, too.* "Let me attach some eggs to that cracker. How about an omelette?"

"Sounds wonderful. And so was last night. And so are you."

"I want to look at your back after breakfast," she said, glowing from his compliment. "Dress it again."

"Only if I get to dress your back. I looked around earlier, hope you don't mind. You don't seem to have much in the upstairs bathroom."

She cracked the eggs. "I use the downstairs one mostly. Coffee?"

"Please. Anything wrong, love?"

"No, course not. Thinking about my early photos made me wonder about your life growing up. Must've been nice having doctors for parents. My father is a builder and my mother a trophy wife—"

"What?" Mark laughed. "What makes you think my parents are doctors?"

She stopped beating the eggs. "An article I read years ago said you were raised in Bath, England. Important parents. Big house. Private school."

"Oh no!" He laughed again. "I'd forgotten that press release, that silly story. A former press agent's hair-brained idea."

Her hand shook as she poured the eggs into the pan. "Then where did you grow up?"

Mark took the coffee and put on the pot. "East Sussex, on the south coast of England. A little coastal village called Rottingdean. My Dad ran a small family restaurant by the shore and we lived on the premises. My mother died of meningitis when I was very young. What?"

Numbed, she flipped the omelette. "How's your hand feeling?"

Mark stood behind her and put his arms around her waist. "You've asked me that before. Oh, a few twinges here and there. Not to worry."

"What do you think it is?"

"Could be a touch of arthritis. Laurel, what's wrong?"

"Honest, nothing. Will you play the piano for me soon, Mark?"

"Of course I will." He nibbled on her ear. "Turban girl."

Play the piano for me, Mark. I love you, my enchanting boy. So how do I tell you about the stone? How do I tell you I think I killed your wife?

7. BLUE DIAMOND

"DAMN THAT DOUBLE for hiding on me now," Mark joked to Laurel, who was giving his hand and arm a heat massage and didn't find this the least bit funny. In the past week she'd nursed his still-undiagnosed cramping through rehearsals, press conferences and studio tapings. She made chocolate marshmallow fudge for him to take to Fraser for an overnight jaunt to New York to see how he was settling in with Annie, his new tutor and governess. He had planned to send for Fraser sooner, but then Laurel got talked into a two-day photo shoot and Sounds had a power outage at the studio.

He'd also planned to stay put at The Banford Arms until the last of the press conferences this afternoon. No doubt the press wanted details of the mysterious woman in his life and his alleged double. Although Justin warned the press to stay clear of questions regarding his and Dale's personal lives, this was like asking Steinway to nix the keyboard.

He hated putting off moving in with Laurel, but preferred waiting until he had Fraser comfortable with the idea. He didn't want him hearing about his father 'shacking up' less than a year after his mother's death until he had several talks with him. That overnight trip to New York was really about having alone time with Fraser to discuss Laurel, although he didn't say as much to her. Fraser didn't mind his having a 'girlfriend' but appeared concerned about his remarrying so soon. He promised Fraser he would not remarry without his wonderful son's approval, and felt a twinge of guilt for it. Everything—him and Laurel—it had happened so fast. And already, the show was Saturday. This was Sunday. Fraser was due in town Thursday afternoon.

He loved how anxious she was to meet Fraser. Laurel adored kids, which was one of the things he loved most about her and he'd begun remembering their talks on the astral shore, talks about her childhood and *his* child. Obviously she longed for family, probably because her family life lacked cohesion. Yesterday she'd surprised him with a silver-framed photo of Fraser. She'd snuck the picture from his wallet and had one of her photographer mates blow it up.

His heart melted when she set it on the coffee table and said, "Okay. All ready for Fraser."

He'd suppressed his anxiety over things moving too fast between them, but really, how fast could things be moving over the course of twenty years? Again though, they'd only been coupled five and a half minutes on this side of the curtain. There were other things as well. She seemed nervous in crowds and with his fame, which surprised him. She was a successful model and well-travelled, did TV commercials, graced magazine covers and knew what it took to produce these shows. Still, she only seemed relaxed when they were alone. He felt confident that she'd fall in love with Fraser, though. Well, mostly he felt confident. An affectionate, loving kid like Fraser would spin rainbows around her. He'd leave them alone, let them come together naturally, not force it. And Laurel could plan for Fraser's arrival however she wanted.

The other thing gnawing at him was Dale's attitude. Dale didn't cotton to Laurel, which was why he never asked what he thought of her. Mostly it added up to the things Dale didn't say and didn't do in Laurel's presence, like act goofy and tease her for incorrectly choosing between the two of them, like asking about her life, her family. Sure, Dale was polite and courteous, even managed an exchange of pleasantries at the small dinner party Guy threw for them last night. But he had never seen

Dale so rigid and controlled and it concerned him that Dale's dislike for Laurel might be reaching the intense stage.

He also found it strange that Dale had become friendly with Laurel's friend, Michael. They'd been out carousing the last few nights. Ever since the party, Michael had been at the studio, at Dale's hotel suite. He even attended one of their press conferences. Dale and Michael had really hit it off. This confused him all the more. Surely the two of them spoke of Laurel. Wouldn't Michael try to present Laurel in a positive light? Perhaps not. Could be Dale hadn't said anything to Michael, either, since it was typical of him to keep his feelings to himself at all the wrong times, this followed by an explosion. And after an explosion came the fallout.

Still, Dale could tell about people. He had a knack. So why didn't he like Laurel? Since it was bothering him so much, he decided to pick his time and just ask him. He had intended to corner Dale at Guy's dinner party last night, but Laurel came over and pleasantly distracted him. Dale took off to the other side of the room then, where he stayed for the rest of the evening.

≈≈≈

Downtown Toronto resembled Times Square on New Year's since Mark Grant and Dale Mith's arrival. The rock legends' month-long stay on Toronto soil gave their fans hope of tracking them, not too difficult a feat for those who'd studied their lives and habits for years. Fanatical fans had insight into their personality and character. They knew Dale Mith liked bourbon and club-hopping late at night. They knew Mark Grant enjoyed five-star dining and browsing art galleries.

It was like Rock Santa in the downtown core. Christmas Mardi Gras in the snow. Properly garbed for long stake-outs, the groupies huddled around The Copa, The Bellair Cafe, the Jarvis House Tavern, The Four Seasons and Royal York hotels and The Ontario Gallery of Art. They even camped outside

Sounds Interchange hoping to glimpse the best in Rock Royalty. Given the brawls, hysteria, drug busts and raucous music, the cops put in overtime writing reports. Angry and worried parents searching for high-strung teenage girls and strung-out teenage boys filled the streets. Street vendors and record stores prospered. DJs promoted the El Mo concert by playing Mark and Dale's music 24/7. In front of The El Mondrago, red-nosed and frozen-eared kids danced in snowy slush chanting things like 'Grant and Mith we're goin' with', 'Give me Heaven, give me Hell, give me Mark and give me Dale'. It was Party Time in Toronto with a few hundred thousand on the guest list.

Mark, Dale and the rest of the band arrived an hour late for the press conference due to the swarm of fans outside the Royal York. Their three-limo entourage had no place to move until the police cleared a path to get them into the hotel unscathed. As they walked through the lobby, a teenaged girl screamed Mark's name.

"Look at me! Please look at me, Mark! Mark!"

When he did look at her, the braless fan tore open her blouse. The cops dragged the hysterical girl past a sea of embarrassed faces toward the lobby exit.

He said to Dale, "Poor balmy thing. What the hell did she expect after that little display? That I'd stop the presses and run her off with me?"

"You love it," Dale said, grinning. "What you have to do is stop being so bloody philosophical about it. Teenage hormones, man. We do what we do and they react the way they react."

"But these young girls," he said, blinking away a camera flash, "they get to me sometimes. I want to shake them and tell them my bathwater gets as dirty as anybody's."

"Yeah, right. They'd bottle it and keep it next to grandma's ashes on the mantle."

"That is so twisted."

The press conference rolled right along in spite of the delay. A dozen reporters, C.B.C. cameramen, concert promoters, DJs and a few of the well-connected beautiful people, including several of his and Dale's entourage, had arrived early to gawk and eat. Bodyguards. Plainclothes cops. Press agents. Managers. With all these warm bodies, the room was thick with humidity, smelling of coffee, cigarettes, cheap cologne and sweat.

He sat to the right of Dale at the head table sipping black coffee while Dale washed down about ten finger sandwiches with a couple bottles of Budweiser. Judging from the whisper vibe in the room, he sensed the press wanted to get Dale out of the way so they could fix on him. Already they'd begun asking the wrong questions.

"Dale, tell us, is it true you've practically given up women since your divorce from Carmen?" This from a cheeky blonde reporter who kept licking her lips.

Dale teased her with a penetrating look. "Since my divorce from Carmen, I've given up only one woman. However, collectively I still adore them. Now if you and your girlfriends are free in about an hour ..."

Laughter.

"Dale, what made you choose the El Mondrago? This could be the concert of the decade and a fraction of your Toronto fans will see it. Surely the *Gardens* would have been the better choice. Do you feel the El Mo stage is big enough to hold the both of you?"

"We wanted a more intimate atmosphere to record the second half of the album. As you know, this collaboration is a first for Mark and me and we simply wanted the informality. There's to be no pomp and ceremony at the El Mo. Just one small party. There'll be other concerts, other tours in future. And as for the stage not being big enough for the both of us–

absolutely true. Carnegie Hall wouldn't be big enough, mate. But we'll have to make do, won't we."

Laughter.

"Fans have been screaming to see you in concert for nearly two years now, Dale. Any idea when you're going to tour again?"

"I don't get ideas. I just get restless. So I'll probably be restless again somewhere around the end of next summer."

"Mark. Kevin McLafferty, *Toronto Star*. I was at your last concert here and loved it, but what really happened at the piano? It seemed to be more than hand cramps. Standing at stage left I noticed you phased out for a few moments."

Mark cupped his hands together and smiled at him. "Battle fatigue. Apart from a recent hand injury, I was rather exhausted. Long tour. Long nights. Besides, the piano puts me to sleep."

Laughter.

"How did you react to this news of a double? How do we know we have the real Mark Grant with us today?" This from the same reporter.

"You don't know. But Dale will vouch for me. I'm the only one who understands his jokes."

"Seriously, Mark, you saw the photographs taken here. Didn't you find the whole thing a bit eerie?"

Justin tilted back his chair and puffed out his chest. "Gentlemen. Didn't we agree to stick to the music business?"

"It's alright, Justin." Mark met McLafferty's gaze. "Of course I found it eerie. Who wouldn't? It was like looking at a mirror reflection. But it seems now that this fellow has had his fun and is done playing. I don't think we'll be seeing him again, so I'm afraid you're stuck with just me."

"Excuse me, Mark. Bunny Jones, *Music Beat*. Any luck locating the lady in the photographs? Rumour has it that a lady strongly resembling her was at a party Guy Sweet threw for yourself and Dale last week."

"We haven't tried locating her, why should we? I don't dispute any resemblance to some woman at Guy's party. Of course it's possible, especially since the two photographs showed only the back of her head and a somewhat hazy profile."

"I was at Guy Sweet's party." McLafferty again. "And that ring on the lady's finger looked identical to the one in the photographs."

"Let's move on," Justin said.

"Oh c'mon, Mark," McLafferty goaded, "Who is this mysterious lady in your life? And there never was a double, was there? It was you all along. Do you have a double working for you, is that it?"

Everybody started talking at once. Dale looked like he wanted to take a swing at McLafferty. Justin jumped up and gestured to the cameraman while he sat back in his seat, legs crossed, smiling at McLafferty. There was always one, it never failed. Perhaps he should let McLafferty enjoy his victory, or at least have it appear that way. It was time to make a move or there'd be no end to these theories, and though Laurel wasn't quite ready for the madness, he had to ease her into his world sometime, but—slowly. If he gave them a little of what they wanted now, they wouldn't hound her too much later. He hushed the room with wile, subtle gestures.

"I can promise you this," he said. "I hired no double to work for me. Who he is or where he is is of no interest to me. In fact, if he wants to carry on the charade he has my permission to do so. If he does carry on, he'll be caught eventually and that *is* of interest to me. Now until that happens, I have more important matters to attend to. Dale and I have a show to put on and an LP to complete. As for the lady in question ... yes. There is a lady. And she assures me she's been out with only one of me."

"What's your relationship with her, Mark?" asked the cheeky blonde reporter. "Just good friends, I suppose?"

He smiled at the crowd, then at her. "Much more than that. But discretion being the better part of valour ..."

Naturally, the reporters fired off the next dozen or so questions simultaneously.

He laughed and politely shushed them. "Marriage isn't a topic for discussion at this stage. As you well know, I've just finished a tour. We've been going at warp speed here what with recording Dale's new LP and the El Mo this Saturday. The lady and I see each other whenever we can and that's it. That's all I can tell you right now because that's all I know."

"Except who she is," someone blurted out.

"Oh, you'll meet her soon enough. Besides, you must allow us some privacy, that's only fair."

"But is she the woman in the photographs?" McLafferty coaxed.

"As I said," he spoke with automatic politeness, "she assures me she's been out with only one of me."

Looking defeated, McLafferty asked no more questions for the rest of the press conference, which couldn't have pleased him more. Well at least this was the last press conference for a bit. He looked over at Justin and Dale. They had been in the limo five minutes and neither had spoken. Dale was crunching the last of the ice cubes in his glass, staring vacantly out the window while Justin absentmindedly twirled his unlit cigar.

"Light the thing and lay it on me," he said to Justin.

"That McLafferty guy," Justin said, reaching for his lighter. "You know, the one you were so glib with? I heard some stuff about him from a couple of people on the way out."

Feeling a narrative coming on, he leaned back and crossed his legs. "So?"

"No secret he's a rock reporter for the *Star*, but he's also something of an investigative one as well. Does a fair bit of ghost-writing. Hangs around cesspools of the rich and famous, then sells the *cess*. He must do well, Mark, he lives in a two thousand a month penthouse at the Harbor Castle. A frustrated songwriter was what I was told. Loves to cause a stink. Not afraid of lawsuits. Gets his rocks off playing in the dirt. He wouldn't tell the world you paid for your grandmother's operation but he'd sell his soul to tell the world you screwed your grandmother in her rocking chair."

"I don't have a grandmother."

Justin puffed nervously on his cigar. "Remember when Danny Devine's career came to an abrupt halt last year? Too bad. That kid was really starting to go places."

"Danny Devine?" Dale said. "Wasn't he the cat who liked to play house with his little stepdaughter?"

Justin flagged his thumb. "That's the one. Seems McLafferty's got smut contacts everywhere, including L.A. Apparently, Devine beat the crap out of his lady and it got hushed up real quick. McLafferty wanted to find out why it got hushed up since Devine wasn't that big an item yet. So he flew out to L.A. and nosed around. Mrs. Devine had threatened to charge Danny unless he paid her an amount he hadn't even made yet. What she got instead was a busted nose, three cracked ribs and a threat she was too afraid to treat as a bluff. By this time she'd left Devine but the lady was feeling lonely, vulnerable, you know?

"So, McLafferty wangles an invite to a private party she's attending and brings along some stud of the year type with him. She and the stud start dating. She gets fried and tells him about Devine and her daughter. The stud tells McLafferty. And so it went. The end of Danny Devine's career. The only thing that kept him out of jail was Mrs. D's decision not to press charges, that and the half million she got from him. But the bad publicity killed his career. He couldn't afford to dispute McLafferty in court and McLafferty knew it. How could he dispute the truth, especially if Mrs. D's lawyer put her little daughter on the stand? And so it went. I hear Devine's playing no class hotels and strip joints in Tampa. End of story. That's what's dangerous about this guy, Mark. He doesn't deal in lies. He deals in truths."

"So what," he snapped. "He's still an invasive asshole, and I'm no struggling young artist trying to get a rung up. He breathes on one of mine and I'll have him sectioned into quarters."

"And he'd deserve it, but that invasive asshole has taken quite an interest in you since Gillian's death. He's been following you rather closely these days. It was put to me confidentially after the conference that somehow, McLafferty miraculously got his hands on the coroner's report. He also found out about Fraser's mishap on the beach at Dale's last month. And he's finding it all very weird. Very weird and very interesting."

Justin paused a moment, then spoke carefully, "Mark, I know you have clout. And because of that clout, the horrific details of Gillian's death were contained. McLafferty would be committing professional suicide if he opened that up now. At this point in time he doesn't have enough legal leverage to sway a one-man jury, and sure, you could put him out of business. Easily. At this point in time."

His stomach twisted remembering the sight of Gil's remains that tragic day, how he screamed at poor Fraser to get out of the room. After catching only a glimpse, Fraser couldn't have made out what it was, or ... who it was. Then, children were highly perceptive, more so than most adults. Fraser knew. He never did say anything. But he knew. *My poor boy. My poor little son.* Why was Justin drudging up this hell now?

"Say it, Justin. Just get to the bloody point."

"My point is this—strange things have been happening to you this past year, Mark, especially the last couple of months.

People are beginning to notice. Right now it's all to your advantage. But for how long? I don't know what's going on. I don't know if *you* know. But Mark, surely in the privacy of your own thoughts you've noticed the similarity between Gillian's death and what happened to Fraser out at Dale's. Dale told me all about it. We're frightened for you. It's all very strange. And now there's this McLafferty business. I just wish the hell I found out about the guy before the press conference today."

"What else did Dale tell you?" he asked, staring coldly at Dale.

"Nothing," Dale said, looking wounded. "I said nothing."

"Well, there's obviously more," Justin said. "And it's also obvious it's personal so I won't pry. Just be careful, Mark. Keep your eyes open."

Justin was meeting a friend for drinks so they dropped him off at the Four Seasons Hotel. In an effort to lighten their mood, Justin said he was happy for him and his new lady, adding that he hoped to meet her soon. He and Dale rode back to the Banford Arms in silence, remaining silent until he slammed the door of his suite behind them. He lunged for his suitcases, threw them on the bed and clicked them open. The first thing out of the vanity drawer was a black satin drawstring pouch. He put the blue stone in it and carefully tucked it inside his toiletry case.

"So, you're moving in with her today," Dale said, squeezing into a chair too small for him beside the dresser. "I figured you'd wait 'til after the concert."

He waved Dale out of the chair and opened the top drawer. "I told you, Fraser's coming in Thursday and Laurel's will be a better atmosphere for them to meet. This will give them a couple of days to get acquainted. There's no need to keep running him back and forth from her place to here."

"But you said you weren't checking out, so I assumed—"

"Annie's bringing him in, so I'm leaving this suite for her."

"What's his governess sticking around for?"

"She's bringing him back here after the show. I don't want Fraser at the party afterwards. It's too late for him and those parties can get wild."

"Mark, why don't you stick around, man? Michael's on his way and I thought we'd throw back a few."

"You and Michael have been chapping it up." He looked suspiciously at Dale. "This Michael, he's heavy into parapsychology, isn't he?"

"That is his business, mate."

"Is he working on a case now?"

"I assume so. He's got to earn a living."

"You're being rather vague, Dale. All this time you've spent with the guy lately and he hasn't told you anything of his business, his *recent* business?"

"We've talked about Laurel if that's what you're getting at."

Mark's stomach knotted. Things between him and Dale had never been this strained.

No sense putting this off. "You don't like Laurel, do you?"

Dale's eyes darted around the room before finding their way back to Mark. "She scares me, man."

"She what! I don't believe what I'm hearing here." Mark masked his unease with laughter. "You? Dale Mith? Afraid of a woman? Come on, why don't you just admit you don't like her. I'm not blind, you know. Even when you don't say anything, you say everything."

Dale stared at him—hard. "Right, okay I'll admit it. I don't like her *because* she scares me."

"Why? Because of the way we found each other?"

"No. Not just that."

"Well then what?"

"It's difficult to put my finger on it. It's a feeling I've got. Her eyes. The way she looks at you, looks through you, past you, to somewhere else or something. The way she walks. It's like she's so stiff she can't relax, like she doesn't know how to relax. She doesn't look at you like she loves you. She looks at you like she owns you. And she looks at me like I'm an intruder with no business being in your life."

He shut his eyes, smiled tight. "You're wrong, Dale. You're freaked by what happened in Malibu, and you've met Laurel exactly twice. She doesn't parade her emotions in front of others. And you haven't seen her care for me. My arm. Especially my hand. You're intimidated by the supernatural, for lack of a better word. It scares you."

"Michael doesn't scare me. Sorry mate, but you asked. There's something about the girl that isn't right and yes, I'm bloody scared. For you. For Fraser."

"That's enough, Dale. You think I'm a fool? You think I would risk my son for anything or anyone, and that includes Laurel. That little voice inside all of us, the little voice we've often talked about, well it's told me to go ahead. It's not sending up any red flags. I can't explain it and damn, it sounds kitsch but we belong together. Like we're destined. For the first time in my life I'm not going to interrogate the fantastic as it happens to me. I'm going to let it go, let it be."

"Mark, maybe what's happening to you is something that's happening to her. Maybe *she's* not happening to you. What if *you're* happening to her?"

"That's the most ridiculous thing I've ever heard you say. It's happening to both of us. Together. Now I bloody well know Michael's been talking to you about Laurel. I can imagine all the crazy things he's saying. Well let me tell you something, this has been happening to Laurel and me long before Michael came around. He doesn't know the half of it. Neither do you. For all his snooping, all he'll ever have are theories because he hasn't experienced what we have. I don't care how many damn visions he's had. How we began, how we evolved together is something even we can't put into words. But we were there. We lived it. We remember most of it. So don't go looking to Michael for answers because I'll tell you right now, he'll never have them. I promise you there's nothing to fear. All my fears vanished after that night in Malibu."

Dale took a deep breath, let it out. "Then I'm happy for you, Mark, if you know, since you strongly feel this is right. Maybe I have been getting carried away. I guess that conversation with Justin got to me or something. All that talk about Gillian and Fraser on the beach. We'll never know what happened to Gil. And Fraser probably got near the water tossing the Frisbee about. You know, this past year has affected me almost as much as you. I liked Gil and I love Fraser. It has been fascinating, this thing with you and Laurel. I admit that. You'll marry her?"

"Of course. I'll give Fraser a few months with Laurel and then we'll marry."

"You setting up house in the U.K.?"

"Hell, no. No more of the quiet country life for me. New York City. Maybe a house on Long Island. I want to show Laurel the best places, restaurants, people. We'll stay in close touch with everybody and everything. I can't wait to see the world again because now I won't have to feel lonely seeing it."

"You said she's been taking care of your arm, especially your *hand*?"

"Laurel took me to see her doctor who tested me for bursitis, arthritis, lupus. Nothing. All negative."

"So what is it then? Did he have any idea?"

"Yeah. He recommended a rheumatologist."

"Shit. How long will that take?"

"There's no point. I only went to the doctor for Laurel."

Dale squeezed back into the too-small chair by the dresser. "What do you mean there's no point, man? Come on."

"This pain is associated with the dreams Laurel and I shared. I'm certain of it."

≈≈≈

When Michael had his physical a couple of months ago, the doctor gave him a little something for his stomach, a horrible tasting pill containing a mild sedative.

"Take them for three or four straight days then forget them until you feel you need them again," his doctor advised.

Today he needed one. After hearing last summer's horrific details of Gillian Grant's death from Dale plus other bits of information not exactly making his day, some of the pieces were falling into place. He couldn't prove it, but somehow Laurel had played a strategic part in all Mark's tragedies. Gillian's death. Mark's father having that sudden stroke, then warning Mark to keep away from his childhood home. Fraser's lungs mysteriously filling with water at Dale's.

Since meeting Laurel, the ocean flowed hot through his senses, slogging them like blue lava. Now, and certainly the reason for the pills, the ocean surrounded him—Laurel's townhouse, the party at Guy's, The Banford Arms. Even the colour blue saturated him, though it wasn't ocean blue, but something quite different. Today, during his meeting with Courtland Ariss, perhaps he'd get some answers. Since Laurel wasn't talking about herself, maybe brother Courtland would.

After cancelling this afternoon's get-together with Dale, he popped a second pill. The more he learned, the more helpless he felt. How could he help Laurel, or Mark, or anyone else who might get in Laurel's way, especially since Laurel wasn't having anything to do with him now. She was suspicious of him. His nervous stomach churned as he recalled Dr. Wieler's words—

'... and should you ever find yourself up against a torrent of negative energy from this woman, do everything in your power to keep her from turning against you. If you feel she has, stay away from her. Immediately drop all hold she has over you on the psychic level or she'll make schnitzel of your mind. I guarantee it.'

Oh if only God would make him drop this case right now, within the next five seconds. Just make him hoof it to that phone and cancel this thing with her brother. Have him walk calmly away and never look back. He stared at the phone for five seconds, then rushed out to meet Courtland Ariss.

Though it was high-end and fashionable, there was nothing phony about Courtland Ariss's west end apartment. Nothing phony about Courtland. He wasn't as neat as his sister, but he was welcoming and friendly. Books and papers cluttered his flipped-up Davenport desk. Opened briefcase on the floor. Necktie on the arm of a massive black leather recliner. Empty coffee mug on the coffee table. Empty wine glass on the bar. It reminded him of his own apartment, except his was one-third the size of this place.

With the exception of gender and eye colour, Courtland was his sister's twin, though their looks seemed to be the only thing they had in common. Given Courtland's understanding, compassionate demeanour, it seemed that he was accustomed to people coming to him about his sister.

Comfortably dressed in a red V-neck cashmere sweater and jeans, Courtland held up a bottle of wine. "I wouldn't pass on this. Marques De Riscal white. Brought it back from Spain."

"Please," Michael said. "Today I could use it."

Before pouring the wine, Courtland glanced sideways at him. "Is my sister alright?"

"I'll know better, I guess, after I talk to you. Thanks for seeing me right away. Since we're strangers, I don't really know where to start."

Courtland handed him the wine, then stretched out on the recliner. "Not really strangers. Laurel's told me about you, Michael. Mind you, recently she hasn't said anything, which leads me to believe she's giving you problems. Laurel has this way of mistrusting people who are good for her. At first I wasn't too keen on the idea of her getting involved with a psychic. But as soon as she clammed up about you, which meant she had no further use for you, I have to admit I'm curious to find out why. My sister used you for something, didn't she?"

Courtland meant no harm by the 'psychic' comment, so he took in a deep breath and let it pass. "We met a month and a half ago. Did she tell you I was helping her with a paranormal problem?"

"Lately my sister's too defensive with me to tell me anything. Let me be blunt, Michael. Are you here to help her or help somebody get free of her? When people come to talk to me about Laurel, it's usually one or the other."

He found that last statement intriguing. "I don't even know if I can help her. To be honest, Courtland, I might even be here because I want to help myself. I'm not really sure. But you're the only family she has here and from what Nancy told me, you're very close to your sister. I don't understand her. I know she had a rotten childhood, that's obvious. But she won't tell me about it. I asked Nancy, but she didn't know either which I thought was strange since Nancy's her best friend. And your lady from what I understand."

Courtland stared into his wine glass. "A long time ago my sister made me promise never to discuss her childhood. With anyone. I've never broken that promise and I can't now, no matter what she's done. But yes, you're right. She had a rotten childhood. Why do you want information about it?"

"I'm afraid that whatever she suffered in the past is resurfacing now, and getting worse. But she doesn't want my help anymore, doesn't want me to help her psychically. I'm afraid for her and I feel guilty about asking you to keep our meeting today confidential. But where could I go from here? You're her brother. You're the only one who knew her when."

"I've always known my sister had this weird gift, but tell me, what is this psychic or *paranormal* problem you mentioned? What's going on with Laurel, anyway?"

"Here we go again," he said.

It was a waste of time coming here. Courtland felt honour-bound not to release information, as did he. Dale knew much of what was going down because of Mark, because he'd been through it with him. And Dr. Wieler knew because, in the beginning, Laurel had given him permission to speak with Wieler. What the hell was he doing here? It was stupid coming here. Stupid.

Courtland seemed to clue in to his thoughts, a family trait, no doubt. "It's a stalemate, isn't it?"

Michael scrubbed a hand over his chin. "I'm afraid so. I'm sorry I wasted your time, Courtland."

Courtland looked concerned for him. "Look, I don't know if I'm doing the right thing and my idea is rather far-fetched, but I do get the feeling you're sincere about helping my sister with her problems, whatever they may be. She's got me going, too. This affair with Mark Grant is extraordinary. I know what happens to her when she gets hurt and guys like Mark Grant eat women for breakfast. I don't know what's going on, but given the publicity and Laurel's patterns, it's simple extrapolation."

He leaned in. "What did you have in mind?"

"You're psychic, right?" Courtland got up and dashed to the bookcase. He glanced back at Michael. "Which means you receive impressions through one or more of the senses. Also right?"

He bounced a knuckle off his chin as Courtland rummaged through books.

"Then how 'bout a gander through a couple of the family albums? I don't know if these will be of any help," Courtland pulled two massive photo albums from the shelf, "but it's the only glimpse into my sister's past I can offer you. Laurel doesn't care who I show these to."

"She might care if it was me." This was one helluva guy.

Courtland smiled and handed them to him. "No. I really don't think she'd mind. They're just family pictures. That's all they are. And like I said, I don't know if they'll be of any help."

They leafed through baby pictures, confirmations, first communions, birthday parties, and polished off the Marques. They laughed through high school pictures, Courtland's first black eye, Laurel at age seven with no front teeth, a second bottle of wine and takeout pizza. It took them two hours to get through the first album because Courtland had an amusing story to tell with every other picture.

Michael noticed there weren't many amusing stories of Laurel, or funny pictures. But he didn't care. Courtland was quite a host, quite the entertainer. He hadn't laughed this much in weeks and an hour ago he'd given up hope of finding anything that might jump off the page at him about Laurel. He didn't even know what he was looking for, but he enjoyed Courtland's company and wondered who might be crazier, Courtland or Dale Mith. Probably Dale, he decided, but only by a hair.

Briefly, he told Courtland about Dale and what a character he was and Courtland said he was anxious to meet both him and Mark Grant. He and Nancy would also be at the El Mo on Saturday. Halfway through the third album, over snifters of Courvoisier, Courtland asked him what Mark Grant was like.

"I've only talked to him twice, briefly. But I liked him. He's extremely intelligent and polished, dresses to the nine's. His charisma makes the guys stammer and gives the girls hiccups. When I'm near him I try to pretend I'm part of the furniture or something. Nobody notices me when I'm around him and Dale, anyway. I could go up in spontaneous combustion around them and nobody would notice."

While Courtland brewed coffee, he came across a picture series of Laurel, Courtland and their father. Looked like somebody's cottage. They were all in their bathing suits. Laurel was sitting cross-legged on a dock in one of them. The image of a middle-aged woman wearing her hair in a ponytail and a man riding an ancient-looking bicycle flashed through his mind. Maybe she and Courtland had pony-tailed, cyclist-riding grandparents. Accustomed to shaking off random images in his head, he continued flipping through the photographs.

He admired Laurel's hair in the last cottage photograph—long, silky black, purplish under the sun. Tanned skin. Although she was smiling in the shot, those big green eyes looked anything but happy. In a close-up of her on the dock, wearing a tiny gold cross around her neck, and hands folded neatly on her lap, a blue stone glistened in front of her. Luminous green eyes. He wiped the bead of sweat from his upper lip. Luminous blue stone.

Suddenly the gush of kitchen tap water transformed to crashing ocean waves. As his eyes jutted back and forth from Laurel's eyes to the stone, the vision clip intensified. The day was clear and cold. Dale was there, hair whipping around his face, long coat ballooning from the wind. Choppy waves. Whitecaps. Dale's eyes watering from the cold—or maybe not from the cold. The vision dissolved and he blinked, then stared trance-like at the stone. Beautiful blue stone. Blue.

Courtland returned with a steaming mug and set it down on the coffee table. "See anything? You alright, Michael?"

He unstuck the sweaty shirt from his back and pointed to the photograph. "How old was Laurel in this one?"

"Oh, seven or eight. A sweetheart, wasn't she?"

"She's still beautiful. What's this?"

Courtland groaned. "Argh, that thing. My father gave it to her. She took it everywhere with her, even to the bathroom. We all got so sick of looking at it. I remember her calling it her

Blue Diamond. She'd play with it and stare at it for hours. Wouldn't let any of us touch it. I was glad when she gave the thing away."

"She gave it away?"

"We were on a family trip in England one Christmas. My father wanted us to experience a true Dickens holiday. So on Christmas Eve, we found ourselves at a little seaside restaurant. Laurel saw this boy playing a piano and became instantly enamoured.

When the kid took a break, she got up and left the stone on the piano for him. We couldn't believe it. I think my mother was especially glad to be rid of it. Anyway, we had to practically drag her out of the place because she couldn't take her eyes off the kid."

Michael blinked his eyes shut for an instant. "Did the boy see her?"

"Funny, Laurel and I just talked about this recently. Well, it's fuzzy now, but I believe he saw her. I remember him looking around trying to figure out who left it for him. And since we seemed to be the only strangers in the place, he probably guessed it came from someone at our table. But Laurel was too shy to go up and speak to him. You know, my sister asked me if the boy came around and if they spoke. I said I didn't know. I'd gone to the head or something. I didn't tell Laurel about his looking around, that he probably saw her. Hmm. Totally forgot to tell her that. Anyway, why am I remembering more than Laurel?"

"Her parting with the stone may have obscured everything else. Did your family take pictures there?"

"Dad took a few but I never saw them. I take it this means something to you, Michael?"

Seeing Courtland and his apartment through a filter of blue, he said, "Yes, I think so."

8. LITTLE BOY BLUE

SHOW ME! HURRY, OPEN THEM UP! Laurel's thoughts scattered at the sight of Mark's three suitcases. *It* was inside one of them. Had to be. The lucky rock Mark spoke of, the one his little son was so infatuated with was her beautiful Blue Diamond, returning home to her after all these years. Tonight she'd tell Mark where it came from, that she loved him at first sight, and she was there before Gillian, before his fame.

Although Mark knew they had shared dreams since childhood, he didn't know she'd dined in his restaurant-home on the English Channel where she first saw him, where she returned to him in the astral. Now they could go home as a family, she and Mark and little Fraser. And they'd live in that wonderful house by the sea.

Already she felt its energy. *It* and she—combined energetic alphas, particles colliding. Were they ever separate? She would be complete now, a whole person worthy of Mark's love. Why was Mark dallying with the unpacking? She couldn't wait to see it again, to gaze into it. *It's my soul, you see, and you've had it for twenty years. And your soul too, Mark. Your soul, too.*

"You want to unpack?" she asked him.

At last they'd finished dessert and coffee and dammit, he still hadn't unpacked. He had been looking strangely at her all through dinner, no doubt sensing her jitters. If he would just hurry the hell up and let her see it, hold it. Mark reached across the table for her hand and kissed it, pretended to take a large bite out of it and she laughed.

"That's the third time you've asked me about unpacking. Don't you believe I'm staying?"

Would it seem smaller? Did it still shine? "Yes, of course I do. I just need to see that we're really together, to see your stuff mixed up with my stuff. If you unpack, I'll tell you a bedtime story." She angled her body towards him, eyes enticing. "A whopper of a bedtime story."

Jet-propelled upstairs by her offer, Mark had all three suitcases on their bed and flipped open in five minutes. He took out a hardcover *The Man from St. Petersburg* from the second suitcase, said, "Fraser's really excited about this visit."

She smiled. She could share the stone with Fraser. Maybe they'd bond over it. She was only three years older than him when she got it. Where was it? It had to be in the small case.

Mark clicked up the lid on his toiletry case and she spotted the black satin pouch. "What's this?" she asked, pulse racing.

"The lucky rock I told you about. I've had it a long time. Open it. Baby, you're shaking. What is it?"

She smiled sweetly at the face of her enchanting boy. She reached for his hand, kissed the bandage covering his wound, then removed the stone from the pouch and held it, held it up for them. The boy seemed frightened. *Oh please don't be frightened.* His eyes expressed concern and she couldn't hear his words. *So beautiful. You've come home.* How long had Mark been holding her in his arms, the crashing waves drowning the sound of his voice? Pounding crashing waves. The sea. The sea at Christmas. She inhaled the brine and salt, wiped breakwater spray from her cheek and broke away from him. *Let it out. It wants to come out, to come back to me.*

"Laurel?"

She squeezed the stone in her fist. "Mark? Mark, play for me. I want us to go back. Only Christmases are happy. Only Christmases. Play that piano song for me again, Mark."

"Laurel, please."

"Ohh," she said, a whimper catching in her throat. "Your finger. You've cut your finger." The bandage looked so old and soiled. "Let me get you a fresh bandage, Mark. Beautiful music, isn't it? You remember the song?" She touched his face and smiled adoringly at him. "My Blue Diamond."

"Your blue diamond? I don't understand you, Laurel."

"You will, sweetheart. I promise, you will."

She fanned out her hand and set it on her palm, held it up to him. How beautiful still. Bigger. Brighter. And it meant more to her than she dreamed, even after all these years. It had never been away from her, not really. It couldn't have hurt Gillian, Mark's father, or little Fraser. It wanted only to clear obstacles between her and Mark. It meant no harm.

She placed the stone in Mark's hands, cupped them around it.

And Mark seemed to know.

"This," she said to him, her voice low and self-assured, "this is how we started. From this we came together. Through this we've been together for almost twenty years. And because of this, we'll be together always."

Her eyes welled as the memory struck Mark's mind. "*You* left it for me," he said, astonished. "*You* were the little dark-haired girl who left this on top of the piano for me that Christmas Eve. My God. I was a stranger. Why, Laurel?"

"From the moment I heard you play in your father's restaurant, I fell in love with you. And I wanted desperately to leave you something of mine, the thing that meant the most to me. I believed it would connect us, bring you back to me one day. It didn't matter that we lived on separate continents. Not as long as you had the Diamond."

They stretched out on the bed and Mark placed the Diamond between them. "I thought you were so beautiful," he said tenderly.

"You saw me?"

"Yes, Laurel, I saw you. Somehow I knew it was from you. Not for any extrasensory reason, probably because we knew all our customers there that night, so it was a logical deduction. I watched you leave with your family and saw this beautiful little woman. You walked like a little woman, so proud and sensitive, so quiet and sad."

She grazed her fingertips along the side of his face. "Why didn't you say anything to me?"

"My father didn't allow me to speak to customers unless spoken to first. I kept hoping someone in your family would say something, maybe request a song. But they never did."

"I didn't see you looking at me once." It was all like yesterday now. So vivid—the tilt of his head as he played, the serious young musician. It had to be the Diamond making her remember, making them both remember. She stroked the stone as they talked.

"At the piano, I watched you with your family, peripherally, caught the tension between you and your mother." Thinking on it, Mark laughed. "You know, I had this overwhelming urge to swat your mother with my music sheets. I remember the emerald green dress you wore with the ribbon bow at the waist. White Peter Pan collar. So sweet and sad you were."

"I was leaving the Diamond for you. In my mind, I was saying goodbye to it. I wanted you to have it so much. And I knew I'd have to wait years for you. You were right—a little woman. I can't ever remember being a child. I never was a child, even when I was eight. I *was* sad that night. I wasn't only saying goodbye to my Diamond when I walked out, I was saying goodbye to you. In spite of the sadness, I knew something magical would happen because it was Christmas Eve, the only time in my life I was ever happy. Never had a bad one, Mark. Never had a bad Christmas."

"And we get to spend this next one together." Mark set the stone in her hand. "I give this back to you. To cherish for us, and when you look at it, don't be afraid to go searching for that

little girl." Mark kissed her cheek. "As you once said, baby—
'To diamonds. Precious. Beautiful. Forever lasting'."

The Diamond sparkled as they exhausted themselves
making love. But its energy had no place here. It belonged to its
dead past. Inside, beyond the sparkle and beauty, that
Diamond world whose ocean they swam and whose beach they
walked was now lined with seagull carcasses, blackened skies,
rabid rats, and stench—an uninhabitable, poisonous world.

≈≈≈

After Mark fell asleep, she took the stone into her Sea Room
and placed it on the blue velvet display stand. How could a
piece of aquamarine-coloured glass outshine a multi-faceted
gemstone? When Mark asked where it got to, she would tell
him she put it in her jewellery box. He wouldn't question that
and if he wanted to see the stone, she'd get it for him. Same for
Fraser. Simple. Once they moved into his father's house, she'd
find the perfect place for it. A display case would do better than
a stand. It could get knocked off the stand. Wouldn't take
much. The bump of a vacuum or a clumsy hand. She had to
protect it because the Diamond trusted her.

Mark didn't have the need to understand the stone the way
she did. To him, the magic inside it was pure romance, *maybe* a
psychic link, or maybe he thought it was nothing more than a
coincidence. She couldn't be sure. Men weren't quick to believe
in these things. To her it was creative essence, soul, one of
God's crumbs. Besides, she had neither desire nor inclination
to discuss the soul and God with her lover. She cringed at the
thought of Mark knowing her and seeing her the way God did.
If God favoured Mark with a mirror to her soul, Mark would
leave, change his name, escape to the ends of the earth and hide.
God disapproved of her.

That *other* Laurel, the one who ended Gillian, had her make
the stand for the return of the Diamond. She knew that now.

But *she* wasn't at all colour-savvy because the shade of the display cloth and the shade of the stone clashed horribly.

'*I* would have chosen black velvet to display it on,' she said, wrinkling her nose at the clashing blues.

Although she could do nothing about replacing the stand now, the cloth was an easy fix. She stepped to the side and squinted. Maybe she should consider white. Or pink velvet. When she took another step to the opposite side, the beaded ornament on her slipper caught the velvet fabric. Unable to snatch it in time, the Diamond toppled off the stand. Panicked, Laurel bent down to retrieve it and examined it carefully. There was a hairline crack at the base. Her throat filled with bile and her eyes watered from the stench seeping through the crack. Hands shaking, she placed the stone on the stand and backed out of the Sea Room.

In their bedroom, Mark was sleeping too soundly to hear her scream.

≈≈≈

On the way in from Toronto International, Fraser Grant couldn't keep still, bouncing from left to right in the limo to catch the sights. "The buildings are so glassy," he said to his father and Annie.

Canada was exciting especially because of the Mounties, the men with the yellow stripes on their pants and the big horses they rode. They had dog-sleds and igloos and Eskimos, but his dad said they were too far north from here, but maybe he'd get to see a Mountie. Maybe he and Laurel would take him to see the Eskimos before he had to leave. They even had Indians and teepees in Canada. He was going to love it here a lot.

He'd be even happier if he didn't still cry for his mom at night sometimes. He'd shut his bedroom door and talk to her, ask her to send a part of her in someone new for Dad. And she said yes. Stories and bedtime kisses. Soft hands and skin. Perfume. Great food smells back in the house. Walks to the school bus. He might even get to go to a real school, have pool parties and have family and friends around the tree again. Annie was nice but she wasn't a mother and Dad didn't love Annie. Annie was too old. But Laurel was beautiful and waiting anxiously to meet him. He drew a picture of her from Dad's description. Why was Dad being so quiet? He was fretting about something. He could tell.

Fraser jumped into Mark's lap and hugged him, knowing his hugs always made his father smile. "Dad? Why can't we go meet Laurel first and then drop Annie off at the hotel later?"

Mark looked tenderly at him. "Because Annie's tired and Uncle Dale's waiting at the hotel so he can say hello."

"It's alright, Mr. Grant," Annie said. "If you'd rather go straight to Miss Ariss', I can carry on from there."

"No," Mark said abruptly. "We'll go to The Banford Arms first. Dale wants to have a visit with Fraser."

Fraser felt himself not being as happy as he was a moment ago. "What's up, Dad?"

Mark propped him on his lap and kissed his cheek. "Nothing, Fraser. Not to worry. Just tired from working hard."

"You sure there's nothing else?"

Mark started tickling him and he broke into peals of laughter. "My kid's such a worry bum. No. There is absolutely nothing else."

"How long will it be before I meet Laurel?"

"A couple of hours. You're very excited and happy about Laurel, aren't you?"

Fraser nodded emphatically. "I can't wait. Think she'll like me?"

Mark's heart fluttered. "I think she'll love you."

It was a happy reunion, with lot of hugs and kisses between Fraser and Dale, even a pillow fight. Mark watched their play in silence as Annie flitted about unpacking. When the time came to leave, Dale suggested to Fraser that he tidy up a bit before meeting Laurel. Fraser knew he wanted to talk privately with Dad. Why couldn't Uncle Dale just tell him that? Adults were so complicated sometimes.

"How's Laurel?" Dale asked. "Are you still worried about her?"

Mark slumped into the tub chair next to the fireplace and stared into the flames. "Yes, I'm very worried. One minute she's fine, laughing and affectionate and playful. Then I turn around and she's gone, sometimes for hours. I never see her go out. She never tells me she's leaving. When she comes back it's always 'I went for a walk to get some air'. But her cheeks are never rosy. She never brings the cold in with her. Her fur coat and jackets never leave the hall closet." Mark closed his eyes and rubbed them. "She's not out for walks, Dale. She's in the house somewhere. Remember that strange noise I told you about the other day?"

"Yeah. A creaking sound you said."

"Right. Well, I didn't tell you this but I figured out what the sound is. I've heard that sound at least a hundred times at the convalescent home my old man's in."

"What?"

"A rocking chair. She's somewhere in the house where I can't find her, rocking and rocking in that blasted chair. It drives me mad when I hear it. What she's doing, I don't know. What she's thinking about, I have no idea. Why is she telling me she's out for walks? Our first morning she told me she had a rocker in the attic. So I went up and guess what—no rocker. No nothing up there, which is something else again."

"Haven't you confronted her with the lie?"

"Of course I have. And she denies it, denies it without explanation. I've told her she's entitled to privacy when she wants, that my feelings won't be hurt. But she gets defensive and teary, accuses me of thinking she's a liar and that I don't trust her. Then I end up consoling her and we make love, then everything's grand again. Yesterday I went all through that blasted townhouse trying to trace the sound, but I couldn't because there's an echo, you know. She rocked in the bleeding chair for three hours, Dale. Disturbing as hell."

"Maybe you're making too big a thing of it, Mark. So she keeps a private place where she wants to go and meditate or something. Fine. Brilliant. Women are into that shit. Probably just needs her space."

He could tell Dale was saying it, but Dale wasn't meaning it. "Right. But why lie about it? No. She hasn't been herself and she won't talk to me about it. Something is wrong with her and I can't find a way to help her. I love her, Dale. It's been brief, I know, but I've never felt this way about anyone. And now there's Fraser. How can I explain her moods and disappearances to a five-year-old when I don't understand them myself?"

"Maybe you won't have to. Your kid'll be there getting to know her. Your kid, man. She may not do it with him around."

Mark crumpled Fraser's baggage ticket and tossed it into the flames. "Oh God, I'll be glad when I get her out of that house. There's something about that house, something in it. The place is beginning to give me the creeps. After the El Mo, that's it, we're leaving for New York. I'm getting her the hell out of there, away from all that blue."

"What's blue got to do with it? What are you talking about?"

"I can't tell you yet."

≈≈≈

She rocked as hard as she could, trying to fight the loathing. Mark's child wasn't part of the plan. She hadn't met the boy yet and already she hated him. Hated him. Why couldn't she change her plan to include the boy? She hated hating him. The Diamond was supposed to be helping her, but it wasn't doing anything. Since she dropped it, it had done nothing, revealed nothing. Maybe it was just for children. Maybe it had accomplished what it set out to do—end Gillian, bring Mark to her. Now, what of this boy?

Perhaps the Diamond had its own plan regarding this boy and she could skip the decision. The Diamond might be doing it for her. And when it was done, its beauty would return. No more killing thoughts. No more storms and drowning and hungry rats biting her. Mark would never have to know about this horrible place. She would have to protect him.

And the son?

"No! I can't hurt the child."

Yes. Kill him. He's an obstacle. Kill him.

"No. No!"

Yesss ...

That *other Laurel* stalked her as she ran crying from the Sea Room. She stalked her everywhere now including their bed. How would she keep her away from Mark? Oh, God. What was happening? *Little girl. Little girl. What happened to you? Give me one more dream with Mark. Please! One last dream.* Hearing Mark's key turning in the lock, she dabbed her eyes and promised herself she would try, try to somehow keep *her* from kil ... hurting his son.

"Laurel?" Mark called from the bottom of the stairs. "We're here, sweetheart."

She walked slowly down the stairs, unable to keep her eyes off the child. He didn't look anything like Mark, except for the smile. The boy's hair was blonder, not sandy like Mark's. She never did like blond hair. Standing there at the bottom of the stairs, smiling at her so cute, all bundled up in his yellow windbreaker and scarf, he seemed the typical adorable child. Gillian's child.

"What, no candlelight this time?" she said to Mark.

Mark put his hand on his son's shoulder, "No more blackouts in this family. Fraser, this is Laurel."

"Hi," Fraser said, still smiling.

"Hello, Fraser." She took his hand. "I'm glad to finally meet you." But she did meet him before, in a way—that ugly afternoon in Gillian's kitchen.

"Well, come on," Mark said, helping him off with his windbreaker, "let's get your coat off and show you your room. Laurel fixed it all up for you."

"This is for you," Fraser said, handing her his drawing. "But you're prettier."

He'd coloured the eyes a vibrant traffic-light green, drew the hair down to her knees in heavy black crayon. A few more art lessons wouldn't hurt the kid. "Thank you, Fraser. It's very flattering." She should probably hug him or something, but didn't.

Throughout the evening, she studied Mark and Gillian's son. She studied them over dinner, during Chutes and Ladders, during the song Mark sang before Fraser's bedtime. She felt uncomfortable, like a stranger in her own home. There was one person too many in this house. She never did learn how to talk to children, having never been one herself. If only she could be a child and start over, but it was too late. *Oh, give me a crying towel, Laurel.* The boy turned around and regarded her uneasily as Mark piggybacked him up to bed. She smiled blandly at him, Mona Lisa-like.

No use fighting anymore. The stone hadn't returned for her. It had returned to claim its rights—magic and power on loan all these years—power and magic inadvertently stolen, maybe? Best to return what she'd taken and let it have its way. God wasn't around. God was never around, so God wasn't handing out new beginnings. He wasn't returning the childhood she never had. How nice of Gillian's boy to remind her of the loss. *Hearts and flowers, Laurel. Ha-ha-ha-ha. Hearts and flowers.* Her life with Mark in the Blue Diamond was over.

Her life with him in this world could never live up to her dream. They could not go back. And they could not stay here.

≈≈≈

The next day, Friday, was the last day the three of them had to spend together. Saturday was the El Mondrago show and he would be gone all day. Dale insisted on a last minute rehearsal at the studio. There were goodbyes to be said, people to thank, a meeting with Justin. He wanted to get hold of some prominent real estate agent out on Long Island and get Laurel out of the townhouse and settled as soon as possible.

Unless Laurel brought it up, he thought it wiser to table the marriage discussion, thinking it too rush-rush for her. After all, they hadn't been together outside the dream for long and the stress of his fame was getting to her. She'd been edgy, blamed her swollen eyes on the winter dryness, told him she found a soothing balm for them. He wasn't buying it but decided to let her be until after the show, then he'd thrash all this out with her. No secrets. They could not have secrets. This was the absolute rule.

It delighted him that Fraser seemed to adore Laurel. She fascinated Fraser who saw her as a combination of Cheetara the Thundercat, even though she probably couldn't run as fast, and Turtle April O'Neil. He loved her eyes. He loved the quiet way in which she spoke. Fraser wanted her love and it was obvious that Laurel wanted Fraser's love because she kept watching him, drinking in their conversations, praising the pictures he drew of her. Dale was right. At least she stopped the disappearing acts since Fraser's arrival. She hardly let Fraser out of her sight now. Last night it touched him to find Laurel sitting in Fraser's room, utterly mesmerized as she watched him sleep.

They got the day off to an early start with a drive to King City, breakfasting in a cozy country inn. Laurel said it reminded her a little of his childhood home. This of course piqued Fraser's curiosity and he decided by way of explanation that less was more. He simply told his son that Laurel once visited with her family when she was a child, then changed the subject. After breakfast they passed by Canada's Wonderland and Fraser's eyes rounded at the sight of Magic Mountain. Disappointed to find Wonderland closed for the winter, Laurel told him he'd see it one day.

"You promise?" Fraser asked. "You promise we'll go in the summer?"

Laurel didn't answer but Fraser took her silence as a promise, telling them he'd mark all the weeks off with red X's on his calendar until next summer. After breakfast they found a small Indian souvenir shop. The place smelled of pine and honeysuckle and had a Christmas tree in the corner with a life-sized wooden Indian flanking its side. Fraser got a miniature wooden Indian, Laurel got a necklace of beads and feathers, and he chose a handcrafted leather photo album.

They spent the rest of the afternoon in Pioneer Village, touring the grounds in a horse-drawn wagon, then walking it again on foot. Fraser loved the pioneer costumes, the snow, the horses, the blacksmith shop. Then, for the second time in twenty-four hours, watching the two of them together tugged at Mark's heart. They were walking along the road, pointing out the sights. Fraser was in the middle. He looked up at Laurel and smiled.

"Take my hand," he said to her.

She took his hand and they walked on a little bit longer in silence.

He told them it was best to pack it in for the day when the snowfall got heavy. Although driving conditions had become hazardous, everything looked like a scene from Currier and Ives. Fresh blankets of packing snow covered rooftops, lakes, park benches. One couldn't tell where one tree ended and the other began. Fraser said they looked like snow-clouds and asked

Laurel to play the Cloud Shape game, but he didn't like her scary monster-shapes and quit after a few minutes.

Near dark, the wind whipped around Laurel's Porsche, rocking it into a sideway skid but he made the adjustment with a few turns of the wheel. The red Thunderbird about a half-mile behind had downshifted to a steadier, slower clip. This seemed to interest Laurel, who kept sneaking peeks in the rear-view mirror.

"That bloke behind us has slowed down but he's not skidding as much," he said, checking out his rear view. "This all looks brilliant, but it's a bugger to drive in."

Fraser let out a little whine when he slid into a half rolling donut. "Dad, I'm scared. I can't see anything."

"It's alright, Fraser. We just have to take it a little slower, that's all. Nothing bad's going to happen to us driving ten miles an hour, is it?"

"Guess not."

"It's a white-out," Laurel said. "I got stuck in a bad one with my father when I was twelve. We couldn't see a thing. Everything was white, worse than the heaviest fog. We couldn't tell what direction the car was going in and spent half the time driving sideways. Ten people died in that storm. Buried in snow. Frozen to death."

Fraser whimpered again and she chuckled.

"None of that, babe," he said. "Fraser, Laurel's just teasing. Don't be a baby."

It took them almost three hours to reach Laurel's, a drive that normally took one. They drove in silence and all that time, for the first time, he wondered what kind of woman he had fallen for. He felt the prickle in his scalp. He should be used to driving in storms. Was there anything scarier than driving on icy roads in a dense London fog? But it wasn't the storm, or the slippery road, or Fraser's nervousness. It was Laurel. From the day he moved in, Laurel was *different*.

Perhaps it had less to do with the obvious stressors he'd discussed with Dale and more to do with her strange behaviour over that stone. He used to be quite fond of the thing, and now, given its effect on Laurel, he rather hoped she'd give it away to someone else, preferably someone on the far side of the planet or one of the Baltic States. Lucky for him she didn't take it out all the time because he hadn't seen it since he returned it to her.

Following a lovely meal of Penne Alfredo with blackened shrimp and Key Lime pie for dessert, he managed to dismiss all dark and disturbing notions from his mind. Laurel seemed happier, laughed at Fraser's attempts to teach Mouth to sing. Things would be good. They just needed time to adjust like all new families. During a Monopoly game when they all got to laughing because he went broke landing on Laurel's properties and Fraser wouldn't lend him any money, his mind was at peace. At least it would be for another thirty hours.

After the El Mondrago concert, his mind would never know peace again.

≈≈≈

Laurel suffered enough pain in life to recognize her limit. Having been conceived by a woman who hated her, although no one would believe that, she spent her youth living in a fantasy world. In her adolescence, three psychiatrists agreed that, yes, she did try to poison her mother, further convincing her it was she who'd killed her mother's cat and not to worry—they were going to help her understand and forgive herself. They would find out why she hated her mother. They would help her, treat her.

She broke down once she believed the lie, and took a small carving knife to her neck. She once asked a plastic surgeon about removing the scar and he fluffed it off saying it wasn't worth the effort since she could cover it with make-up. But covering up the half-moon scar would be a daily reminder, she argued, "Every day I'll relive the whole nightmare." And the guilt—always there was the guilt.

"But it's my mother who hates me," she insisted for the next two years. "She framed me. She poisoned herself and made me take the rap. She did it again with the cat. She's jealous of me. She can't stand to see my father love me. If I was a boy it would be different. But I'm not and there's only room for one woman in my father's life. She's the sick one. She did all those things. He's not keeping me away from her. He's keeping her away from me. Go on, ask him. Make him tell you the truth. He's afraid you'll put her away, put her in jail. Make him tell you, please, because I can't stand anymore!"

She was so convincing, they went to her father and they did ask him. Was the girl right? Was it Mrs. Ariss who needed treatment? "No," he told them, believing it at the time. "It was Laurel."

After a while it seemed easier for her to believe it too, forgetting the hazy memory of her mother entering her room that night, a week after her fourteenth birthday.

"Keep this for me," Santina told her, placing a small vial of liquid in her hand. "It's my cold medicine. I'll only forget to take it. So you give it to me. A half teaspoon every three hours in my tea."

The cat horror happened just days later. She woke up one morning and found it lying on the edge of her bed, the roast string it had been playing with the night before tied in a neat little bow around its neck. Its eyes were open and it lay there staring at her. It seemed like an hour before she realized it was dead. How could she not remember killing a little animal she loved? But she did, because they told her she did.

After her father buried it, she dug it up, applied enough make-up to age herself way beyond her years and took the cat to a taxidermist. "Make it look as mean as you can," she told the taxidermist, at the time entertaining the idea of wrapping it up so she could give it to her mother for Christmas. But she never got the chance to give it to her because her father decided, surprise surprise, to take Santina on a trip. After the cat episode, her father took Santina on lots of trips.

The earlier years were just as bad although she had no memory of the nightmares. She'd awaken crying and could never remember the dream. Sometimes her father would sit and hold her through the night, sometimes her mother, and those nights she didn't dream much because she was always too afraid to sleep.

Then came the tiny drop of rain on the desert—the Blue Diamond, the Christmas trip to England. And Mark. Years followed with the hatred intensifying between her and Santina. She had given up on God by the time she was seventeen. A Catholic girl giving up on God so early in life was unforgivable, not that she had any role models. Santina used to attend Mass regularly and stopped suddenly before Laurel reached her teens. Her father and Courtland went at Christmas.

Except for Courtland and Nancy, she couldn't trust the few friends she made long enough to keep them—because she was selfish and self-centred, Santina never failed to remind her. So the modelling and the few nondescript relationships she'd had along the way kept her busy and well-travelled. Unlike Courtland, university didn't interest her since she didn't seem to have interests, except for music. She adored all kinds of music, especially classical piano, and braved the crowds to catch a favourite band or concert pianist. To this day, crowds of people still made her nervous.

The one thing she carried in her heart was the memory of the enchanting boy, his music and the dreams they shared through the years.

Laurel kissed Mark as he lay sleeping. Was he real? Maybe she had been in an insane asylum all these years and this was a dream. Maybe she was in a coma. Maybe Gillian was the lady in the next cell. Maybe Mark was the sexy psychiatrist trying to get through to her. Maybe the Blue Diamond was the tool he used to hypnotize her, or a simple light figure on a wall. The stone could be almost anything.

Gently pulling down the covers, she ran her hand along his slim, muscular body. He had such thick, silky honey-coloured hair, not stringy and blond like his son's, the son no longer welcome in their lives. This was her dream and because this was her dream, she could have it any way she wanted. Fraser had to go. He had to go join his mother. She and Mark had to go too, but not with Gillian and Fraser. They had to go somewhere else and she knew just the place.

Stabbed by fear, she turned to the shadow leaning in the corner by the window—watching her—always watching her. *These are your thoughts, not mine. I won't touch him!*

She drew back and clung to Mark as the shadow lunged toward the bed. *My time to be alone with him now. The boy goes.*

And the reporter in the red Thunderbird who'd been following them today—he had to go, too. He'd been sticking his nose into Mark's business, and hers. Everybody had to go it seemed. They couldn't stay here anymore. Too crowded. Too hard to hold on. She'd have to try and hang on for one more week. One more week, max. She'd have to bear the crowds, the reporters, the pain and the guilt, but if she could make it through, everything would be alright. Then she would have the life she always wanted—with Mark.

Starting tomorrow.

≈≈≈

The first phone call came in at nine a.m. Dale said he'd pick Mark up at noon and they'd head over to the El Mo to load-in and sound check. Dale insisted on being present while the musicians perfected their sound for the space, a lunch meeting to follow then more discussions on set length. Justin phoned. C.P.I. was hosting a late-afternoon spread for them over at the

Harbour Castle. The Long Island real estate agent phoned. She'd lined up three homes for Mark to look at. Brilliant, he told her, adding that he and Laurel would be there to meet with her in a couple of days. She agreed to immediately put her townhouse up for sale and Courtland promised he'd handle it for her.

"Start packing, baby," Mark said. "We leave for New York first thing in the morning. Nine-twenty flight."

Every nerve-ending in her body was on slow burn. Long Island? Living in New York State was never in the plan. But did she have a minute to tell him this? Oh no. Did he have a minute to listen? Certainly not because he was too busy staying famous. Oh, if only she could get out of going tonight, but it was necessary to be with him when ...

"What about tonight?" she asked, studying him as he threw his kit together. His hand seemed to be bothering him again. "How do we do this?"

"Have Fraser pack up his things. I'm sending a car for you at seven-thirty." Mark shook out his hand absentmindedly. "Annie'll be in it and she'll take him back to The Banford Arms after the concert. They'll meet us at the airport in the morning. I've arranged for your friend Michael to meet you here and ride to the El Mo with you. Have Nancy and Courtland join you as well if you like."

At ten after twelve, Dale's driver announced his arrival, ticking Mark off that he didn't bother coming in to say hello to her, which was perfectly fine with her. Mark looked around for Fraser. No answer came when he called him.

"Where'd my kid get to?" he asked, throwing on his coat.

"He's upstairs giving Mouth another singing lesson," she lied, knowing Fraser's real whereabouts. She'd known for the past half hour. "I love you Mark. I love you so much. Be great tonight, darling."

"I'll do my best." He pulled her into his arms. "Tell Fraser I had to run and I'll see you both tonight. Make him wear a tie. I love you, Laurel. Everything will be alright, you'll see. You'll feel better as soon as we get away from here. This place isn't right for you, it never has been. We're going to have a real home, a real life together. No more dreams, baby. And no more nightmares."

He kissed her tenderly, whispered *ma chérie* in her ear, and raced out the door.

After standing there a moment staring blindly at the ceiling, she turned and walked slowly up the stairs toward the hall closet, each step heavier than the last. This would be less fun than it was with Gillian. Feeling the other Laurel tugging inside her mind again, still fighting to dominate, she wondered why this was so. She should surrender—let *her* handle it. Like mother like daughter. She turned the knob to the Sea Room and said goodbye to God. He had never been there for her. He wasn't around now to fix things up. He wasn't handing out any miracles. So why the hell even bother saying goodbye to Him?

She creaked open the door.

Gillian's child had huddled himself into a corner on the rollaway bed. Hugging a blue satin pillow to his chest, his confused, frightened eyes peered up at her. He whimpered as she approached. A teardrop trickled down his cheek as she smiled and took the pillow from him.

She kept her voice soft. "I see you've found my secret room."

"Mm-hmm," he said, a second tear trickling down.

"What are you so afraid of, Fraser?"

The child cringed when she touched his hair. "This room. It scares me."

"What is it about the room that scares you?"

"Everything. The cat. All these pictures of my Dad, especially the one of him standing in the water. They seem funny in here. And that's his lucky rock over there."

"Does the lucky rock scare you, too?"

"No. It's the only thing in here that doesn't scare me."

"Why didn't you leave the room if you were scared?"

"I don't know. I couldn't."

"Do I scare you, Fraser?"

"I don't think you like me."

She grinned at the kid. "It's just that I know you'd rather be with your mother."

"Mom's in heaven," he said, trying to hold back the tears.

What a whiny kid. "No she isn't, Fraser."

"Where is she then?"

"She's right over there. Inside the lucky rock. There's nothing to be afraid of with your mother here."

"Then how come I can't see her?"

"You can't because I have to arrange it for you. Would you like to have a visit with your mom?"

"Can I bring Dad?"

"No. Your dad is working tonight. You know he has to sing and you and I have to be there. But I'll tell you what. If you promise to keep this room our secret, I'll let you visit with your mom right after we hear your dad sing. Would you like that?"

Fraser hesitated. "Guess so." He wiped his snotty nose with his hands. "Will you be with us?"

"Just long enough to get you there. Then your mother will want to speak to you alone. She loves you and misses you so much."

"When can I see her?"

"I'll bring the lucky rock to the concert with us tonight. And right after, when you go with Annie, I'll give it to you. When you get back to the hotel, you go into your room and hold it tightly in your hands. Then you'll have a nice visit with your mom and you'll see that she isn't in Heaven at all, but right here with all of us. Do you think you can keep our secret?"

"Yes, Laurel. You won't let anything bad happen, will you?"

"Of course not, Fraser. I want this to make you happy. And you will be, I promise."

"Laurel?"

"Yes, Fraser?"

"You do like me, don't you?"

She stroked his hair. "Of course I do, Fraser. I like you very much."

9. LOVE YOU—HATE YOU—LOVE YOU

COURTLAND, WHO COULDN'T BE LATE to save his life, arrived at six on the dot with a chilled bottle of Cristal tucked under one arm and Nancy on the other. She was relieved her famous man-of-the-hour had included them. Now she wouldn't have to be alone with Michael. Certainly he had to be feeling the depth of her turbulent emotions, and hopefully, didn't know the cause. Did he? If she was near the breaking point, would he know? Would he know about her stalking shadow? Okay, no more obsessing about any of that tonight. Michael couldn't know her plans and in a few days she would never have to see the guy again. And Mark's gauzy-headed kid would be with Gillian. So, she and her rockstar were outta here.

Michael left Courtland and Nancy in the living room watching Fraser and Mouth play Chase the Bone and followed her into the kitchen.

"What's wrong, Laurel?" he asked, taking the Cristal from her and popping the cork. She caught Mr. Psychic Private Eye checking out her shoulder bag on the counter. "You nervous about going public with Mark?"

"I'm just sad about Mouth," which was half true because she would miss Mouth terribly. Michael couldn't take his eyes off that purse. Could he feel the stone's vibe inside? "Courtland's taking him tomorrow. I don't know how long I'll be gone."

"We don't have much time," Michael said, "so I'll come to the point. Laurel, I know about the Christmas trip to England. After a talk with your brother, I put it together. I know about the boy on the piano, the boy with the bandaged finger. I know about your blue diamond. I know you left it for the boy and I know who the boy is."

She narrowed her eyes as she poured the champagne into four flutes. "You know quite a bit then. Will you take these in to Court and Nancy?"

He took the glasses. "Don't move," he said, and returned before Courtland and Nancy could make the toast.

"Hey, you two," Courtland called, "What gives? Get out here."

"Alrighty!" Michael said. "Give us a minute! Laurel? I know Mark is the boy."

Bully for him. "So you said. Do you also know I've got my blue diamond back?"

"I figured as soon as I walked in here. The house reeks of sea air, more pervasive than Halloween. Laurel, I fear for you and Mark and Fraser. Very much so."

"Would you like to see it?" she asked, ignoring the caveat.

"You know I would."

≈≈≈

Michael almost passed out when she took the stone from the pouch and handed it to him. Wieler was right. The damned thing was filled with the energy of a lifetime's pain and sorrow, the pain and sorrow of a little girl who hadn't the knowledge of the power she possessed. And the negative energy had compounded over the years, making it lethal now. Was he already under its spell? Was Laurel standing over there using it on him? No. It had no mind of its own. It was only an object as Wieler had said. He shook off the distant sounds he heard inside his head. The laughter of children. The tooting of a bicycle bell. Intuiting the dark purpose instilled into the stone and the mysterious protective force around it, he wondered if Laurel had connected with it in some way.

"Has this revealed itself to you in any way?" Seeing the shrewd smile cross Laurel's face, he realized he'd been given the shut-out. "Laurel, this is important. Please."

Courtland joined them in the kitchen as Laurel snatched the stone from Michael's hand. "It's time to motor," he said, looking questioningly at them. "Mark's car is here and so is Annie. Nancy's getting Fraser together. So? Your limo awaits, your highness."

Michael let the others go ahead to the car and tugged Laurel back. "Laurel, I know you're in trouble. Before you harm yourself or anyone else, let me help you. Please. First thing tomorrow let's get together and talk. You asked me to help you once. I still can."

Laurel looked at him defiantly. "Impossible, Michael. Mark and I are leaving for New York first thing in the morning."

≈≈≈

Though the El Mondrago packed as much security as a caucus convention, the atmosphere remained cheery and Christmassy. The tables were decked with mini-tree centrepieces and a huge wreath hung over the stage with a picture of Mark and Dale in the middle. Everyone was having a great time, including the staff, donning Santa hats and white fur-lined aprons for the ladies and white fur-lined vests for the guys. The staff swished away ribbon and wrapping on the floor while balancing trays loaded with jugs of draught above their heads. Santa had arrived early.

Given the Diamond's proximity, the festive atmosphere had done nothing to improve Michael's mood. Laurel seemed a million miles away at his right, and to her right sat little Fraser. He was such a sweet child and he couldn't figure out why he pitied him. Maybe it was Laurel. She seemed distant with Fraser. Distant. Cold. And icy polite. Not unlike the way Dale treated her. And he knew Dale didn't like Laurel, an understatement for sure.

Guy and Katherine were at their table, along with Justin, some big shot from Sounds Interchange and his party of four. Courtland and Nancy sat to his left and the result of this was his having to lean back every time Nancy wanted to speak to Laurel.

"Everybody in the place is looking at you, Laur," Nancy told her, full tilt smile. Michael enjoyed Nancy's radiating warmth. "They all know you and Mark are a thing. You're gonna be famous, you know that."

"But I don't want to be famous," Laurel said, childlike.

"That's okay," Fraser assured her. "I'm not famous, so you don't have to be either."

Michael smiled. Fraser was trying hard to please her. Too hard. A tall, stocky-looking man with a moustache and slight overbite stopped at their table.

"Hello again," he held out his hand to Justin. "Kevin McLafferty. We met briefly at the Royal York last Sunday."

Justin stubbed out his cigar and stood to shake McLafferty's hand. Introductions passed all the way around the table.

"Mark's a lucky man," McLafferty said to Laurel. "No one would have to tell me you're a model."

"Thank you," she said in a hollow voice. "And no one would have to tell me you're a reporter. Nice Thunderbird, by the way. '62 or '63, is it?"

"'62. You're very observant, Miss Ariss," McLafferty said with a hint of sarcasm.

"I do my best."

McLafferty exchanged a few more words with Justin, telling him he'd catch him at the party after the show. Another exchange transpired before McLafferty excused himself, a silent one between him and Laurel.

Everyone wondered what that was all about and Courtland leaned over to pose the question when the lights dimmed. He turned around to check out McLafferty who happened to be staring at Laurel. All other eyes were glued to the stage. The room shook from the vibration of stomping feet and applause. Necks cranked upwards. Eyeglasses were given the once-over with tissue. Ladies crossed their legs and finger-straightened their hair. Men hooted and raised their glasses. Then the drum roll, followed by automatic, drop-of-a-pin silence.

Dale strutted onto the stage first before introducing Mark, not that he needed an introduction, but this was the first time the two artists had performed together. Of course no one in the room knew that the beautiful, raven-haired lady at the head table was responsible for this event. The audience was generously receptive, so much so that Dale had to shout to get heard. And a few minutes later when Mark snuck on stage and stood behind Dale with his saxophone at the ready, they went wild. It took fifteen minutes to settle them down amid flashing bulbs, tossed roses and one fainting girl.

Michael sat through the entire show battling anxiety and dread, fighting off old visions and new, trying to interpret the raging ocean and red piano no one on stage was playing. Sensitized by Fraser's intermittent cough, the dread intensified as he absorbed Laurel's emotional reaction to the audience, particularly, to Mark and Dale's bond. No hint of competition. Pure warmth. A loving friendship destined to continue to the death.

He bore Laurel's hatred of the audience, of Dale, of Mark's son. And herself, which he got directly after his meeting with Courtland Ariss. Laurel hated herself for not knowing how to love, and the more she tried, the more it eluded her. Her greatest sadness lay in the knowledge that her love for Mark was about as real and precious as the synthetic stone in her purse.

A security guard escorted Michael to a private washroom backstage and he took Fraser with him.

"You getting a cold?" Michael asked him.

"I don't think so," Fraser said, trying to plunge his ear with the palm of his hand. "Sometimes my ears get water in them and it makes me cough."

"Does it happen a lot?"

Fraser shook his head. "Last time was at Uncle Dale's on the beach. I was showing Dad's lucky rock to Heathcliffe, that's Uncle Dale's dog."

Michael tested the waters. "Does Mark have his lucky rock with him tonight?"

"No, but ..."

When Fraser cut himself off, Michael knew the boy was keeping some kind of secret concerning the stone, a secret between him and Laurel. He decided to keep Fraser in his sights for the rest of the evening.

Following the intermission, his condition worsened. Unable to move, he sat helplessly watching the visions take over like some powerful hallucinogen. He couldn't feel his legs to walk, couldn't see the room to exit. So he prayed, fervently, securing himself in the knowledge that God would soon put a stop to this. Even his own spirit seemed alien to him. He looked at his hand and saw a sapphire ring on the marriage finger while his other hand clutched an object he couldn't see.

He looked over at Laurel and saw himself watching the stage from inside her body, saw the *young* boy on stage singing his heart out, a blue stone glistening at him from the piano top. Michael's hair felt long and heavy, his legs short, his heart small and pulsing while he watched the girl materialize on stage beside the piano—a young girl with long black hair and big adoring eyes for the boy.

The mental images felt worse than the hallucinations. From youth to adulthood, then back to youth. A little girl blocking out the sound of her mother's hateful voice ... tears of guilt and anguish ... a knife cutting into her neck ... doctors examining her, locking a door behind them ... tears, pain ... beautiful blue

... a release ... a young girl and boy swimming and laughing ... a tooting bicycle bell ...

Before he came out of it, as the last encore wound down, he received the image of the stone, but the stone was on its side—and on its side it resembled a square. Actually it was a square. A *lopsided* square. Of course—Ben Sidenko's photograph. His brain had processed the shape as a square that day. But the shape was never a square, it was a diamond. The *Diamond* was the lopsided square.

When the house lights flicked on he looked again at Laurel who happened to be looking not at the stage, not even at Mark, but *through* the stage. She seemed vacant, lost. My God, how could one person survive so much pain? What could she have done to merit it?

Laurel had lived almost every day of her life filtering sludge from her mind and emotions. He was never a praying man, but he'd asked God for guidance and God guided him into an empathic transfer with Laurel. Agonized, he realized there was nothing he could do. A little girl had tapped into her mind looking for a release from the reality of a miserable life, choosing to remain a child the day her Blue Diamond came into it. Dual life on another plane began. Life on Earth ended. And what of Mark? What devastating thing was going to happen to him?

Mark's wife was dead because of Laurel's Diamond, his father had suffered a stroke and Fraser had already experienced one near miss at Dale's. Clearly out of control, it was Laurel who needed guidance here and it didn't look like she'd be getting a miracle any time soon.

Laurel stiffened during introductions to the big wigs and press after the concert, nervous fingers brushing her lips. She hated the attention and during the camera flashes, he caught sight of a combative glance between her and Dale, undoubtedly captured by several photographers. He watched Laurel, he watched McLafferty watching Laurel, and he watched Fraser until their group split into two waiting limousines bound for the party at the Harbour Castle. He reached the hotel half an hour after them and immediately noticed the conspicuous absence of Annie, Fraser—and Laurel.

The band and co. looked fresh off a Super Bowl win, staggering around drinking from champagne bottles and clapping each other's backs. Dale appeared to be holding his own with the Jack Daniel's while Mark was off in a corner discussing something heavy with Justin. Hmm ... business or personal? The dread had lingered, cold and sinister like demonic vapour.

He strolled over to Dale. "Where's Fraser?" he asked, trying to keep the tone casual.

"Annie took him back to The Banford Arms. Here, mate, have a swallow of this. It'll relax you."

"Pass, thanks Dale. Actually, I wanted to say goodbye to Laurel since I won't get the chance to see her before she takes off tomorrow. Have you seen her around?"

"Saw her sneak out the door a while ago for a whizz or something. What's wrong, Michael?"

Although he assured Dale nothing was wrong, he felt Dale's eyes on his back as he left the party room in search of Laurel, locating her in the hall about fifty feet away. She seemed to be staggering a little and when she saw him, she stopped and leaned against the wall for support. By the time he reached her, he could tell she was severely disoriented and not from alcohol.

"Oh Michael, please. Just leave me alone. I'm used to these blackout things."

"What blackout things? What did this to you?"

She laughed weakly, wiped the perspiration from her neck and rambled some more. He understood little of her fragmented speech because nothing flowed. Nothing connected. Drops of sweat covered her brow and upper lip and her body was slightly convulsive. She was in no state to walk back into that party room. Maybe if he could open her up, open her up to calm her down.

"Santina," she said, repeating the name several more times. "Santina did it. I didn't. They all told me I did. It's a lie, you know. Do you hear me? Psychotic hateful woman. Destroyed me."

"Laurel, focus, hon. We can't attract attention here."

"Destroyed. No place to go but the Diamond. MARK. He's all I ever wanted. Just Mark and me. No more left to destroy. I killed Gillian."

She'd said it like she was apologizing for leaving the cat out in the rain. "Laurel, no. You didn't even know Gillian."

"I may have killed again tonight. Gotta get him away before more happens. Leave me alone, Michael. Got to get to Mark!"

He grabbed her gently by the shoulders and pushed her into a club chair. "Laurel, listen to me. You're not the one in control here. You never have been. Something in the Diamond ... the past ... has a hold on you. It's important we speak privately before you leave. You have to let me explain the Diamond. But please, not here. Listen to me. You have to get yourself together now. Some of the press are in there."

Laurel narrowed those green eyes into a fevered stare that chilled him to the bone. "If you tell Mark what I told you about Gillian, I'll kill you. Or maybe I'll make you live with what's inside me. I'll make you live with no control, not sure of which world you're living in half the time. I saw you during the concert tonight. You felt it, didn't you, Michael? Keep away from Mark and me. I may be the only one left for him to love."

"What do you mean by that, Laurel?"

"I don't know." She said it childlike, sincere, and seemed to have come around some. He wondered if she remembered her little rant of a moment ago—and her threat. "If Mark leaves me or if we don't go far away together, I'll die. It's that simple. I won't go back to hell. Seen it already, thanks. You know I've seen it."

"Going away with Mark is not the answer. Trust me on this."

"Then what is the answer, Michael? We both know no doctor can help me. No doctor can help Mark, either. Mark and I are one in this now. So you see we have to go. Something is happening to us. Something's been happening since he brought the Diamond back to me. I've decided to let it be because Mark and I are in the hands of something else, or someone else. And now that I've let go, I won't have to fight much longer. Because it's happening fast. That's why Mark and I have to get away from all of you. I have to protect Mark from the Diamond. He's famous. What would happen to him? We have to get away, Michael, don't you see?"

Michael was too emotionally drained to answer, or sense that someone had been listening.

≈≈≈

Laurel pulled herself together and let Michael take her back to the party, a party with no music, movement or voices. Had everyone left? Maybe they heard her. Oh God, they heard her outside in the hall! Her heart started hammering. Something was wrong here. Who was Mark talking to on the phone and why was he pacing? And Dale, invading her space as always, was right at his side, practically standing in his shadow. She knew it! Something was about to spoil their getaway in the morning. Light-headed and shaky, she rushed over to Mark. And the subtle move he made was like a knife in her heart. Ever so slightly, he turned his back on her.

"I'll be right there," Mark said, struggling with the words. "Tell him Daddy's coming." Then he hung up and turned to Dale, not her, Dale. He hadn't looked at her. "That was Annie. They're rushing Fraser to Sick Children's Hospital. The ambulance arrived as we spoke. I've got to get there right away. Security! Please have a police escort meet our ride. Now!"

She wasn't aware of the speed at which they cut through traffic, nor the kaleidoscope of lights, nor the hour of the morning, not even the sound of the police siren piercing her eardrums. All she could hear was the torment in Mark's voice as he spoke mostly to Dale. Her chest ached and her posture drooped at the sight of him.

"... and his lungs are filling with fluid. Coughing, then choking, Annie said. I wasn't there when it happened to Gillian. Now I'm not there for Fraser. He's going to die, Dale, I know it. It's happening again, all over again. They're going to tell me he's suffocated. They're not going to know what caused it. Christ, please tell me this isn't happening."

She sat across from him in the limo, desperately trying to find consoling words, but nothing came. Nothing. And he seemed to not want to look at her. Their eyes had met once briefly since leaving the hotel, and there was detachment in them, distance. Oh God, couldn't she stop thinking of herself for one damn minute, even now? Couldn't she find it in her to care about the kid?

"When I was performing tonight, I saw him coughing," Mark said, hunched over. "I actually saw my son sitting there coughing and smiling at me and all I could think about was the way my muscles ached, if my legs would make it through the next tune. And my son was coughing. Now he's dying without me, dying alone."

"Mark, don't," Dale said. "Fraser will be fine. He's young. He's strong."

"No," Mark glanced at her, then turned and stared blankly out the window. "What have we done? My God, what have we done?"

She leaned forward and put her hand on Mark's, and though he didn't move or retract his hand, she felt him recoil.

≈≈≈

By the time they reached Sick Children's Hospital, Fraser Grant was all over the news. The press had already found their way to the hospital and a crowd had formed in the street and lobby. They kept their place though, remaining courteous as Mark and his party met up with hospital security and slid through the crowd without incident. Two doctors were waiting for him the moment he stepped off the elevator in ICU.

"Is my son dead?" he asked, shaking.

"No, Mr. Grant," one doctor said. "But it was close. We've drained three pints of fluid from his lungs and he's stabilizing now. We don't in God's name know how to explain this, but his lungs kept filling as fast as we could drain them. But they're clear now so we'll take you in."

"Thank-you. Yes, please get me in to him."

Laurel waited with Dale, Annie and Justin while two doctors took him into the room, where another doctor and three nurses unhooked Fraser from a massive aspirator. Unable to get near the bed, his eyes filled with tears at the sight of his son's ashen face. His body appeared swollen and although he was semi-anaesthetized, Fraser's eyes opened slightly when he called to him.

"I love you so much, Fraser," he said as a smiling nurse cleared a path to his son's bedside. "You're well and safe now. Nothing more to be scared of."

Fraser blinked, his eyes smiling.

He took Fraser's hand, kissed it. "Dad's here and the worst is over."

Before drifting off into a peaceful sleep, Fraser smiled, first at his father and then at an empty spot at the foot of the bed.

He sat quietly at Fraser's side through the night, holding his hand while he slept. "He must have been so frightened and I wasn't there," he said at 4 a.m. to the doctor on call. "Was Fraser conscious when admitted?"

"He'll be fine now, Mr. Grant."

"Tell me," he asked, not sure what he was looking for, but he had to know something ... anything. Fraser had survived but Gillian hadn't. He had to know how to prevent this from happening again. "Tell me, Dr. Keenan, was my boy conscious? Did he say anything?"

"He was thrashing about trying to catch his breath, so we had to anaesthetize him to attach the aspirator. We tried to get him to tell us what happened as he calmed but all he said was 'oral' or 'choral'. And then something about a rock. A 'choral rock'? Does that help?"

Mark's jaw tightened. "Might the word have been *Laurel*?"

Fraser had nearly suffocated to death and not one doctor had a credible explanation. They advised him to keep the boy in hospital for more tests and he agreed, though not for the reasons the doctors assumed. His plan was to get Laurel as far away from his son as possible. Though he had no proof she was somehow connected to the loss in his life, for which he blamed himself as well, somehow their supernatural pairing had had deadly effects on his loved ones. And Laurel's family remained unaffected. Why was this? Also, the fluid that filled Fraser's lungs as fast as they could drain them mystified the doctors further as it came from an unidentified source.

The following day, the head paediatric surgeon met with the press at Sick Children's Hospital and told them the boy had collapsed from *Pneumorrhagia*, severe lung haemorrhage, adding that he was not permitted to disclose further details by request of the boy's father. Early that evening, Fraser Grant's file along with the sample of meticulously examined fluid, conveniently disappeared. Given the press's incessant speculation of Gillian's death back in the U.K, Mark had every intention of keeping his son out of that circus. Unknown to him as yet, someone had already beaten his people to both the file and sample. Soon the world would know that the tiny vial containing the fluid from Fraser's lungs was labelled *Sea Water*.

Late that evening, he and Dale were back at The Banford Arms collecting Fraser's belongings for the hospital when he saw Laurel's stone lying on the floor by the bed. Had she given it to Fraser to play with? Fraser would never have taken the stone without Laurel's permission. Fraser had it at the beach at Dale's, and now here in this room. *Bloody stone*. The sight of it was beginning to sicken him.

He confided to Dale, "I haven't been back to Laurel's since leaving the hospital. I came back here."

Dale had their glowing El Mo review from the *Toronto Sun* with him and threw it aside, giving Mark his full attention. "Here? I thought Annie took this suite?"

"She did. I took 504 last night. I'm on my way to Laurel's now."

"Why didn't you go back to Laurel's last night?"

"You mean this morning in the wee hours? Yes well, I talked to her on the phone. I'm making plans, you see."

"What plans, Mark?"

Mark covered his mouth, studying Dale for a moment. "To keep my son safe. To get Laurel away." His eyes softened. "Dale, I need you to stay here ... with Fraser."

"What's this? You're leaving Fraser behind in hospital while you abscond with loony Laurel?" Dale twirled his finger at the temple. "At Christmas? Mark, I'm not processing this. This isn't like you at all."

"Will you stay with him, Dale?"

"Only if you tell me what's going on. What your plans are, where you're going."

"Back to where Laurel and I started."

"And where the hell would that be?"

"I can't tell you that yet. But we have to get back there, and fast. Bloody doctors insisted on examining me at the hospital, but I told them Laurel's physician checked me out already."

"You're having those weird pains again?"

"Yeah. In my joints now, too. My muscles are stretching out or something. Crazy because it feels like growing pains, but last time I looked I wasn't any taller."

"So you still think the pain's connected to those dreams with Laurel?"

"I do." He rolled the stone aggressively in his palm, fingers stiffening over it until its sharp edges punctured his hand. "I've been lost since the day I found Gillian blue and bloated on the living room rug. Haven't thought clearly since. Haven't been able to reason all that well. I've been living in a dream with a woman I couldn't escape even if I wanted. I blindly charged into this affair, didn't I? Five minutes after Gillian died. Where was my mind, Dale? For all I know she could be psychotic. Actually I could say that of me as well. Right?"

"Mark, stop it. Remember, you never gave yourself time to grieve for Gil. You were too busy taking care of Fraser, your dad, managing the press, your career. No wonder you got caught up in this barking affair with—that woman. Ease off yourself."

Mark looked about the room for the velvet pouch and when he found it in the night table drawer he shoved the stone inside, drawing the string tight enough to snap it. "Sure. I plan to do just that."

"Good," Dale said, squinting at him. "Listen man, I need to know more about this mystery mission, where you're going. For Fraser. Oh and bloody yes, for me, too."

"I will call you and Fraser on Christmas. I promise."

"Right. Brilliant. And what am I supposed to tell Fraser?"

"I explained to him tonight that I need him safe back here while I go off and play detective. Told him I need to find out what made his mum so sick so fast. I asked him to please understand."

"And did he?"

"He's still groggy, but yes, I think so." Mark smiled at his best friend. "I told him his Uncle Dale would stay with him while I'm gone. Knew you wouldn't let me down."

"Right." Dale stared at him, nodded absentmindedly like the little plastic dogs with the bobbing heads. "I'll call Carmen. See if she'll join me here."

He clapped Dale on the shoulder and took Fraser's overnight bag into the living room. "That would be brilliant. Fraser adores Carmen."

"Did you find out anything more from Fraser about his ... episode?"

Though he wanted to, he couldn't tell Dale about the *choral rock*. If Dale suspected Laurel was involved with Fraser's accident, he'd never agree to help him, never let him go. Besides, he needed Dale safe and as uninvolved as he could keep him. "No. As I said he's still groggy. You'll probably get him to open up in a few days. Don't push him, though."

"Course not. What do I do with Annie?"

"She might as well go back to New York. She's got the flat happening there. I was going to keep it until Laurel and I found a house." Mark collapsed into a chair.

"And if they release Fraser from hospital before you get back from mystery-land, you want me to bring him to Malibu or New York?"

"I want him with *you* whether it's at the beach house or New York with Carmen. I want him with you, Dale." Mark looked searchingly at him. "We've never talked about this ... but, if anything happened to me ... would you take Fraser?"

Dale rounded his eyes. "You need to ask? Of course, man. I love Fraser. You know that."

"I know." Then he said it again, "I know."

"Alright then. That's settled. And you and Laurel?"

He had to laugh at that one. Good question to which he had no answer. Yet. "My son almost died, Dale. Did she save him? Or did she try to ... harm him? We're going away, Laurel and I. We're going to get some answers."

≈≈≈

It was close to midnight when he got back to the townhouse. Stopping outside the wrought iron gate, he set Fraser's bag down on the walkway and looked up. Almost a full moon. The wind whistled around his ears, the cold stinging them. There was something frightening about the sky tonight, although it stretched upward toward eternity, it seemed too close, as if he were really inside and the sky was just a painting on a mural. This could be a large freezer with plastic scenery, icicles made of sugar, a hidden phonograph playing the wintry sound effects. A stage for him alone. Or was there another player?

He'd heard footsteps crunching snow behind him since he stepped out of the cab. A fan maybe? Some of them had been ingenious enough to track him anywhere and he couldn't be rude or curt to a fan. They were his life's blood back in the beginning, and in many ways they still were. Laurel's place wouldn't be hard for them to find, now that they knew who she was, no thanks to him. He was daft to have her photo taken everywhere with him except the bloody bathroom these past few days. Fraser's photo, too. Fraser. Did he really understand his leaving him alone in hospital for Christmas? A twig snapped about fifteen feet away.

"Who's over there?" he shouted, feeling the cold attack his lungs. "Feel free to say hello. Don't have much time, though, my son's just out of emergency."

"I'm sorry about your son, Mr. Grant." A tall, shadowy figure stepped out from behind a cluster of pines.

He narrowed his eyes at the approaching man. Where had he seen him? "I know you," he said, shivering. "Where from? Who are you?"

"The name's Kevin McLafferty, Mr. Grant. Our paths have crossed more than once these past two weeks."

They never quit, these people. "Oh, yes. I remember now. What do you want?"

"I have something you and your lady might want, Mr. Grant." McLafferty held up a large brown envelope. "Can we discuss it inside? The light's rather bad out here."

"Tell me what's in the envelope, McLafferty, and we'll see."

"Reports," McLafferty said, smugly. "Past and present."

≈≈≈

Laurel had the door open for them before they reached the back step. "Well, if it isn't the man in the red Thunderbird," she said, relieved at the sight of Mark. Then she took Fraser's duffle. Mark must have found the Diamond. Lord, what did he think when he found it? Did he pack it? She slipped the duffle in the hall closet and challenged McLafferty.

"I was watching you with Mark from the kitchen window. You're up to smut aren't you, McLafferty? I've seen you following us. What do you want with Mark and me?"

"I think our friend is about to blackmail us," Mark said. "Come on then, let's sit by the fire. I want to be blackmailed in comfort."

Moving aside for Mark as he led McLafferty into the living room, she searched his eyes for the smallest hint of warmth, a sign that he'd missed her last night, that he needed to be with her now. There wasn't one.

"The bottom line is this, Mr. Grant," McLafferty said, handing Mark the envelope. "I believe that somehow you and your lady are responsible for the death of your wife and near death of your son. Now I don't know how you did it and I can't prove it, *yet*, but I do have a copy of your wife's autopsy report and your son's lab tests, several in fact—"

Enraged, Mark flew at McLafferty and was ready to take several swings at him when she wedged herself between them.

"Let him finish, Mark. He has squat with that information. In fact, I'd enjoy hearing him explain how he got his hands on it in the first place."

"Oh, they might let me off the hook, Miss Ariss, when they piece together everything I've compiled." McLafferty helped himself to a chair and crossed his legs. "Seems your son almost died the same way as your wife. Lungs inexplicably bursting with sea water. Sound familiar? Now we all know you had an alibi, Mr. Grant, but what we don't know is that you have an accomplice. I can easily testify to that after overhearing a conversation between Miss Ariss and Michael Johnstone the other night. And from what I found out about him, he's a pretty decent guy, would never think of perjuring himself."

Overweened, materialistic little prick. She hardened her voice. "What is it you think you heard?"

McLafferty shifted leg positions and cleared his throat. "Enough. I heard you tell Michael Johnstone that you killed Gillian Grant. That's a confession, Miss Ariss. I also heard you tell him that you may have killed again, that you and Mr. Grant are one in this now. There's no need for me to go on."

Mark had just heard McLafferty say she killed Gillian, and he hadn't reacted. He was stone cold and distant, hiding his emotions behind the barrier he'd put between them. For the first time ever, she couldn't come close to reading him and it terrified her. What was he thinking now? Had he turned against her?

"Mark, I also told Michael I'd die without you. I can explain about Gillian. And Fraser. I tried to fight it, to stop it, but another part — something from the Diamond took over. Something inside it—"

Mark cut her off and gestured for her to sit. "Not now, Laurel. Don't say anything more now. At this moment we have Mr. McLafferty here to deal with. And surely he knows you were with Michael and me the other night. You were nowhere near Fraser."

"Maybe so, Mr. Grant. But she did confess to killing your wife. Now I know I could go down harder trying to bring you down. But I've assembled a useful portfolio that will prove fascinating for some. It could cost you a Grammy-load of trouble."

"You want to retire, McLafferty, is that it? Give it to me."

"A cool million you won't even miss," McLafferty drawled nervously, "pounds."

Mark stood up and threw the envelope at him. "I just wanted to hear you say it. You know, you were right a moment ago when you said there was no need for you to go on."

She enjoyed watching the blood drain from McLafferty's face.

"Scare tactics won't work, Grant. You're not the killing type. You'd have someone else do it for you. And it's obvious your lady here is unstrung. Maybe not drugs. But she's strung out on something. Now I'm sick of earning my living from trash. So my only escape is to hand it over to you. The last of the trash, Grant. For a price."

Poor Mark hadn't much of a choice. Toiletboy was quite capable of ruining lives. Their only chance was to get the stone out of theirs. In order to do that, they had to go back to their beginning. And the stone was going with them.

"Alright," Mark said, weighted down by sadness. "But there's a condition. We are leaving tomorrow. And who's to say you won't take my cheque and go running off to the bobbies with it. You might tear up the cheque, say I paid you off. I can't have that."

She could practically feel the chill circling McLafferty's spine.

"What's the condition?"

"You're to be our house guest for approximately ten hours following our departure. We lock you in a room with enough water and food to sustain you. When we arrive at our destination, we make a phone call. A close friend will come and let you out. You'll have your cheque and we'll be long gone.

"Approximately two days from now you can cash the cheque, but you'll never write the story. My accountants will explain the cheque as publicity and marketing services not yet rendered. Think of it as a retainer from a new employer. You will write me a receipt explaining it as such."

McLafferty thought about it, obviously didn't like it, but of course went with it. "Okay, Grant. I'll meet your conditions. Lock me up and throw away the key. Just lock me up with the cheque. And keep your woman away from me."

"Do you have a lock for the attic?" Mark asked her.

She leered at Kevin McLafferty. "I have a better place for our guest."

≈≈≈

Mark shuddered at the sight of the rocking chair, shuddered at the shrine she'd erected to him. So this was where she spent all those hours while he paced the bloody house trying to source the sound. Obviously she hadn't planned on a guest spending the night or his seeing it for the first time in the presence of a third party. But it was the perfect place to stash this greedy bastard. McLafferty couldn't get out on his own, not with both doors in this twisted room and closet doors locked after him.

He froze in the centre of the small room, feeling like he was floating backwards, passing through every dream he had shared with this woman. For the first time he saw the clearer picture of Laurel as a little girl. The first night they made love he had recalled their beginning—seeing her walking into his father's restaurant with her parents and brother. But up to now it was surreal—he was never in his skin. Up to now. Looking at his finger, he saw two ghostly stitches, the result of a broken wine glass earlier that day.

He was peering out the kitchen door into the restaurant when she walked in. The prettiest little girl he had ever seen. And that beautiful stone she carried had caught the beginnings of sunset, refracting light everywhere in the room, light he now realized only he and Laurel could see. He felt warmth in her presence and awareness that life existed away from his comfortable world on Rottingdean's shore. He heard the gulls, the tide coming in, and plate rattles mingling with *The Nutcracker*. A tune popped into his mind, a tune he wrote that night after the restaurant closed. All because of her.

"Don't be a tourist, please," he had whispered to himself. "In the name of whoever's listening to me right now, don't ever let her go away."

"Mark," his father had been calling him. "Mark, stop your ogling and play something out there. The restaurant's filling up. Get a move on, son."

He saw her from the corner of his eye as he headed toward the piano. She had noticed him, too. *This song is for you, pretty little girl*. Then taking his place, he played the first song they ever heard together, not a Christmas tune, a song that had haunted him from manhood. Until now, he never knew why.

Suddenly he was back in this Sea Room place, as she called it. Laurel was leaning against the wall looking embarrassed. McLafferty, visibly shaken, stood at the far end of the room opposite them, eyebrows raised, facial muscles tight.

"A Charles Wildman composition," he said, amazed at the sudden recollection. "The first song I played for you. It was *Riviera Concerto*."

"I know. I hear it in my sleep."

"Look," McLafferty said, "don't you two have an attic I can stay in? I'm not into stuffed cats and shrines. I feel like I'm on holy ground or something."

"No something for nothing," Mark said. "This is it, McLafferty. Stay or go. Your choice."

"Then get me a bottle of your strongest, Grant. A bottle and a cheque."

"Don't worry, you'll be comfortable enough here. You'll even get room service. How do you like your eggs, McLafferty? Scrambled, I hope. Laurel's good with scrambled."

"Yes," Laurel said, eyes misting. She set the stone carefully on the display stand. "We'll leave this with you tonight and pick it up before we leave."

"Just pick *me* up before you leave, lady."

"Concerns?" he said.

"What do I do for a men's room, Grant? There isn't even a window I can piss out of."

"We'll give you a bucket to shit neatly in. And take your shit bucket with you when you go." With that, he bid McLafferty a goodnight.

≈≈≈

That evening, Laurel wrote the note. Michael would be the one to come and release McLafferty. But they wouldn't phone him until they reached Heathrow—

Dear Michael,

It's been hell for both of us, that's why we must go. A friend of Mark's has arranged a private plane to take us to London. Mark wants to see his father before we move on. From there we're going back to our beginning and taking the Diamond with us, to a place where it can't harm anybody ever again. As for the harm it's done to us, well,

that's irreparable, Michael. The stagnant energy of two young souls is locked up in that Diamond and you know I've experienced its fallout. The Diamond world is an ugly, insane place. And it doesn't seem to want us to live happily outside of it, either. We don't understand it completely, but we're almost certain that if we bring it back to our beginning, it will release us.

Michael, two nights ago Kevin McLafferty successfully blackmailed us. He believes I killed Gillian and attempted to kill Fraser. And although he hasn't said, not yet anyway, I think Mark believes it too. I'm sure McLafferty will be eager to share his theories with you. But please form your own theories, Michael. You know of the hell I've been through. And Mark isn't far behind me. I have a plan of my own that, if it works, Mark will never have to suffer again. I'll do anything to spare him that.

McLafferty agreed to stay with us until we could get away. He had no choice, actually. We couldn't take the chance of being stopped when we're so close. The keys to the closet door and McLafferty's room are outside the back door, under the pebbles in the blue flowerpot. The room is at the top of the stairs, hidden behind the hall closet. Feel around for the knob approximately in the middle of the back panel. The smaller gold key fits into the knob.

After you rescue McLafferty, call Courtland and tell him to go ahead and arrange for the sale of the townhouse. The realtor has my signed papers and she'll be calling him. Tell my brother goodbye, that I'll miss him, that I'm not returning. I can't speak for Mark. Insist he make Daddy tell him the truth about our mother. Daddy must know by now. A very disturbed lady. Like mother like daughter, eh, Michael?

Hopefully, Dale is right there with you now, reading this letter. If he isn't, find him and let him know that Mark has made him power of attorney and he's couriered personal letters to him and Fraser at his New York office. But for now, he wants you to tell Dale that he loves him, that he was always more than a best friend. He was a soul mate and a brother.

Goodbye, Michael. Thanks for caring.

—Laurel

10. RETURN TO THE SHORE

IMMEDIATELY FOLLOWING MARK AND LAUREL'S sudden disappearance, Dale hi-tailed it to Sick Kid's Hospital and spent every moment with Fraser, explaining, reminding the boy why his father couldn't be there. Camped in the lobby and annoying as hell to everyone were the reporters. "Hey, Dale!" they shouted every time he walked by, "where's Mark!"

Dale scooted into the elevator, flagged on all sides by security so the press couldn't get near him. The headlines kept coming ... and coming ...

Mark Grant goes off with lady friend while son convalesces in Toronto hospital.

Dale felt grateful for one small favour—that pesky Kevin McLafferty had left Fraser alone, hadn't once bothered him.

On the fourteenth he called Carmen and asked her to join him for a few days at the Banford. Carmen had holiday plans from the sixteenth until Christmas Eve, but agreed to fly in and spend a couple of days with him and Fraser, then fly back to New York, do her thing, then return Christmas morning. They hadn't fought since the divorce and he found this encouraging. Maybe they could take another go-round. He couldn't wait to see her. She had a way of bringing him around when he was lonely or depressed or frightened. Carmen had her hands full with him this time because he was all three of those things.

Unfortunately, Carmen was going nowhere. The snow began falling heavily in New York City on the twelfth and all weather reports warned that the heavy snowfall would turn into white-out and blizzard conditions by late evening. The next day, Buffalo was buried in snow. With ten people dead and some entombed in their cars, the count was rising. Toronto and the Great Lakes region were next to get hit.

By eight o'clock Tuesday evening, the fourteenth, Toronto International shut down, detouring incoming flights to Vancouver. Just his bloody rotten luck that Carmen was delayed in New York and it took his driver an hour and a half to get from Sick Kid's back to the Banford Arms. He was stuck and alone. Wherever Mark was, he had made it out by a hair's breadth, him and that wanker he was in love with.

Miserable with fear and loneliness, he almost jumped the phone when it rang. Conversation with the devil would be gratifying about now. But this was better than a ring-up since the front desk wanted to know if he would receive Mr. Michael Johnstone.

Finally, a bit of cheer. "You tell Mr. Johnstone to get his grim carcass right up here. Then follow him with a bottle of Amaretto, will you?"

This was no social visit. Michael's lips were nearly blue, his head and coat were soaked with melting snow and his eyes harbingers of bad news. Suddenly, Michael seemed a lot older than his years.

Dale poured him a double Amaretto. "What in blazes brings you down here on a night like this? What's wrong now? Has anything happened to Mark?"

Exhausted, Michael slumped over on the sofa, nervously tinkling the cubes in his glass. "I left the office early today to get in some Christmas shopping before the storm broke. I haven't even been home yet, but I never go anywhere without my pager. A couple of hours ago I called home to check for messages. The last message on the tape blew me away. It was from Laurel. She was calling from Heathrow and naturally Mark was with her. I thought you might want to be in on this so I came straight here."

"Blew you away, right? Then let's have it, mate."

Michael got up, dialed his number and told him to listen. Activating the playback message, he passed him the phone—

"Hello, Michael. This is Laurel. At this moment I'm calling you from Heathrow Airport in London. I'm glad I got your machine. You would've asked me too many questions. Michael, there's a letter I've left you on the kitchen table in my townhouse. It's important you get there right away to read it. After you read the letter, you'll see that it may be quite impossible to keep the police and press away for too long. But try, Michael, if you can. Mark and I need a couple more days and then we'll be out of London. Hurry to the house, Michael. A man's sanity depends on you. Sorry to involve you, but given your psychic gift where Mark, myself, and the Diamond are concerned, you may know best how to help him. You'll find the key to the front door taped to the bottom of the pumpkin can in the milk box. Goodbye."

Because of the distance and all the noise in the background at Heathrow, he had Michael play back the message twice. He fought the urge to hit something especially with Michael standing there dripping in dread.

"We'd better get right over there, Dale. It took me two hours to get here in this mess and I was only twenty minutes away."

"That friend of yours is crazy," he said, slamming through drawers looking for his hat and gloves. "If Mark suffers any more or in any way because of her, I'll wring her bloody neck. You hear me? I swear, Michael."

Michael ignored the outburst. His car, double-parked in front of The Banford Arms with hazard lights flashing was already half-buried in snow. The wind had people sliding and stumbling up and down the street. Tire marks in zigzag patterns covered the roads. No one noticed that one of the two men clearing snow off the white Cressida was Dale Mith. Only a few days ago, some of these same people had practically camped in the area just to catch a glimpse of him.

Under normal conditions, it was an easy twenty-minute walk from The Banford Arms to Laurel's townhouse. These were not normal conditions. The few people walking out on the streets could barely see two feet in front of them. Fortunately, there were few cars out on the road and Michael and Dale made their way to Laurel's driving an average of eight miles per hour the entire time. When they reached the townhouse, approximately an hour and a quarter later, their nerves were raw.

Michael had to heat his car key in order to break into the milk box, welded shut by the ice. Even with Dale cupping his hands around Michael's lighter, it took them six tries before the key got good and hot. Finally inside, Dale spotted a full bottle of Courvoisier and two brandy snifters on the coffee table.

"Come on, mate," he said, twisting off the cap, "obviously she left this for us."

Michael stood in the hallway staring blindly up the stairs. Still shivering, and not from the cold, he felt the hairs stand up on the back of his neck. Every time they stood up like this, he knew...

"We're not alone here, Dale." With the howling wind as a backdrop, an eerie, creaking echo filtered down from the top floor. "Can you hear it? Laurel said a man's sanity depended on how fast we got here. Let's get that letter."

"Kevin McLafferty? Bloody hell!" Dale shouted, after they'd finished reading the letter. He stared at the ceiling. "McLafferty's locked away somewhere upstairs? Police, a man's sanity, blackmail, Mark going back to their beginning? The Diamond world? Shit."

The letter trembled in Michael's hands. "We'd better get McLafferty, then find Laurel and Mark. They've got the

Diamond with them. And they've disappeared. I don't like the feeling that gives me."

"I'll go dig the key out of the flower pot." Dale's voice trailed off from Michael. "Poor Mark must be almost as crazy as she is by now. Why in blazes didn't they just leave the closet door keys by the letter? We're already inside the house. Not thinking straight, not thinking straight at all ..."

While waiting for Dale, Michael re-read the same two sentences in the letter—

From there we're going home, back to our beginning. We're taking the Diamond with us, to a place where it can't harm anybody ever again.

We're going home. Back to our beginning. He had to know where home was, where their beginning was. *Gah!* This was maddening. He'd discovered the proximity of their beginning, but not the place. Maybe the answer was upstairs with McLafferty, locked away in that room. What secret did the man know? What did he have on Mark and Laurel? What the hell was taking Dale so long?

"Man," Dale said, bringing in the cold with him. "Had to hack through more ice to get under the damn pebbles in the pot. Anyway, here's the keys."

Michael grabbed the keys and they dashed up the stairs. The creaking sound intensified the second they unlocked the closet door. Startled, Dale took a quick step backward.

Michael stumbled on a garbage bag and then shoved the clothes away from the middle of the closet rack. He called in, "Hello? Hello, are you alright in there?"

The creaking stopped.

"McLafferty!" Dale yelled over Michael's shoulder. "Pound on the wall where the door is, man. We can't let you out 'til we find the door."

No answer. They called McLafferty's name twice more. Still no answer.

"Laurel said to feel around for the knob in the middle of the back panel," Michael said. "Hand me the other key, Dale. I'm going through."

Without light to guide him, it took a couple of minutes to locate the door knob. Thinking about McLafferty sitting in the dark for two days made his hands shake, and the small skeleton key slipped from his fingers. Dale was squatting right behind him and retrieved the key.

"Hurry, Michael."

The lock clicked and he eased the door open. Dale recoiled from the stench of vomit and excrement, while he smelled crag and sea water, and heard piano music off in a distant dusty corner of his mind. But it wasn't one of Mark's compositions, yet it was so familiar. They stared into the dark room.

Hearing the reporter's uneven breathing, he called softly, "Kevin? Don't be afraid. It's Michael Johnstone and Dale Mith. We've come for you. Everything's going to be alright. We're coming in now."

"There's gotta be a light in there somewhere," Dale whispered. "See if you can find a switch around the door."

They heard a voice whisper, pleading, "Nohhh. Nohhh light. Pleeeese."

Terrified, both men felt along the wall for the switch until Dale located it. In one intrepid move he switched on the light. And there he was—down on all fours by the rocking chair, the nape of the taxidermied cat clutched between his teeth, arms and neck scratched and scabbing. He whined and backed into the corner when they approached him. McLafferty's face looked ... *different?*

"Come on now," Michael said, inching closer. "It's all over. We're here to get you home."

McLafferty whimpered like a child. "They left me. They left me with the rats. They made it hurt me. Then they took it away with them. But it still hurt me."

Michael helped him to his feet and sat him down on the edge of the cot while Dale stood in the centre of the small room looking at McLafferty, the pictures on the walls, the cat, McLafferty, the wallpapered clouds on the ceiling, the display stand, McLafferty, Mark's pictures, the strands of blue twinkle lights, McLafferty ...

"Dale? Dale! Snap out of it. Help me get him downstairs."

"I tore it up!" McLafferty cried, gesturing to the floor. "See? Look at all the small pieces. I tore it up in front of them when they took the crystal thing, but they still left me."

"Dale!"

Dale exhaled deeply and picked up two pieces of paper. "Mark's handwriting. This is from his cheque book. Bank of London."

"I tore it up," McLafferty repeated, tears streaming down his face. "I wasn't going to use it. I told them and I tore it up in front of them."

Dale gathered the pieces and shoved them in his pocket, then looked at the reporter like he was a grease fire he had to put out. "Where's Mark, McLafferty?"

Still sobbing the man shook his head. "I don't know. They left me. They left me here alone!"

Dale rushed him and slapped his face. "Where is he? You must know where he went, you were blackmailing him."

Michael grabbed hold of Dale's arm. "Not now. He doesn't know anything, believe me. I know what he's been through. Help me get him out of here. Now, Dale."

It was a struggle getting McLafferty's dead-weight body down the stairs and after laying him on the couch, Michael stared absently at him while Dale fetched the bottle.

"We've got to get him to a hospital," he said, tilting McLafferty's head to get the brandy into him. "He's going to need a tetanus shot for these scrapes and he's still in shock."

"Bloody right," Dale snapped. "We can't have an ambulance coming here. There's gotta be people out looking for this guy, people who worked with him, people who helped him spy on Mark. I don't want to be caught with a missing reporter on my hands, especially with Mark having disappeared." Dale looked at McLafferty with disgust. "Why don't we just administer some first aid and dump him somewhere? We'll call an ambulance then take off."

Michael studied McLafferty's face. He barely knew the guy, but his face ... had it changed? "You can't get near the hospital, that's for sure. And if I check him in there's still going to be questions. You're right. Let's get him in his car and park him in a Yorkville lot. You follow in my car. We'll leave him in the driver's seat and call for an ambulance. We can pretend we're passers-by who saw the guy sick or worse behind the wheel."

"How the hell are we supposed to find his car? We've got to make fast tracks outta here, Michael. Like I said, there are dicks out looking for him. Somebody's bound to lead them here before long."

"At the concert Laurel said he drove a red T-bird. It has to be in underground parking. That's the only place for guest parking around here. Why don't you make sure the car's there before we take him down."

"Then what? This guy's gonna be trouble when he straightens out. Laurel said in that letter that he believes she and Mark killed Gillian. He could easily start an investigation. And with Mark and Laurel nowhere in sight, it will look bad, man."

"He can't tell all without implicating himself too much, Dale."

"Reporters have a knack at getting around that sort of thing, I know. Oh he'll talk, alright. What gets me is that he probably knows more than I do. And he must know a lot to risk going after someone of Mark's stature."

"All conjecture," Michael tried to assure him. "Besides, McLafferty'll be in the hospital incoherent as hell for the next couple of days at least. So nobody's going to be taking him too seriously for a while. That will give us time to locate Mark and Laurel. I have a couple of ideas of my own and after we have a talk with Courtland, I know we'll find them, Dale."

While Dale checked on the T-bird in the Circle Court underground parking, Michael rinsed the brandy snifters, put them away and locked the Sea Room door. All Laurel's keys were leaving here with him. Then he wondered why he bothered locking the door. In a day or two, the house would smell like sewer sludge.

If the police believed McLafferty's babble and searched the place, it wouldn't take them long to source the smell. Once they found that room, they'd have no trouble believing they were looking for a mad woman, given Laurel's psychiatric history. But there wasn't time to clean it up. Dale was right. They had to make fast tracks out of here. Two and a half days was a long time for a reporter to be missing.

Michael tried to think positively. Maybe McLafferty would never talk. Right now the police were only concerned with his whereabouts. In the meantime he would ask Courtland to clean the room and take it apart—fast. If McLafferty insisted on an investigation once he recovered, if he ever did, the police would find nothing incriminating, at least nothing to suggest that the proprietress was anything beyond eccentric.

As he waited for Dale to return, he sat with McLafferty, listening to more and more of his gibberish. The man seemed to have regressed to the adolescent stage. He cried for his mother, whimpered and whined, and complained about the aching in his arms and legs. Michael didn't want to say anything to Dale until he was certain of the change in McLafferty's appearance. Now under the proper lighting, the differences were alarmingly obvious.

The grey was gone from his beard and eyebrows with less definitive laugh lines around his mouth. The small mole on his right cheek had disappeared. His eyes were clearer with only a faint trace of crow's feet at the edges. Where deep creases lined his forehead before, a single crease remained. A week ago he might have guessed McLafferty to be around fortyish. At this moment, the man did not look a day over thirty.

A battery of thoughts, questions and visions assaulted his brain and he worried that they may not have rescued him from the Sea Room in time. To what extent did that hellifying experience affect his mind? The crusts of blood under McLafferty's fingernails meant his scratches were self-inflicted. What horror had the Diamond world revealed to him? A horrific experience generally aged people. How could he be younger? What did Laurel really mean when she said *back to their beginning*? Her brother would know. It had to be somewhere in England—the place she gave the Diamond away to the enchanting boy. Courtland Ariss had to remember where this place was.

≈≈≈

December 15, Brighton, England

Lyton Stokes cycled four miles from his antique shop in Brighton to his home above Rottingdean's chalk cliffs six days a week and every other Sunday. At the halfway point, he put down the brakes on his old Raleigh, lit his pipe and looked out at the English Channel. The smell of the sea, marsh, and chalk refreshed him as much as the two cold beers Sara had waiting for him.

Lyton stayed at the halfway point longer than usual tonight. How could Sara turn down a surprise Hawaiian vacation to welcome in the New Year? He zipped down his cycling parka and fingered the plastic leis. Since there was no way around their grief except straight through it, wouldn't it be preferable to grieve in the South Pacific, away from Chris's room? Their nephew, Chris had passed from leukemia four months ago and prior, Sara had been helping him with his college entrance exams. His passing had left a gaping hole in their hearts and lives.

At the outskirts of Rottingdean Village, Lyton cycled past village greens and frozen duck ponds, waving at neighbours out for their late evening walk along the beach. About a quarter mile from home, he noticed all the lights on at John-Philip's. Last he'd heard, old John was still in hospital recuperating from that awful stroke. Lyton entertained the idea of pulling up to welcome John-Philip home then considered the time. It was close to eleven thirty. If John was just home from hospital, he'd be far too knackered to receive callers. Besides, Sara kept closer tabs on John's condition. Better to wait until she filled him in.

"Hello, sweetheart." Lyton gave Sara's ponytail a tug and kissed her cheek. "Saw the lights on at John-Philip's. How long has he been home?"

Sara, a tiny bird-like woman whose 4' 11" frame came up to her husband's chest, poured his mug of beer without her usual enthusiasm. "Isn't John-Philip." Avoiding his eyes, she set his beer mug on the table and cut him a piece of strudel. "Mark rang ahead to ready the house and set the lights for the holidays. Seems he's on his way with a friend. Quite unfathomable why he's coming, with his son in that Toronto hospital. Almost died, poor thing. The Grant family has had their share this past year."

"Maybe the boy's recovered and Mark's bringing him. Was John well enough to fill you in?" Lyton remembered how proud old John was of his famous son, how he liked to go on about him, the same way he used to go on about Chris. But John wasn't talking well these days because of the stroke.

"Didn't hear it from John-Philip. I saw handy-Randy and Joey in town at Foster's this morning getting lights. Mark called last week from Toronto and asked them to decorate and set up the tree. And Paula's stocking the fridge and tidying the house. Randy told me Mark called two days in a row and asked him to do the same chore. Isn't that odd?"

"A lot on his mind with his son, I expect. When is Mark arriving?"

"He's on his way now. Night flight, which is why Randy left the lights on for him. Take off your coat, Lyton."

Sara didn't notice the leis. Her mind had already trailed off someplace, some sad place. Chris was more like a son and there were times he didn't feel like hiding his grief for Sara's sake and this was one of them. "What is it, love?"

Sara slouched at the kitchen table, fingering the cross pendant on her neck. "Jean rang up a little while ago. Late for her to call but she's having a bad night." Jean was his sister-in-law and Chris's mother. "I've been thinking of going on in to London and staying with her a few days, dear. After Christmas. We'll do Teddy's party and then ... would you like to close the shop for a bit and join me?"

"I've already arranged a two-week cover for the shop." Lyton took off one of the leis and placed it around Sara's neck. Her face brightened. "Jean has Billy and Sue and all her other friends at the club. You and I are going to Hawaii. Don't say no. I've already bought the tickets and we leave on the twenty-eighth. Happy Christmas and aloha, love."

≈≈≈

Their arrival in the quaint, sleeping Rottingdean Village brought clarity of mind for the first time in her life, even in her gloomy state. The most depressingly significant thing Mark had said on the plane was, 'You might want to reconsider selling your townhouse,' which he said again an hour prior to landing. This being Mark's first Christmas separated from his son, he missed Fraser like hell and his sadness brought her near to tears. This too, a new emotion because never had she empathized so deeply with another's feelings.

She hated the glancing blows brought by this developing clarity of mind, thoughts of past injuries to others stabbing her like thousands of tiny needles. Her hatred for her mother, a mentally ill woman besought with demons of her own, had possessed her all her life. Now she found herself considering gifts of understanding, even mercy. Though she loved her father, she'd had no pity for the hell he must have suffered, unable to choose sides between wife and daughter, and Courtland, her whipping boy, forever caught in the backlash.

The nearer they got to the house, the more self-deprecating her thoughts became. At this moment she preferred the dark cage of her past, still a cage, but familiar even in bondage. What had this house in store for her? Would this sojourn back to their beginning have its price?

Up the incline they drove, to the overcliff facing the English Channel. And there it stood, the Grant house, poised to welcome angels. It was nearly six in the morning as they drove past the five-foot lighted candy canes lining the long ascending driveway. The twin silver birches in front sparkled behind multi-colored lights. A period cottage, as the Brits liked to call it, was wide and three-storied, clearly larger than a cottage by anyone's description.

Finally she was a threshold away from being inside Mark's childhood home again. She craned her neck to spot the stretch of shore where they first made love in their dream and her heart lurched when she saw the place where they lay. This was her home too and she'd treasured it in her heart and diamond world since that Christmas Eve twenty years ago.

She smiled at Mark and touched his hand, which lay cold and unmoving beneath hers. "It's beautiful, Mark. Just like our diamond world, only it's winter."

Mark agreed with annoying politeness and forced a smile. "Paul," he leaned forward to talk to Paul, probably as an excuse to unleash his hand. "Drive round in back and we'll bring the bags in there. Then kill the lights please, while I get my son on the phone."

"Mark, it's one in the morning in Toronto."

"The hospital's expecting my call," he said with more frost in his voice than the air outside. "Fraser wants to feel part of our arrival."

Paul pulled up to the rear entrance and turned off the ignition. "Sir, will I be taking you back to the airport directly?"

Her stomach dropped. "Airport? Aren't we staying here?"

"Of course." Mark looked sheepish, different somehow. She couldn't quite tell in this dusk, but his skin had a pinkish glow. "But you'll be on your own for most of the day. Come on, let's get in and have tea while I explain. You're going to need to sleep all day, anyway."

"What about you?"

Mark's face tightened. "Let's just get inside, Laurel."

Once upon a time he had wanted to please her, having had this marvelous century home decorated with a Scotch pine that reached the beamed living room ceiling. Old-fashioned holly and ivy lined the mantle fireplace where four monogrammed stockings hung—Mark, John-Philip, Fraser and *Laurel*. Still rigidly polite and quiet, Marked helped her off with her coat. Yeah sure, he had wanted to please her. Once upon a time.

"Mark, how beautiful. When did you set this up? We'd originally planned to go to New York for the holidays."

"I thought I'd surprise you with a trip back to—what do you fancy calling it, *our beginning*?" The question lacked emotion and hinted of mockery. "Warm yourself by the fire while I call Fraser." He whipped off his coat and scarf and dashed off at breakneck speed.

Biting on a raggedy cuticle, she stared into the flames. Here she sat in this Currier and Ives heaven while her lover drifted farther away into the Land of Without Laurel. Her eyes welled. He was calling his son and for the first time she wished to speak to Fraser and hear his kind little voice. 'Take my hand' he sweetly ordered her that afternoon at Pioneer Village. He had been trying so hard and in return she'd given him nothing but ice and fear.

Obsessing over Gillian's death had caused an endless drumroll in her ears. Had it been real? How could she have done this horrific thing? The evil shadow twin could be a metaphor for a life of selfishness and grudges, self-absorption and emotional tyranny. Was there the remotest chance that that could be true? Like the cat? Most of the time she believed she didn't kill the cat.

Maybe she could believe, most of the time, that she didn't kill Gillian Grant. But what about Fraser? She would *never* have hurt Fraser and this time, no one but no one was going to make her believe otherwise. Too bad if Mark didn't like it. She needed to hear the boy's voice.

"Mark?" Following his voice down the hall into a cozy den, she reached out her arm and he stopped talking, mid-sentence.

"... and tell Uncle Dale to behave him—"

"Let me speak to him before you hang up," she said.

"Fraser? You up to chatting with Laurel?" Narrowing his eyes, Mark passed her the phone. "One minute only. It's late for him."

"Fraser? How are you, my friend?"

"Laurel! Almost good enough to travel."

He was happy to hear her voice, but she had to talk fast with Mark patrolling like a Foot Guard at Buckingham Palace. "Well that's great because soon you can join us then."

"Oh yes!" he said loud enough for his father the watchdog to hear.

Mark wagged his fingers for the receiver.

"Fraser, your Dad wants to talk to you, but I'll talk to you again soon, too. Get better quick, okay?"

She returned the phone to Mark, noticing the natural daylight's emphasis on his complexion. Again, something was different about his face, perhaps in the pinkishness or plumpness in the skin. She left Mark alone, closing the door behind her.

It wasn't only his face—he'd stopped rubbing his arms every few minutes since they hit Rottingdean Village. Could the pain have subsided? He hadn't said. Then, he hadn't said much of anything these past few days. She found a washroom at the end of the hall and looked at her lifeless eyes in the mirror. Same old Laurel.

At least in this house, in this *home,* from their astral world to this very moment, she could look in a mirror without seeing the lurking Santina. How many times over how many years had she stood in front of a mirror, brushing her teeth or putting on make-up, only to catch the reflection of her mother's leering face? She started closing doors, but continued to see her mother in all things reflective. Pots. Pans. Kettles. Toasters. It got so she'd see Santina's spying face in the mirror after she left home. As the years passed, the mirrors became smaller.

She hurried to the living room and stood by the window, letting the morning sun wash over her.

God, let me fix this.

≈≈≈

Mark stared at the Rottingdean cliffs that brought him so much joy as a child. The chalk cliffs looked more like mottled grey sheeting this morning, something you'd toss on a floor before priming the walls. Abstract and bland. Certainly not the wonder they used to be at this magical time of year.

If he'd crossed that threshold with Laurel only two weeks ago, they would be upstairs making love now. Afterwards on a town walkabout, he'd have regaled her with stories of Rottingdean. The townies never bothered him, but only tipped their hats and smiled, said hello and passed right on by. Laurel would've liked that. They'd have stopped for a pint or two of Christmas grog in Carry's Pub, laughed and planned their future. And he'd have reassured her about meeting John-Philip because she'd be nervous.

But he wasn't taking her to meet his father. He wasn't taking her anywhere. Not to bed. Not to the village or Carry's Pub. And not into the future. He opened the door a crack and heard her rustling about in the kitchen, probably fixing tea, trying to get a proper start into making things right again. He had to tell her things would never be right again.

He had to tell her it was over between them.

≈≈≈

Laurel didn't have to see Mark's reflection in the tea kettle to know he'd been standing in the doorway watching her. She could smell his Calvin Klein, the hypnotic scent she smelled in their astral dreams and before rising. She used to love to lie in bed with her eyes closed and pretend he was still lying next to her.

"Found the teapot." Her throat constricted as she placed the steeping pot on the long harvest table. Where was he off to without her? "You said I'd be on my own for most of the day?"

He sat across from her and scrubbed his face with his hands. "I want to see my father. Have a visit. I'll be back by tonight."

"And I'm not to go with you?"

"He's not doing well, Laurel, and I don't want to confuse him with strangers."

She was a stranger now? "You were so quiet on the plane, since the hospital, actually. Mark, I know you're exhausted and worried and this is probably me being selfish again, but ... I need to know what's going on with you."

Mark poured them both a cup. "What's going on with me." He repeated the words, not as a question, and not to her.

"Mark?"

"The pain has stopped. Did I tell you that?" A spark of boyish delight flashed through his eyes.

"No. But I can see—"

"It's the stone, you understand. It's carrying part of me inside. But mostly it's carrying you, isn't it, Laurel?" Finally he focused on her, eyes sad, jaw clamped.

"Yes. I ... my father gave it to me when I was eight. So ... yes."

"And your childhood, unlike mine, was a sad one. I've come to believe that what's inside the stone is a potent negative force, growing all these years until it reunited us. I also believe you've kept information about it from me. And information about your mother. Tell me please if that's true."

Finally, the *stranger* gets to speak. For the first time she wanted Mark to learn the truth about the stone, about the darkness inside it, about her mother's darkness. From childhood she could hardly separate Santina's darkness from her own.

She wanted him to know it all, only thing was she didn't know it all herself, especially the horror of Gillian's death. Oh God, did she really take part in that, or had she witnessed? *Please God, let me have witnessed.* Mark was right to return here and destroy the stone, of this she was certain. But would the *thing* that united them ever let them go?

As if in answer to the question, she felt its breath on the back of her neck. Startled, she turned around.

"Seeing shadows again?" Mark asked.

"Always. But it's different here. I feel different here, like I belong. Even in our dreams I was always drawn here. Remember, Mark? I never wanted to leave our shore."

"You didn't answer my question."

She took too large a gulp of tea and coughed, noticing how he just sat there glaring, and silently waiting. "Yes. Yes, I've kept information from you. I didn't want to scare you. Back at my townhouse I walked around anxious, afraid, feeling like some horror inside the stone was going to shoot out and possess me. There was two of me there, Mark. And the second person I didn't recognize. I thought maybe some *thing* invaded my dreams disguised as me. I couldn't tell you because I couldn't explain it. I still can't. The night you returned the diamond to me, it cracked. It slipped off the stand in the Sea Room and cracked at the base." *Oh and yes—I watched your wife die that night.* "I don't remember much after."

"You're stalling me, Laurel. Holding out."

"Yeah, okay. I am." She picked at the same raggedy cuticle and tore it this time.

"Your father gave you the stone when you were eight, you said. Where did he get it? Did you receive any impressions from it?"

"Somewhere in the States. He was on a business trip. Impressions? Yeah, of course. I loved it the moment I saw it. I never let it out of my sight. Took it everywhere."

"Did anything unusual happen before you gave it to me?"

"I was eight, Mark." She sucked the blood from the torn cuticle.

"So you don't recall this precious, marvelous stone you never let out of your midst?"

She resisted the urge to fling the teabag at him. "Of course I do. I remember having dreams, some good and some bad. I remember my parents coming to me in the night, once or twice."

"Parents? So this includes monster-mother?"

"Why are you being so sarcastic?"

"Why have you been so evasive?"

"Who likes to brag about their dysfunctional family? I didn't want you to think I was, you know—troubled?"

"And ... did you grow up—troubled?"

"We weren't *The Cleaver's*, Mark."

He glared at her. "Tell me about your mother."

Oh, God. "Don't you have to go visit your father?"

He glared at her some more.

In her mind's eye she saw Santina's eyes forever shadowing her. "I think I was the first to notice her weirdness. Which began when Dad gave me the stone. It brought my father and me closer and my mother didn't like it. My mother—" It had been years since she referred to Santina so personally. "—was raised in a home where she was alienated. When she misbehaved, my grandparents would ignore her. They never hit her or locked her in a closet. They never starved her. They ignored her, gave her the silent treatment. She left home at eighteen feeling insecure and paranoid. She left hating her parents. They were uneducated people who knew nothing about psychology. They didn't know what they were doing."

Mark leaned back in the chair and stretched his legs under the table. "Did she punish you the same way?"

"Yes, when my father wasn't around. Then she'd feel sorry. Then she'd feel nothing. Then she'd do it again. And after Dad spent time with me I always knew I was in for it with my mother. She'd have to think up some way to steal my happiness. And the best way she knew was to pretend I wasn't there. She'd play with Courtland in front of me. And when he wanted to include me in a game, she'd say, 'Mothers and sons only, Court.'"

"Who told you about her childhood?"

"My grandfather. I think he developed a serious case of the guilts in later years. I was about twenty-five when he told me. All he ever wanted to talk to me and Courtland about was the awful way he treated Santina. I think my grandmother felt remorse but she never said much."

"Your mother had to be terribly afraid to repeat the past."

"I guess she was afraid she'd end up alone and ignored all over again. For once in her life she had to be the center of attention and couldn't be with me around. I was Daddy's little girl and Court's baby sister. I was her competition."

"How did you end up in that hospital?"

"You're talking about the dream you had, the girl, the dumb daisy and sunflower picture over the hospital bed?"

"That's the one. Of course we both know you were the girl."

"I know that, Mark." She sipped her tea and the cup shook when she set it down. "When I was fourteen two incidents happened days apart. Dad was away on a business trip and Santina couldn't join him because she had a bad cold. Courtland was away at school. For days she stalked me around the house and I thought it was because she wanted me to catch her cold.

"She had this little bell by her bed that she used to summon me, which I can still hear ringing sometimes. You'd think she was dying from pneumonia the way she carried on. She asked me to medicate her and gave me a little vial of cold medicine. That *cold medicine* was strychnine diluted with tea, by the way. She had me administer enough to land her in the hospital for four days. Dad and Courtland rushed home and within a week, a lot of people were hovering around asking me questions."

"Your mother tried to frame you?"

"Yes. At first I thought she wanted to kill herself and didn't have the guts. But after 'the cat episode', which was a week to the day afterward, I knew she was out to get me."

"The cat episode?"

"We had this affectionate, sleeky black cat that adopted us. We didn't have it long, hadn't even named it and Santina could see I was taken with it right away. A few days after she got home from the hospital she was hanging out in the kitchen watching me help my father cook a pot roast. When he took the string off the roast I dangled it at the cat and played with it until Dad called us in to dinner ..."

"Go on."

Was she on the witness stand now? "I left the cat playing with the roast string. The next morning I woke up and there it was ... lying there on the edge of my bed. Lifeless. The roast string tied in a neat little bow around its neck."

"My God."

"I screamed and Dad and Santina came running in. 'What did you do?' Santina asked, eyes tearing up. She was so very dramatic. I insisted I'd done nothing and there it began. My story against my mother's. Within days I was under observation in a private psyche ward, not before I dug up the cat the day after my father buried it, put it in a pillow case and took it to a taxidermist. When I got home that day I cut my neck with a nail file. Stupid thing to do because my father thought I was the mental case and rushed me to the hospital, where I spent the better part of six months."

"But you'd obviously broken down."

"Yes. On one weekend outing from the hospital, I picked up the cat at the taxidermist's with the intention of giving it to my mother for Christmas. But Dad took Santina to Italy that Christmas, which suited me just fine. I think he wanted to keep us at a safe distance until he figured things out." Mark's look of pity and concern scared her. *Just like you're keeping Fraser and I at a safe distance now, eh Mark?*

"Surely though, you'd noticed your mother's emergent mental illness. I should think you'd feel more abandoned by the healthy parent. How was it with your father?"

"He was torn and I was needy, and they all had me convinced I killed the cat. Nearly convinced. I thought *how could I do this horrific thing?* People came at me from all sides then. I was a mess and my father was sympathetic. Then in the hospital, the dreams with you had started. More and more I escaped into the Diamond world. And in case you're wondering, Mark, my mother killed that cat."

"I'm sorry, Laurel. Really. Did your mother admit it to you or did you hear it from your father?"

"Admit what?"

"That she killed the cat."

"She admitted nothing to me, Mark."

"So who did she tell?"

"Tell what?"

"How did you find out she killed the cat?"

"I didn't find out."

"Then how do you know?"

"Oh come on. It wasn't my father. It certainly wasn't Courtland. What? You think I did it?"

He tightened his face again. "I didn't say that."

"But that's what you're thinking."

"You know what I'm thinking now? I'm just saying you can't know for certain that your mother did it, Laurel. And that doesn't mean I believe you did it."

Ah, but he did believe it. "Fine."

He sipped his tea and looked at her apologetically. "I should be off to see my father."

"So you're leaving. What? In five minutes? And you're leaving without me. We spoke of marriage a week ago. And now you don't want your father to meet the *stranger*. I don't believe I'm the only one holding out, Mark."

"You're right, I'm sorry. I feel like such a bloody coward."

Oh no. "What do you mean?"

"For a while now I've had concerns about the diamond's Jekyll and Hyde effect on you. I've seen the darkness in you and talked myself into believing that if we could get you out of that townhouse, you'd feel better. I blamed my pain and your anxiety on the stone with its twisted magic and hold over us. And in Malibu I was so enrapt with our development that I completely overlooked Dale's warnings and Fraser's accident on the beach. And then ..."

Where was he going with this? "And then?"

"And then Fraser got hold of the stone somehow that last night. And we know what followed. You gave it to him, didn't you?"

Mark's look of pity and defiance leveled her with such a feeling of worthlessness that she had to look away. He deserved better than her. "I remember giving it to him, Mark. I believe something in me pressed to harm him, but with my mind filled with dark shadows, I can't recall it all—except that I fought for Fraser and me. And I remember Michael approaching me in the hall during the party. That's all that comes to me. Mark please, I've been selfish my whole life, but I never set out to hurt anyone. I would never hurt a child."

Mark slid the chair back from the table. "Convenient memory, yours. My God, you might have killed him. And I'm equally responsible."

"No, please! I was the one who came into your life all those years ago. I left you the stone. It was all me."

"You entered my life *here*, in *this* house. We had the dreams in and around *this* house. And here we are again with me mysteriously pain-free. And while the pain has stopped, I'm feeling strange here, like my childhood home is uncharted territory. I'm also having difficulty staying focused. Wasn't I leaving to ... I'm off to..."

"To visit your father." She stumbled out the words. Already he was forgetting. *What to do, what to do?* For his sake she couldn't let him alone, not now. "I should go with you, don't you think?"

"I don't mean to be cruel, but no, I don't."

She used the tea to mask a hard swallow. "What is it you do want, Mark?"

"I know some supernatural thing had hold of you, as I know it had hold of me. Seems it still does. You already know I brought you here hoping that by destroying the stone, it would release us. I also brought you here to get you the hell away from Fraser, which I suspect you've figured out by now. So, we destroy it as planned. On Christmas Eve."

She braced against the cold drifting through her body like a migrant flash freeze. "And what happens to us after that?"

Again he looked at her with pity. "After that, my dear Laurel, I'm afraid we'll have to go our separate ways. I'm sorry, I really am. But I can't marry you."

She pressed in on her stomach. He knew what he was saying, she could tell. Love wasn't supposed to injure the way her love had injured him, his son, his ex-wife. *Oh I love you so much. But I can't let you go now—for your sake.* "I do love you, Mark. And until recently you loved me. Have we the right to toss it away? Even though I don't deserve—"

"You call what we have *love*? I thought we had a good crack at it anyway, until that vile paranormal darkness made puppets of us. Really, Laurel, what do you expect from contaminated soil besides toxic waste?" Mark got out of his chair, paced and stopped. "Not only did I almost lose my son, who's recently lost his mother—he might've lost his father. That could still happen. Did you take a good look at Kevin McLafferty yesterday morning?"

Thrusting open the kitchen window, Mark pointed outside as the morning chill swept the room. "Hear that? That bleeding ocean hammering the shore? You have any idea how disturbed I am by a sound I used to love? So help me God, I will never forgive myself for diving into this devil's swash of yours, exposing Fraser to it without turning a hair." Mark slammed the window shut.

There was nothing left for her, true. But she could give Mark his life back. He'd always wanted what was real, what already belonged to him, what he'd earned. Nothing more. Even in the dreams he'd wanted out.

"I know what I feel for you is real. And I will fight for you, but not in the way you think."

"What does that mean?"

"It means no more hurt. For any of us."

"You're not quite the tempest I thought you'd be."

Sure, right. Because he couldn't see the emotional avalanche inside her. "Did you think I'd put up a fight, pelt you with pots and pans? Well, shock is merciful. Maybe you'd better dig yourself up a helmet in case I snap out of it."

"I am sorry, Laurel. I wanted this to work big time."

"When did you decide to end us?"

"Probably since that first morning I heard you rocking, though I wasn't aware of it. It was gradual. The more time we spent together the more I came to realize how little we knew each other. Even in the dreams, even when I first visited you in that hospital, we never really spent time together. It was all sex and magic and expectation and lust. We'd moved into this castle in the air, played our roles, read our lines. And our first night in the castle the princess leaves the prince in bed and disappears. And in the morning I get some bullshit explanation. Tell me now, Laurel, why did you leave me to spend the night rocking in that chair?"

"I had a vision. A horrific one."

"Go on."

"I saw Gillian ... I saw what happened to her."

For a moment, Mark seemed afraid to ask. "Was she murdered?"

"I don't ... know ... the diamond on the mantle. Glistening like ... like it was alive. Then I saw a black shadow...of myself, of something that was me but couldn't be me. It forced me to watch as something from the stone took her breath, and her life. There was energy around her, a swirling mass of dark energy. It entrapped her, caught her up in this vortex. And that was it. I couldn't take anymore. At least I don't remember any more because I got out of bed then. I was horrified. I went into my Sea Room to think, to try to reason out what I saw ... then the crack in the diamond..."

Mark gripped the back of his neck. "And where was Fraser?"

"He'd already left with your driver."

"Were you there when Fraser had his accident on the beach?"

"No. And I was a witness with Gillian. Had to be."

"Oh excuse me. So your evil clone wasn't around, either?"

"I don't know, Mark. I wasn't there to see."

"Why did you always seem to be fighting Michael's help? Dale said you sloughed him off after you and I met at the party."

She closed her eyes, shook her head. He was siding with Dale now? *Sure. Why not?* "Michael believes we're in danger and I didn't want to listen. For the first time in my life I was happy and I didn't want to listen. And he was speculating, didn't seem sure about anything."

"Did you extend him the courtesy of listening to a spot of his theory?"

No. There were no courtesies. I'm sorry, Michael. "I never gave him much of a chance, no. Michael said he feared for me, that the past and something in the Diamond had a hold on me. And something did. Michael was right about that but I was in no shape to listen. Next thing I knew, we were rushing to the hospital. You blame me for Fraser, don't you?"

"You're. Bloody. Right. I. Do." Mark punctuated every word, cutting her like diamonds into glass. "You knew I had a child. You should have ditched that cursed stone the day after I returned it and stayed the hell away from me. Well, we have a few more days together and then we can be done. Now I'm going to ask you to do one last thing for me. A promise I want you to make. I think I've earned it."

She could barely breathe. "What is that?"

"No matter what happens, no matter how this plays out, when it's over—I want you out of my dreams and out of my life and my son's life. And since I'm forced to share this house with you until Christmas, I'll try my very best to be civil. So? Do you give me your word, your promise to make no attempt to re-enter my life when this is done?"

No and yes. I will always look out for you, even from a distance. "If that's what you want, Mark."

"That's what I want. Thank-you. That's it then, Laurel. The disposal of that precious stone of yours will be the last thing we ever do together. I'm going to see my father now ... in ... he's in ..."

"London, Mark. A convalescent home in London. I heard you tell Paul to pick you up at nine. It's just after eight."

"I'm all muddled," he said, squinting at her. "I'm calling Paul to fetch me now." He headed to the doorway and froze there, hesitant.

"Put if off until tomorrow, please. Paul's already clued in that something's wrong. You kept repeating yourself in the car."

"I trust him," Mark said, blinking rapidly. "More than I trust you right now."

He could hack away at her all he wanted. Since it was over between them anyway, she had nothing more to lose, and she had to protect him. Like it or not, she was going with him and just let him try and stop her. "Something could happen on the way. It could all end up in the papers. What if the hand pain returns once you're out of Rottingdean? Do you want to worry your father?"

"There's doctors there," he said stubbornly.

"You've been to doctors, Mark. In Toronto, remember? It was me who insisted you get checked out."

He softened a little. "Why are you unaffected?"

"Told you, I ... it's affecting me emotionally. I'm different here. Always have been."

He walked halfway into the room. "So what is this, like *Lost Horizon*? Are we going to die as soon as we go beyond Rottingdean's border?"

"I don't know any more than you do. But Michael did warn me."

"Oh so now you're listening to Michael. A bit late, isn't it?"

"Listen. I got you into this, so I'm getting you out of this. Like it or lump it, Mark. If you insist on driving into London with Paul, I'm strapping myself on the outside of the car if I have to. But I believe you're wisest option is to compromise."

He walked up to the table and tapped his fingertips on the edge. "What do you mean, *compromise*?"

"Was that your father's car in the garage?"

"Yes."

"Is it driveable?"

"Course, why?"

"Then drive me just outside Rottingdean Village. In the astral, you told me your father taught you how to drive when you were eleven. So—you're not likely to forget. Drive me past the border, Mark. Let's see what happens. I dare you." How could he resist a dare? What *boy* could resist a dare?

≈≈≈

She snuck a peek in the garage an hour later and found him asleep on the backseat of his father's Vauxhall Cavalier. Best to let him be for a while. She curled up on the couch by the fire and awakened at noon to a clanking sound in the garage. Tooling around with the car seemed to distract him from his troubles and he gratefully exchanged his expensive London Fog for an old military jacket of his father's.

"I'll fix us coffee and sandwiches before we leave. Can I help here?" His skin was smoother, his hair silkier, more so now than just hours ago.

"No, thank-you," he said, wiping his hands on a rag. "She'll need petrol, though. We'll have to stop in town."

She? His manner, too, had changed. Was it friendlier? Her stomach turned over. Mark was no longer hers. But he could change his mind, couldn't he? Women didn't have the monopoly on that prerogative. And he did listen to her about putting off the visit with his father for a few days. Her shoulders tightened and her mouth went dry thinking how he couldn't remember if his father was lying in bed expecting him, couldn't remember if he called him before leaving Toronto.

She had to put her personal fear and heartbreak behind her now and focus on Mark. She had to take care of Mark. And oh God, maybe driving to the town's border wasn't such a hot idea. Maybe go after dark. She fixed the sandwiches and tried to shake it all off for at least one blessed hour. She was exhausted. Bad dreams. Bad frame of mind. *Bad, bad, bad Laurel.*

There's something to be said for self-involvement, right, Laurel?

Damn voice of conscience, if that's what it was. And Mark was at the end of a long list of people she'd hurt. Yeah, sometimes life was easier when you didn't care about anyone but yourself.

Mark climbed in behind the wheel and checked the wipers and headlights, checked her out from the corner of his eye, checked his thumbnail. "I have this un-bumpy thumbnail," he said, randomly.

"What?"

"I lost a thumbnail ... well, *whenever*. Recently, anyway. And it grew back so bumpy I had to file it down. It's perfect now. See?" He swung open the car door and hopped out to show her.

"Yes, it looks perfect."

Mark smiled and flicked the thumb around like it was a separate appendage. "Thanks for the sandwiches. I'm a lousy cook. Do you cook?"

"Do I ... yes I cook."

Fear flashed through his eyes. "I should know that, shouldn't I? But I called Fraser, didn't I? Soon as we got here?"

She pressed a palm to her heart and nodded. "Maybe we should stick close to the house. Forget the drive?"

"No. It's a good idea to investigate this phenomenon. I have to know what's happening to me and I always feel better with a plan. Why are you unaffected?"

Again. He was asking this question *again.* "I am affected—morally, ethically, while you seem to be affected physically. Like Kevin McLafferty."

Mark leaned against the Vauxhall and scratched his cheek. "Should I know Kevin McLafferty?"

≈≈≈

Her heart was still thumping when they pulled into a weary but cozy little station for 'petrol' at the edge of town. Fake Christmas wreaths and strings of tacky red bulbs hung haphazardly about and it was all so corny and lovely that she wanted to cry. Mark grazed her thigh while reaching for his wallet in the glove compartment and for a flicker of a moment their eyes locked.

"I'll fill up," he said. "You warm enough? You're shivering."

"I'm fine. I'll crank up the heat when we're done." Like more heat would help.

From the rear view mirror she watched him insert the nozzle into the tank, wind ripping through his hair and coat, the blush of winter on his cheeks erasing the fine lines around his eyes and mouth. He stood taller and straighter and looked oh so much younger. About ten years younger.

On the front panel of the gas pump, a loosely-fastened sheet of ancient stainless steel rattled in the moaning wind. Jolted by a gnawing feeling of sadness she opened the car door and got out. Her coat flapped around her legs and arms. Several Christmas bulbs popped and red debris skittered along the ground. It was like walking into a dream.

"Mark?"

Mark set the nozzle back into the gas pump and the sheet of steel detached as he made a grab for it.

"Blast!" Mark shouted. Blood spurted down his sleeve and an attendant zoomed out of the tiny diner.

"Mark!"

"Oh, lordy lord! You all right, son?"

"I've sliced it. Sliced my finger good."

"Mark, let's get inside and look at that," she said.

The attendant, about as antique as the shoddy piece of steel, put a gnarly hand on Mark's elbow and rushed him inside the diner. "You might need a stitch or two in that finger, son."

"Where's your medical kit?"

Had the floor dissolved beneath her? The man nodded to a shelf above the sink and within five minutes she had his wound cleaned, which, thank God, was superficial. She let out a huge breath. How she wanted to hold him. But Mark hadn't said more than a dozen words since it happened. He looked from the attendant to her with a clouded gaze.

The attendant, Neville, put on tea.

"But we don't have time," Mark said. Finally he *said* something. "We have to go to Brighton."

"I think we should turn back."

"Wind's kicking in worse," Neville said, rattling cups. "Your friend's right, son."

Mark studied his hand with a blank look. "Sliced it."

"My doctor's in Brighton, miss. Be happy to ring him, seeing you're headed that way."

He kept calling him *son*. And Mark didn't need a doctor, didn't need the recognition. And they sure as hell didn't need to cross the town border. Not now. But it wasn't her call. Hadn't she made enough dumb, stupid calls?

When Neville set down the tea, Mark snuck a glance at his watch and pretended to come around. She knew he was pretending because he'd nodded at the watch, at her, at Neville, even the tea, and Mark was not a nodder.

"It's just after two," he said. "We won't bother your doctor friend. It's just a cut and I'm fine. But tah very much." He gulped down the tea and rounded his eyes at her.

"Thanks for the tea," she said. "What do we owe you for the gas?"

"Oh, no charge, miss. You've had enough trouble. Some blokes would sue."

Mark cleared his throat. "No worries there."

"We'll be going then," she said.

"Happy Christmas to both of you. And that cut'll mend in no time, son. You teenagers heal in a nip."

≈≈≈

He insisted his finger had gone a bit *gammy* and refused to turn back—he had to get across the county line into Brighton—just to see. It was all of five miles and *your idea* he kept saying. Her mouth went dry as she listened to him repeat it four more times in four miles along the blustery coast road, his British jargon thickening with every mile as the Vauxhall rocked against the wind.

"A kilometre away now," Mark said, steering with his left hand. "What's wrong? Isn't this what you wanted?"

Not so much now, not so much. Her dry mouth had turned sour. "I've had issues with my wants over the years. I'm so sorry, Mark."

Mark glanced at her like he didn't know what she was talking about. "Hang on, turban girl. Almost there."

Turban girl? Had he forgotten their fight?

As the Palace Pier came into view, Mark pulled over to the side of the road and turned off the ignition. "See? Nothing. You're fine and I'm fine."

She dropped her face in her hands and laughed. "Ahh. All's fine. Now we can get back to the house and decide the best way to put the Diamond to rest. How's that gammy finger?"

"All sorted. Need a stretch, though." He checked his watch. "Going on 2:30. Let's take that stretch to the end of the pier and then back to the car. Fifteen minutes."

Before she could say 'Can't we skip this adventure and go home,' he pulled out and sped into the Pier parking like a teenager late for a drag race. "The handful of people out braving the wind up on that pier might recognize you." Not that the crazy people traipsing about on that pier would recognize him since he looked about fifteen years younger. God, how was she ever going to help him?

She studied her hands, then flipped them over. No changes, unless realization was change. She'd wrecked Mark's life, his son's, maybe even Gillian's and Santina's. But Gillian was beyond help, Fraser still had his dad, sort of, Santina couldn't help being nuts and Mark would always be good. And her? Well, here she was, stuck inside her old, selfish self.

"Storms destroyed it twice," Mark said, playing tour guide as they swayed on the pier in a storm of their own. "In December of 1896 and in '73, a seventy-ton barge broke loose and damaged the pier head, mainly the theatre. Sad because the theatre was never used again. But do you know it has eighty-five miles of planking and considered the finest pleasure pier ever built? Sort of your answer to ... to um ..."

"Canadian National Exhibition."

"Right. Believe I've played in the CNE Stadium."

"Several times, Mark."

She looked ahead at the domed amusement arcade, roller coaster and multitude of kiosks, now closed for the winter. This carnival atmosphere might be wonderful in summer but right now she wanted to escape, to feel safe again. She didn't feel at all safe here. A black cloud of birds swooped and wheeled in unison above the pier.

"Ever seen such an amazing spectacle? It's called *murmuration exaltation*. In autumn and winter, the starlings mass and turn the sky black." Mark craned his neck to marvel at the sight. "Uggh! Arrrgh!" Wincing in pain, he hunched forward clutching the sides of his face.

"Mark! What is it?"

"Ohh. Shooting pains up and down my sides."

"Back to the car. Right now!"

He leaned on her for support as they turned around on the pier and into the wind. "P-people coming. C-can't ... let's get by them."

In the small group of teens heading toward them, one girl's jaw dropped when, dammit, she recognized Mark. "Perform, Mark. It's what you do."

"Oh my God!" the girl cried to her friends. "Oh my God, Mark Grant!"

Mark winced, straightened, and somehow managed to smile as they passed. "Wish I were," he said to the fan-stricken girl. "Not for the fame, for his bob."

"That's not him." A boy in their group stubbed out his cigarette and walked on. "He's too young."

"Can we help?" a concerned couple asked as they exited the pier.

"I've got him, thank-you," she said. "Twisted ankle, I think. Our car's right over there."

Mark headed straight for the backseat. "God Almighty, what's happening to me? Take the keys. You'll have to manage the car."

Was she ever going to stop causing him pain? "Oh, Mark. I'll get us back. But driving on the right side? I-I don't know—"

"Hurry, Lara. Please."

Lara?

Her hands shook on the wheel as Mark moaned and thrashed in the back seat. This was all her fault. Wasn't everything always her fault? Ten minutes later when they had crossed into Rottingdean, things got quiet in back. "Mark?"

"Pull over, please," he said, calmly.

She almost pulled off to the wrong side of the road but caught herself. "Mark? You okay?" She turned off the ignition. As the hair lifted on her neck and arms, she looked in back.

He was sitting up, the picture of composure, though his expression was slack until he took a good look at her. He wrinkled his nose, then apparently pleased with what he saw, smiled.

"Are you still in pain, Mark?"

"Pain?" He looked curiously at her. "It's just a cut." He jumped out and took his place in the front seat. "I'd better drive the rest of the way," he said, examining the bandage on his finger and the blood drops on his coat sleeve. And without explanation or reason, he pulled off the bandage. Coldness smacked her at the core as she searched for the cut that was no longer there.

"Odd," he said. "I'm sorry, I'm a bit muddled. Forgive me. Where do you live, Lara? I'll drive you home."

11. GOODBYE, CHRISTMAS CARDINAL

AFTER SEEING McLAFFERTY half-crazed and blathering in that sea room, they had to find them, help them, and get them home. Michael and Dale kicked themselves for not putting the pieces together sooner, and once Michael talked with Courtland, it didn't take them long to locate Laurel and Mark, to find 'their beginning' as Laurel so passionately phrased it. How stupid could he be? After learning Mark was the enchanting boy to whom she had given the Diamond all those years ago, Michael recalled Courtland's Christmas Eve story about the little seaside restaurant near Brighton. From there, Dale ran with the ball. Dale had been at Mark's childhood home. He knew his father. He knew the Grant home had once been a restaurant from 1959 to 1969 or '70 in the quaint hamlet of Rottingdean.

Unfortunately they could not leave for England the moment they put this together on the fifteenth. In preparation for a meeting with Justin in New York, Dale had to fabricate a believable story about Mark's little impromptu 'vacation'. He had used Fraser's accident, which wasn't entirely a lie and told Justin that Mark had slipped quietly off with his lady to live in peace for a few months or however long it would take him to get his life together again, and Fraser would of course be joining them soon. Suspicious that Mark took off with Fraser still hospitalized, Justin pressed for more information but Dale managed to distract him. A score of Mark's people had to be notified. Business managers. Financial advisors. Press agents. Record distributors. The list was endless. Dale spent more time with Mark's affairs than his own.

Michael, in the meantime, tried to console Courtland and Nancy. He wanted to keep a discreet check on McLafferty's condition and the last report was grim. McLafferty wasn't telling the world that Mark Grant had locked him up in his eccentric girlfriend's hidden room for two and a half days. He wasn't telling the world that Laurel Ariss killed Grant's wife, nearly killed his son, and that Grant was mysteriously linked to these tragedies.

McLafferty wouldn't be telling the world anything because he couldn't remember last month and now he couldn't remember last year. Although the physical aging had ceased, his mind was reduced to that of a fifteen-year-old. Sadly, Michael realized Kevin McLafferty was not about to be cured any time soon. What a horrible way to stop worrying about McLafferty.

≈≈≈

Per Laurel's instructions, Courtland listed the Circle Court townhouse. The only thing in the house not listed was Mouth and the taxidermied cat. While Katherine dog-sat over Christmas, he entertained the idea of the cat accompanying Nancy and him to Cordoba. A little Christmas gift to the folks. A little reminder of the goings on inside their daughter's head from the time they'd taken up globetrotting.

After taking the Sea Room apart, he made the dreaded call to his father in Spain. He explained that Laurel had run off with a rock star, likely never to return, that she left a note raising the issue of their mother's mental state in the early years. Courtland told his father he expected the truth about Santina when he joined them in Cordoba. That's when Santina grabbed the phone and told him a little *truth* of her own.

"Find Laurel," she said, voice trembling. "Tell her *this,* Courtland. Tell her I'm so sorry ..."

After his mother dropped her little bomb, he asked her, "Does Dad know?" He heard his father moan in the background. "Guess he knows now, eh Mom? Well, I would love to tell her if I could find her. But how do you find somebody who's been lost for years."

Soon as he hung up, Courtland made one more call.

≈≈≈

Michael reached for the phone on his night table just as the clock changed from 2:59 to 3:00 a.m. Oh Lord, was Dale calling with bad news of Fraser? Bleary-eyed, he clumsily picked up the receiver. Fraser was doing great, Dale said yesterday afternoon. So who the hell ...

"Hello?"

"Michael. It's Laurel."

He switched on the light and bolted up in bed. "Hey—"

"Michael, he broke up with me. Just like that. And two hours later he changed. Forgot everything. Us ... everything."

"How did he change, Laurel?"

"Michael, I need to know about McLafferty."

"How did Mark change, Laurel?"

"It's like something blotted out the middle of his life. He looks younger, like McLafferty. For the last three days all he does is surf, swim, wax his surfboard. And tomorrow he insists on giving me lessons. It's two below zero here. Michael, tell me about McLafferty."

He swung his legs out of bed. Did she really need to hear this? Hell. He wasn't there, she was, and Mark needed help now. "He's regressed as well. But his regression seems to have stopped in your absence. Laurel, I believe it's all about the type of energy projected into the stone. When you locked McLafferty in that room, had he and Mark come to blows?"

"No. McLafferty was scared, sure. Mostly of me, I think. And naturally, he and Mark argued. But he agreed to Mark's terms, agreed to let us hold him until we got away. Is he going to be all right?"

He couldn't tell if she was genuinely concerned for McLafferty or afraid for Mark. In any case, she seemed least concerned for herself. Definitely un-Laurel. "He'll be all right eventually. I don't know how long it will take. But I do think the emotional state around the stone quantifies the change. A terrified McLafferty becomes a mind on the brink."

"Yeah, so what was Gillian Grant's emotional state?"

"I can't know that, Laurel. But listen, I have to tell you—"

"Yeah, well I know. I was there. I saw."

"Not from Mark's house you didn't."

"No. But the little re-enactment scene on the ceiling in *my* house was enough to convince me I was there."

"How was Fraser when you last saw him?"

"You're asking if I gave Fraser the stone, Michael?"

He didn't want to answer, didn't want to piss her off. But it was important to know—seeing it was all coming together. "Yes, I guess that's what I'm asking."

She was breathing heavily. "Yes. I gave Fraser the stone. Sure. And he was nervous but excited. A little wary of me but happy to be seeing his mother. God help me, that's what I made him think."

"Did you give it to him at the El Mo?"

"Yes. So what happened after he left with Annie, I couldn't tell you."

His stomach knotted. "Why did you give Fraser the stone?"

She laughed pathetically. "I'm not sure it was me who did." When he started to query her further she cut him off. "Michael, Fraser's fine. Mark isn't. So here's the thing, I got away from McLafferty and he's on the road to recovery. I got away from Fraser, and he's fine now."

Knowing where she was going with this, he stood and stared into the tangled fringe around the bedside mat. "No. It's different with Mark. The both of you are like one cell now, your energy moving through the same nuclear pores. And the stone is the skin separating your inner cell from its surroundings. Listen Laurel, you were right to go to Rottingdean. Stay put."

He heard the hitch in her breath. "How did you find out where we are?"

"Dale and Courtland figured it out. Listen, Dale and I are coming after Christmas. But right now I have to tell you—"

"What? No! No one else gets damaged. You and Dale better bloody well stay where you are until I call you again. If I so much as hear a car or one footstep on this road, Mark and I disappear. You hear me?"

Damn, he shouldn't have said they were coming. But she caught him fricken asleep. So what the hell did she want him for? "Why did you call me, Laurel?"

"I have a feeling that if I get Mark back to our astral world, he'll be himself again."

"That's the last thing he'll be." God, she could be crazy. Maybe she was crazy. "You and Mark shattered that world when you left. It'd be like returning to a war zone. You really want the fall-out from that? Mentally, you may never get out. Say you understand." He gripped a section of mat fringe with his toes and watched the blood drain. "Laurel, you hearing me? Wrong feeling. Okay? Returning to the astral—crazy bad idea."

"I feel it's the right thing to do."

He slumped down on the bedside. "So as usual, you're asking for my advice and not taking it. I'm not clear on why you called me, Laurel."

"I'll call you again, Michael. Maybe. Remember, don't come here."

"Reconsider letting me come. I could come alone—"

"I'm hanging up, Michael."

"Laurel! Please, don't hang up. I have a message for you. You there?"

"Yes. What message?"

"Promise you won't hang up until I'm done?" She didn't say yes. She didn't say no. "Courtland called me today. What he told me doesn't make much sense to me but he said you'd understand."

"Understand what?"

"He spoke to your mother who insisted you know something. No, now *wait*. Wait. She said you didn't kill the cat. Nor did she. She said the cat choked on a roast string it'd been playing with. She wants you to know she's so very, very sorry."

Laurel took a deep breath and released it. "Merry Christmas, Michael."

"Merry Chr—"

She hung up.

≈≈≈

While waiting for Julian Wieler's call, Michael filed his nails down to the nub. He'd left a message in Vancouver with the housekeeper an hour ago, who suggested he call Dr. Wieler at the student faculty Christmas party.

"He won't mind, Mr. Johnstone, seeing it's urgent."

"Thank you," he said, hoping Julian wouldn't be partying into the wee hours. "I need him to tuck himself somewhere where he won't be disturbed. I'll be right here waiting for his call."

He wrestled with his conscience. Laurel wouldn't like him discussing her private business with Dr. Wieler but to hell with it because he needed Julian's take on this, especially now. She had to know that at 3 a.m. she'd catch him unprepared. A very Laurel thing to do. She'd sounded scared but in control, and some mysteriously different quality lingered in her voice. For an instant he'd wondered if it really was Laurel. Maybe it was her double. Maybe it was her double *listening in*.

"We're going anyway," he told Julian after he'd reiterated Laurel's call. "I mean, how fast can they bolt? How far can they get once they see us coming? I didn't tell Laurel that I know Mark hasn't visited his father yet."

"And you found this out, how?" Wieler asked.

"Dale called the neighbours because Mark isn't answering the phone. And he's stopped calling his son. Add to that what Laurel said and I'm fairly alarmed here. So, Dale and I are flying into Gatwick the day after Christmas and Rottingdean is only thirty miles from there. Julian ..." He paused to think. He needed one lousy second to think. "I'm not sure what we're going to do when we get there, what we're going to find. I fear what we might find."

"Which is the fear of finding them with the same affliction as Mr. McLafferty," Wieler said."

Michael sensed Wieler's reluctance, and quite possibly the futility of it all, as though it was over, that he was too late.

"Let them go, Michael. Truths are at stake here, simple truths. Their existence together and apart has been the only truth they have known all these years. The truth of the Diamond world. The truth outside the Diamond world. Whatever their choice—limbo.

"Laurel infused her essence with that magical world when she was a child. She placed all her negative and loving energy into that stone. Then that energy grew in Mark until they united in that world. Recall the object theory we spoke of months ago, Michael. That misplaced energy had stagnated for nearly twenty years and when Mark returned it, she was forced back into it again, back in time with it.

"Mark, the boy, was living in that same time, the same world with her even though they'd been separated by an ocean for twenty years. The power in her mind, the longing, that intense misplaced energy, her past trauma—all these overwhelming factors revolved around the destiny she and Mark created for themselves. When an individual charges after his destiny, placing too much emphasis on his own knowledge and power, the results can only be tragic. Destiny must be left to God."

He wasn't sure he agreed. Didn't one create destiny through one's choices? Good choices-good destiny. Bad choices-bad destiny. And to the best of his knowledge, unless asked, God kept out of it.

"Laurel and Mark must regress because they have no place left to go," Wieler said. "Their minds are not equipped to handle past and current trauma. They were able to live in the world of the stone all these years because of its obvious stimuli—intensity of attraction, sex disguised as love, mystery of the supernatural. Then the energy returned polarized and the stone emptied when they reunited here. And on this plane, the world also empties when one lives solely for one's self.

"Yes, you have reason to fear for them, Michael. The beginning, before all the pain, is the only world in which they can exist away from the limbo of two worlds. There they don't have to know and remember death, guilt, fear, the waiting for that perfect world outside the stone. Their minds have had enough waiting. And they've been forced to relinquish control over obstacles threatening their perfect, illusory world. McLafferty is an example, as is Mark's wife. They were serious obstacles."

Michael gave his head a shake. Wieler had to be overzealous in his conclusions.

"Be assured there is hope for Mr. McLafferty. When their minds completely regress, he will be released. This I think will happen. But Mark and Laurel will never be released, Michael. They cannot exist in either world. The energy in the stone has released Kevin McLafferty and little Fraser. But it will never release Laurel and Mark, who breathed life into it. I'm sorry, Michael, but institutionalization is the sad path on which they tread, and this is where they will remain until their eventual release from both worlds. So is this what you want, Michael, you and your friend, to go and find them in this state? Perhaps it's wiser, yes, to have someone else locate them, have someone else ... help them?"

Institutionalization? "Then it's over. But how do I abandon them to strangers? I can't. And I know Dale can't. He would never agree to let Mark go. Mark has been his dearest friend for years. And there's one other thing that's really bothering me."

"What is that?"

"In retrospect, my conversation with Laurel didn't flow, had no rhyme or reason. Sure she wanted to help Mark, but she has another agenda. I know it. I mean, I got the impression she'd already made up her mind to return to the astral. So why call me? No. Something's off here. We're going to Rottingdean, Julian. I have to see them again."

≈≈≈

He'd been sleeping in his boyhood attic room, bed under a slanted ceiling with paint faded from sticky tape and ghost covers of Surf Magazine. His father hadn't changed the room much. An antique school desk stood in one corner and lined along the floorboards beside it was a vast collection of books including the complete works of Sir Arthur Conan Doyle and picture books of airplanes and trains. There were stacks of music sheets and surfing magazines from around the globe, National Geographic books on Canada, high school yearbooks and photo albums. Swim meet trophies, ribbons and medals covered the shelves, dresser, desk and corkboard.

Eye-catching and imposing on a shelf at the opposite end of the room stood the British Typhoon Hawker Hurricane and Lancaster models he had made when he was fifteen, plus two favourites — the American designed Corsair and the German Stuka Ju 87G—with no dust under them or anywhere else in the room. Had *she* been in here tidying? The lovely Christmas Laurel?

His favourite thing was still on the desk, looking as new and shiny as it had when he opened the box on his seventeenth birthday. The CPR Royal Hudson was an exact replica of Engine No. 2850 and he used to imagine himself as a passenger on this train in 1939 when their Majesties King George VI and Queen Elizabeth toured Canada. For years, that's where he kept her stone at night—on the desk beside the Royal Hudson. In the mornings he'd tote it back to the piano and set it on the same spot Laurel left it for him that Christmas Eve. By the time he was twenty, the stone had replaced the Royal Hudson in his affections. How could he remember all this boyhood stuff and not remember life after this house?

This morning she told him about his fame, his son, the life *temporarily* left behind because his memory would return, she'd promised. He clung to that, plodded over to the phone and gripped the cord they'd disconnected a few days ago—if it was a few days ago. At the time he remembered why they'd disconnected the phone. What reason did she give? Something about 'alarm'. Yeah well he felt fairly alarmed now, but didn't know why. He'd flipped through the photo albums ten times this past hour and except for the fact that he and his father had aged, he didn't recognize one face outside of Rottingdean. And the kid in the pictures. And the smiling bloke with his arm around the smiling kid. *My kid. Me in the future.*

"Laurel!" The sound of her rushing footsteps centred him until she stood at the door, eyes rounded, beautiful face taut.

"You okay?"

"Sorry to alarm you," he said, considering that word again as the cord hung from his hand like a mangled snake. "But ... I don't know who I'd ring up."

She hurried across the room to him, cradled his face. "We'll fix this, Mark. I promise."

Somehow he believed her. He always believed her. He let out a breath and sat on the bed, deflated. He reached for her and she sat beside him, a bothersome distance away. "A doctor wouldn't help?"

"No," she said.

"Did we call a doctor?"

She hesitated. "No."

"I'm quite gutted, you know. Not just the brain. But my spirit and heart. It's like waking after surgery not knowing what was cut out. Tell me again how you remember, how you're ... okay."

Though swollen, her eyes were wonderfully intense. "I'm not okay, Mark. What you've lost in memory, I've gained in conscience. I dodged a bullet, you see."

He had no idea what in blazes she meant. "I don't understand." He slid a fraction closer and she tightened up on him again. *Cor!* He wanted to hold her and not because she was such a tidy miss, for an older woman, but because he saw nothing bad in her. There was only warmth, care and concern, and he so much wanted to sop up every ray of light she'd spare him.

"I told you. I'm responsible for the state you're in."

"The stone?" That part he remembered so well, remembered the night she left it for him. And he was *older* than her. She touched his shoulder, sending tiny shock waves through him. "But if not for that stone, I might not've gone on to fame. That has to be true."

"You're so sweet to say that. But it's not quite that simple."

He rubbed his hand over hers and she blinked her eyes out of passion—he hoped. Then she pulled it away. "What? Why don't you let me get close? We've been lovers, I know it. Don't deny that, Laurel."

"It's true. We were lovers." She went to the window and straightened the red Christmas apron she'd tied over all that depressing black—black knee-length cardie, black stretch pants, black loafers. "And now we're friends in a very serious predicament. Help me stay focused, Mark. I need to reconnect you with your life. As it was. Please understand the priority."

"It's simply that when I'm near you I feel a shadow of my recent past." God, he was crazy mad to jump her. What it must've been like between them! And with his heart hammering against his ribs, she made him forget he was scared spitless. He walked over and touched the cat brooch pinned to her collar. "I like these feminine things on you, though you don't need them. You quite sparkle without them."

She sighed, blinked her swollen eyes again. "Dinner's almost ready. And tomorrow night we'll have our Christmas Eve dinner. Play the piano for me tomorrow night, Mark. Play *Riviera Concerto* for me."

"Of course I'll play for you," he said, anxious to please her. "But no need to wait 'til tomorrow. I'll play it for you tonight."

"No." She flexed her jaw, stiffened her shoulders. "Christmas Eve. Like you did twenty years ago tomorrow night."

"It's about tying the stone into everything on Christmas Eve, isn't it? Except for the magic it held for me growing up, I believe there's something dark in it now. Wonder what we did to darken it. The details are fuzzy but I remember the night you left it for me."

"On the plane ride here we talked about getting rid of the stone." For an instant she turned abruptly away, like she was checking for ghosts. "Mark, don't worry, by next week you'll be reunited with your son. You'll have your life back."

What secret was she keeping from him? He felt the sadness in her secret and the tenderness in his heart, as deep as he sensed the viral wasteland around the stone. Observing a thunderous look pass briefly in her eyes, like a storm cloud ducking behind the chalk cliffs of Rottingdean, he asked her, "But will we have it back *together*?"

Laurel kissed his cheek. "Yes. We'll have it." She left him then, left him with his photo albums full of strangers and a boyhood room full of ghosts.

Riding the waves was about the only thing that filled his mind with peace, well, riding the waves and obsessive thoughts about kissing Laurel. But when he caught her talking to herself in the kitchen while mashing potatoes, he decided she wasn't quite receptive to kissing. She'd been pounding those potatoes in the bowl like they were the last angry thought when he heard her say, "I knew you'd be pleased. So happy I could help." He held back from approaching her. But to be fair, he talked to himself, too. They would work this out. It was Christmas and they'd work it all out. He believed it because he had to believe it, because belief would make it so.

"Yeah yeah, you've given me no choice. Yes it's going in with me, okay? Enough already. Just let me have Christmas with him."

Mark ducked back into the hall. That last remark required an explanation. He wouldn't startle or embarrass her by asking her now. Over dinner he'd ask. "Quite the swell out there," he called in from the hallway, giving her a chance to pull herself together. "Do I have time for a surf before dinner?"

"Sure," she said. She gave him one of those interrogative looks, like she might be wondering if he heard her talking to herself. Her eyes were watery, probably from a fresh batch of tears. Once he got on the waves he'd figure out how to help her. He hadn't been much help so far and that had to stop because he ached seeing her so unhappy and frazzled.

"Half hour. I'll put on some Christmas music and light a fire when I get back. And my turn to do the dishes."

She smiled sweetly. "Half hour then."

Out in the choppy surf, he decided to be more forceful, get her to open up so he could help her. He'd insist on carrying some of the burden. Losing his memory hadn't made him helpless. And maybe he'd ring up his father and wish him a very quick Happy Christmas. Quick indeed! He laughed and positioned himself on the board. He had no choice keeping conversation brief, really. He'd tell his dad not to worry. He'd be round to visit soon. Then he'd encourage Laurel to call her family. It was Christmas.

She'd lit candles and a fire, even dug out an old Christmas album of his dad's when he found her hunched at the table flipping pages. Mark moved a chair close to hers and recognized his much older face on the page. The *rockstar* was playing the saxophone. He didn't even know he played the saxophone. And there she was, coveting his picture with those swollen, blasted puppy eyes. Was it possible to be jealous of himself?

"Did you love me very much?" he asked, instantly regretting the stupid question.

"Of course." She slid her fingers along the table to him, gently squeezed his arm. "Though it wasn't real at first. It was all about possession and lust. And magic. Then one day you were telling your son a story and I realized I'd forgotten myself. There was only you and the joy around you."

She closed the album and pushed it aside. "Time to eat. Not too fancy, I'm afraid."

Mark followed her into the kitchen, trailed her to the table carrying meatloaf and gravy so he could watch the way she moved. So straight and upright. So sure in her stride. But she couldn't be sure, he knew that now. He told her to sit and when he returned with the salad he pretended to laugh. *Keep it light, Mark. Keep it light for now.* "I heard you chatting to yourself before. I do that, too. Glad I'm not the only one."

She stole a sideways glance at him. It was a new look and it unnerved him a little. She portioned the meatloaf onto their plates, saying nothing.

"I heard you say *I'm taking it in with me and that's that.* Then you said *just let me have Christmas with him.*"

"I often pray out loud," she said, doling out the much-mashed potatoes. "Another scoop?"

"No that's fine, thanks. That wasn't prayer, Laurel. Please?"

"Okay, so I have a dark side I talk to, more like argue with. What's on your mind, Mark?"

So much for keeping it light. "You're not confiding in me, not telling me things, because I think you're worried for me and ... well ... I insist on sharing more than meatloaf and potatoes with you—"

"There is definitely something you can share with me," she said, swallowing and grinning sheepishly. "You can do me a little favour. Tomorrow night."

For the first time he didn't quite trust her. He narrowed his eyes and set down a forkful of loaf. "I aim to please. If I can."

"After you play the piano for me, I want you to take me surfing. After all, you bought me the winter wetsuit, gave me the lessons."

"You've had three lessons, two off the water. And all three in daylight."

"You'll be with me."

"What is this about, Laurel? First *Riviera Concerto* and now surfing in the dark? You started to tell me earlier that on the plane we talked about getting rid of the stone. I want to know your plan. It concerns us so I insist on knowing." He set down his knife and fork, sat back and crossed his arms in front.

She tilted her head at him like she was talking to a ten-year-old who wanted to open his Christmas presents early. "I can't, Mark, sorry. I don't have it all worked out yet and you'll have to trust me. And go along with me, please."

"I can't take you out into those swells at night. You're not a strong swimmer and you can't surf. So, sorry," he protested, proud for sticking to his guns. "You'll have to come up with another plan."

She stabbed a cherry tomato on her plate and laughed. "I can do that. I love to see you on the water, though. I never heard of winter surfing before and it fascinates me. *You* fascinate me when you do it."

"You can stay on the shore and watch me then." She looked so sexy and mysterious and she seemed to be breathing hard. He liked that. A lot.

"Tell you what." She picked another cherry tomato from the salad bowl and placed it in his mouth. "I'll bring the binoculars and paddle out beside you to the first wave. Then I'll stay put and watch. How's that?"

"You'll stay put?"

"Cross my heart." She crossed her heart.

He'd surf though a tsunami for her if she asked him, but how was that helping her? "Tell me why you've been crying."

Laurel searched his eyes. "I'm going through a break-up, Mark."

A stone dropped in his stomach. "I don't ... a break-up with whom?"

"My poor Mark. With you. And you're the one that broke it off."

≈≈≈

As soon as Sara hung up the phone after wishing John-Philip a happy Christmas, Lyton gave into her about the Christmas cake. Every year she made an extra Christmas cake for John and took it to him Christmas Eve, but since John wasn't home this year she insisted on giving the cake to his son. Mark would certainly be interested in hearing about the chat she had with his father, though it really wasn't much of a chat. Poor John was still having difficulty with his speech but there was absolutely nothing wrong with his ears. When the head nurse seemed reluctant to ring her through to John's room, Sara promised not to keep him. All she wanted to do was tell him their thoughts were with him on this holy night.

"I felt so bad," Sara said as Lyton took the cake and helped her out of the car in the Grant driveway. "He didn't seem to know that Mark and his friend were staying at the house and I certainly wasn't going to tell him. You'd think he'd ring up his own father on Christmas Eve. I know Mark's just separated from his son who's ill, but John's separated from his son, too. And John learned of his grandson from *staff*. He was trying desperately to talk when I mentioned Mark. How sad. I'm going to suggest to Mark that he ring his father tonight. My mind's made up. Don't care if I'm meddling." Sara pressed the buzzer.

Lyton smiled adoringly at her. Wasn't it like Sara to put aside her own heartache. "You do that then, love." Lyton peered through the window. "That is if we get to see Mark at all. Doesn't look like they're about."

Sara squeezed in beside Lyton at the window. "Someone's in there, I'm sure I saw movement between the drapery panels. We'll wait another minute."

"You know," Lyton said, lowering his voice, "on the way home from work last evening, I saw Mark prepping on shore with his surfboard. I took a jaunt down trying to catch him before he hit the water, but didn't manage in time. Called out but he didn't hear. Caught a glimpse of him though, before he got all goggled up, and cheese and crackers he looks dandy. The years have been good to him. Mark's hardly aged since he left."

"All that exercise, I expect. On stage, too." Sara buzzed again.

"No one home. Don't know what you saw but it's black as crow in there."

"But the house lights were on just moments ago. I saw them when we flicked ours off. Where could they have gone in five minutes?"

"Could be a timer, Sara. And the tree lights are off. Come on then, we'll be late for Teddy's."

"I think I'll call later from Teddy's. Something's not quite right in there. I could've sworn I saw a silvery flicker, like jewellery or something."

"Come on, dear, I'm freezing. If they're in, they're probably at it and we're intruding."

"Lyton."

"What? They're young and it's Christmas."

≈≈≈

"Okay they've gone, you can switch the lights back on," Laurel said, watching the Stokes' drive off. "I heard him say he took a jaunt down to catch you. I thought your beach was private."

She seemed panicked at the prospect of a public beach. "Tis." He switched on the tree lights and motioned her away from the crack in the draperies. "It's all right, they're neighbours and there's no access to the beach from down there—only down the flight from our overcliff."

"But what's to stop people from driving up here? It's not gated and—"

"There's private signs everywhere, Laurel. Be naff of folks to try."

"Be what?"

"Uncool," he said, smiling. "They don't do it here. You worried we'll be robbed or something?"

"No, but we're surfing later and—"

"*I'm* surfing. *You're* watching."

"—and if you're recognized and approached, well with your adult memory gone ... I'm sorry, Mark."

"It's all right, really. May not recall playing the saxophone but I could manage a bluff on the rockstar stuff. I'm sure."

"But you look ... well never mind." She twirled around for him. "How do I look? Got my Christmas best on for you. No black tonight."

He loved the spunky silver jewellery set on the blinding red cowl neck woollen dress and she must've towed the high-heeled patent leather boots over on the plane because he'd never seen her in them, not that he could remember. She had her hair up in one of those posh styles and she certainly looked that—posh and sexy and he wished he could have her upstairs right this minute. "Wicked fit you are."

She laughed and took a seat at the *re-enactment table* she'd set up in front of the piano. "I'm guessing that means you like the way I look." She sucked on her lower lip, took a deep breath. "Play that *Riviera Concerto* song for me, Mark."

He noticed she'd placed the stone on the table in front of her. She'd obviously gone hunting and found the ancient restaurant furniture and paraphernalia. "Funny how I remember all this stuff and nothing from the present. Dad kept a catch aquarium over here." Mark nodded to their right, uncomfortably aware of the butterflies and pounding heart. "Was it really twenty years ago tonight?"

"Mmmm, yes," she said dreamily, cupping her hands over the stone. "Ready?"

Mark took his seat at the piano, noting the absence of sheet music. He closed his eyes, praying to capture the moment for her, to remember the song's elaborate flourishes, hoping he'd play it one-tenth as well as Roger Williams. Maybe if he tried to forget *her* sitting so close, so close and so captivating, he could abandon himself to the piece.

He smiled shyly. The stone in her cupped hands glistened like some universal shaft of light. He glanced at his right hand. It felt numb, almost frozen. Was it happening now? Did he actually see a ghost-bandage on his finger? He felt sure he remembered something of this before with Laurel, away from here. Now he recalled more of that Christmas as he played, reliving it exactly as he had twenty years ago ...

... "Dad!" he called to his father from the kitchen that Christmas Eve afternoon, "I've sliced it. Sod it!"

His father ran in and asked his assistant to call the doctor. "Oh bugger, so you have. Broken glass?"

Mark nodded. "Will I need stitches?"

"Think so, son. But only one or two."

"A pair," Dr. Poynter said an hour later in their kitchen. "Be quick as nettle in a dog's rear. Don't you worry, Mark."

"But my meet? My 400 metre? It'll throw my timing off."

"You can still compete, Mark. That's the main thing," his father said.

He had intended to win that meet. He knew he'd win that meet. No one could touch him, not in the 400 metre. And after he'd won, he'd planned to confess to his father that music wasn't his dream. 'I'm an athlete', he'd say. 'I surf. I swim. And one day I'll win Olympic gold for my country. That's where my heart is, Dad.'

That's how he'd intended it to go. But after the doctor left, and his father said what he said, the conversation took a different turn. His dream was ruined. His life was over.

"Son, listen to me. You are an athlete. No-one's taking that from you. You're great in the water and perfect in the 400 freestyle. But your coach says you don't have the stamina for the 1500."

"I can develop my stamina."

"Mark, you have a greater aptitude. A great gift."

"I'm not interested in the piano, Dad. Or studying voice."

"It's in you like it was in your mother. One day—"

"No, Dad!"

His father gave him a hug. "Tell you, why not leave this until after the holidays? We'll sort it all out, I promise."

A few hours later, in 'she' walked. The prettiest, most adorable, sad little girl he had ever seen. He was bussing tables as they approached and assumed she was accompanied by her parents *and brother. Father and brother in back. Mother and little girl in front. Standing behind the mother was a large shadow of a woman. It gave him a start, he remembered, because the shadow cast itself as high as the ceiling. Then in a blink it was gone.*

The lovely little girl was carrying something blue, glistening at him like a prism. His hand did not ache so much now. Instead, he felt a tingling, and a shifting sensation similar to an earth tremor. He savoured the restaurant smells and ocean sounds—the gulls, the tide coming in, waves pounding the shore, as a kind of destiny overture. Permission to lift the veil and peek inside.

As he cleared the table, he watched her take her seat and set the blue stone down in front. The woman-shadow returned suddenly and stood behind the mother again, inanimate, but startlingly real. Touched by the girl's sadness, the beginnings of a tune popped into his mind, a tune he would finish composing tonight after the restaurant closed.

"Don't be a tourist, please," he thought as he unloaded his bussing bucket in the kitchen, then opened the door a crack to spy on her. "In the name of whoever's listening to me right now, don't ever let her go away."

Mark heard his father calling him, as though he were here with him now, in the next room—

"Mark? Mark, stop your ogling and play something out there. The restaurant's filling up. Get a move on, son."

He knew what he would play for her. He had been practicing this song for weeks and now he was ready to play it in public. He hadn't cared to be a prodigy like they all said—his piano teacher, the neighbours, friends. He was sick of hearing how accomplished he was at thirteen-and-a-half.

"I'm going to play Riviera Concerto," he said to his father, forgetting that his Olympian dream was over.

As he walked through the empty restaurant, it seemed to echo, soft echoes of a room filled with people, echoes of the ocean, echoes of his footsteps as he walked by the little girl. Passing her table, he stole a glance then took his seat at the piano, placing the sheet music he didn't really need for Riviera Concerto on the rack. He felt her eyes on him, the warmth of her presence. So, bandaged finger and all, he began to play but it was awkward at first and he struck the wrong key. Embarrassed, he stopped and cleared his throat, thinking he wanted to hop on his surfboard and disappear in the swells. But he could not disappear and since his father taught him never to run from anything, he took a deep breath and resumed playing.

This time his fingers sailed over the keys and as he played he felt her eyes on him. He stole another glance. How it pleased him to see those eyes grow big and round, to feel her pleasure surge around him like a great rise in the sea. This ability, this talent— maybe it wasn't such a curse after all. Apparently, few people were prodigies. Perhaps he should take seriously this talent everyone insisted he had.

He would always remember this magical Christmas Eve and the beautiful little girl so moved by his music. If he had his way, he would keep her here forever.

"Beautiful," Laurel clapped when he'd finished. "Encore, Mark!"

He played for her again, and a third time, touched by the tears she kept dabbing away. When he'd finished he stayed at the piano for a moment, admiring her, wanting her, loving her. It was all Laurel—she was the reason he was here, the reason for his life-choice, the reason he finally relinquished the all-important Olympic dream for something much grander.

Laurel shuffled over to him and placed the stone on the piano, setting it down like a sin she wanted scraped off her hands. "I'm putting this back here where it belongs," she said, lines drawn at the mouth and a look of disgust impossible to imagine. "It's such a paradoxical thing, isn't it? It brought us together and will keep us apart. I should never have left it with you twenty years ago. We would've met without it. I'm sure of that now. Too late."

Seeing the devastation in her eyes about ended him and he wanted to handspring over the piano to get to her. He'd intended to kiss her breathless, but Laurel threw her arms around him and hung on tight.

"Don't," he said over her shoulder. "You're overwrought. That's all that's wrong with you."

She broke from his embrace and he saw how angry she was with herself. "Oh Mark, if I hadn't come into your life you'd be back in your life."

She still hadn't the vaguest notion what she'd done for him. Mark rushed to the table and heaved the scrapbook to his shoulder. "See this thing ... and what's in it? Laurel, truth is I never wanted to be a singer, not at first. Probably you don't know of my Olympian fancies. If not for you I'd be a leathery soggy mess with swimmer's shoulder and bad hair. Hold out your hands." She held them out and he placed the scrapbook on them. "Feel the weight? And we know my father has more of these around here."

"You accomplished what's in this book, Mark. Only you."

"Don't you see? None of what's in this scrapbook would've come about. I received your passion so strongly that it made me take a look at my real gift. My father couldn't get through to me. But you did. You did that for me, Laurel."

He explained how the memory surfaced while he played, told her about the conversation with his father and the depth of his dream. But he couldn't explain the intermittent shadow standing behind her wretched-looking mother and how it cast its pall on her, maybe on all of them.

"Obviously I've forgotten everything you've told me of your mother."

Laurel stepped back from him and walked over to the tree, crossing her arms on her shoulders like she was protecting herself from the world. "Tch, my crazy mother. I was first to see the craziness, being her target and all, and instead of helping her I accused her. The craziness started when we came here that Christmas. Maybe you glimpsed the energy field around her, which would've been dark, certainly unstable. And I remember the hell I experienced leaving you that night, leaving Rottingdean. Life changed for both of us that night, didn't it?"

Mark massaged the hand with the ghost-cut and stitches, imagined he felt the freezing take effect in his finger. And he thought about the words that might've passed between them in bed during the hours and hours they would've made love. He joined her at the tree. She was sure worth ignoring the hand, the lost memory, the fear. How could he have ever broken off with her? She had explained yesterday, and again this morning. And already he'd forgotten.

She smelled of sandalwood and reminded him of a time when he woke knowing something extraordinary was about to happen to him. "I want to help you. Let me. It's Christmas, you see. Magical things happen. It did for us, right?"

≈≈≈

Mark was the magical thing that happened, until she came along and siphoned the magic from him like some saltwater snail. In spite of his loss and the horror he must be feeling, he thought to help her. God, he was good—loved by the world, his friends, his son. Her. Or maybe with her it was never really love. What the hell did selfish people know about love, anyway? Mark deserved to get back the love he'd lost.

"I hung something for you on the tree." Laurel reached up to a high branch on the Scotch pine and picked off a gold saxophone keychain. "I saw it in a little shop near Rudy's in Yorkville." He didn't remember Rudy's or Yorkville and he clearly didn't remember barely speaking to her on the flight over, could care less when she took out the stone and slept holding it in her hand. She pretended to sleep while rushing through stench and gloomy dusk, past carcasses along the astral shore, what was left of it, to McLafferty's hospital room.

She swallowed the stubborn lump in her throat. "I didn't know if we'd be Christmas shopping here. Do you like it?"

Mark flushed, dangled it from his finger. "Love it. Especially now that I know I can play it," he laughed.

He looked so tall and strong standing in the shadow of the twinkling tree, so certain of his claim on the good in the world. Mark was on the verge of world renown and here she stood— once his inspiration. At least she'd accomplished one good thing in her life. *Yay, Laurel. We'll pin the medal on your halo.*

"You do much more than play it, you have no idea. You do everything with love, Mark. Your son is so crazy about you."

"And I'm crazy about you," he said, and her breath caught seeing the man surface in that instant.

"You know that, do you? Fair to remind you, you called it quits with us just a few days ago."

"I have an excuse. I'm not in my right mind. Don't move away from me anymore. Please?"

"Okay." Would it be amoral to kiss him to pieces the way they used to? Mark was certain of his feelings, always had been, and the feelings he had the other day to break it off were the right feelings. Even in his present state he possessed courage and confidence. And faith. Mark believed everything would be fine again. How could she tell him or even convey to him that it was impossible for things to be fine again ever? On this Christmas Eve standing near this beautiful tree with Mark inching closer for a kiss, she hadn't the heart to tell him this was a no-win scenario.

If she took him back to their astral shore they'd die, or worse, be trapped in some shattered netherworld. If she kept him here in present day Rottingdean, he'd remain an amnesic adolescent for the rest of his life. If she got him back to his life as it was, they'd lose each other. Simple choice, really. *A kiss is all I have left to give you. A kiss and your freedom.*

Mark caressed her face with his hand and she kissed his palm, kissed the bandage on his finger. *Bandage on his finger?* She was going crazy. Dammit, as crazy as her mother. "No bandage," she whispered as his soft shining eyes filtered the dark thoughts out of her.

He grazed her cheek with his lips and tilted her chin up to him as she wound her arms tightly about his waist. "So beautiful," he said and damned if she could stop the watery eyes as a picture of Fraser the Forgotten assaulted her mind. No thanks to her, Mark had lost the memory of his son.

"Forgive me, Mark."

"Don't," he whispered, tightening his grip. "Kiss me. Please kiss me."

"Oh but we really shouldn't." And she kissed him, feeling his hunger for her, heart rapping in his chest. This *boy* was the man she made love to one short week ago. Oh God, little more than a boy. She pushed Mark gently away. "We can't. Oh Mark, I'm so sorry."

"What's wrong?" He stumbled back a step and held his breath. Could she ever do anything except hurt him? "You don't want me anymore?"

"Mark, I'll never stop wanting you," and when he lunged for her she turned her head away and looked down. "We have a mess to straighten out. I think I can fix things tonight if you'll help me. Will you help me?"

Mark grabbed a fistful of shirt and gave her a long, pained look. "I've been asking you for days to let me help. What can I do?"

"When we paddle out to that first pocket as you call it, you know, the spot you want me to sit and watch you take off from?"

Mark eyed her suspiciously. "Yes?"

"I want you to take the stone as far out as you can and toss it, Mark. Bury it in the ocean. Please. I wanted to do it but you won't let me."

"That's right," he said with a satisfied smile. "I won't have my Christmas Laurel buried in the ocean along with your stone. I feel it's the right thing to do somehow," Mark lowered his voice, "but are you sure you want to part with it? It has us in it. I grew up with it on that piano over there. Boyhood I do recall."

She couldn't wait to part with the stone. It was Mark she couldn't bear to part with. "Get the thing out of our lives, Mark."

≈≈≈

Since sunset, she'd felt the Diamond's menacing presence enveloping her like a second skin. Muscles tensing around her eyes, she took a slow choppy breath. "I need to, how do you Brits say—gear up?"

She asked Mark to get into his wetsuit. "I put my wetsuit upstairs," she explained, not to overdo it. "I want to rub some petroleum jelly on a couple spots first."

She waited until she heard Mark going down the basement stairs before scooping the stone off the piano. But it was about more than grabbing the stone so he wouldn't see or rubbing on petroleum. It was the note she wanted Mark to find long after she was out of his life. Still weak where he was concerned, she propped the note behind Mark's beloved Royal Hudson. It might be years before he discovered it in the old attic bedroom, but that was okay, she needed to leave that tiny piece of herself here with him. She re-read the note one last time—

My darling Mark, I ache with sorrow for the pain I've brought you.

Please try to remember only the love. Laurel

"Laurel!" Mark shouted up while she struggled into the suit. "Your body heats the water trapped behind the neoprene. Not that you'll be needing it on for long."

Seeing Mark waiting for her at the bottom of the stairs reminded her of the night he came into her life at Guy's party, except he was considerably younger now. He smiled up at her and stopped singing a Christmas tune to giggle as she plodded down the stairs in the wetsuit. At Guy's party they were in the dark. As they would be again in a few minutes.

As always, she trembled at the sight of him. "Sorry. Us girls and maintenance. All that. You remind me of the Christmas cardinal with your song and red stripe in your wetsuit. I've heard it said that a glimpse of the cardinal brings hope and inspiration. Nature's reminder to focus on our faith."

Mark smiled, continued singing like the Christmas cardinal, "*O Holy night, the stars are brightly shining. It is the night of our dear Saviour's birth. Long lay the world in sin and error pining ...* sing, Laurel ... *'til He appeared and the soul felt its worth.* Hey, why so teary?"

"You have such a beautiful voice." She hung her arms at her side, hiding the small protruding lump in her pocket while Mark fastened the hood on her suit.

"*... Fall on your knees. O hear the angel voices. O night divine. O night when Christ was born. O night divine. O night, O night divine!*"

The carollers' music carried far along the overcliff. Laurel's heart swelled as they hauled the boards down to the beach. She thought of all the things she'd say to him if Fraser were here, if their families were joining them for their first Christmas. Maybe this was the spot he'd propose and slip on the ring. "*Of course, yes,*" she'd say. "*Your heart beats in my chest, too. I love you and I'll do right by you, my love. Always.*"

"I'll always do right by you, Mark," she said as they propped their boards in the sand.

"Then stop looking so sad."

"Oh no." She pretended to pat an empty pocket. "I was ... I can't believe it. I'm such a dummy. I left the stone in your attic room when I changed into the wetsuit."

He raised his brows and grinned. "Good. Like to think I've got you all knotted up. Want to walk me in? We can have a virgin toddy before we set out. We're not on a schedule."

"Naw. I wanna get this over with. I'll wait here and enjoy the fresh air. Haven't been out all day."

"Right then, won't be a moment."

When he was a scant two feet away she ran after him and tapped his back with playful, nervous fingers. "Hey, I forgot."

"Forgot what?"

"I haven't paid you."

"Again?"

"For the concert. Will you take a kiss, handsome man?"

Mark hardly took a breath as he pulled her into his arms and kissed her hard, exploring her tongue with his. She ran her hands through Mark's hair and along his back, hungrily returning his kiss. This was the man's kiss, and somehow the memory of her touch had returned to him. *Love you love you love you love you. Remember me, darling. Remember me.*

She stopped kissing him and gazed into his adoring grey-blue eyes. "You deserve to have the world love you," she said, physically weakened with desire. Was he staring into her very soul? Oh how it seemed so.

"You make me *know* I had a big life," he said. "That I'll have a big life again."

"The photo albums ... in the house—"

Mark placed his finger on her lips. "No. I'm not talking about the big life in the albums. You weren't in those albums. You're right here. And you know what? Already my life's getting bigger. Come inside with me?"

She kissed him tenderly. "After we get this done, I'm all yours." She flung her arms around him and they held each other firm against the wind as the waves snuck to their feet, the carollers' voices far in the background, fading now. "Pretty sure I left the stone on the bed. I'll wait here for you."

He turned away happy, singing along with the distant carollers as she watched him for the saddest seconds of her life. *Your son is waiting for you, Mark. Hurry home to him, baby. 'Bye.*

When Mark reached the steps, she pulled up her hood and raised the surfboard over her head. For a moment she considered kicking the fin off Mark's beautiful board but didn't have the heart. Besides, it wasn't necessary because she had more than enough time.

"Never a bad Christmas," she said, paddling out. "Never." Focusing on a whitecap fifty feet ahead, she took a deep breath and paddled into the frigid water. "One, two, three, four," she counted. He must be in the attic room now, looking for the stone. "Five, six, seven, eight..." Either he'll keep looking a moment longer or he'll guess what she's up to. She paddled to the first swell with all her strength. "Nine. Ten!"

Catching her breath, she lay on the board. She had only to pass the first wave and heave the wretched thing into the waters of oblivion before the next wave hit. She'd have time. Mark had taken her out this far on three occasions. But in the light of day. Laurel's heart hammered as she pushed forward, thrashing through a wave as high as a house into calm water. Oh beautiful lovely calm water. She wiped away the spray and tears, sat up and removed the stone from her wetsuit. Mark would have guessed that she'd tricked him by now, but no way could he locate her behind this hidden swell.

Resisting the impulse to kiss the stone before burying it forever, she gripped it until her knuckles whitened. "Once you're buried in the sea, our connection severs." She raised her arm and took aim. "As it should be."

She flung the Diamond into the sea and sat mesmerized, following its fading glimmer over the whitecaps until it disappeared like a shooting star across the sky. "There. The end."

"Laurel!" the stone's essence seemed to call, "No, Laurel!"

In a feeble attempt to turn the board around in the choppy water, she leaned into the voice and slipped off.

"Laurel!"

Mark's voice? Mark? Had it been this windy a moment ago, the water so choppy? She managed to climb back up and right the board in the direction of the voice. Blinded by spray, she held tight as the squall rocked it like an angry bear against a tree. Another wave struck her right side and knocked her into the water as invisible claws gripped her ankles and yanked her down. What had hold of her? Oh God.

"Laurel!"

Mark's voice calling!

"Go back, Mark." Marshaling all her strength, she hefted a leg onto the board. "Only I can do this for us."

Mark's voice was closer now. "Undertow, Laurel! Hang onto the board, I'm coming. Hang on to the board!"

She clung to the board and called to him. "Oh go back, Mark, please. I have to make it on my own." *Dear God, keep him safe.*

Somehow she got her other leg onto the board when she caught sight of Mark taking Olympian strokes toward her, cutting the water like a straight shear through stainless steel.

"Let me do this for you," she begged as he neared. "I can do this. Go. I'll follow you back, Mark." She wanted to promise but that would have been another lie.

"I won't." He was a foot away, about to reach for her.

She slid off the board. Mark's saving her wasn't an option. She had to save *him*. But of course she was no match for him in the water.

"No, Laurel," he said, clamping his arms around her waist. "I let this happen, too. And I won't let you go. We're getting out together."

She stopped struggling and turned to see his face. Of course he meant it. Now. But the past would never completely die because a loved one had died in that past. The memory, even if forgotten, would always shadow his mind. There was no escape, not from this past. Anguish. Guilt. Fear. And it wasn't suicide when you offered your life for another. This was the only way to save him. Mark had to live. Mark had too much to give back to the world. And ... Mark was ... *is* ... innocent.

"I love you so much," she said, yielding to the undertow. "This is all I have to give. Goodbye, my en-chant-t-ting b-boy."

She unclamped his hands from her waist and slid beneath the surface, bobbing up to check on him one last time. Was he swimming away from her? Well, yes that was best. Sweet relief. He would be okay. He'd get out. Circles of waves came at her, multiplying, and she let the undertow have its way. *Mark, my love.* At least *she* was gone. Finally destroyed. She let her body go limp, quit holding her breath. Time to go. Time to go now. The undertow would take her down for the last time and soon it would be over.

She slid under.

Below the water, she agonized over the place she'd be going in just minutes, after her last heartbeat. Would there be mercy? Mark was safe. She had that. *He will be okay, right, God? God, let him be okay.* Laurel repeated that prayer once more then smiled—because she was not alone under the water. Mark was right there with her, but he was not Mark as she knew him. He was her Mark of twenty years ago. Her enchanting boy.

≈≈≈

Teddy set down his guitar long enough to remind his guests that the grandfather clock struck twelve. It was Christmas. Sara and Lyton Stokes had already begun the countdown since eleven-thirty. It had been a tradition in Lyton's family to make what they called their 'Christmas Wish' every year, one minute before midnight. When he married Sara thirty years ago, they carried on this tradition together. So while Teddy had been plucking, they had already begun their silent wishes, holding hands and pretending that Teddy had their undivided attention.

Sara noticed something different in Lyton this year during their wish. She felt a subtle electric jolt moving through his arm to hers. It lasted about eight seconds, after which Lyton's complexion paled. He seemed restless and nervous, unable to sit still. Sara felt strange herself and wondered if she was imagining it because she was sensing it in Lyton, or whether they had actually shared something when the clock struck twelve. When Teddy resumed his guitar playing and the small number of houseguests began milling about again, Sara motioned Lyton off to the side.

"What is it, love? What's the matter?"

For a second, Lyton squeezed his eyes shut. "I feel a little ... I need some air, Sara. Something strange. I don't know. Crikey, I guess I'm not making much sense. You think Teddy and Rose would feel bad if we left?"

Their neighbours understood the moment they saw the pallor in Lyton's face, adding that Sara seemed a little peaked herself. Sara told them there was no need for concern, tomorrow's Christmas brunch was still on. Five minutes later they were driving along the slippery Beach Road, humming along with Elvis to *If Every Day Was Like Christmas* on the car radio. It wasn't until four years later that they spoke of the strange electric current that shot up both their arms at exactly midnight.

Sara did all the driving and Lyton did all the bicycling in the family. The only time he took the car was when he had to transport antiques from Gatwick to his shop in Brighton. He always enjoyed looking down at the shoreline from the car at this angle, especially tonight. With the three-quarter moon, the whitecaps shone like speckled jewels under its glow. Yes, especially tonight ... seeing as that strange feeling of anticipation had returned.

Lyton took notice of how high the driftwood had piled below the undercliff at John-Philip's. Oddly black, rounded pieces. Strange shape for driftwood. Strange ...

"Sara! Over at John-Philip's! Stop the car. Hurry, Sara!"

As he took the last few steps down to the beach, Lyton heard a faint cry of someone calling for help over the wind and pounding surf. Using the moonlight and echo as guides, they came to the spot where two forms lay, half in and half out of the water.

"My God, my God. Are you all right, son?"

"I t-think s-so. No b-breath. My friend, p-please help my friend. I think she's-s d-dead."

Lyton prayed to remember how to do this, turning the girl first on her stomach, then on her back, still praying as he resuscitated her. It seemed forever before she coughed up the small amount of water and gazed at him from the most beautiful green eyes. Lyton's heart fluttered. She was the loveliest little thing, couldn't have been more than eight or nine years old.

Sara had her coat and arms wrapped around the quivering boy who made a beeline for the girl as soon as she came around. "Hello," he said, kneeling over her in the sand.

"Hello," she said back to him, smiling for the first time. Both Lyton and Sara noticed the adoring way they looked at each other. "What's your name?"

"My name is ... it's ..." and then the boy frowned. "I don't know."

"I don't know, either," she said, her eyes filling with tears.

"Hush," the boy soothed her. "It will be all right. I'll take care of you."

≈≈≈

Lyton and Sara rushed them home, called the police and awakened their local Dr. Poynter out of a dead sleep. By three a.m. they had the children examined, snugly tucked away and sleeping soundly. They were fine, the doctor said, with the exception of the mysterious amnesia. There were no bumps on the children's heads, no concussions or broken bones. He guessed the boy to be around thirteen, adding that it shouldn't be difficult to locate their parents, though they didn't look at all alike and the girl was American, the boy English. The police assumed they'd have word for them within a few hours.

"What about the amnesia?" Sara asked.

"Have yourself or their parents bring them in to see me in a couple of days if their memories haven't returned." Then Dr. Poynter assured them, "They'll be all right, you two. They're in glowing health otherwise. Bloody miracle there's no hypothermia, I'll tell you. Odd, though."

"What's odd?" Lyton and Sara asked as one voice.

"The suture." Dr. Poynter began shoving things into his medical bag. "The boy's had a recent cut on his finger and both stitches had come loose, so I removed the old suture and re-stitched his finger."

"What's odd about that then?" Lyton asked.

"Haven't seen suture like that in years. Swear the way that second stitch was tied off, that I did the work meself. But the suture we use now is lighter in weight and colour. Usually it's dark blue or brown. This was black and heavy. Extremely wiry. Gotta be goin' back, oh, 'bout fifteen years since I've seen suture like that. Might be wise to inform the police of that.

These children could be tourists. Well, good morning, Sara. Lyton. Happy Christmas to both of ya."

Neither Lyton nor Sara got any sleep that night. Minutes after the doctor had left, the phone rang. John-Philip had quietly passed just before midnight. Would they please help to find his son and notify him? So Lyton got dressed again and walked over to John's house. The front door was wide open, the house was obviously vacant, and feeling as though he were in a dream, Lyton felt compelled to take a seat at one of the five tables. He sat until dawn, thinking about this strange evening, wondering what had happened tonight in this house, and grieving for John-Philip. His tired mind flooded with the events of the past seven hours.

Unable to keep his eyes open any longer, Lyton switched off the lights and closed up the house. Mark Grant was nowhere around here, he could feel it. Perhaps he'd been located and was in London seeing to his father right at this moment. He couldn't think anymore. He would wait for word tomorrow, word of Mark Grant and more importantly, word of the children's parents. Lyton fell asleep thinking of what the doctor had said about the suture. Then he dreamed of the children growing up around him.

Unknown to him, Sara was having a similar dream.

12. LOVE ME TOMORROW

THE CO-PILOT OF THE *CARMEN TOO* welcomed Michael aboard Dale's eleven-passenger Gulfstream III. Never having flown in a luxury private plane, he would've been excited under happier circumstances. Still, dazzled by the surroundings, there were worse ways to travel. On board, Frank said to make himself comfortable. Right. No problem.

"We won't be taking off for an hour or so," Frank said, laughing at the gaping crater that used to be his mouth. "We're fuelling and Mr. Mith and the captain are due shortly."

Lost in the thick carpeting, white onyx illuminated bar, plush black leather sofas and recliners, he deadpanned to Frank, "Does it have a sauna?"

"No," the co-pilot laughed, "but I think Mr. Mith's considering one."

He poured himself a soda and lime and as an afterthought, added an ounce and a half of vodka. This latest news had about fried his nerves. First Gillian, then they almost lose poor little Fraser. Now Mark's father passes away early Christmas morning. His entire family in less than a year and Mark and Laurel nowhere to be found. No wonder Dale was loaded when they spoke on the phone last night. Dale had also mentioned something about a letter Mark left for him but said he'd wait until today to fill him in. "I'll be more *hocherent* in the morning," he had said.

"Hi," Dale said, looking drawn, moving slower than usual. He headed straight to the bar. "Welcome aboard the *Carmen Too*. You impressed or what?"

"Oh sure, I often fly Air Mogul," he said, noticing the puffy eyes and dark circles. "How are ya?"

"I feel like something's crawled up my ass and died. Sorry about last night on the phone, mate. I couldn't have made much sense. Just that I got properly pissed when I heard the news about Mark's dad. I always liked him a lot. I'm still feeling guilty about leaving Fraser with Carmen and Annie. Now John-Philip's gone. Never even got the chance to look after him for Mark." Dale shook an angry fist and hollered, "I could throttle him for taking off! Ach! But he's in bloody trouble, isn't he?"

He forced a nod. There was no way to comfort Dale. "The purpose of this trip was to find them and now we discover they've been and gone again. You said you got a letter from Mark?"

Dale decided against pouring an extra shot into his Bloody Mary. "Mark had the letter couriered to the hospital. And the courier was days late because of the storm. Hospital's releasing Fraser today, by the way, and Carmen's taking him back to my place in Malibu. Fraser loves it there." Dale paused, rubbed the cold glass across his forehead. "I didn't have the heart to tell him about his grandfather. Couldn't."

"Poor kid. At least he's out of there today. And Mark still hasn't called him?"

"Not since last week." Dale sat across from him, eyes tightening. "His letter to me was dated around that time. So your call from loony Laurel was the last anyone's heard from them."

Michael didn't care for the slur against Laurel but let it pass because how the hell could he blame him? And Dale's accepting her *someday maybe* was the least of their worries. "I'd like to hear more of the letter ... if it's not too personal."

"No, it's alright. Mark wrote that he was losing it. Bit by bit. Chunks of memory. He went on to explain about the hand cramps again, said the cramps were subsiding since they reached the house and thought it strange. Everything he described, Michael, sounded like what we saw with McLafferty. The letter was a bit of a heap. I mean of course, he's a grieving mess not being with his son. But what he wanted to say mostly, because he repeated it a few times, is that he wanted to get his words to me on record. *Lock this letter away, Dale,* he wrote. *Keep it in your safe at home.* But there wasn't much I hadn't heard before. He talked about that blasted stone, Malibu, his changing feelings for Laurel."

Dale stopped and made eye contact, probably guessing he wanted to hear more of what Mark had to say about laurel. He'd be right. "Does he blame Laurel for Fraser?"

"Think so, Michael. He kept saying *my poor little son, my poor little son. Take care of him, Dale. Laurel's damaged. Maybe insane. It's all as much my fault for rushing into this with her.* But then he insisted she had to go with him. The letter was a collection of random thoughts of this nature."

"Guess he didn't mention Laurel's condition."

Dale set down the Mary and rubbed his brow. "No, though he did say *we* instead of *I.* '*We* don't know when we're coming back but *we* have to fix this before we can ever come back'. He ended by repeating that I tuck the letter safely away again, then spoke about business and wrote affectionately about our friendship. That's pretty much it."

Michael guessed Dale was excluding a few details, but no one was more entitled. Or maybe Mark wrote some hateful things about Laurel and Dale didn't want to upset him. "Who exactly are the Stokes'?" he asked.

"Neighbours of Mark's father, next door a ways. Apparently, they'd been looking in on John-Philip while he was supposedly convalescing, so the hospital rang when he died Christmas morning. The Stokes' then tried to reach Mark. John-Philip had given them all his numbers. Obviously they couldn't reach Mark next door at the house, but kept calling his London and Manhattan numbers until they got hold of Annie yesterday.

"Annie gave them my number and they called me. They told me they'd already made funeral preparations when no one could locate Mark. Said they saw Mark out surfing a few days ago. Can you believe that? And he still hadn't been to see his father." Dale took a healthy swig and continued. "I told them I'd take care of all the funeral expenses. But I missed the service, Michael. It was today, UK clock."

"Did they say anything else about Laurel and Mark? You were a little fuzzy on the phone last night."

"Mr. Stokes told me they went over on Christmas Eve with a cake or something and there was no sign of them, even though the lights were on minutes before. But get this, all their clothes and luggage are still in the house. That's where we're staying, by the way. John-Philip gave them a key and they're leaving it under the mat by the side entrance."

Michael reached for his seatbelt. "The first thing we do is pay a visit on the Stokes'. "The second we get there."

Frank walked back and asked them to buckle up, forcing Dale to shout over the roar of the powerful engines, "You're forgetting the time difference, mate. It's 3 p.m. now, our time, which means our ETA at Gatwick will be four in the morning, their time. Our talk with the Stokes' will have to wait until tomorrow."

He waited until they were in the air four hours before telling Dale the news about McLafferty. Dale awakened after a much needed nap and took a hefty club sandwich and bowl of soup into him. Halfway through his second cup of coffee, Michael said, "You weren't the only one on the phone with hospitals yesterday. I called Saint Michael's Hospital again to check on McLafferty."

Dale looked wary. "And?"

"And he showed a remarkable improvement early yesterday morning, so much so that he was able to have visitors. So before Christmas dinner at my parents, I went to see him. You know, to check out his headspace, to see how much our friend was remembering."

"Just what we need, more bad news. Go on."

"He remembers everything, Dale."

"Oh well, let's raise our glasses in celebration."

"No, hold on. McLafferty isn't talking. Seems the guy's still paranoid about the whole experience. He doesn't want to have anything to do with Laurel and Mark. In fact, he said he'd be quite happy if he never heard their names again. Besides, the man's together enough to know that nobody's going to be interested in his theories now, especially since he's on his way back from a crack-up. Mark's lawyers would crucify him in court." He stared pensively at Dale.

"What's wrong, Michael? Mark won't have to suffer through a scandal now. Neither will Laurel. So what is it?"

"Have you ever thought that someone was brought into your life for a purpose, that that someone was there because they needed your help or vice versa? Then you find out you were never any help at all, that it was all for nothing?"

"You're thinking about Laurel?"

"Yes. I've pasted so many people's psychic consciousness' back together and I did nothing for Laurel. I was totally useless throughout this whole thing. She came to me for help when we first met and I told her I would help her. But I did nothing. All I did was study and observe, raise questions, find some of the answers and lecture her some. But I never did help her. I never even knew how to help her. I was too late every step of the way. I accomplished nothing. I helped no one."

"You helped her brother learn the truth about his mother. About his sister. And you helped me, Michael. It would've been hard lines for old Dale if I had to go it alone. Laurel always hated me, I could feel that. I posed a threat to her relationship with Mark. But there you were. My shield. To get to me, she had to go through you and you knew too much about her.

"I think she stayed away from you in the end specifically for that reason. The less you knew the better. And I could tell by that letter she left you and the phone calls that she was genuinely fond of you underneath it all. Michael, if you ask me, this creepy paranormal thing between Mark and Laurel has always been absolutely out of our hands. Always. But we followed through because we cared very much about two people. It's that simple. So don't think you were useless, you weren't. Especially to me, for what it's worth."

"Does Mark have any other kin?" he asked, touched by Dale's words.

"There was a maiden aunt on his mother's side, but she died of cancer five years ago. His father was an only child just like Mark. So there's no cousins, no anybody."

"I guess someone with his wealth would always have a will handy."

"Of course. Almost all of it goes to Fraser. He mentioned once that he was leaving a great deal for cancer research and other charities. Why do you ask?"

"What if Mark never shows up again, Dale? He could be declared dead, living incognito with Laurel in some obscure part of the world with their names changed. Another life. What would happen to his estate then?"

"Well, there would be a lengthy investigation and search for him. If I'm not mistaken, I think a person has to be missing seven years before they're declared legally dead. In that event, all his money would go in trust to Fraser. But he'd have to be completely out of his mind or have suffered a conk on the head to leave Fraser behind. What's gnawing at you, Michael?"

"I don't know. It's just that Mr. Grant's death and Fraser and McLafferty's instant recovery concerns me. Both of them on Christmas. Mark and Laurel disappearing on Christmas. If we do find them, I'm worried what we will find. In a way I feel what Julian Wieler hoped might be best for me, for us ... that we not be the ones to find them. Then I wonder if they've run off to start a new life together, do they have the emotional and mental capacities to elude the populace for the rest of their lives."

"Unless you're having some psychic thing happening now, I can't see Mark leaving the life he loved to run off with that woman. Unless, God help us, he's gone bonkers. And if he did plan to run off, he would've sent for Fraser by now."

No way would Mark be sending for Fraser. Not now. Not any time soon. "I keep hearing Laurel's voice on the phone telling me he left her. *Just like that.* And returned two hours later—changed. Then she mentioned his preoccupation with surfing. Water has been a core obsession for both of them. What if there's been an accident in the water?"

A wave of sadness passed through Dale's eyes. "You're thinking about their dreams and Gillian, all that?"

"Yes."

"Mark's bloody Flipper in the water. Even this time of year. Nope. Can't see it. Though I have come to trust these feelings of yours. So lay it on me. What do you feel, Michael? What are your feelings right at this moment?"

"That they've changed so much. That if it weren't for their appearances, we might not know them. I haven't slept proper since that little psychic anxiety attack at the El Mo. Shadows. Darkness—and tons of water."

≈≈≈

They taxied to Rottingdean from Gatwick Airport, arriving at the Grant house shortly before 5 a.m. A familiar scenario, without the snow, without Kevin McLafferty locked away upstairs. Unable to resist the impulse, Michael called their names the moment they crossed the threshold. Though he sensed the couple's physical absence, he felt saturated by their spiritual presence, unescapable like fog rolling over the harbour.

When Dale switched on the lights, he ran to the stairwell and shouted for them. "Laurel! Mark! It's Michael. Michael and Dale. Laurel! Mar—"

"They're not here, Michael." Dale clasped his shoulder. "They're not here. Remember?"

Unable to keep still, he moved about like a whirling dervish, up the stairs, down the stairs, out the front door. Back door. Kitchen.

"Michael?"

"No, you don't understand. They're somewhere around here, I c-can feel them. I can smell the crag and the seawater. The sound of the ocean's hammering my eardrums." Michael pressed his palms against his ears. "Piano. Loud. Near us. I h-hear children laughing. They're close by, Dale. I know it."

"How? Surely he would've shown up for his own father's funeral yesterday."

"No, they *are* here. Let's tear the place apart if we have to."

The old restaurant dining room in the rear of the house stopped them cold. The room was proof of Mark and Laurel's attempted excursion into the past, back to their beginning. They had re-enacted the scene of their first meeting—then disappeared. Fighting a dizzy spell, Michael braced his hands on the back of a chair to keep from passing out.

"You're coming into the kitchen with me," Dale said. "I'm fixing you a strong cup of English tea with a hit of brandy. That'll cure anything. After that we sleep until noon. Then we'll talk to the Stokes' and find Mark and Laurel. I told you I've come to trust this psychic thing of yours. If you say they're around here, then they're around here. That means they're alive and physically well, at least. So come on. There's nothing we can do at five in the morning."

While Dale put the kettle on, Michael noticed the latest copy of **The Brighton Sentinel**, obviously left for them by the Stokes'. Scanning the front page, his tired eyes skimmed over Margaret Thatcher's New Year greeting to the Commonwealth, President Hissene Habre's warning of a new rebel thrust from northern Chad, photographs taken locally of two children with missing parents, over toward the obituary at the bottom right of the page.

John-Philip Grant, father of the famous singer, died of stroke complications early Christmas morning at Saint Camillo's Nursing Home, London. Funeral service will be held December 26th at 2:30 p.m., Basset and Grey's Funeral Chapel, Brighton.

"This paper's gonna have a lot more than a small blurb come tomorrow," Dale said, slumping in the chair. "Mark didn't show up for his father's funeral yesterday afternoon. And he wasn't at his son's release from hospital in Toronto. Everybody'll want to know why. In a few days the question of his whereabouts will be headlines. A statement is forthcoming and guess who'll be giving it? I told Justin to hold off saying anything in the States because I wanted it to come first from England. After all, this is his home."

With the brandy kicking in, Michael strained to keep his eyes open. "What are you going to tell them?"

"That Mark has quietly retired from the industry and has gone off with his lady to live anonymously in blessed peace for a time. That his son will be joining them soon as he's well enough. That I don't know where they went or how to reach them, so the world will have to wait until we hear from him again."

"Suppose the press already got to the Stokes' and told them Mark and Laurel just vanished from here, leaving all their things behind?"

"When I spoke to the Stokes' on the phone, I told them not to say anything to the press until I got here."

"Good thinking."

"Right. Now let's get some sack."

≈≈≈

At noon the next day, Lyton Stokes greeted both men by his living room fireplace over steaming cups of coffee. It was obvious to Lyton that they hadn't had much sleep and one of them, Mr. Johnstone, seemed unusually nervous and distracted.

"I'm sorry. This must be such a sad time for you," Lyton said to Mith. "The accident of Mark's son. John-Philip's death. I hope you find Mark soon. I can't help but wonder if he knows his father has passed."

"I've wondered about that, too. But now I don't think he does know. Mark would have shown up for his father's funeral. He loved him very much. You see, Mr. Stokes, Mark *wanted* to disappear. He and Laurel left a note telling us exactly that. They were going away to live quietly for some months. But now I need to locate him for personal reasons. He has business to settle in the States and must be told about his father.

"And I don't want the press to know I'm looking for him. More importantly, I don't want them to learn how he abruptly vacated his father's house, leaving all his things behind like that. Mark would loathe the headlines. He and Laurel would prefer to be left alone."

"But what if something's really happened to them? Surely you'd want the police to begin investigating in that event."

"We have reason to believe they're all right," Mith assured him.

"I see," Lyton said. Mr. Johnstone seemed curiously preoccupied with the red toy piano under the tree. "So you want to keep false rumours from circulating."

"Exactly. We don't want his disappearance sensationalized. That's why I'm giving a large press conference tomorrow afternoon in London."

"Well, I must admit I'm relieved you've got the matter in hand." Lyton lit his pipe. "We have our own hands quite full at the moment. My wife and I were off to Hawaii in a couple of days but we've cancelled. You see, the Brighton authorities are busy trying to locate the parents of two children. We found them on the beach just after midnight Christmas morning. Almost drowned, they were. The children are physically fine, but seem to be suffering from amnesia. My wife is at the hospital with them for a follow-up at this moment."

"Are they staying with you and your wife?" Mith asked.

"Yes. Caroline Trilby, a friend who works for a London social services agency has been wonderful. Sara and I have temporary custody until the parents are located."

"How young are they?"

Mith phrased the question oddly, Lyton thought. And his nervous friend looked like he needed something stronger than coffee. "We've estimated the boy to be around thirteen and the girl eight years thereabouts. They're such beautiful children and in great spirits, which is odd considering what they've been through. We've been calling them Audrey and David. You should see Audrey. She's the most beautiful and loving little thing and she's got the biggest green eyes I've ever seen."

"Green eyes?" Mr. Johnstone said.

"Yes, she's so beautiful and David is such a handsome lad. Talented, too. Plays the piano exceptionally well for his age."

"They related?" A second odd question, this time from the distrait Mr. Johnstone.

"No. They've had blood tests. Besides which, David is English and Audrey speaks with an American accent."

≈≈≈

Michael gulped down the rest of his coffee and asked for more, anything to get Lyton Stokes out of the room. "My God. My God," he whispered to Dale, visibly shaking all over.

"It can't be." Dale refused to consider the notion. "This is insane. We must be suffering from jet lag or something. It can't be, Michael. No. No—"

"I've seen photographs of Laurel as a child. I would know her. And you've seen pictures of Mark, so you would know—"

"Stop it. It's mad. I won't acknowledge it."

"Maybe not so mad."

"Alright then. Bloody impossible! Michael, get a grip."

"We've got to hang around and see those children. For our own peace of mind. I don't believe you. I saw your face a few moments ago when he spoke of their appearance and backgrounds. You know we've got to see them. So wangle us an invitation to lunch or something. Use anything to keep us here until they get back."

"Michael, I don't know about you but I'm slightly terrified here."

"I know. But I believe we've found them, Dale. They've come home."

Shortly after Lyton Stokes fixed a light lunch, which they hardly touched, the weather took a sudden turn for the worse. It began snowing, snow mixed with freezing rain. The wind rattled the small home and rain pelted the windows. Michael stood against one of the windows staring at the shoreline. The ocean had become angry, a vision he had seen many times in his mind. He felt consumed by it the night of Mark's El Mondrago concert, only those feelings belonged to Laurel. The fear, loneliness and guilt he experienced that night emanated from Laurel through their empathic exchange. With her emotions as turbulent as the sea was now, he knew she couldn't live with them much longer. If only the children would come home.

Lyton called the hospital and learned Sara and the kids left an hour ago. They were probably no more than a mile or so down the beach road when the weather turned nasty. Unable to hear the car in the drive because of the storm, Michael jumped up from his seat when the front door slammed behind what had to be the voice of Sara Stokes. Two small blurry figures raced by them down the hall.

"Hurry now. Into some dry clothes."

Lyton introduced his wife, who apologized for her absence earlier. "I had planned to be here to welcome you both and felt sure I could make it. But there was an emergency at the hospital and the children's appointments were put back an hour."

"Oh, of course," Dale said. "The important thing is the kids. Your husband told us what happened. Are they alright?"

"They're in perfect health," Sara beamed, "and in great spirits. Dr. Poynter's a bit concerned about the amnesia, though."

"Anyone can see they're fine," Lyton said. "The amnesia will clear itself up in its own good time. Did he check David's stitches, dear?"

"Stitches?" Michael asked.

"In his finger," Sara said. "He had them when we found him, but two had to be re-stitched. They'll be in for another five days."

Dale stood alongside him when he heard the children approach. Friendly, though shy, the smiling children appeared on the threshold, quietly waiting for introductions. After they exchanged hellos, he and Dale got tongue-tied and looked to the Stokes' for help, but the couple were busy exchanging curious glances. Dale kept nodding at the boy and Michael took a step forward toward the girl—and froze. So the little girl padded right up to him in fuzzy bunny slippers, gave him a glowing smile and extended her hand.

"You talk funny like I do," she said. "Are you from near here?"

Rifling through his bewildered brain for words, he shook his head like a moron. *Come, come words. Nice words.* "I-I'm from Canada. That's a place way across the ocean."

"I like that name," Audrey said. "Canada. Do you have pictures?"

"Not with me. But I'll be happy to send you some."

"Thank you. Canada. Yes, I like that name."

David and Dale were quieter. David couldn't take his eyes off Dale and it was Dale who drew him out.

"So I hear you play the piano," Dale said to the boy.

"Mr. Mith is very famous all over the world, David," Lyton said. "He's a singer and a musician."

"Do you have records?" the boy asked him.

"Yes I do. I'll drop some by to you before I leave for America."

"Tomorrow?"

"David," Sara laughed, "that's not very polite."

"That's alright," Dale said. "I'm flattered that you want to hear my music. Maybe someday I'll be listening to yours."

"I hope so," David said dreamily. "I should like to become famous so I can get very rich and buy Audrey all sorts of furs and jewels and things. But I want to make music, all kinds of music when I grow up."

"I'm certain you will. David. Anything you want badly enough you can make happen."

They spoke of many things. Music for David. Canada and clothes for Audrey. She seemed to have a natural aptitude for colour and fashion and loved ploughing through Sara's magazines, expressing her opinion. When he asked what her favourite colour was, she didn't hesitate.

"Blue."

They took their leave as soon as the rain stopped. Dale's eyes were watering slightly and explained it was the smoke from the fireplace. They watered heavily when he shook David's hand and said goodbye, promising to drop off those albums for him the following day, before his trip to London and home.

While Dale took deep breaths on the Stokes' front walk, he glanced up and caught David and Audrey watching from the top floor. If only he could read their minds. Instead, Dale's raw emotions pulsed through him like small electrical currents. How could he console Dale? What could he do to help him?

"I can't tell Fraser his father's dead," Dale said, eyes glistening. "And I won't let him think Mark left him. And if I tell him his father has amnesia, he'll wonder how I know. He'll want to see Mark."

He motioned Dale down the walkway. "You're going to tell Fraser the truth?"

"Yes. He's honourable like his father. And like his father he keeps his secrets well."

Happy for Laurel, but hurting for Dale, he regarded the Grant home. "I see them—the *children,* spending time in that house. Will you sell it now, Dale?"

Dale rubbed the drip from his nose. "Not mine to sell. The house goes to Fraser and he's too young to decide what to do with it. But, yeah. Mark'll get to grow up near there all over again. And you, Michael? *Her* family?"

He didn't know Courtland like Dale knew Mark, and he wasn't mourning the loss of his best friend. With the ocean calmed in his mind at long last, the vision he'd had at Laurel's townhouse the night they met became clear. He'd seen a small grim-looking group shivering on the beach. They were crouched over something, which Michael couldn't see until now.

Two surfboards washed ashore.

≈≈≈

Dale decided to postpone the London press conference until he broke the news to Fraser. Once the authorities identified the surfboards as Mark's, Dale had to modify his original press statement. He agonized over what he was going to tell Fraser, since he was ill prepared to tell him so soon. Dale hadn't adjusted to the idea himself yet, not that he ever would.

"I still refuse to tell him his father's dead," Dale said, en route to the airport. Courtland was on his way in and Michael thought it best to stay on with Courtland and accompany him back to Toronto. Dale was anxious to get home to Fraser in Malibu. "So he's going to get the truth. Now."

"I wish I knew Courtland Ariss as well as you know Fraser."

He had hoped Courtland's flight would be delayed. Facing a similar dilemma as Dale, he still didn't know what to tell him. Laurel's family had a right to know. But a right to know what? That Laurel was now the little girl next door? She had a right to this fresh start more than her family had the right to return and possibly screw it up. Again. He couldn't believe it. He'd decided what to do in this very moment.

"I'm not going to tell him, Dale. I'm going to let Mark and Laurel be."

≈≈≈

The following spring, the Stokes' hadn't learned any more about the children or their families, and it would take three more years to finalize the adoption. But Lyton and Sara knew the children were theirs. In their hearts, they believed no parents would be coming to claim them.

David and little Audrey hadn't regained their memories and the Stokes' believed this was somehow a mysterious gift from God. The children were happy, had many playmates and did exceptionally well at school. But mostly they had each other. Though Lyton found it unsettling the way David would sometimes drift off and stare at little Audrey with a bothered look, this for no reason until he snapped himself out of it and told Audrey to hurry and grow up so he could marry her.

Audrey would tell him she loved him and was hurrying as fast as she could. She loved her new parents and was now calling them Mommy and Daddy. Yet for one so young, much to Sara Stokes' consternation, Audrey's world revolved around David. But knowing Audrey had been traumatized, Sara decided to be patient. Eventually, Audrey would make a life of her own.

Following an exhaustive search, a London paper wrote that the only things surfacing in the Grant/Ariss alleged drowning were surfboards and speculation. Maybe it was a stunt. Why the boards and no bodies? The press learned that Mark Grant was a crack swimmer with a fondness for winter surfing, that he'd won medals in his youth. Was he giving Ariss a lesson? In December? In eight-foot swells and near-freezing water? Unlikely, was the general consensus.

Rumours circulated about the couple living the quiet life somewhere in the South Pacific. Some said they had become Hindu mystics. Some insisted they were dead and to let them rest in peace. Dale was astounded at Fraser's reaction to the secret truth. He'd accepted the miracle in all faith and was happy to hear his father was alive. But he cried for Mark at night.

"Can I watch Dad from a ways, then?" Fraser asked Dale.

Dale smiled and gave him a hug. "Not for a time. But life is full of miracles, little bud. Your Dad's had one. One day it'll be your turn."

Given the theories and speculation, Mark Grant was more famous than ever, his music enjoyed worldwide and albums outselling everyone, except for Dale Mith. Many said Dale knew more than he was telling but for the most part they left him alone about Mark. Dale's image had softened and he'd become the elusive family man. He was touring now and often sent postcards to David and little Audrey. David had come to idolize Dale, playing his music day and night. In his last postcard, Dale promised that he and Michael would visit next Christmas with Mark Grant's son, Fraser.

Every Friday after school, Sara picked up the children and brought them to visit Lyton in the shop. David would slip away with Audrey to his favourite music shop across the lane and always buy a new record with his allowance. David loved the poster-papered walls in the music shop, especially the ones of Mark Grant and Dale Mith. The clerks who'd become friendly with David and Audrey, encouraged David in his musical aspirations. One clerk commented on David's resemblance to Grant every time she saw him.

"Your eyes are the same," she said. "Remarkable."

David handed his purchases to the clerk and drummed his fingers on the counter. "I'm going to work hard, and then one day maybe I'll resemble his talent as well."

Little Audrey elbowed her way into their space and gave David an affirmative nod. "For sure true," she said, and her conviction made them smile. "Someday you'll be just as famous as Mark Grant was."

THE END

Thank you for reading! Word-of-mouth is crucial for any author to succeed. If you enjoyed *The Astral Shore,* I'd love it if you'd leave a big fat review. Or an itsy, skinny review. Even if it's only a line or two, it would be a huge help.

Another big **Thank-you** for your support!

Did you love The Astral Shore?

Then you should read *Dark Angels Prey*
by Elizabeth Genovese

Dark Angels Prey

Signs and wonders can deceive ...

Devastated by a heartbreaking loss, empath, Joe Ross accepts a strange, hypnotic priest's invitation to convalesce at a Quebec monastery. When Joe admits he heard voices as a kid, directing him to save a child in a place called Marion Lake, the priest says, "I will bring you to *Marianlake* Dominican Monastery. A child lives nearby, a child who's waited a long time to meet you."

Inside a world of supernatural confrontation and demonic cutthroats, an engaging cast of characters draw Joe closer to the discovery of a lifetime: the mystical child, Alain Duprielle; Dina Amodeo, the soft-hearted rocker with a dissociative identity; Carol Ann Page, love of his life, a woman capable of destroying them both; Maggie Page, the great catalyst, the artist whose horrific drawings lead to a long-lost friend and a world-rocking document.

Below the cover of darkness and above a mantle of light, Joe faces a showdown with an old demonic enemy. In a land more inscrutable than Marianlake, he uncovers the startling secret behind three soul-saving paintings. And when events explode in a surprising climax, Joe Ross finds his destiny—and a gift for humanity. But he must outwit the forces of Hell to get it.

Dark Angels Prey ... a standalone tale of supernatural suspense.

Frankie G's Miracle

A Supernatural Novella
by Elizabeth Genovese
FREE to subscribers on elizabethgenovese.com

Only Two Men Hear the Music...

In the 'summer of love' 1967, old school buses painted with psychedelic graffiti head West while liquor rep, Frankie Gallagher buries his wife in Boston. Guilt-ridden, sick and boozing too much, Frankie settles in the mysterious town of Angelfish Cove, believing life has little to offer.

Until he witnesses a miracle.

But when a sadistic teenager exposes his secret shame and the glow from Frankie's miracle fades with the threat of scandal and prison, he opts for a supernatural solution—and faces the fight of his life.

Acknowledgements

Thank-you to the many who helped me, touched me, inspired me, changed me, advised me, guided me, baffled me and challenged me well:

Irene Alexander, Karen Lukas, Dave Thomson, Dee Dee Hayes, Shirley Traynor, Susan DePlanche, Kathi DePlanche, Vicky Plante, Elaine Tennyson, Bev Licastro, Jim Prue and Linda Warner. And in memory of Pierre Berton, who kept me from chucking this book out the window.

Cover Design: Jennifer Quinlan, Historical Editorial, historicaleditorial.blogspot.ca

Let's connect on Twitter:

twitter.com/lizgenovese

A lengthier note, maybe? I'd love it! Zap me an email at: Liz@elizabethgenovese.com

Website: elizabethgenovese.com

About the Author

In the mid-eighties, nervous novice writer, Elizabeth Genovese attended a taping of Toronto's *Front Page Challenge* where a friend introduced her to Canadian icon, Pierre Berton. When Mr. Berton said he was interested in reading her novel, Elizabeth said she 'just happened' to have a manuscript in the trunk of her car. "Up front I'll tell you, if I don't like it I'll say so," he warned, "I will not embarrass myself by submitting a bad manuscript." Two weeks later at 7:00 a.m., the phone rang: "Elizabeth! Pierre Berton here. I think you've got yourself a book." Following a previous publication, a title change and several re-writes, that book became *The Astral Shore.*

Elizabeth's books combine supernatural suspense, mystery, and time travel with recurring themes of obsession and idol worship. *Dark Angels Prey* is a supernatural tale of suspense and adventure. The book's companion, *Frankie G's Miracle,* highlights the life of a character briefly portrayed in *Dark*

Angels Prey. Though the novella introduces DAP's main characters, they can be read and enjoyed as standalone books. *Frankie G's Miracle* is free on *elizabethgenovese.com*. Elizabeth lives in Napanee, Ontario with her exceptionally green-eyed cat, Valley Girl.